LEGACY

LILAH LANCE

UNDERWORLD KINGS BOOK I

*To the girl who'd rather be with a
Prince of Darkness than Prince Charming*

WELCOME TO THE UNDERWORLD

This series explores the stories of the O'Hara family.

You've met them in the world of Titan.

Now you'll get to explore the world of the O'Hara's in depth.

Be warned, the stories ahead are dark, morbid, slightly
unhinged, and have violent themes to them.

CONTENT WARNING

This book contains:

- A morally gray Alpha-male
- Mature themes
- Explicit content
- Graphic and explicit language
- Mentions of human trafficking/kidnapping
- Violence
- Graphic descriptions of domestic violence

KILLIAN

"MOTHERFUCKER."

Running across a rooftop at midnight to catch a criminal was not the way I wanted my Friday night to go down. Not exactly.

I was going to kill this motherfucker.

I leapt off the building I was in, the wind whipping in my hair, as I gained on the fucker running from me.

The skyline around me stretched out the lights guiding me towards my target. A maze of concrete that I knew would hurt if I splattered on it.

Street pizza was not what I wanted to be tonight.

Not when I was chasing a potential perp.

God, when I got my fucking claws and fangs into him—he'd scream for a completely different reason.

I was bolting down and right before he hit the next building, I caught him at the edge.

"Not so fast, fucker." It was a growl ripped from my throat as he elbowed me. With a snarl I had him on the ground. But he was a fighter.

He maneuvered in a way that I felt the elbow coming at my throat and ducked, landing on my back.

He took off, leaping over the edge. I shouted as I drew back and took the jump with him.

I thought he'd make it.

He kinda did, but he groaned as he hit the ground. I definitely made it the air whooshing from my lungs as I rolled smoothly.

Or I would've. I landed wrong.

I felt a searing pain in my shoulder that ripped right through me as I groaned. But my other hand moved. My gun yanking out as I took the shot.

With confidence. He groaned going down as I saw him get hit.

"Fuck!" I groaned dropping onto my knees. I shot him again taking him out as I heard someone land next to me.

"Boss, you good?"

Landon Donohue.

My right hand most of the time when I was working.

I looked up into dark eyes and darker hair whipping in the wind as another man dropped down next to him.

Derek Macall, shaved head, piercings and tattoos. My team. Sean was downstairs in the car.

I let out a breath.

"Straight." I would get Kieran to set it.

Three days later, Kieran did not in fact set it and the pain was getting too excruciating to ignore.

I couldn't. But I didn't wanna go to the hospital and deal with another presumptuous doctor or nurse ever again. But I couldn't stop myself.

Sean watched me one evening struggling to put my jacket on.

"Just ask for Nisha Graham when you go," he muttered. His clear blue eyes watched me wincing a little. "She's solid. Nicest lady there."

"Just because you got favorites, doesn't mean I trust them." I bit out. "You fuck her or something?"

He made a noise. "Nah, she's cool." Right. He just looked uneasy as I groaned about my shoulder. "Just go check it out tonight."

"Fine. I'll go."

"Nisha Graham." Sean repeated. "Trust me. She's good."

We'll see about that.

A CAT PHOTO FROM KIERAN LIT UP MY PHONE SCREEN ON THE WAY TO THE hospital with Nisha.

It was of a chubby gray cat with a bandaged paw, frowning at the camera.

> That's you.

Another photo appeared of a regal black cat with a crown rolling its eyes.

> That's big bro.

I snorted.
I sent him back a photo of a tombstone.

> Keep texting me annoying shit and this will be you.

> BWahahah. Nice to see you getting on board the meme train.

> Such a fucking idiot

> You didn't fix my arm

> I'm not a doctor

> That was your first mistake with me

I groaned.
Little brother's fucking sucked sometimes.
Even if I loved the little shit.
Right now, my shoulder throbbing in pain?
I couldn't focus on anything else.

> Such a shit

> Go to the hospital, bro

2

NISHA

"Nisha, you've got a patient! O'Hara in Room 3."

I glanced up, the summer sunlight slightly blinding me in my efforts to see straight from the window. I covered my face with an arm as I heard directions given out.

He hasn't been back in a while.

I hadn't ever seen O'Hara before, but I'd *heard* of him.

Some nurses were terrified of him, their whispers echoing in the corridors, but I didn't pay them any mind.

People's opinions were meaningless at the end of the day. I tried not to listen to other people's judgment calls about others. I knew just how inaccurate they could be.

And how wrong.

Life with my adoptive parents had taught me things I didn't want to remember. Judgment calls couldn't be made accurately about anyone.

On paper, I was perfect.

On the inside?

Not so much.

Maybe he isn't so bad.

"He's back," one of the older nurses grumbled, the lines on her face deepening. "I swear if he yells at someone else again…"

"I don't know," someone else said. "He's kinda cute. Got that tall, dark, and scary thing…"

I glanced at my friend and resident doctor—Adam Whittaker. Most of our patients were Agents, their bodies bearing testament to the dangers of their profession.

They worked with Adam's brother, Reed Whittaker, who owned the company, Titan Security. This ward in the hospital was for them.

But Adam rarely spoke of him, his eyes clouding over whenever the topic arose. I didn't press. I didn't want to know since I had my invisible boundaries too.

We'd both moved up together to the Titan ward together and had stuck close ever since.

His usual dark blonde hair and warm eyes comforting more than anything else. "Want me to step in? You just finished."

"No, I can handle it."

"Let me know if you need me."

And so I headed towards Room 3.

My hand gripped the cool metal of the doorknob, and I took a deep breath, steeling myself for whatever—or whoever—waited on the other side.

As soon as I knocked and stepped in, I was in trouble.

The man before me was leaning against the wall while sitting on the hospital bed, his head tipped back, exposing the strong line of his throat.

As I entered, he dropped his gaze forward, cradling his arm to his chest.

Impeccably dressed in a suit that hugged his broad shoulders and lean form, his hair was mussed like he'd run his hands through it over and over again. But his movement drew my attention to his arm, making me acutely aware of how he filled the small space—and how he was in pain.

"Mr. O'Hara? I'm Nisha, your nurse for today." My voice sounded steadier than I felt. His eyes met mine, sending a spark coursing through my body.

This is Killian O'Hara?

His eyes caught me first. He had heterochromia eyes—one aqua, one amber—gazed back at me with a frightening intensity.

"Are you all right?"

He's hurt. I have to do something.

His limb was still held protectively against his chest, the fabric of his shirt stretched taut over tense muscles.

5

"You're in a lot of pain…"

"It's not serious. Just need it looked at."

"Doesn't look not serious to me."

As I said it a muscle ticked in his jaw, his lips pressing together like he was biting back a comment.

Which I hoped he was because I didn't want to deal with his infamous temper today.

Men like him didn't usually come to the hospital unless they were dying or so severely injured it took everything they had not to admit it.

I needed a different approach.

I took a step back, my shoes squeaking softly on the polished floor.

The small sound seemed amplified in the quiet room.

"Would you mind confirming your name and birthday?" I managed, focusing on the task at hand.

I was determined to maintain my professionalism despite the attraction simmering beneath the surface, like a current threatening to pull me under.

He's a patient. And one who won't hesitate to swipe you down.

Focus.

Killian Liam O'Hara. Twenty-seven.

Five years older than me, but in an entirely different world.

He worked for Titan Security, the private company that owned this hospital.

And he worked in a particularly dangerous sector. I'd heard of some of them frequently coming in for all sorts of injuries.

Killian…he came in very few times.

And when he did, he erupted on everyone.

From what I had heard.

Nobody mentioned if they had been decent to him.

I reached toward his arm. "Let me take a look—"

"No—" His brows slammed down in a frown, his eyes flashing with a mix of pain and defiance.

Annnnnd that might be why he put everyone off. I took him in—brows furrowed, watching me with an intensity I hadn't imagined—and felt my professional demeanor wavering.

Enough for me to know…he was definitely a man.

And I hadn't really found myself attracted to a man in a long time.

Not since…everything had happened. Those mismatched eyes

boring into mine. And I felt a flicker, a nudge, just something rushing through me I couldn't explain.

It almost hurt to look at him. But his eyes, it was his eyes that hurt the most. Despite being different, they were the most striking eyes I'd ever seen.

And I knew he was enormous compared to me, easily six-two or three.

Focus, Nisha.

Don't be afraid of him.

"I'm going to have to take a look—"

"I don't need that shit—"

But I caught a flicker of something else in his eyes, a vulnerability. Rumors of his temper aside, I wasn't afraid. I could see he was hurting, and I was determined to do right by him.

"I want to be able to do my job and help you. I can't if you don't let me."

Stay calm. He's like a bear.

Don't move.

And he won't eat you.

"Fuck this. I need to go—" He started to push off the wall, but I saw him bite back a grimace of pain.

"You're hurt."

"*Move back.*"

"I can't—" I stood my ground.

He looked even more pissed off. "*Why don't you just–*"

"I'm trying to help you–"

"*It's not helping!*"

"*Then quit acting like a big baby!*"

I clapped my hand over my mouth, eyes wide.

Those mismatched eyes widened, and his jaw went slack. My chest was heaving, and I was aware of his eyes darting to the fabric stretched tight across my scrubs.

One eye was amber, bright, and watchful, his other one blue and disarming. *Oh my God.*

It was like he'd short-circuited, blinking rapidly as if rebooting his brain. He looked like a toddler who'd just eaten a lemon, his lower lip working in his mouth.

"I...what did you just say to me?"

His voice was deep, settling somewhere deeper in me. I had to ignore that.

Do not laugh right now.

The taste of my cheek filled my mouth as I bit the inside of it, trying to maintain my composure.

Do not laugh.

But gosh, he's adorable.

The fabric of my scrubs felt too tight, too confining. Part of me wanted to apologize and backpedal.

But another part—the part that got me through endless night shifts and difficult patients—stood its ground. Doctor Perla hadn't hired me to be walked all over.

"You came to the hospital to get help. I'm trying. It doesn't help you or me if you refuse any treatment," I rushed on, the words tumbling out in a breathless stream. "I don't want to see you hurt. And I'm not trying to hurt you."

Something about him got under my skin. Somewhere I hadn't felt since high school. Years ago.

"Let me help you. Tell me what happened. You're here for a reason."

He stared at me for a long moment, those mismatched eyes searching my face.

The confusion in them slowly gave way to something else—curiosity, perhaps, or a grudging respect.

"I…fell," he admitted slowly, his eyes dropping to his injured arm. "Landed badly on my shoulder."

"Can you describe the pain for me? Is it sharp, dull, or throbbing?"

Killian hesitated, his jaw clenching. A muscle ticked in his cheek. "Sharp. Feels like it's on fire."

"Can you move your arm at all?" I asked, reaching for him slowly. I watched closely as he attempted to lift his arm, my eyes tracing the ripple of muscles beneath his shirt.

"No, it's…it's too painful."

I leaned in closer, my eyes scanning his shoulder, my breath mingling with his. Even through his shirt, I could see the telltale deformity.

"May I?"

As I gently palpated the injury, I could feel the abnormal protrusion of the humeral head.

"Does it feel numb or tingly down your arm?"

"Yeah, a bit," he admitted through gritted teeth, his breath hitching slightly as I continued my examination. *"Fuck."*

"What about weakness in your hand? Can you grip my fingers?" I offered my hand, palm up, the fluorescent lights casting a soft glow on my skin.

He hesitated for a moment before reaching out, his rough, calloused palm sliding against mine.

Don't move.

His grip was weak, but the warmth of his skin lingered on mine long after he let go.

"I think I dislocated it...My brother tried to set it, but it hasn't stopped hurting..."

"Your brother tried to set it—"

"Kieran's not exactly the best, but—"

"Mr. O'Hara, a dislocation needs immediate medical attention. The longer it's out, the more damage it can cause." I took a step back, the cool hospital air rushing between us. "How many days ago? What did you take for it?"

"Not sure. Pain-killers." The way his throat worked, I knew he was lying. I didn't know how I knew. I just knew.

"What did you take for your shoulder?" I repeated.

His throat worked again as his eyes closed. "Nothing."

My chest tightened at the expression on his face. *Oh Gosh.*

"We need to get this properly set and imaged," I said, my voice steadier than I felt. "Take off your shirt. I'll get you fixed up."

3

KILLIAN

GETTING HURT WAS A PART OF THE JOB.

Didn't mean it was a part of the plan.

But work for Gabriel usually fucking meant I got hurt.

The de-facto head of Titan Security, the company I worked for on paper, had a knack for sending me out on gigs that required...*finesse*.

To say the fucking least.

As in the kind of work that never fucking saw the light of day on paper.

I straddled both of my worlds—for Aidan, my older brother, and the mob, for Gabriel and Titan—equally.

After Aidan had taken over for my father, Cormac, and had him off'd I'd been balancing a tightrope. Of legality and loyalty.

Reed, Gabriel's best friend and on paper CEO called it, the morally grey area.

I didn't give a shit what it was called—that was *my* area.

And despite offering all the legitimate trappings it could, beneath the underbelly of Titan was me. And my reality. The other half of the truth and jobs. Gabriel wanted cockroaches eliminated? I took care of it.

He didn't like the mess. I didn't like to fuss.

I was Gabriel's personal hitman.

And it worked.

Give me a corpse any day. At least they didn't talk back.

Gabriel, had been my mentor since my twenties. He'd saved me from myself more times than I cared to count. The shadow. And his ghosts.

When he said jump, I jumped. I leapt.

Only this time...I jumped too high.

I'd been running after a target. And the motherfucker had vaulted off a larger building onto a smaller one. Not a fan. I'd landed all right into a smooth roll.

Or what would have been a smooth roll.

I fumbled and hit my shoulder. But I'd got the motherfucker and off'd him and thats all that I'd cared about then. Three days ago.

Now?

Now my shoulder was a live-wire of pain. Now it ached. Throbbed. And hurt so fucking bad.

Chasing targets, dodging bullets, staying alive—it was all part of the job description. But this? *This* wasn't part of any plan. I hated getting hurt.

Hated getting fucked over like this.

Hated the hospital.

Hated the self-righteous stares of doctors.

Hated how they quipped about a big-tough-guy needing to toughen up. Hated it.

And now...The florescent lights of the hospital burned my eyes, the antiseptic smell turning my stomach. And then—*there was her.*

Her.

Nisha.

Fucking.

Graham.

The nurse my team wouldn't shut up about.

In the flesh.

Sean, and a bunch of the other guys yapped about her non-stop. I'd dismissed their infatuation, rolled my eyes at them.

Oh, I got it now. I fucking get it.

Her scent hit me first—warm, spiced, unfamiliar.

It cut through the sterile hospital smell, making my head spin.

All five feet five inches of curves and warmth, and suddenly I couldn't breathe. Couldn't think. Nisha Graham was fucking *gorgeous* in a way I had no business noticing. Long midnight wavy hair, soft green

11

scrubs hugging every curve, those dark eyes batting at me from where she was.

Every. *Single.* Curve. *Jeez.*

The moment I saw her, I fucking knew who she was. Those hips? Her *tits. Motherfucker.*

I was in hell.

Her entire body curved and dipped and fuck if she wasn't beautiful. In a way that made me want to strip her right there. Sink my teeth into her. And just like that my cock was responding to her.

The pain in my shoulder faded to background noise as a different kind of ache took hold. One that made my dick throb.

Fuck me, I just want to kiss her.

She looked golden and pink. Soft. *Too* soft. The kind that didn't last in my world.

"Take off your clothes," she said, all professional efficiency.

Jeez, luv. Say please at least.

The thought flickered through my mind, surprising me with its playfulness. I swallowed hard, off-balance in a way that had nothing to do with my injury.

She called me a big baby, and I almost laughed.

If she only knew who the fuck I was.

Heir apparent to the soon-to-be *former* Irish mafia.

A man with blood on his hands and darkness in his soul. A man who had no business wanting someone like her. Someone who looked warm. Like she glowed.

Those mocha eyes met mine, and she looked at my shirt. And my eyes dropped to her chest several times. Her breasts straining against the v of her top.

I wanted...I did. *I do.*

Her voice was soft, professional. Innocent. "Do you need help?"

Oh. Fuck.

My dick responded to that voice.

The light arch of her brow. The cheek-bones looking delicate and her lips parting.

Oh. Fuck. Me.

I knew she was just doing her *job.* But *fuck me* Nisha was pretty. Experience had taught me hard lessons.

No woman who looked like *that* approached me without ulterior motives.

I wasn't gentle in bed. And women loved that.

Pussy was just that—a commodity, easy to use and discard.

Kieran's policy was never go back twice, and between Aidan never settling down with any woman. Kieran, with too many women. I had zero intention of ever being serious.

Ever.

Except…something was different this time.

A foreign feeling stirred in my chest, one I couldn't name. *Didn't* want to name. I felt off-kilter, like the ground beneath my feet had shifted.

Her name alone conjured images of something other-worldly. Dark eyes like pools of midnight, framed by long lashes. High cheekbones and delicate features that begged to be traced with my lips. Waves of silky hair cascading down her back. Naked. *Lush.*

Her hips curving into handfuls I'd grip fucking into her—Her breasts heavy and full and—*Holy. Fucking—Shiiiiiiitt.*

"Mr. O'Hara?" She reached for me, and I tensed instinctively.

Touch meant pain, betrayal, weakness. But as she drew closer, her scent enveloped me. *What the fuck was that?*

Why did it smell so good?

Something unfamiliar stirred within, and I had to bite back a growl.

Call me Killian, luv.

Women rarely phased me. And the kind of women I fucked—were into whatever I put out.

I hated being touched. Fucking hated it.

I tied up my women so they wouldn't feel any part of me but what they needed. But as she approached, I found myself fighting a different urge. Her scent clouded my senses, making it hard to think straight.

Say that naked. Get on your knees.

My throat worked, suddenly dry. "I need–"

"I understand. Let me help you."

And then she reached for my shirt, her fingers whisper-soft against my skin as she began unbuttoning it. My dick reacted instantly, hardening painfully. I willed myself to calm down. I couldn't.

"I got you," she kept her voice low. "I can take care of that, let me…" and then she started fucking *talking*. "Move this way—"

I obeyed. I didn't even bat a fucking eyelash since Nisha was…she was so fucking distracting. All plush and pink cheeks.

And I was in pain.

Vulnerable.

As she slowly slid the shirt off my good arm every instinct screamed to push her away, to maintain control, but her proximity short-circuited my brain.

I could easily haul her into my lap, suck on those…let her ride me til she came—*No. Fuck no.* I clenched my jaw, willing away the thoughts. This wasn't me.

I didn't lose *control*, not for anyone.

"It's all right," she whispered, her husky voice soothing. The scent of her infiltrated every fiber of my being. Amber. Lush. Soft.

My entire body responded to her. My dick in question was loving her.

"It'll be over soon, I promise…"

Oh, fuck me. She can say whatever the fuck she wants to me.

"Do you want me to cut into your shirt…no? Okay. Breathe for me, exhale…"

The last time I'd dislocated my shoulder, Kieran had snarled at me to stop being a punk bitch as he wrenched it back into place.

But Nisha's soft reassurances?

They had me harder than I'd been in years.

I didn't get it. I shouldn't have craved it. Craved that voice.

I gritted my teeth, desperately trying to focus on anything but the pain. *Anything but her.*

Locking my eyes onto the way those soft green scrubs stretched across her, her fingers grazed my skin. And I bit my cheek to not fucking make a sound. *Fuck.*

When did a hospital visit turn into…*this?*

"Breathe for me. It's okay, I have you. Nothing's going to happen to you. I have you…"

It was foreign and unsettling how her voice washed over me.

Nisha undid my sleeve, and agony flared white-hot in my arm.

"Shhh, it's okay, I got you. I know…I know…it's okay," she whispered, her breath warm against my ear. "Breathe…once more."

The pain was still there, a searing, relentless agony radiating through my entire body.

14

"I'm going to reset it now," Nisha said softly. "Breathe for me."

I steeled myself, jaw clenched. I'd been shot, stabbed, tortured. Abused. This should be nothing.

"Ready? On three. One...two..."

Before "three" left her lips, her hands moved swiftly. White-hot pain exploded through my shoulder, vision blurring.

A sound I didn't recognize tore from my throat.

"Fuuuuuucck."

Nisha's voice cut through the haze. Her arms were around me, and I was powerless to push her away. Amber invaded my senses and I stayed there not moving.

"I know it hurts," she murmured, drawing me closer. "You're doing great. Just breathe with me...You're doing so well. Good job..." Her fingers carefully probed the area. I found myself leaning into her, forehead against her collarbone.

Her warmth seeped into me, grounding me in ways I didn't understand. "Breathe for me...good...another one, there you go, baby. You're all right."

Fuck. Call me baby again.

When the fuck did pain ever hit me this hard?

And why the hell was I letting her see me like this?

As my senses slowly returned, I became acutely aware of my surroundings. Of *her*.

Of how dangerously close I was to crossing a line I'd never even considered before. This wasn't me.

Soft and vulnerable were for *other* people—the *normies*—not Killian fucking O'Hara.

Yet here I was, breath syncing with hers, stripped bare in ways that had nothing to do with my shirt being off.

"Shhh, I got you..."

The throb in my shoulder was a distant echo compared to the ache blooming in my chest, an alien sensation I couldn't—*wouldn't*—name.

My fingers were twisted in her scrubs, clutching the fabric like it was the only thing keeping me from drowning.

Shame burned hot in my gut.

Weakness.

I'd spent a lifetime building walls, learning to be harder than whatever life threw at me.

15

And right now?

Right now at my lowest this fucking woman had me stumped.

But Nisha…*Christ.* Nisha was dismantling everything with each whispered word, each touch. Was that me shaking?

No. Couldn't be.

"No, no, it's okay," she murmured, her grip tightening. "You're okay. It's all right, breathe for me…*breathe, Killian. I won't let anything happen to you.*"

My name on her lips was the last straw.

I was moving. Moving. Grabbing. Stamping my mouth over hers before I even realized what I was doing. I wanted to taste how sweet she was. A noise left her lips as I did.

Part whimper, part gasp. Part something all her. And I turned into this animal.

I tasted her heat, her lips against mine. And I groaned not even hesitating taking her further.

Taking advantage of the way she gasped to thrust my tongue into her mouth to hear her moan. Low.

But she did.

My dick responded hardening, my entire being aching to hear it again. I kissed her longer, every bit of her inching into me.

Another small noise left her as she held onto me. Nearly pulling back in shock. *"Killian—"*

I didn't give her a second. I kissed her again.

Softer. Seizing my moment. *Her.* She made a soft noise as I explored her mouth, tasting something sweet and groaning louder. She tasted like candy.

I didn't know why I was breathing so hard.

Or why I wanted to strip down every layer of her…right there. Lust. It was just lust.

That's all it was. One taste and I'd be good. Solid. Except all I saw was her dark pupils dilated and the flush on her cheeks. Her eyes taking me in surprise. In wonder.

A soft look in them as I watched her. My throat worked as I brought her closer, my hand gripped her hip and my other lifted to her face. Or it would have. Had my shoulder not chosen that exact moment to scream in pain.

"Fuck, luv—"

"Sorry," she whispered. "I'm sorry. I forgot..." Soft noises left her as she held me again.

"No..." I don't know why *she* was apologizing.

She did nothing wrong.

I just kissed Nisha Graham. My nurse. Holy—

"Killian...your shoulder—"

The way she said my name...like it was everything. Like I was everything. Her hands on my skin left trails of fire, and suddenly I wanted to devour her.

To possess every inch, to lose myself in her completely. Sink deep into her and stay there.

She was...*indescribable.* I licked my lips, biting back words that threatened to spill out. Promises. Pleas.

Things I had no business saying or feeling. *And I just fucking kissed her.*

"I'm going to get you some ice," she said softly. As she moved to pull away, panic flared. My grip tightened involuntarily.

Nisha stopped moving like I was an animal she had to be wary of.

"Killian." I couldn't meet her eyes.

I kissed this girl.

"I'm not leaving," she whispered. "The ice packets are in the fridge to my right. I won't leave you. But you have to let me get it for you."

I knew that.

"Killian, you have to let me go. I promise I'll come back, Killian. You have to let me go..."

I was starving suddenly, out of the blue. For *everything*. For her.

Her voice came again. *"Killian..."*

I know. I know. I know.

I promise. I'll behave.

As Nisha's fingers traced soothing patterns on my skin, memories flickered—cold nights, scraped knees, bruised knuckles. Always alone, always picking myself up.

But now...I groaned at the sensation of her fingers in my hair rubbing gently.

"Breathe, Killian, I'm going to get that ice pack. I'm right here."

I held on for a heartbeat too long before forcing my fingers to uncurl from her scrubs. Couldn't even look at her.

The fridge door opened. Ice packets rustled, the sound sharp and jarring in the sudden quiet.

Each second stretched, an eternity of cold air against my skin where her warmth had been. *Finally*, mercifully, she returned. Her warmth was all over me again, and I reached for her before I could stop myself. Curling myself into her.

Not realizing what the fuck was happening as Nisha's arms curled around me and my face tucked into her neck.

"I know." Her voice was a whisper. "Breathe for me."

I did. Hating my weakness even as I craved more. My good hand found the curve of her waist.

"It's okay," she murmured, low and soothing. "I'm right here. I'm not going anywhere."

"I don't need this shit."

Fuck.

Why did I say that?

Am I stupid or dumb?

"Do you want to hold the ice pack yourself?"

No.

I did not.

Say yes, punk bitch. Say it. Be the man you're supposed to be.

The voice in my head was a snarl, all too familiar.

But for the first time, it didn't feel like mine. It wasn't mine.

So I said nothing. Nisha turned her head to me to say something, and my entire being reacted to it.

"You just needed a hug, I know."

No. I needed more.

I *snapped*, kissing her like some wild animal, hungry to get his way into her. I was craving her. That softness, that touch, that lightness to her.

Why does she smell like cookies? Like sugar?

Why does she feel so good?

If Nisha was a bunny under my fingers, I was the ravenous wolf ready to devour her. I couldn't stop.

I want more.

Disarmed.

I was disarmed.

18

I'd faced off men in a crowded room ready to die.

And suddenly I was disarmed by a five-foot-five woman with the softest lips in the world I couldn't stop tasting.

4

NISHA

I had thrown professionalism out the window when I kissed him back. *Killian O'Hara.*

If kissing me wasn't bad enough?

I'd kissed him *back.*

And now he showed up again and again with a little smirk on his too handsome, too pretty, too sharp face. The man was lethal, his jawline cut from marble, and eyes that saw too much.

The first time he returned after our initial kiss—the one I liked more than I should have—something shifted.

When he entered the room, a quiet anticipation stirred within me, a gentle pull I couldn't ignore.

Those eyes locked on mine and I shrunk backwards a little.

After my experiences growing up, I knew better than to fall head-first into anything, but that didn't stop my body and my mind from warring with each other.

His lips parted as he watched me.

"Mr. O'Hara—"

I barely managed to start before his lips were on mine again, urgent and demanding.

I didn't even move as he closed the distance between us, his mouth hungrily over mine leaving me scrambling to grip his shoulders.

He easily lifted me up into his arms and set me on the bed as he kissed me.

I gasped a little as he thrust his tongue into my mouth and a noise left me. This wasn't gentle like the first time.

No, he seemed to have patiently waited for himself to get better before he came after me.

I was a little breathless when he finally broke apart. Like I was caught, pinned, and helpless in his arms.

He was staring at me a little confused and in wonder.

I swallowed not sure where to look as my fingers clung to him. Ducking my head I took a few breaths to steady myself unsure of what to say to him. He didn't like that.

His nose was brushing against my cheek as he watched me.

"Wait—" I cautiously whispered. "I need a second."

He was like a big baby in disguise, seeking comfort in the most unexpected ways. Brushing his lips over mine. Unable to stop. And I yielded.

I had to ask, my throat working uneasily.

"Do you have a girlfriend?"

He shook his head, and then his lips found mine again.

This time, it wasn't the hungry devouring of before, but a tenderness that took my breath away.

My body responding to his, my nipples harder than ever, brushing uncomfortably against my scrubs. I felt how wet I was through my panties. And I arched into his touch.

I'd run my fingers through his hair, and he'd brush his lips over mine again and again. I wondered if he was trying to seek comfort through me, which should have bristled my professional sensibilities.

I didn't think he had a girlfriend...but what if he did?

"Aren't you going to ask me if I have anyone?"

I didn't.

"Do you?" The shift in the air was tense, the energy between us changing. I told him I didn't, and he nodded quietly.

"Well...no, but, do you kiss everyone who treats you?"

"Do you kiss everyone you treat?"

We both paused. I blinked.

"No," we both answered simultaneously, pausing watching each other carefully, and then he reached for me again.

It was absolutely out of line.

Unprofessional in every sense of the word.

And yet, the moment he kissed me, I was gone, lost in a world where only Killian and I existed.

I knew I was crossing a line I could never uncross, but in that moment, with his arms around me and his lips on mine, I couldn't bring myself to care.

"We should stop," I whispered. He nodded without stopping, and I breathed his name. "*Killian.*"

I was lost in his world, his tongue thrusting into my mouth, my entire being responding to him.

I felt even more protective of him time and time again.

When he went to get his blood drawn and the nurse there accidentally kept prodding him. I stepped in calmly even if I wanted to strangle her.

Or when we got into the elevator to get his prescriptions and two of the hospitals doctors with cops, were eyeing him—I just stepped in front of him calmly pushing him back a little with my shoulders. They'd looked away after that.

He didn't utter a noise of complaint with me in the room ever. And people noticed but I ignored everyone.

At the end of one of his visits, I finally took a step back.

His eyes flared wide, and I caught the way he moved his head, tipping it slightly like a curious wolf.

"I don't think we should do this—" I broke off, unable to form a coherent sentence around him. "I can't—"

Even as I said it, I knew we already *had*, multiple times.

I didn't know what I was saying; I just knew that even though I had moved back, he still took up all the space in the room.

He didn't say a word, those mismatched eyes of his taking me in disarmingly. He wasn't happy with it. I knew that much.

"You're a patient," I whispered, grasping at straws. "I work here. I don't know…" I didn't know what I was doing or why. Why he did it… why I let him…and how out of place this was.

I never did anything like this, and he just watched me quietly, hungrily, without saying a word. My throat worked as he did.

"I'll just hug you…from now on…" Even though all of me screamed.

I can't even form the fucking words.

His brows drew down, but even then, I knew I was crossing a line. Tremendously so.

And I felt so stupid for saying it.

Killian had been back four times in the last two weeks. Instead of kissing me he sat through and accepted my ministrations.

The last time, he'd had a burn. I didn't know from where and I didn't ask. I'd been a little upset—at his injury, but mostly at how he had waited for hours before coming to me.

"Why didn't you come sooner?"

"Needed to handle some stuff."

I frowned at him not hiding my displeasure. "What was more important than this?"

But he had seen the furrow in my brow as I'd walked away to grab what I needed, cursing myself for getting attached to him.

He was just supposed to be a patient.

Who you kiss to comfort.

The burn on his arm was clearly bothering him. He looked perturbed as I asked him that and I didn't know who moved. But he was cuddled up to me again.

Words of comfort left my lips and I knew I was so stupid for turning my back on what I had said. Because I did want to kiss him.

"It's okay…it's just a burn, I got you. You're all right. Does it hurt anywhere else?" I checked him over.

He looked at me and that was when I broke at the look in his eyes. Like he was holding back and he didn't know how to say so.

I was on him so fast, brushing those inky locks back, lips on his cheek, his lips. Comforting him. Knowing he needed it.

"I'm sorry," I murmured into his skin. "I wish you came sooner. I'm not upset with you. You're going to come sooner, next time?"

He didn't say a word and I couldn't even feel guilty for kissing him *again* as he nodded into me.

I brushed his hair back kissing him steadily, gingerly exploring his mouth with my tongue.

The moment he sucked on my tongue I moaned almost drawing back, but those steel bands of his arms wrapped around me—until he hissed a little. I pulled back looking down at his bandage.

"Sorry," I whispered.

He'd all but melted into me then, and stayed lingering. I only flew apart from him at the sound of a knock on the door and my heart racing wildly. Or I tried to. He just held on tighter.

23

He made no comment.

And that was the thing about Killian. He rarely said anything. If he needed me, I knew.

And I didn't understand it *at all*.

5

NISHA

IN THE DEAD OF NIGHT, MY PINK SHEETS TWISTED AROUND MY LEGS AS I tossed and turned, sleep eluding me yet again.

Nightmares plagued my mind.

Earlier that evening, I'd come home to find letter in my mailbox and the stamp on it immediately made my stomach bottom out.

Besides struggling with my anxiety on a day to day; nothing got my heart racing than seeing a letter from the jail that my adopted father was in.

Eugene Graham might be released thanks to some legal loophole allowing him to walk free.

He, and his wife, Michelle, had been missionaries abroad. I had thought the story they told on paper was the one they believed.

I had been rescued from a family that didn't want me and they had. So I should've spent the rest of my life being grateful. That gratitude hadn't played out in the best ways.

They insisted that my birth parents hadn't wanted me and that they were giving me a better life in America. But that couldn't have been further from the truth.

The news, combined with the sweltering summer heat and my finicky HVAC system, made for a restless night.

But it wasn't just the temperature keeping me awake.

No. I just kept imagining Killian. His amber and blue eyes. Unsettling but not so much anymore. Not when I knew he was a freaking softie. Underneath it all.

But I didn't know how to talk to him or turn to him. And what would he do even if I did?

"My adopted parents molested me, and now my father might be getting out of jail. Help?"

Would he tell me I was being stupid, that I wasn't worth his time or concern?

He was a busy man with an important career. He worked for Titan.

I didn't know under what capacity but he was important.

And I was Nisha Graham.

Just Nisha.

After an hour of futile attempts at sleep, I threw off the covers in frustration.

My skin felt too tight, my body thrumming with an energy I couldn't dispel. Padding barefoot to the kitchen, I welcomed the cool tiles against my feet as I flicked on the lights.

The microwave clock blinked at 2:17 AM, a reminder of yet another sleepless night courtesy of Killian O'Hara and my dreams of his muscles and body. And well—my nightmares.

Seeking a distraction, I decided to be productive and use my hands. An old therapist had once told me that I thought best when engaging both the anxious and rational parts of my brain.

With music no longer an option, cooking and prepping food seemed like the next best thing—certainly better than going to work in my current state.

But I was too tired to rummage up any recipes so I just opened up my laptop on my island.

I made coffee and began working through my food blog.

I'd started it years ago in college. It had been a way to find comfort and a practice that didn't involve me eating pans of cakes and brownies just for the hell of it.

Wherever I went taking photos of food. What started out on social media ended up with me running a blog called 'Slice of Life.'

I could always go and take some photos and brainstorm some ideas. A little cheesy, but I liked the vibes, I liked the audience it attracted— lots of wholesome folks and good things.

I wanted to bring good things into my life.

In my world where chaos was…well everywhere? It was nice to come home to something calmer.

Not a house where your adoptive father touched you sometimes. Or put his hand down your shirt. Or down your pants.

Not a house where your adoptive mother told you, you were asking for it. Not one where she told me it was my fault her husband couldn't himself.

I was eight.

I shook myself out of my thoughts about my past choosing instead to focus on the task at hand. A recipe. Something to focus on other than my trauma.

"I need to post more, it's been a few days," I muttered to myself.

My last post about lemon possets and lemon bars garnered a lot of likes. In the summer I did a 'Citrus Series' and it was a hit all the time.

Sunshine. Good things.

Good things after a lifetime of bad ones.

I had made a few friends on my blog, girls and women all over the world I talked to but the longer I sat on there scrolling, I needed something to do. Otherwise my mind was go stir crazy.

So I moved to the kitchen with my phone and set up and began chopping a colorful array of fresh fruits from the farmers market.

It was halfway through the process my adopted mother's voice filled my head, drowning me in shame.

Do you really think he likes you?

How could he ever like you?

Attention seeking whore.

This is all your fault, you ruined my entire life, I took you in and you repaid me by seducing my husband.

My throat closed up on me a few times as my hands shook. A side effect of everything.

I dropped the knife several times, panicking at the sound of her voice and the feeling of my adopted father's eyes on me—the source of my nightmares.

Samuel was evil incarnate.

While the details of my early childhood remained hazy, I remembered with crystal clarity the moment I decided to leave the Graham's.

The police had torn apart my adoptive parents' house, uncovering evidence of my adopted father's acts. *Photos.* Images of me he'd taken.

I had thrown up over and over again. The detective on the case at the time had been a man named Cameron Giroux.

He'd been there for me and guided me along the way. He had been such a huge help and on occasion we still kept in touch. He was a Lieutenant now in the NYPD.

The day I ran away, I swore I'd never let myself be vulnerable again —and Lt. Giroux had gotten me help from a few people to ensure I never had to go through it again.

Until now.

Could I allow myself to want *someone* simply because it made me happy? Killian felt too intense, too real, too close to a happiness I wasn't sure I deserved.

At twenty-four, my teenage self seemed like a distant memory, another life entirely. I didn't feel my age.

I felt older. I felt trapped in my body sometimes. I ate my feelings through it.

I couldn't remember the last time I had been with someone or wanted anything like this burning desire I felt for Killian. Being called names for wanting to date another boy in high school haunted me.

You're such a fucking whore with your body.

Only whores have breasts like yours.

Did you honestly think any boy would ever like you?

I adopted you for what to be a whore?

Michelle's voice was shrill and it burned my blood to hear her.

I would scream, I would stay out late, I would react—because that was my reality every single day.

Everything had haunted me for a long time after I had been freed. Shopping. The doctor. My emotions.

Coming out of an abusive household meant you questioned your reality, your truth, trusted no one—and spent your time alone.

Because it was easier than ever getting hurt. And Michelle's voice in my head *hurt.*

I don't know which subsection of hell Michelle's voice came out of. But I did know that women like her had filled my life for so long when I finally broke free?

I got to be someone better.

I got to be this version of me.

I heard her in my mind talking about my body, how big it was getting even at size eight. I knew it wasn't big at all.

It was average at best. But I found myself remembering all the times she let me starve to get rid of that baby fat.

My hips. My breasts. My everything.

Michelle wanted to *erase* me.

And it stung more than I cared to admit.

All because her husband was attracted to me.

He felt uncomfortable with me wearing a bra. Or shorts. Or a dress.

"Can't you change? Why do you have to seduce my husband? Why are you such a whore?"

I'd been twelve.

I spent my years understanding Michelle would never see him as the problem. My existence was.

And so I made myself invisible. Smaller. Escaping to school and eating my feelings, just like I was doing now. I learned to fade out and live in my head.

All because I wasn't welcome. Eating alone in my room because I'd have to listen to Michelle saying things like. *"I just don't understand why she eats so much."*

The weight gain that followed my escape had been challenging to accept, but over the years, I'd grown to embrace my curves.

I wasn't tiny, but I was healthy.

I didn't have to hide my breasts anymore. I could wear dresses. Skirts. Anything. And everything I wanted. I was free. It took time to accept. But I was free.

And I struggled.

Killian likes your body.

Initially, I had been given a chance at a better life, until everything unraveled, and I realized I'd been robbed—not just once, but multiple times.

And finally, I stopped running. I heard my thoughts telling me things but I recognized it wasn't my voice. It was Michelle's.

And it wasn't my voice telling me to be grateful. It was Eugene's. And I felt nothing but nauseous.

Do you really think anyone would ever like you? You?

A failure. A disgrace.

Nobody wanted you. Nobody loves you.

Your own mother never loved you.

So I picked you up off the street.

And now you want to accuse my husband of something he didn't do?

Dirty. Little. Liar.

I saw Killian's eyes flashing in my mind before the image faded away.

When Dr. Perla informed me that I was the only one allowed to treat Killian, it felt surreal, almost like a cruel joke.

"Mr. O'Hara placed the request," she had said. *"But it's not really a request since whatever the Titans say goes. I can assure you, you'll be the only one seeing him."*

Then, because Dr. Perla was who she was, she had to ask. *"Is everything okay? I know sometimes he isn't the easiest—"*

"I just think he's in extreme pain," I had interrupted. *"I can imagine I wouldn't be pleasant company if I ever dislocated my shoulder."*

Perla had nodded understandingly. *"I hear you on that."*

She didn't press further, simply stating that she was aware of the Titans having preferences and she accommodated all of them.

There were patients only she was allowed to treat, like Reed Whittaker, Adam's older brother, and a few others who came directly to her.

But if I was honest with myself, I understood the situation all too well.

The way Killian's eyes roamed over my figure when he touched me, hauling me close and kissing me steadily, made it clear that he appreciated every inch of me.

During his visits, he lingered, tucking his nose into my shoulder or arm. And I, weak for him, gave in every single time.

I held him for long moments, hugging him close, unable to stop myself. And then there were his kisses—slow and steady, drugging and soft.

After the initial note, I didn't hear much from anyone on my adopted father.

But I would be lying if I said it didn't give me anxiety.

How did they have my address? Did he have it?

Not possible.

Right?

I didn't know much about Titan Security or Killian's role there. But it was clear he had influence.

His ability to request me specifically proved that.

Killian would watch me with those mismatched eyes—one aqua, one amber—his gaze soft and hazy.

It made my hands shake, suddenly aware of him as more than just a patient. Sometimes I'd see the hint of a smirk on his face. Enough to let me know, he knew the effect he had on me.

I covered my face breathing in and out.

When he'd lie down and I'd lean over him, his breathing would hitch, a subtle change that didn't escape my notice.

It had been weeks now, maybe a month, since our first encounter.

Perla said you requested to see me...just me...

I did.

Why? You won't see anyone else?

I don't want to see anyone else.

And he was still watching me like a patient wolf. Not letting me go.

"All done for today."

One side of his mouth quirked up a bit as I realized what he wanted. I went to tug myself out of his arms, and he smirked.

Only to have him catch me and haul me closer.

A squeal left my lips as I gasped against his mouth, not missing the way he drew me closer.

Until I was moaning into his kisses again.

"We should stop," I whispered.

"Mhm." And he kept going.

6

KILLIAN

I was making out with my fucking nurse like a teenager in heat, and I couldn't stop if my life depended on it.

All I wanted were her kisses, those little noises I'd tasted on my tongue half a dozen times now. I wanted it all.

Neither of us said shit about it, we just fell into each other every fucking time.

Was I fucking strange?

Maybe.

I wasn't like my brother's. I couldn't just—tell her. I couldn't say what I wanted to say. With work? I was adept.

With Nisha?

I was like a fucking *idiot* who couldn't string anything together so I just made out with her like my world was ending.

Every single time I told myself I'd stop?

Nisha would run her fingers through my hair and I'd just lose my fucking mind. Holding her close, tighter against me, using her like some kind of fucked-up comfort blanket. And she just *held* me.

And then she gave me one of her fucking heart bandaids and I wore that shit all the time. Obsessed was putting it lightly.

The greatest frustration was not being around her, the greatest peace was being held by her. And I didn't even fucking know the lady! Nothing compared to Nisha, her voice, soothing me, calming me down —and I was now fucking imagining her *everywhere*.

I felt like a *goddamn idiot* for finding peace with her.

Maybe it was just because she worked in the hospital. No big deal. I was emotionally attached to my nurse. No big. Deal.

But.

Nisha's gentleness was foreign to me.

Nobody treated me like she did.

Even medical professionals regarded me with wariness. Growing up, gentleness wasn't something I'd known.

Not in my world.

Never.

Dark dreams of my mother...an image of her I couldn't quite make out. Aidan blocking me from seeing her for some reason. And then images of my father, beating his kids, until Aidan and Gabriel finally off'd the son of a bitch.

But before they did his disgust at my 'freak eyes', his fists and words that shaped my fucked-up childhood.

You're not my fucking son.

I knew my mother's eyes were blue. His were amber. I got spliced in half by both their genes. I had just enough of her to be reminded I wasn't exactly like Kieran and Aidan.

I had never been like my brother's.

Not my fucking son.

Not his fucking brother.

You're a bastard to me.

And I didn't know what the fuck he was talking. I looked a tiny bit like Kieran. I was family. Right?

The solo memory in my mind was of my mother. Dark. She was...I couldn't remember. It was all black.

Her brushing her inky hair, crying her eyes out. She was always crying especially after having Kieran who she didn't really go near. I remember her avoiding him. And I couldn't explain why.

I remembered Aidan though, his eyes changing at a young age.

Hardening until there was nothing left. Aidan had been the one who hadn't said a word. He'd been quieter than both me and Kieran.

Just stay close to me, yeah?

Making us grilled cheese sandwiches before school because that's all he could make at the time.

We couldn't afford much so Aidan taught us how to spend what little we had wisely. Aidan took care of me and Kieran more than our father had. Aidan dropped out of school and he sacrificed everything so we could have the life we wanted.

Any money he got he'd pitched it back to me and I had been responsible for my baby brother.

Now that baby brother was stirring up trouble in New York in my playground. Thankfully, he didn't know about Nisha.

During the month I met her, my team noticed the change in me.

I fucking knew one of them would smell the faint trace of women's perfume that hung on me after seeing Nisha.

Because maybe she was the first woman in years who extended some kindness to me.

The bandaid I tucked away carefully. And the way I chilled out? Even I felt it.

They knew better than to say shit, but I caught Sean's sharp blue eyes and curious eyes as he looked me over.

"You look better, you go to the hospital?" Sean asked innocently.

His blonde hair was combed back into a ponytail, looking way too put-together next to how I felt.

I wasn't sleeping well at all. Not with the thoughts of her.

But the moment Sean asked me the question, both of the guys in the car quieted and eyes darted to me.

Motherfucker.

Nobody gossiped more than men.

Most of the time, the guys who worked for me gave me space. We were a mix of the old O'Hara clan and the new Titans, all thrown together into one unit.

I ran them all, unless they worked somewhere else like Teasers—Nate took over then.

Landon and Derek, my current shadows, had been staring out the van window like statues, now turned to me.

"Are you fucking serious right now?" I looked at Sean who ducked his head.

"Sorryy," he shrugged. "You smell like her. It's kinda hard to ignore." As he said it, I stiffened.

"I thought you put on perfume," Derek muttered. "And then Sean over here filled us in on your girl. Never took you for the type to fuck with her—"

"Not a *single fucking word* about her," my jaw clenched as Derek's pale eyes moved over me and then looked away.

I felt a wave of possessive fury take over as I sat back in the passenger seat and Sean looked away in the driver's side.

Landon watched me now. "We wanted to tell you in case you wanted any of us on her in the future."

I breathed out. As in protection. He wanted to know so Landon— the planner—could factor Nisha into anything for me.

I was quiet.

If I admitted it? They'd know I liked her.

If I didn't? They'd think she was fair game.

And Nisha Graham was fucking fair game.

"Yeah. Put her into your plans."

Derek raised a brow and Sean smirked. Landon hid his in his fist.

Motherfucker.

"Mr. Monroe wants us on the ground?" Landon asked gruffly, his dark eyes raked over me and I could see him fighting his grin.

"He does. He's got a few jobs," I said tersely. Damn. Had they all taken bets or something?

"Mr. Monroe doesn't like roaches," Derek murmured. "I bet he's got a plan for that Congressman."

Gabriel *didn't* like cockroaches.

And neither did I.

"He does."

From day one, I knew someone had royally screwed Gabriel over in his past life. He'd spent seven years wiping out enough of them for me to know he was gunning for something bigger.

Something out of reach but just there.

The faint scent of Nisha's perfume still clung to my clothes, a constant reminder of what I couldn't have. And I had kissed her. Marked her as mine in a way I couldn't take back.

Landon's dark hair peeked out from under his beanie, his breath fogging up the window as he spoke.

The intricate tattoos on Derek's neck shifted as he swallowed, waiting for my response. His shaved head gleamed under the street-lights as we cruised through the city, his eyes a flat grey made of ice.

He was the one I went to for the ugly shit.

Sean was softer than the three of 'em but he had the most heart.

Landon was whatever you needed him to be.

"Focus on the objective." I kept my voice firm, the words echoing in the confined space of the van. "Derek, you're on perimeter. Landon, back exit. Sean and I will take 'em out. No stragglers. No survivors."

Gabriel had odd jobs for us here and there. This was different. Information brokers weren't good to have around at all unless they were in your pocket.

And most problems—I took care of.

Sean tossed in the smoke bombs. Within seconds people were screaming and running out.

We were in and out in quick minutes in the chaos. It was a higher end club, but they didn't stand a chance.

The guys and I always moved like shadows. And I had a guy under-cover as the bartender. Easy kills.

I moved my mask over my face taking out anything I needed to.

Derek got grazed in his side, but other than that? My eyes swept through the carnage we'd wreaked havoc in a few minutes.

Not too shabby.

After, I coughed up my lungs from the amount of smoke.

"Boss," Sean held up a man squirming in his hold, begging.

"Please, please, I wasn't working with them—" he broke off when Landon taped over his face.

Hard eyes met mine from Landon. "What do you want to do with him?"

I shrugged. "Just kill 'em. They're all the same." And Gabriel didn't like cockroaches. Neither did I.

You let one live—it became an entire infestation that I had to get rid of. I ignored the screaming.

I always did.

I got back to the van aware the cops wouldn't be coming out here ever. Perks of having an older brother in league with them. I didn't think rival gangs or anyone knew the level of power we had.

Gabriel and Aidan worked on opposites of the coin—and I ran down the center of it.

When I did get back to my car to check my phone, I thought about her for a second. Just a second to breathe.

I didn't want her out of my head, even though I knew I should.

Her face haunted me, stirring up memories I thought I'd buried deep.

Something warm and soft, just out of reach. Like my mother's perfume, fading as she walked out on us.

Or the way I remembered her brushing my hair back. Faint memories of a woman who had given a shit. Held me. Was there. Before she wasn't.

I remembered her crying to Aidan, remembered Kieran clinging to my side, barely three years old.

The images were fuzzy, but Aidan's eyes remained clear in my mind —hard and cold, a man trapped in a boy's body.

Aidan was thirty now.

Did he ever think about what we lost? We never talked about it.

Never talked about anything that mattered.

At twenty-seven, I felt a chasm growing between us, wider with each passing day.

I couldn't tell anyone about Nisha. Not Gabriel, not Aidan. Nobody.

How could I explain those dark eyes that saw right through me?

That quirk of a smile, the apples of her cheeks were fucking adorable when she did it. Her eyes fucking sparkled with this light in them. And her body—*Jeez*. Nisha was…something else.

She was fucking edible, and once I got a taste, I had been addicted.

I wanted more. Needed more.

Her voice was the only thing that could quiet the chaos in my head, drowning out the echoes of gunshots and screams that usually filled my nights.

I blamed it on not getting laid recently. But even then, empty sex had turned into just that.

My brother were down for any kind of empty sex. But…I didn't want that. Not anymore.

Aidan, ever serious, never letting anyone in; Kieran, wild and untamed, chasing his next high like his life depended on it.

And me? I was chasing Nisha.

Because…I didn't fucking understand why she got under my skin. But she did. When she looked at me with those eyes, I felt seen. And then she'd hug me, and I'd lose my shit all over again.

I'd practically snarled at Doc Perla, demanding that only Nisha tend to me. Everyone else could fuck right off. And Perla being trained around the Titans knew better than to argue.

Gabriel always said I was a creature of habit. A reliability guy.

I'd had the same routine, same weapons, same everything for years. I knew what I wanted and saw no reason to change.

But Nisha...she was shaking the foundations of everything I thought I knew about myself.

7

KILLIAN

TONIGHT, I WAS HOME, AND I DIDN'T WANT TO BE.

A penthouse I'd gotten off my cash, high above the city's chaos. Panoramic views of the city skyline combined with soundproof glass and privacy screens helped give me some solitude.

The place was all sleek lines and minimalist design—and it felt more like a hotel than a home.

An open-concept kitchen, all stainless steel and marble, absolutely spotless. I barely used it, save for the coffee maker that kept me functioning.

Combined with a reinforced door, soundproofed walls, state-of-the-art security system.

Nisha wouldn't fit in here. She liked pink.

Cartoon lanyards. Her fucking cartoon bandaids I wore even though nothing was wrong with me. Like some fucking pussy I was.

Her nails clean and short. Nothing gaudy for my girl. And she smelled like...the softest spiciest—I didn't even know what *it* was.

Her entire being...soft. Every inch of me was hardened to a fault. The cold perfection of my state of living was nothing like her.

None of it was warm.

My phone buzzed, the screen lighting up the van's interior. Lara Ford's text glared at me:

Your brother is being an idiot.

Can you come get him before Nate shoots him?

Fuck.

Followed by a video of Kieran making out with Gianna May, one of the girls at Teasers. *To cat-calls.* I swore.

He there now?

Please tell me this was a recent video and my brother is still fucking there

Negative.

Kieran was out again, and Nate Wyatt—a fellow Titan working under Reed—was at his wit's end.

I pinched the bridge of my nose, feeling a headache coming on. I wanted to think about Nisha, not deal with my brother's bullshit.

Nate kicked him out.

He left to De Nuit with his friend Teo?

Matteo?

The pretty boy with the blue eyes and fast cars.

Teo. Yup.

Motherfucker.

I sighed. I didn't want this tonight.

But I couldn't ignore Lara's message. Lara wasn't just another player in our twisted game—she was the reason for everything we'd become.

Years ago, Lara had been the catalyst for Gabriel's grand plan.

A power play that changed all our lives.

It started simple enough: Gabriel's brother had asked him to keep Lara safe. That was it. But from that simple request, an empire was born.

I didn't know much about Gabriel's past.

On paper, Gabriel Monroe didn't exist.

No record, no history.

Just a ghost living in his quiet manor in Greenwich, far removed from the world of normal people.

I knew enough to understand that horrific things had happened to him, things that made him erase his entire existence.

Lara's safety had been his request. In exchange, Gabriel promised to elevate my family. In power, in name, in influence.

All it took were a few calculated steps. Seemed simple at the time, but it set off a chain reaction none of us could've predicted.

Our bastard of a father had owned the club where Lara worked—the old Teasers. Just another piece in his empire of filth and corruption.

In exchange for setting Lara free, Gabriel negotiated with Aidan.

Gabriel got Lara. Aidan got the family name.

He teamed up with Aidan, offering a way to break free from our father's iron grip.

I can still see the cold efficiency with which Aidan and Gabriel, barely out of their teens, carved through half the organization.

And because Gabriel was a fucking political mastermind with his fingers in every pie, we learned to make amends with all the folks our father had pissed off.

We kept our darker operations—Gabriel's thirst for necessary bloodshed hadn't exactly dried up—but on paper, we were clean as fucking whistles.

Gabriel always played his cards close to the chest, never fully explaining his grand design.

So Aidan started working with Lucas Devereaux. Taking up properties across Chicago, New York, and the whole damn East Coast like it was a game of Monopoly.

Meanwhile, Gabriel hunkered down in his fortress of a manor and birthed Titan Security with his best friend Reed Whittaker.

The Devereaux fortune flowed through Aidan's shrewd investments, circling back to Lucas and then back to us. And into Titan.

It was pure fucking insanity.

Every business was connected, each thread strengthening the whole fucked-up tapestry. And at the center of it all was Gabriel and Lara. She was a force of nature on her own.

At twenty, I found myself being put through the wringer by a guy barely older than Aidan.

With Aidan busy running an empire, he couldn't focus on me and

Kieran. But Gabriel? He had people for that. So we trained under him. Mostly me.

I'll never forget that first sparring session.

Gabriel, a six-five behemoth with blonde hair gleaming in the sun and those eerie pale blue eyes fixed on me.

He was the scariest motherfucker I'd ever met, and that's saying something in our world. But he was *there*.

Gabriel's methods were brutal—punishing martial arts, endless strategy sessions that felt like mental warfare. *Get up.* He was ruthless.

Don't be a punk bitch.

You're supposed to be able to control your fucking anger. Not piss off everything in sight.

Kieran's sharper than you.

For a while I hated him.

Until I realized how much better I felt to not have my fathers influence in my life. Gabriel was an obelisk. And I was molded back in his image. Less angry. Less all over the place.

My hair-trigger temper replaced and tempered over time. A year of quietly training under his ruthless efficiency—I was better.

Gabriel had killed my father, and here I was, training under him to be a better fucking person.

The irony of the situation never escaped me. Being molded by the guy who'd murdered your old man—*twisted* didn't even begin to cover it.

He broke me down and rebuilt me, piece by agonizing piece.

My phone buzzed. *Aidan.*

If my older brother texted me, I was solid. If he called? He was pissed. He only talked to people when shit hit the fan.

And if Aidan showed up in person? Everyone was fucked because he was worried. Something he rarely did.

"Yeah?" I answered, keeping my voice level despite Nisha's brown eyes flashing in my mind.

"Why the fuck is Kieran shitfaced and chasing after one of Lara's girls?" Aidan's voice was ice.

Shit. He knew. No doubt Nate told him.

Nathan 'Nate' Wyatt, the Titan overseeing security for Lara's Teasers, worked hand in hand with my guys.

I inhaled slowly, pushing thoughts of Nisha aside. "I'm handling it.

42

Lara gave me the heads up." But they had to notify Aidan when Kieran did stupid shit because Aidan didn't want the youngest of us washing up in the Hudson off a bender.

I got why Kieran had lost his fucking mind in so many ways, but I also didn't.

He'd checked out, lost in his fantasy of freedom. Years ago, it would've been me in his place if he hadn't switched spots with me. My father had liked Kieran better, but Gabriel and Aidan?

They saw something in me. In turn, Kieran offered me the spot I never had.

I'd found my purpose in Gabriel's fucked-up structure, in this empire we were building.

The "normal" life Kieran was chasing? I had no use for that shit. Not anymore. But my new normal only existed because Kieran didn't want it.

And Kieran had ditched Teasers for Matteo 'Teo' DuPont's place, De Nuit.

It wasn't quite a hotel, more like an old property they'd turned into their personal playground.

Matteo and Kieran were like gasoline and matches—they fed each other's worst habits. I knew exactly what kind of shit went down on Matteo's desk. And what he and Kieran were into.

"Find him before he does something stupid."

Pinching the bridge of my nose, I felt the familiar weight of responsibility settle onto my shoulders. "I'm on it."

"Let him know if he wants out I have conditions..." I paused, listening as Aidan talked to me about everything he wanted out of me and Kieran. He couldn't have Kieran getting killed.

Or worse. And so he wanted me to temper him. Or Gabriel. Either way Aidan needed to come down to the city. He grumbled about that.

"I don't fucking understand—"

"You don't have to," I cut him off. "He's been like this for enough that at this point it shouldn't even surprise you."

"I know." Aidan wasn't happy. "But he can't be doing this bullshit. This isn't the first time." No, it would be the last though. I'd make sure of it.

"You're letting him go. That's enough."

"It better be. I'm tempted to off him myself at this rate."

I bit back a laugh. Aidan said that about both of us. But that wouldn't ever happen. He just didn't get it.

Unlike me or Kieran, Aidan didn't let loose with drugs or alcohol. I didn't know what he did. But I had a faint idea I wouldn't be thrilled at how much blood he spilled.

Aidan made me look like a saint.

"Try not to murder everyone in Chicago."

"Alexei does that all by himself."

My brother's head Enforcer and guard was something else.

Alexei Markovik had been another casualty of my father. Someone Aidan had taken in and now he was loyal to Aidan. Not exactly a guard. Not exactly a son. Or a brother.

Somewhere floating in the middle ground after Alexei had been a teenager who tried to rob Aidan. It had taken Aidan two seconds to catch him and keep him.

Now? The kid was important to us. We'd all adopted Alexei in some way shape or form watching him grow with us.

In Chicago, Aidan was closer to the side of the family that wasn't legit. The side that I would *never* in a million years go back to.

This was my life now. I served Gabriel. I served Lara.

And the Titans. Pausing at the threshold of my apartment, the weight of my decisions pressed down on me. Bringing someone like Nisha into my world was reckless, dangerous.

Something I didn't do.

I didn't even know how to. Yet as I stood there, I couldn't shake the image of her smile, the warmth of her touch.

She represented everything I couldn't have—everything I shouldn't want.

And everything I wanted anyway.

8

KILLIAN

Maison De Nuit.

I arrived parking in the underground garage, the lights twinkling in the French style of an elegant building.

Having a little brother who owned a sex-club wasn't exactly something I'd pictured Kieran doing. But given his recent escapades I wasn't surprised.

Lucas Devereaux had sold a French styled hotel to Kieran as a club. Matteo DuPont had invested into it turning into…well…the sex club of Teo and Kieran's dreams.

Kieran and Teo needed a debauched playground to do anything and everything they wanted.

The two of them had plenty in common.

The grand lobby stretched out in front of me, vacant front desk, and I walked up the balcony into the upper floors.

Luckily, I knew where Kieran might be tonight.

I used to come here so the sounds of sex didn't phase me anymore. Not when I only wanted one fucking woman and those soft eyes of hers watching me.

Kieran's playground for sex and drugs didn't bother me. But being here when I didn't want to be did.

Kieran's door was labeled 'Topaz.'

One of us was a pampered private school trust fund kid who got his company handed to him by *his* older brother.

45

And the other? Was a street rat who became a hitman to survive under *his* older brother.

We couldn't be further apart.

I had a thing for rules. For reliability.

Teo said fuck the rules and did his own thing.

Nobody of ours hit on anything under Lara's roof.

We had rules about it after my father was removed from power. He had used Teasers as a venue to traffic underage girls.

And now? Now I was committed to never repeating a hint of that shit ever again.

I promised Lara I'd never put her through that shit again.

As soon as I walked into the suite and entered the code, I saw Teo first.

Naked in the kitchen with two women, one of their high-pitched giggles grating on my nerves while she made out with him.

The other was bent over naked, Teo grinding between her legs unmistakable in what he was doing. Leave it to Teo to fuck women without giving a shit.

His alien blue eyes, pupils rimmed in black, met mine as I stalked in. His smirk was wide.

One of the girls licked his neck. I caught the lines of white on the back of the other girl.

"Big brother to the rescue," he grinned, tipping his head back. He was high as a fucking kite.

"Where is he?"

I knew Kieran wasn't far from Teo. Between the two women passed out on the couch in front of me and the other two with Teo?

Kieran was close.

"You could almost pass for normal." I didn't say anything. Not because I judged him.

But because I was worse than both of them. Which was why I hadn't done anything with Nisha. I'd tear her up.

Teo fisted the hair on the girl he was fucking hauling her up to her moans, her eyes glassy and tits shaking with every thrust, the other girl making out with him had stopped watching me avidly.

"You should try her out," Teo motioned to the girl next to him who was licking her lips now.

"I'll pass. Where's Kieran?"

Teo watched me not stopping as he took the girl in his arms. None of this phased me anymore. He motioned to the right. The back.

Got it.

Tipping my head I moved past him. I didn't hate Teo. Not at all. He was an irritation at best, but I couldn't judge him since years ago? I was where he was. Before Gabriel.

Before Titan.

I got why he was fucked. Between his own family feuds and what little I did know about his older brother, Andrei?

It made sense Teo needed an outlet.

Just not enough to kill *my* brother.

But just as I was about to go to Kieran, another woman wound her way around me, giggling and trying to lick my neck. Jeez.

"I'm good." The scent of her perfume almost made me gag. Nisha didn't smell like these women. Nisha smelled warm and inviting. Not this cloying plastic shit. I grimaced.

I found Kieran in the bedroom in the back, identifiable by the black clover tattoo I knew all too well.

Sprawled on the bed, his skin slick with sweat and god knew what else, Kieran was losing his mind in pussy like he always did.

One riding him, back arched, head thrown back. The other making out with him.

I swore softly at the guns and knives on the floor. Fucking. Kieran.

Years ago, this might have stirred something in me.

I was a part of this world and I'd been into the same things. And now?

Now my visions were filled with raven hair, dark eyes, and soft smiles at me, softer kisses. Fuck. I would never go anywhere near her with a knife. In the past…maybe.

Back when Kieran and I had both given into vices that were beyond toxic, with Aidan unable to control either one of us. I had been worse than him. Darker. *Once.* Now all I knew was my fist and dreams of Nisha's lips all over me.

All because she was the softest thing I'd ever had in my life.

"Get out," I snapped, tossing clothes at the women, wishing I could as easily discard the life I'd built.

"What the fuck," Kieran slurred. "I'm not finished."

"You're finished, little brother. All of you. *Out.* Now."

47

One of the girls, a brunette had the audacity to suggest I join them.

"Nope." I had thrown a wad of bills at them along with their clothes. "*Out.*"

Money talked, and I had plenty to make them scream.

Kieran had glared at me like I was the villain in his drug-addled narrative, his eyes struggling to focus. *Jeez. When the fuck did it get this bad?*

"Get up," my voice cutting through the haze of his high. "I heard about Teasers. What the fuck were you thinking?"

I privately knew she was fucking Nate Wyatt, and that might be why Nate had lost his mind a little at Kieran all over her.

"What the fuck is wrong with you?"

"Lara's girls are off-limits. Always. Nate was ready to put you in the ground tonight."

"Why the fuck are you like thi—"

"Shut. The. Fuck. Up." My patience, already threadbare, had snapped. "Aidan called me. You want out? Fine. He'll cut you loose. But you better have a fucking plan beyond chasing pussy and getting high."

I laid out his options, including the one I knew he'd hate most. I felt nothing but frustration for some reason. Like I was on the edge of something I couldn't name.

"Aidan's not letting you waltz away scot-free," I watched him. "He wants mandatory check-ins with either Gabriel or himself. Your choice."

After our mother left, I took care of him. I raised the kid.

He was my brother and something more. I'd been his saving grace for so long...I didn't know anything else. Aidan had shouldered the pressures of keeping us safe. And even now?

The three of us were a trio fucked up beyond repair coping in unhealthy ways despite life getting better for all of us.

Kieran had money now. We made sure of it.

But it wasn't enough. Growing up the way did?

We all had issues and our demons. And Kieran needed his own ways of coping. I got it. But I also didn't.

"Aidan wants to set up a meeting," I continued, my tone brooking no argument, even as part of me wanted to shield Kieran from what was coming. "But first, he has a list of demands."

"Of course he fucking does."

I didn't let Kieran's voice grate on my nerves. Not when I could smell the room on me. And not her.

As I finished laying down the facts to my brother, all I could think about was Nisha while Kieran's amber eyes processed what I said.

His wide eyes were blank without the light that was usually in them. He didn't always get like this.

But the fact that he did told me he wasn't in a good place.

And all I wanted? Was her. That was my good place.

Your only fucking good place.

Wanting Nisha meant acknowledging that I wanted out of this life.

It meant admitting that I was tired of being the responsible one, tired of cleaning up Kieran's messes, tired of living up to Gabriel and Aidan's expectations.

For the first time in years, I allowed myself to imagine a different life. A life with Nisha.

The idea of introducing her to Aidan, to my family, made my stomach turn. In our world, bringing a woman to meet Aidan wasn't just a casual thing.

It was as good as declaring her family, marking her as mine.

The thought of exposing Nisha to that life, to the darkness that clung to us like a second skin, made my stomach sink further.

"That's it?" Kieran said. "He wants me to either work for him or Gabriel?"

I tipped my head.

"Aidan wants me to be a Titan?"

"Did I fucking stutter?"

A hysterical laugh came out of Kieran. "And do what? Be some bodyguard and save people—"

"Keep your ass out of trouble. That's it. That's all he wants." Aidan had goals. None of them involved a little brother hell bent on getting in trouble. Or ending up dead. I fucking *knew* he'd pick what he thought was the least morbid option.

Nobody killed people the way Aidan did. He didn't believe in letting cockroaches roam. As the leader of the family?

Aidan ruthlessly cut his way through things.

"Gabriel won't let you work for him without getting your act together. So pick your shit up. Get the fuck out of this place. And clean up."

I told him Aidan wanted to meet a few weeks from now. A few weeks. Time flew. I'd been stumbling around Nisha for a little over a month now.

As I stepped out of *De Nuit,* the summer night air enveloped me like a thick, humid blanket.

It was close to ten o'clock, and the darkness seemed to pulse with the rhythm of the city.

A distant siren wailed, its echo bouncing off the buildings and fading into the night.

No, what I want is Nisha.

I could almost feel her hands on me, gentle yet firm, working out the knots in my shoulders.

Nobody touched me like that. Women didn't want me to comfort me. I wasn't a stranger to women. Plenty of them wanted me.

But not like her.

The memory of her scent—clean and amber and warm, so different from the acrid smell of drugs and sex that clung to me now—made my throat tight with longing.

When she touched me? I felt peace. I felt warmth. Like I belonged somewhere in life other than the darkness of my soul—and for that alone I wanted her. It was just sexual. That's it. If I fucked her? I'd have enough.

I told myself I'd kissed her so many times it should've been enough. She should've been it.

No dice.

It was the way she looked at me, really looked at me, like she saw past the name, past the violence and the darkness. She didn't give a shit what anyone else said. She felt like mine.

Like she saw me.

And she was kind.

The stench of everything clinging to my clothes competed with the night air. Sweat beaded on my forehead, whether from the muggy heat or my inner turmoil, I couldn't tell.

She was so fucking nice.

All I could think about was getting back to the hospital. Back to Nisha. I wanted to bury my face in the crook of her neck, to feel her fingers running through my hair.

I understood Kieran's desire for freedom. But I also didn't.

Hell, I'd wanted the same thing once.

I'd buried that desire deep, accepting the role that he so casually tossed aside.

The irony wasn't lost on me—I'd kill for what he threw away, and he'd die to have what I longed to escape.

But Nisha…she was something else entirely. I couldn't tell Nisha who I was unless it was serious between us. And even then, the double edged sword was—if she knew? She might hate me for being a monster.

Wanting Nisha meant wanting *more* than just her.

It meant wanting a different life, a different me.

And suddenly I didn't want to be…*me* anymore.

9

NISHA

He was back.

The days had melted into weeks, into a month, and summer found Killian a frequent visitor to our ward.

Today, it was just a small cut, but the moment he entered the room, my world narrowed to his presence alone.

And I didn't know how it made me feel anymore after the lifetime of...my parents.

My life.

The longer he came the longer it broke down my defenses.

Because he was...just himself. Not expecting anything from me.

The note of Eugene's release faded and became less important to me with Killian in my life.

He makes me feel safe. To just be.

I felt protected when he held me. And nothing else existed anymore.

Today, Killian didn't move towards me right away. And that stirred some anxiety in me. Just enough for me to know that something was off.

"Who got you flowers?"

He'd noticed those. I thought I'd told the girls to take them away. I turned to face him, feeling my cheeks get hot. His eyes burned with something I couldn't name.

"It's not a big deal." But judging by the look in his eyes he thought it was.

He couldn't be jealous.

He kissed me.

But I also kissed him back. My fingers tingled as they brushed his skin, each point of contact sparking with an energy I couldn't explain.

The warmth of his body seeped into my hands, and I was lingering longer than necessary. Dark swirls of tattoos covered his hands.

Symbols, shapes, a wolf on his pec.

That's what he was—an enormous, patient wolf with those eyes, just sitting there, watching me. Devouring me.

In ways I wanted more of, outside of this place.

I didn't even question it when he first kissed me.

From day one, it felt as natural as breathing, as inevitable as the tide.

Killian O'Hara was turning into something that I couldn't shake and I didn't think I wanted to.

My eyes drifted to his hand on his thigh, and I noticed a tiny cut.

Better fix that too.

My heart raced as I reached for his hand, the silence heavy between us as I wrapped a silly bandaid around it.

I'd been doing that more often lately.

Sometimes he lost them. Sometimes he came back with the bandaid still on. He held it out for me as I placed it on.

This one had little hearts printed on it.

"They're just...from patients," I stumbled over my words, my usual calm crumbling under his stare. "I left them out there for everyone to share the donuts."

I wanted to tell him that none of it mattered, that he was the only one who made my heart race like this, who was in all my thoughts and dreams.

"People like...men."

Oh. *Gosh.* He couldn't be jealous. Out of *everyone?*

"Sometimes."

All the time. I didn't pay attention.

The room felt smaller, his presence filling every corner, leaving me dizzy. His shirt half-done, belt loose, suit messy—he looked incredibly handsome and dangerously intense.

"Men send you flowers?"

Why did he say it like he was going to murder anyone who did? I couldn't even look at him.

"It's nothing…We should get you that x-ray—"

"Why?" A muscle in his jaw twitched.

"Your knees. I'm worried about the pain—"

"I'm talking about the flowers." Oh.

My chest was pounding a little. In the enclosed space, Killian's presence swallowed the area whole. Dark and dangerous, he took all the words from my usually articulate mouth and turned them into mush. I turned to look at him to find those eyes on me with a glint in them.

"It doesn't matter."

He paused, his gaze raking over me.

"Mr. Walker isn't here today, so that would be good," I continued, words tumbling out. "I know you don't like him and so—"

"Why doesn't it matter?" Killian's voice sliced through my rambling those eyes watching me. Unsettling in a way that sent a bolt of lust to my lady bits. "Lots of men send you things?"

It felt like his voice was *all* over me.

How was I supposed to lie? Could I lie to him? *No, better not.*

"Sometimes, but it doesn't matter to me—"

"Why?"

I paused. Focusing on his shirt. His hands. Anywhere but those disarming eyes of his.

To say Killian was intense was an understatement.

That was like saying a tiger in a jungle at night wasn't hungry and roaming for its next prey.

And me? I felt like I was caught in that jungle. I was his prey.

They don't make me feel the way you do.

Confusion flickered across his face, quickly replaced by something hungrier. Darker.

"Do you—" His eyes dropped to my lips as he tipped his head.

"No." I don't why I rushed to reassure him. Like I could make out with all my patients?

The butterflies in my stomach were losing it. Losing. It.

"Just you." Even if neither one of us knew how to navigate what this was—it was just him.

I wasn't usually *this* awkward but around him? I lost all rational thought. And this was *awkward.*

"We need to go get your knees and calves x-rayed." I motioned to his legs clad in tailored pants. My throat worked as I asked. I turned to find his intense gaze fixed on me, pupils dilated. I was rightfully embarrassed now.

"Do you need help with your clothes? Does your arm hurt—"

"Just me."

His eyes, those mismatched orbs of stormy blue-grey and warm amber, never left mine.

"Just you...we should leave the tie off since...*sometimes* women come by for Adam, but he's always with a patient. It doesn't mean anything. It's just flowers, not a big deal."

I was rambling.

Killian remained silent, but his body leaned into my touch, almost imperceptibly. As I finished the last button, I dared to look up at his face, my heart racing.

"All set for the—"

A sudden knock on the door startled me. I jumped, and in an instant, Killian's arms banded around me, pulling me close.

His nose pressed against my cheek, his stubble grazing my skin. I felt more than heard the low rumble in his chest—protective, possessive.

"*Yes?*"

"*Sorry!*" Said the outside voice.

Killian's arms tightened fractionally, and I felt the curve of his lips against my skin.

"You're all right! I'm almost done!" I said, though whether I was reassuring the person outside or myself, I wasn't sure.

His arm tightened around me and I stopped thinking, his scent in my lungs as I inhaled shakily.

"That scared me."

A soft noise left him.

One I didn't imagine him making.

I felt his nose moving, nuzzling my cheek, my jaw. My breath caught as his lips found my pulse, rapidly fluttering beneath my skin.

His lips brushed over it. "Just me."

I stood frozen between his thighs, feeling my breathing slowly calm under his touch, even as my heart raced.

"Just you."

Killian held me tighter if possible, lips brushing over that erratic flutter, legs spreading to accommodate me in between them as he held fast.

He wasn't letting go of me anytime soon and I wasn't sure I wanted him to. His mouth moved over my lips.

"Only me."

He *was* jealous...

I looked into those eyes of his watching me.

"You can't be jealous," I whispered. "Do you really think I kiss everyone?" At the words his gaze dropped to my lips.

He was quiet for a long moment. "Only me." He repeated it. Something darker was in his eyes making mine widen the shock fluttering through my chest.

"Only you."

I didn't know why I knew I needed to confirm it. Why would there be anyone else?

"Do you like flowers?" That look never left his eyes.

"I've never met a woman who doesn't."

"But do you like them?"

I swallowed hard around the unfamiliar lump in my throat. "I love them."

"Which ones?"

"Pink. Anything pink."

His eyes flickered to my lips with a soft look to them, like he wanted to smile at that. He tipped his head like he was taking notes. He wasn't the type to walk in here carrying pink flowers.

Not him.

No. *Don't be silly. He doesn't wear color.*

"We should go," I said, my voice unsteady and breathless. "Get you taken care of. Come on."

10

KILLIAN

SHE WAS A LITTLE NERVOUS.

She reminded me of a deer. Terrified. A little jumpy.

I didn't think she understood my need for her.

Hell, I didn't understand why I fucking needed to know that nobody else was after her. Of course, people—*men*—got her fucking flowers. I could just find them and kill them—and then they'd never send flowers again.

Unhinged was one word for how I felt about Nisha fucking Graham.

Unbalanced.

Lunatic.

Confused.

I wanted this woman. And my mind and my body didn't understand why her. I could have anyone.

I could pluck any fucking dark-haired woman out of De Nuit and fuck her until she cried. Tie her arms and legs up and make her cum until she lost her mind.

But the only one I wanted to do that to, was Nisha.

The one who was currently a little startled by me. I never usually let anyone in.

Even opening up to her a tiny bit about my jealousy. The one that flared up like a wild animal in my chest over someone—*anyone*—daring to even try for her attention?

I didn't understand.

Someone slammed a door and Nisha jumped a little. Right into my way. I didn't even blink, catching her up in my arms, before setting her right again.

Like I said.

Jumpy.

But beautiful despite being startled. Her skin was so soft, the pulse of her body under my lips felt so…perfect. I pressed my lips to the erratic flutter finding it against the column of her throat.

I pulled back. Those doe eyes bat up at me a little. A lot. And I felt my lips twitch at her nervous energy.

I couldn't stop myself. I wanted to *devour* her.

Sink myself so deep into her skin that she didn't know what it felt like to be without me.

Her figure pressed into me in elevator when others walked in. This was why I *liked* Nisha.

She defended me without even knowing she was doing it. Instinctively.

She moved in front of me, pressing that lush ass up against my thighs because she was tiny compared to me.

I towered over her and her dark hair I dipped my head down onto inhale that scent.

Amber. Cotton-candy. Pink flowers. Something spicy. Nisha smelled like a whole snack. And combined with that body of hers?

I wanted to sink my fangs into her.

I didn't hesitate to kiss her softly, when I caught someone watching her, to move her closer to me.

She didn't even protest instead easing her entire body into mine and I held her tightly as people got on and off.

Her lips parted like she wanted to say something and then bit it back and I felt a smirk curve my lips.

We'd skipped past professionalism a while ago.

And all of my fights had been abandoned the moment her hands had been all over me soothing me. Kissing me. I was insane. But I knew what I wanted.

I wasn't pretending for shit.

"It's colder down there," she looked at me. "Are you going to be all right?" I nodded. A little cold never bothered me.

Once, my father had wanted to punish me for stealing food.

I didn't remember much of my childhood, but I knew I'd gone hungry, and he'd kicked my stomach until I'd passed out in the freezing Chicago snow to teach me a lesson.

I'd thrown everything up and blacked out. Aidan had found me and taken me to his room.

He'd gotten his ass beat, but he and Kieran were more favored than I was, so he got off easier than I did. Which wasn't saying much.

Nisha looked out for me. Like Aidan did.

And maybe that was what I saw in her, too. A sense of...something familiar I knew. Family. Life. But better.

She'd put another one of those bandaids on my finger.

On a paper cut. And I fucking adored her for it. She thought I needed soft. It was the first time in my life I'd ever experienced that.

"How does your leg feel right now?"

"Not too bad."

I didn't think I had shin splints but we should check with all the falls and landings I took. Nisha would want to check.

I watched her carefully, tracing the lines of her face with my eyes. The smooth curves of her cheeks, her skin glowing under the lights a little, lips full and lush and she looked around.

I knew something was bothering my knees. And my calves.

I didn't want it to get worse, but until Nisha said something, I didn't know what to do. I fucking hated coming here until her.

And now her midnight hair was in my vision as she scooted closer to me when more people got on. I moved her gently behind me, keeping me as her wall.

To look out for her.

My hand brushed her lower back, and I felt her leaning into me, her hand moving to my chest, sitting there squarely as people moved in and out.

The scent of amber was in my lungs and I bent down a little playing with the ends of her softer waves.

When the elevator cleared out I didn't hesitate pulling her back into my arms despite it being empty.

Nisha just sighed a little contented and damn if that didn't do something warm to my chest. She wanted to be in my arms.

"We're here now."

I followed Nisha into the X-ray room, my eyes immediately drawn to her graceful movements. And the way her scrubs hugged her figure.

She turned to look at me, her fingers grazing my arm as she passed. And then I saw who was in the room.

Eugene fucking Walker. X-Ray tech.

Mother. Fucker.

If there was anything I hated more in the world than everyone else —it was fucking cowards like that idiot.

The scrawny technician stood hunched over the equipment, his ill-fitting scrubs hanging off his bony frame.

His appearance was as unkempt as ever, but I found my attention drifting back to Nisha.

Nisha's presence beside me was calming, her subtle amber scent cutting through the hospital's antiseptic smell.

As she leaned in to whisper instructions, her breath tickled my ear, reminding me of the gentle kisses she'd placed there just days ago.

Her lanyard around her neck had flowers on it.

The thought returned from earlier despite her reassurance. Men brought her flowers. Men wanted her.

You want her.

I did.

I do.

But...I didn't know...I didn't know how to do anything. Women didn't want me for sweet nothings and flowers.

But the image of Nisha's face lighting up at the gesture was tempting.

Cold seeped through my clothes as we entered the room where I was about to get my X-ray done. She was worried about my legs.

Nobody fucking worried about me. Harsh fluorescent lights cast an unforgiving glare on the medical equipment, and I realized how fucking uncomfortable I was until she brushed my arm again. And my eyes landed on why.

"I thought you weren't in today, Eugene," Nisha said in a louder voice, like she was alerting me.

Nisha moved around me to my front as if she could shield me from him. There were a few times in my life I saw someone I wanted to punch in the face. He was one of those times.

"Plans changed," Eugene mumbled, his gaze darting between Nisha and me.

"Mr. O'Hara needs an X-ray for his legs," Nisha explained, her professionalism being in stark contrast to Eugene's demeanor.

Eugene nodded, his movements jerky. "Right. Well, we'll need to, uh, get a clear image. Mr. O'Hara, you'll need to remove your pants for this." The cold air seemed to grow even chillier at the prospect.

I locked eyes with Eugene, a smirk playing at the corners of my mouth.

Turning to Nisha, I asked. "You'll stay." It wasn't a question.

Nisha's cheeks flushed slightly, a hint of pink against her olive skin, but her voice remained steady. "Of course. I'll be here with you the entire time, Mr. O'Hara."

Just say my name, luv.

Nisha sent me an apologetic look. She hadn't known he was here. "Let's get you into the smaller room…" Her hands touched mine gently on my belt. "Come on."

When I came back out after changing into just my t-shirt and briefs, my eyes met Nisha's, who turned a light shade of pink, glancing down my chest.

She looked at the corner of the room, and I smirked. Nisha liked my tattoos. She thought I didn't know how much until I caught her rubbing at the skull on my back a little.

If Eugene fucking Walker wasn't in the room right now, I'd kiss her again.

And then, like an opportunity coming around, Eugene turned away to adjust some equipment.

I seized the moment, pulling Nisha close and pursing my lips to her. Her eyes widened and she shook her head, darting to Eugene and then back to me. I pursed my lips again. Nisha's brows drew down but she did it quickly.

Brushing her lips against mine. And I didn't even hesitate to deepen it with a small grin.

She gasped softly against my mouth, those eyes of hers widening, her hands instinctively gripping my arms. She shook her head.

"Behave," she mouthed. And then she kissed me again quickly.

When I emerged, Eugene couldn't look at me directly, and when he did, his eyes widened noticeably.

I wasn't as wide as Aidan, but I was pretty fucking big coming up from that scrawny boy with Gabriel to this. And I wasn't afraid of nobody. Not a single fucking person had shit on me.

Maybe a tiny bit Aidan, but that was more respect for him and his taste for violence. But if I could take Gabriel in a fight? I could take this little shit.

As I positioned myself on the cold, hard table, memories of our last encounter flooded back.

Eugene's fingers had dug into my injuries, the unmistakable intentionality behind his actions. That's why I didn't come back to the hospital.

Not Nisha.

Nisha's touch was gentle. Calming. Soothing.

I lay back, my body taut with tension, every muscle coiled and ready.

The thin paper covering the table crinkled loudly with each small movement. I was hyper-aware of every sound, every shift in the air around me.

Eugene's voice crackled through the speaker, a slight tremor betraying his nervousness. "Move your leg to the left...sir."

Nisha was there instantly, her hand gentle but firm on my leg, guiding me.

"Sorry, I promise it'll be over soon. Your right leg looks fine; I'm more worried about your left. Breathe for me..." I did, inhaling deeply and taking in the air and her scent.

Nisha's hands lingered on my legs, my calves, her touch softer now, almost caressing. My body responded to her, every nerve ending alive, but I was acutely aware of Eugene watching us.

Nisha appeared over me again. "Killian, breathe for me. Breathe..." Her eyes drifted over mine then, and she held a soft smile on her lips. "It's almost done. I promise."

I followed her lead, my gaze never leaving hers. Her hands lingered on my knees, shifting here and there. The cold of the room seemed to intensify, seeping into my bones.

"I'm here," she mouthed, her eyes locked on mine. "I'm right by you. Don't freak out." I heard her.

I did.

But I hated being here.

But whatever relief I felt was short-lived. Once Nisha went inside the other room and closed the door, it took a few moments for me to hear it. After I had been told to take a deep breath, to adjust, to hold my breath again.

And then I heard it.

My head turned to see Nisha beyond the glass as I did.

"He's gotta be what? Six-two, maybe three? Two-twenty?" Eugene's words passed on to the speaker. *Two-forty. All muscle.*

"Didn't take you for the type to fuck with someone like that?"

This motherfucker.

"I beg your pardon?"

Red-hot rage surged through me.

"You ghosted me—"

"I *never* gave you my number—"

He didn't mute himself. *Idiot.*

"I called—"

"*Eugene.*" And then I heard it. That little sound she made. And my brain took maybe a second to register it. Nisha. In distress. She made these tiny, pleased noises when I kissed her. But now?

He doesn't get to say anything to her.

The threat wasn't just in the room with me anymore.

No, all I saw was my father's face, his fist, his belt—and everything in me reared up to make sure Nisha wasn't next.

The threat wasn't after me.

It was after her.

In an instant, I was off the table, the paper cover tearing with a loud rip that echoed through the room.

My feet hit the cold floor, but I didn't feel it.

I didn't feel anything but the urge to tear into that son-of-a-bitch.

That made her make that noise.

My hands clenched into fists, knuckles white with tension. My knees and limbs ached, but the pain was distant, irrelevant. I was ready to lose it.

Not her.

Never her.

Nothing registered except Eugene's face, now drained of all color.

The room seemed to shrink. Eugene backed away, stumbling over his own feet, his eyes wide with terror.

Gonna kill this motherfucker.

11

NISHA

"Say that shit to me. Not to her. I fucking dare you."

If I thought Killian was imposing before?

It didn't compare to who was in the room with me.

The look in his eyes as he focused on Eugene. The air in the room was sucked out replaced with an electric tension that sent my stomach lurching.

Outside, he was darkness, shadows, with the hint of dangerous that drove me wild whenever he kissed me.

But now? Now he was downright frightening.

His eyes usually calmer and a mix of mesmerizing colors now burned like ice. And I knew in that moment Killian was going to kill Eugene—and nothing he did was an idle threat.

Everything now was a very real thing.

"I didn't—I didn't mean—" Eugene stammered.

"Yes, you fucking did." I could see the muscles in his jaw working as Killian clenched his teeth, his hands balled into tight fists at his sides.

Eugene stammered, his earlier smugness replaced by fear. "What the fuck do you want—"

"Nisha. What did he do?"

I had never heard him sound like *that*. I met those eyes head on.

"Nothing," I said quickly, trying to defuse the situation. "He asked me out. I don't know how he got my number, but I blocked him—"

I moved between them, placing a hand on Killian's chest.

He's going to kill Eugene.

"If you so much as *look* at her again," Killian snarled, each word dripping with lethal intent. "I will put a bullet in your brain."

"Are you fucking serious—" Eugene sputtered. Who said—"

Killian's eyes flashed, wild and dangerous. "I fucking did."

I needed to get him out of here.

I tugged at him, pulling him to me.

Out the door. In all the time I'd known Killian as a patient, I had never heard him speak like this, had never seen this side of him. He was a completely different man.

No, this is who he is outside of this place.

Outside of the hospital walls where he didn't have to be around me. And I didn't know what to do about that.

Eugene's mouth snapped shut with an audible click, his eyes bulging out of his head. *"I'm going to Perla about this—"*

"You can go to whoever the fuck you want," Killian cut him off, his voice razor-sharp. "You're fired. Get. The. Fuck. Out."

He tucked me closer to him, his arm tightening around my waist. "I need my clothes. We're done here."

❀

AS KILLIAN PULLED HIS SHIRT ON, A KNOT FORMED IN MY STOMACH, A nagging sense of unease that I couldn't quite shake. The tiny room around us seemed to close in around me.

"Please talk to me. W-w-what just happened out there?"

He turned to face me, his mismatched eyes searching mine, a slight frown on his expression taking me in. He was faster than I gave him credit for, hands gently cupping my face.

"Breathe with me," he murmured, his thumbs stroking my cheeks. "In and out, slowly."

I couldn't think. My mind was racing. It was absolutely out of it. I couldn't stop myself from freaking out now. Michelle 's voice rang in my head.

Why are you causing problems?

We should've had a boy he never would've caused all these problems.

If I had known you would've been so problematic and difficult to be around, I would've had you killed on the spot.

What an ungrateful girl.

I could hear my harsher breathing in the tiny space. Swallowed whole entirely by his presence. The floor tilted a little under me and I heard Killian swearing as he held me tight to him.

He was saying something in a language I didn't understand. Harder syllables moving over my skin.

"*Nisha.*"

Harder sounds that softened with his voice as he moved over my temple, over my cheeks. I didn't know what language that was,

"I feel like I'm in trouble." My voice was a squeak. "I don't know what happened..." One second Eugene was threatening me and the next Killian had *fired him.*

"You're not in any trouble, luv. Breathe for me. I heard him through the speaker...you didn't do anything wrong." I heard him. I did.

But his voice was at war with Michelle.

You are so ungrateful. Why can't you just be grateful?

I was spiraling. Like my vision was fraying at the edges, and I couldn't see.

"*Nisha.*" This time his voice was a growl and I felt his hand clamp the back of my neck as my chest rose and fell too quickly.

I felt him grip that part of my neck and turn my head up to look at him. When he saw my eyes, his own widened.

"Fuck," he whispered. And then his lips stamped onto mine.

A noise left me as his tongue thrust into my mouth. Taking over all my senses, every thought in my head obliterated with his scent alone.

Killian was immovable and strong, and I was hauled into his arms feeling everything release from me.

A gruff sound left him as I felt his other hand roaming my body, and I gasped at how quick they were.

"Look at me, luv." He gripped my neck to stay looking up at him while his other hand tugged at my scrubs. "Look at me. There you go—"

I gasped as his hand slid down faster than I thought possible into my pants. *What was he—*

A noise left me the moment he grazed my swollen soaking clit.

I gasped against his mouth as he found me soaking wet. It would've been embarrassing if I hadn't wanted him so bad.

"Breathe—"

"Killian—" My eyes locked onto his. One aqua. One amber. Burning into me. All I focused on was his eyes. Calming me down.

"*Breathe.* I'll make it better," he whispered against my lips. He already was. I was too acutely aware of him to see anyone else.

Oh God.

I kissed him like a starving woman.

"I'll make it better, luv."

Tongue and teeth and nothing but desire. His finger now gently rubbing the entrance of my body.

A noise left me as he banded his arm around me, bringing me closer as that finger pushed deeper. Deeper. I cried out a little into his mouth.

"*Killian—*"

"I know, luv." Killian kept kissing me as he curled it inside of me, and only then did he stop. "Fuck, you're soaked…"

I was? I couldn't think anymore.

Not a single ounce of rational thought was in my brain.

He pulled back there to look into my eyes as I panted wide-eyed, feeling pinned and like I was wriggling.

Those eyes watched me with an intensity that told me he felt for me as I did for him. He adjusted his hand, rubbing his second finger as he slid it into me, stretching me out.

His eyes never left mine as I closed them.

"Better."

A noise left me as I parted my lips. I was all too aware of him.

"Mhm." *Ohgoshthatsogood.* A whimper left my lips as he pushed deeper.

Unable to stop myself, I let out a noise, nearly giving out at the knees. It didn't matter when his arm banded around me, holding me up as his mouth moved over mine. "*Shh—*"

"*Kiss me, please.*"

Gosh, was that my voice?

He didn't hesitate as his fingers curled in me. Another noise left me as they began to move. Not in and out.

They curled inside of me and gently rubbed somewhere so sweet, a muffled scream left my lips into his mouth. Low and slow. Just enough for me to know they were there, like he was discovering me.

"You're soaked," he growled against my mouth. "Hold onto me, luv."

I did. I didn't plan on letting go completely disoriented now at this. All I could focus on was his fingers and nothing else.

My mouth opened for his tongue as he thrust it into my mouth the same way he moved his fingers.

I was squirming a little, unable to stand properly. He backed me against the door as he ate at my mouth, fingers working relentlessly then.

Curling and stimulating that sweet spot. Every nerve ending in me was on fire, focused on that.

"OhGodbaby."

"I can feel that, keep going—"

"I can't like this—" I was in a closet. I couldn't have an orgasm like *this*.

"Yes, you can." And if possible he rocked his fingers harder and I moaned at the glint in his eyes. "Come for me."

Oh, God. I closed my eyes as I felt it in my body. Rising to the surface.

"Please—" I didn't know what I was asking for. My hips rocked into his hand. "Killian…please."

My forehead pressed to his the moment his thumb ground down on my clit, sending white-hot sensations coursing through my body as he thrust his fingers against that spot, and I felt my orgasm building quicker.

"Oh God…" it left me in a whimper. I was going to lose it. *"Kiss me."*

His lips stamped over mine as I screamed a little at the sensations.

"Mmmphmm."

"I know, let me have it."

As soon as he said it, my body obeyed.

My orgasm felt unable to control. Not mine at all.

But his.

I closed my eyes as the waves of pleasure crashed over me. My forehead pressed to his. Holding onto him.

Pressing my lips together, I stifled all sounds as he pressed my mouth into his chest. My muffled screams quieted against his pec as he worked his fingers harder.

I clung to him, sobbing a little as it went on.

"There you go," he encouraged with a dark voice. "Just like that…

Move your hips, luv…" If possible, it ratcheted up my orgasm ten-fold hearing him.

Oh God, it should be illegal for him to speak.

I moved a hand over his mouth, not missing the wicked glint in them as I shook. I bit down on my lip. Hard.

All while his fingers moved. Rocking against. *That.* Spot.

"*OhGodstop*," I whispered, the stimulation growing too intense. Slowly, he stilled, holding me close as he brought me down from the peak.

I reached for him then kissing him again. And again. Squeezing on his fingers still in me.

"Oh my gosh. I can't believe I did that."

"I can do it again." There was a wicked glint in his eyes.

At the look on my face, his mouth quirked up a tiny bit. A soft noise escaped me as his fingers gently withdrew, and then he brought them to his mouth, licking, his tongue darting out to taste me.

Seeing his tattooed fingers touch his lips was the hottest thing I'd ever seen him do.

He should be illegal.

We were both breathing harder as he watched me through those eyes. "Better?"

I was clinging to him tighter confused at how I even got here.

For long moments I stayed like that attached to him. Kissing him slowly until my heart calmed down. His lips moved down my jaw, my throat—lower. He was moving too fast.

"No," I gripped his shoulders knowing exactly where he was going and I didn't think I could take anymore.

He rose up slowly like he was catching his breath.

"When do you eat?" The question caught me completely off guard. He licked his lips. "You have to take a break…?"

I blinked, my lust-addled brain struggling to process the abrupt change in topic. His fingers moved to my scrubs, drawing them up just a bit while still holding me tight to him. I was shaking, holding onto him still.

What was happening? I just came in this room.

On his fingers.

"When do you take a break?"

"Killian," I started again, forcing myself to focus. "Why…" I looked at the shut door, aware he'd just exerted authority in a place I hadn't imagined. I just came all over this man after a panic attack and he wants to know when I take a break?

Why did you just do that?

Why did you stop Eugene?

Why are you...why are you with me?

Before I had a chance to respond, he spoke, his tongue darting out, his tattooed hands gripped my hips as he drew even closer to me.

"I can bring you lunch."

"What?"

"Today?" His intense gaze made my breath catch. *Today?*

"Are you asking me out?" My eyes met his.

"I am."

And what was I supposed to say? *No? Not right now?*

"You have the worst timing," I whispered. But I was still shaken up by what happened. "Tomorrow."

His eyes widened slightly, a flicker of something passing through them.

Maybe asking me out after firing a man who threatened me and making me come was his way of telling me he liked me? A laugh bubbled in my throat I suppressed.

"Or maybe not—" I backpedaled, suddenly unsure of myself. With my...whatever he was.

"Tomorrow."

"Tomorrow." I said it quickly.

If he knew he didn't say a word and held me quietly.

"Why did you...how did you just...do that?"

His forehead pressed against mine.

"Nobody is going to hurt you on my watch. If someone so much as *looks* at you wrong—*tell me.* And I will make sure it never happens again."

NISHA

Today, whispers of the firing spread like wildfire through the hospital.

Killian told me before he left that he'd have a talk with Perla. She wouldn't be happy, but she was professional about it.

Adam, on the other hand, was pleased.

"Thank fuck," Adam murmured, his voice low. "I know he worked for the general hospital, but he made everyone up here hate him."

He huffed out a breath, his blonde hair worn longer than normal, tousled more than usual made him look younger than twenty-five.

"Did he?" I whispered, keeping my voice down, fidgeting with my scrubs.

"He fucking sucked, Nisha."

I liked Adam. We had a candid relationship, and I knew my words wouldn't leave this conversation.

But even still, I didn't know how to tell Adam what Eugene had done.

Adam nodded, his warm eyes drifting to meet mine. Something flickered in them as he took me in. A softer look to them.

Did he know?

"Listen, it isn't my place," he began hesitantly. "But I heard…"

He glanced around before continuing. "Did he say something to you? Someone mentioned Killian was walking out of there. If that's the case—" he broke off, his gaze fixed on me.

I was the only one it could have been...
Oh. Gosh.

I was the only one who saw Killian regularly. It wasn't hard to connect the dots. I didn't know what to say to Adam.

"I can't—" I broke off shaking my head.

Reed was his brother, but I wasn't sure how close they were.

Adam never talked about him, and I didn't think many people knew about their connection.

But it was Adam. He'd never given me a reason to doubt him before. Slowly, I nodded, confirming his suspicions.

Adam's eyes filled with understanding and he looked away a little stunned.

"I'm sorry. I figured as much..." He shook his head, his warm eyes sympathetic.

"It's all right," I didn't know what else to say. Changing the subject, I asked. "How are you holding up?"

He smiled, a hint of weariness in his eyes. "Another day of patients, you know how it is."

"Someone dropped off snacks for you again?"

Adam blushed, looking away as I grinned. He hated talking about the many women who had a crush on him, preferring to pretend it didn't happen.

"Easy, Casanova," I laughed. "Save some women for the rest of the residents waiting in line."

"Says you, you got another round of flowers for you." My heart lurched—not from Killian were they?

"I'll check later," I forced out.

In the break room I found them rolling my eyes at the giant bouquet.

I went to toss it or put it so that anyone else could have it when I caught the note. It was blank.

Usually, people wanted me to know. I didn't think twice.

I tossed the note and stilled at the address. It had been sent by a florist near my old address in Queens.

What were the odds?

After that one letter, I hadn't heard anything else that worried me, and even with his release from prison?

I had no rational reason to worry. I had separated myself from my family. They didn't know where I lived.

I told myself this as I looked down at it, my heart still ratcheted up.

But the rest of my day passed in a dizzying spell of patients. At one point an entire team came in needing shots and other things so I just went down the chart of twenty-four.

A broken arm, serrated cuts and some minor burns—and then there had been a surgery Adam had been in.

Everyone was juggling and learning rapidly.

I enjoyed this as much as my blog or playing instruments. Working with my hands was the only way I stayed focused in the present.

I was so busy, Adam came to get me to tell me Killian was here for lunch. The clock did read noon. But the day felt quicker when running around.

"Your favorite patient is here," Adam said with a knowing smirk as I drank water in the back room. "Are you dating him now?"

Technically, it wasn't illegal or immoral to date a patient.

There was no rule against it.

Just the unspoken one to not mix work and pleasure.

Even if I trusted Adam to not say a word, I didn't know how to put my words together to tell him I didn't know what this was.

I hadn't been on a date since college.

"*No*," I said with a little too much emphasis. "He brought lunch."

"That's technically a date."

Adam sat back on a bench as we talked in a break area.

"I don't want to call it that," I shot back with a frown.

"Why?" Adam smirked looking too adorable for his own good.

"*Because*. It's lunch. In *uniform*." I motioned to my scrubs.

He shook his head like he didn't know what I was talking about, the sun glinting off his dark-blonde hair worn too long. "It can still be a date."

I puffed out a breath. "Where is he?"

"In the hall. Where everyone can see his prince of darkness self looming over the corridor waiting for his lady love."

I threw a pen at Adam who ducked playfully and laughed while I smoothed a hand over my scrubs, my hair, to go to meet Killian.

Adam smirked at my motions again.

"I take back what I said about you being a decent man."

He only laughed harder.

The moment I saw Killian standing there leaning against the wall, his head turned and caught me.

I felt like a deer in headlights as I nervously walked up to him. Memories of yesterday washed over me.

"Hi."

"Hey." His eyes raked over me, one blue-one amber, as his scent washed over me. "You solid?"

"Have you been waiting long?" I almost tripped to get to him and I felt him move smoothly closing the distance between us, wrapping his arm around my waist to help. My heart skipped a beat and then another.

"No." He turned his lips down and shook his head, turning to Adam who was still standing there grinning at us. He was such a little brother. Now I got it. I had never met his older brother Reed but I imagined this is how he was with him.

I shooed him as I said to Killian who looked a little bemused.

"Shall we? It's warm outside so the courtyard might be best to eat in." I took in his dark presence dominating the space around me. He moved quietly for a man his size.

There was a glint of something in his eyes as he held the doors open for me each time, with me moving past him brushing against his body.

The closer I got the more he seemed to gravitate towards me. And *I* had a freaking orgasm on him *yesterday*.

"Are you having a good day today?" I asked, unable to keep silent any longer.

My cheeks must've been flaming hot but thankfully, I sounded reasonable. Calm. Maybe a little affected but nothing to freak out about.

"No." His eyes met mine with that delivery. And something shifted in his eyes as we entered the courtyard where it was kept oddly neat and pretty. "But it's better now."

Tall, shaded oak trees that gave enough of a reprieve from the sun. I found us an empty table to sit at.

I turned to him then nearly bumping into him chest to chest...or... my chest to his abdomen. I craned my head up to look at him and those eyes of his latched onto me.

"Why's it better?"

He moved so quickly I didn't see him coming. His lips stamping over mine right there, his hand gripping my hip and pulling me close.

I gripped his bicep, holding onto his muscles.

Every inch of his body was ripped and tatted, and it made my body lose it around him. Him in his briefs and shirt had been sexy, but now? In a suit?

He was devastatingly handsome.

Like a dark prince taking up his residence.

He let me go and blinked down at me softly. "Better."

It was. "I get anxious. How do you know to do that?"

"Lucky guess," he murmured over my lips. I knew my face was flaming at this point. "Lunch?"

He held up the bag now and I could actually see the label.

"You went to *Butterscotch's?*" My eyes widened. "I love that bakery!"

There was a hint of amusement in his eyes as he set it down.

"They have fresh basil—Did you get the one with mozzarella—*You did!*" I rambled on about the cafe's artisanal bread and locally-sourced ingredients. "It's *really* good. Have you had this place before?"

Killian shook his head, a hint of warmth in his voice, his eyes softening on me. "I just looked it up."

"I get excited about *good* food. I love to cook and bake, and let me tell you, this bakery is good...Which one do you want?" I asked, holding up the sandwiches. "If you like this one, I'll take the other."

"The one you don't want."

"That doesn't seem very fair," I chewed my lip. "What if you like the one I pick?"

"I wouldn't." His eyes met mine, and I saw the heat in them from yesterday. His lips tipped up a fraction, enough to make my heart skip. "You can have the one you like."

I didn't know if that sat well with me.

"What if we just shared?" I bit down on my lip feeling nervous, brushing my hand over my scrubs. He looked down at where my hand was moving over my scrubs. And then back up at me.

He nodded, his tongue darting out to lick his lips and I squirmed a little remembering the last time he did that, he tasted me. I should've felt even the slightest bit nervous. But I wasn't.

Because I knew better. I trusted him. His eyes calmed me down.

I ducked my head, pulling out the food wondering if he was even aware of what he was doing. "Hang on, I gotta take a picture of this, the aesthetic is so pretty."

I snapped a few photos before handing him one of each.

He blinked at my phone and a wave of embarrassment washed over me. "Right, sorry—it's for social media."

I didn't want to tell him about my food blog just yet. I handed him one of each and sat down with mine as I asked. "Why did you have a bad day?"

Killian's hands fumbled with the sandwich packaging as his eyes took me in. "Social media?"

I opened my half catching the brief flashes of ink peeking out through his shirtsleeves, some on his knuckles.

"Mhm, it's pretty." I didn't want him to know about 'Slice of Life' yet. But my eyes also caught his tattoos. On his knuckles.

I knew most of them now. On his ribs, one on his hand, his calves even. But my bandaid stood in stark contrast on his index finger. I bit back a smile at the hearts out of place among the black ink.

He wore them all the time.

He was struggling with not tearing it open entirely with his larger hands.

Even the tops of his hands had some tattoos...I thought maybe after being around him all the time half naked, I would be used to them. But I never was.

Those tattoos were inside of me.

And my stomach dipped again as I swallowed.

"They always pack their items so securely," I commented, trying to lighten the mood. "You'd think someone was trying to rob them. Here let me..."

His mouth twitched.

"There," I said softly, successfully tugging open the packaging. His eyes, those two shades, focused on me like he'd just seen me for the first time. "Well...?"

Killian blinked, taking a bite of his food as if suddenly remembering where he was.

A passerby caught Killian's attention, his gaze snapping to assess our surroundings with predatory alertness.

He took a bite slowly, his mismatched eyes wide, and focused on me. He swallowed his bite before answering.

77

"It's not a bad day. Just…bad jobs. Yours?"

"Honestly…until now, I haven't even gotten a chance to sit down."

I began chattering about my hectic morning and various patients, all too aware that I might be talking too much.

"I'm sorry, is it…Am I talking too much?"

He shook his head immediately, his eyes warmer as he watched me. "You can keep going."

I felt the warmth burst a little in my chest as his brows rose at my smile. He bit into his sandwich, watching me a little wide-eyed as I kept talking and telling him about my day.

Through it, he occasionally nodded and murmured his agreement with something I said, making me smile.

Lowering my voice, I decided to approach the subject. "I think a few people heard about Eugene…"

Killian slowly stopped chewing. "He should be gone. If anyone says anything, tell me."

"Thank you," I whispered. "But even Perla hasn't said anything to me. I don't understand how you have the power to do that."

He paused for a moment as he looked down at his food.

"Or why…you'd do that for me." There. I said it. I was staring at my gift horse aware I felt the anxiety brewing. But I had to ask him. "Why do you do what you do…for me. We don't really know each other…"

Even as I said it? It felt like a lie. Because I knew him. I did. I knew his heart. I knew this man.

His brows rose in surprise, like he didn't believe it. Because we kissed? Because I came on his hand?

He looked like he was thinking about it. About me. The questions and for a moment I wondered if he would even answer.

His reply was slow. Measured. "When I was injured…my shoulder. You didn't make me feel like shit. You were good to me—"

"It's my job—"

"Other people don't do your job like you." He paused his eyes drifting to my lips. "Not everything is your job." I swallowed and I swear those eyes of his focused on my rapidly fluttering pulse in my throat where he always found himself.

He protected me…because I did right by him.

If someone said anything to me? He'd take care of me?

No. Not everything was my job. But he...he wasn't the one I was expecting to come along.

"It's that simple to you?"

He nodded.

"You're good at your job."

"Some people make it easier than others."

A ghost of a smile played at the corners of his mouth, encouraging me. Our eyes connected then and something warm blossomed in my stomach.

"Do you work close by here?"

I noticed Killian's gaze drop momentarily before snapping back to my face.

Someone walked by us, looking at our table, and his eyes tracked the movement before returning to mine, reminding me of a patient wolf, always assessing, always alert.

"I work all over the city sometimes."

"Do you enjoy it? The variety then? I don't get to leave the wing."

Killian paused, considering his words carefully. Like he did everything. *Save for kiss me...*

"It has its moments."

There was a hint of something in his tone I didn't recognize, his eyes watching around us before coming back to me. "But it's not the same every day."

"Oh, do you think you'd want it otherwise?"

"No, I—" he paused looking a little off. "I never thought about it being anything else. It just is."

"Hm," I considered that. "You don't believe in complaining?"

"I believe in getting it done."

"You'd make for a good doctor."

For some reason he smirked. "Not unless you want people to get even more hurt—"

"You don't think so?"

Killian shook his head but I caught his smile at my laughter. "I don't have the fucking patience to deal with people like you."

"Sometimes I don't have the patience to deal with the people I do."

We shared a quiet laugh.

"Did you have a good day?"

I looked up as he asked the question, surprised by it.

"Did I have a good—"

The shrill sound of my phone timer stopped me.

"I'm sorry, that's my time. I have to head back."

"That's thirty?"

"Not quite. Five minutes to go. Time flies and all that. Adam always takes his break after me or before me so I should go but this was great."

I was *rambling*.

At the mention of Adam, Killian's entire demeanor shifted, his jaw tightened imperceptibly.

"Adam?"

"He's…Reed's younger brother," I explained, watching Killian's reaction carefully. "I know you said you work with Reed. But Adam's great. He's a resident here…"

I went on to explain how we'd both moved up to the Titan ward from another one, and how we traded breaks because it was easier coordinating with each other.

"This was nice though. Thank you—" I started, trying to wrap up our lunch.

"Tomorrow?" Killian interjected, catching me off guard.

Tomorrow?

I paused, suddenly very aware of our proximity. When had he gotten closer? I didn't even hear him.

"Tomorrow…I'm off tomorrow. I'm at home."

Why did I say it like an idiot?

Killian's eyes met mine and for a moment I was thinking about the closet. The way his eyes met mine and when I came. All over his hand. *Oh.*

I felt the heat creep up my face as he blinked, his brows dropping a little like he knew. His eyes turned a little darker.

"I mean…if you want…We can still…go out. Do you want to take my number down so we can get together if you're not busy…"

He was pulling out his phone before I finished my sentence.

13

KILLIAN

"Do I want to know why you fired that idiotic kid over Nisha Graham?"

"Why?" I said gruffly. "You never liked the little fucker."

Nobody did.

Gabriel's voice sliced through the quiet of my gym, sharp and direct as always. "I'm surprised *you* did it."

The *over her* part went unspoken glowing in the air like an ugly neon shaped sign.

I *knew* Gabriel didn't give a fuck about that shit x-ray tech. No.

He called because he knew about Nisha.

Gabriel was…invested in every detail of everyone's life. I'd known this since I met him.

"He was a dick."

"So are you."

I didn't even resist rolling my eyes.

There was a reason why Nate Wyatt called Gabriel Reed's work wife. Somehow, the image of Gabriel being a homemaker after I'd watched him put bullets in people's brains wasn't processing in my head.

I grunted, setting the weight down in my hand with a heavy thud that echoed through my penthouse gym.

Sweat clung to my skin as I straightened up, the New York skyline stretching out before me through the floor-to-ceiling windows. I pressed the phone between my ear and shoulder, my jaw clenching involuntarily.

"Is that why you called?"

I had been working out to keep my thoughts from drifting to her.

Fuck. I knew this call was coming. I always answered Gabriel's calls quicker than Aidan's.

"No. I have questions, but that was my first one. Perla was curious. She says you spend time with your nurse."

And there it went.

All my cards out there. It didn't mean I had to tell him about Nisha. But he knew. He knew enough.

"Nothing's going on."

I heard his snort. "Is that why Nisha is the only one allowed to see you? Because *nothing* is going on?"

Shit. I fucking knew he'd look into it.

"What the fuck do you do when she's not there?" he asked.

Wait until she comes back. The truth hit me. I *waited*, like some lovesick idiot, for Nisha to walk through the door.

But I couldn't admit to Gabriel, or to myself, just how much I needed her.

Growing up in the shadows of my father's empire, I'd learned early that attachment was a weakness.

I'd watched Aidan harden himself, saw Kieran lose himself in fleeting pleasures. Me?

I'd buried everything deep, locked it away where no one could use it against me.

Needing someone meant vulnerability, and vulnerability was dangerous in my world.

"It's not a big deal. Don't make it into one."

"It's not a big deal—" he broke off, sounding incredulous. "You can't just steal a nurse from the hospital—"

"I haven't kidnapped her—"

"—in broad daylight—"

"She came willingly—"

"So you asked her out."

Motherfucker. That was the thing about talking to Gabriel.

It was always a fucking mind game. And he was going to corner you regardless of what you thought. I let out a breath.

"Is this why you left the Agency?" I had to ask. Gabriel was former CIA. "By irritating the shit out of your subordinates?"

He made a noise like he was amused. "That little shit you fired went to Perla, who called me. You can't shoot everyone who threatens your nurse. Reed would've handled it—"

"I handled it—"

"Too well. He wants to talk to higher-ups—"

"About what?" I fucking hated guys like Eugene. "Why did you hire him anyway?"

"Perla didn't know he'd be a dick—"

"You would do the same if he did anything to your—" I broke off. Motherfucker. "Is this why you called? To drag me into your pit?"

He was silent, and he sighed like he was bored.

"How fucking long—"

"What?"

"How long have you been dating your nurse? Shows you showed up for a dislocated shoulder. I told you not let Kieran set it. What the fuck was he going to do?"

"I'm not seeing her—"

"Yet. You had lunch with her—"

"It was one time—" But I want so many more.

"I didn't even know you ate cookies—"

I was going to shoot him. *The end.*

"Gabriel—"

"Reed and I took bets on how often you'd talk—"

"I said five, didn't I?" Reed yelled in the background. He didn't deal with our family too much, but he was polite when he did. I could tell he wasn't thrilled about our dealings, our reputation, or anything else. But Aidan was determined to be better than our father.

"Fucking assholes," I growled. If they weren't people I'd respected I'd just shoot 'em. "I can't fucking believe you two—"

"We counted."

"Gabriel—"

I heard both him and Reed chuckling.

They got off on this shit so much. All the time.

I knew they'd been friends since they were teenagers, and they got along well enough. Reed had been solid for Gabriel since they were teens.

And I liked when Nisha liked to talk.

I liked to listen to her talk.

I'd never looked up a nice, cozy restaurant to get food from, my suit-clad self looking out of place among the bohemian crowd there.

But one guy eyed my bandaid on my finger with curiosity. I fucking loved Nisha's touch on me, but not when other people watched.

"I know what I'm doing," I snapped. "I don't need you to meddle or get involved."

Do I? Do I really know what I'm doing with Nisha?

"Do you?" Gabriel's question was pointed, cutting straight to the heart of the matter. "Because from where I'm standing, it looks like you actually like this girl."

"It's not serious—"

Who was I trying to fool? Gabriel? Or myself?

"So I should fuck her then? I mean, I could." He continued like my blood pressure hadn't lost its ever loving fucking mind at the idea of Gabriel even flirting with her. "What is she? Five-five? Four? Selena's height right? All that hair—"

"You shut the fuck up."

White hot rage filtered through me then at the idea of fucking Gabriel anywhere near her.

"Don't you fucking touch her." He's not her type. I am.

The moment it left my mouth I fucking knew I got played.

Big time. Because that was what Gabriel wanted. Me to walk into him doing this shit. And I'd fallen for it.

"Motherfucker."

I sighed as I heard laughter. This is why they couldn't handle him.

"You don't even eat lunch."

I stopped talking, my eyes locking with my own in the mirror. "I eat. Are you done?"

Just on the go. I never sat down. Not until her. Not until Nisha walked into my life and turned everything upside down.

I blew out a frustrated breath. *"Fuck."*

"That's what I thought."

I wanted to find her and sink myself into her until nothing else existed. To lose myself in her warmth, her light. I shouldn't.

"Does she know…"

Did she know I was sort of second-in-command of the mob? No.

"I'll tell her if it ever gets serious."

"You had lunch with a nurse in the middle of the day. And you don't think it's serious?"

"Gabriel—"

"I already know where you're going with this. Do not get involved if you don't plan on being good to her. She's had enough shit in her own life—"

"What do you mean, she's got enough shit in her life?"

The idea that Nisha might be dealing with something, might be hurting in some way I didn't know about, made something in me want to lash out, to protect her from whatever was causing her pain.

"You don't think the moment I saw you two, I found her file?" I didn't think he'd care.

"How the fuck do you know so much about my—" I broke off, realizing what I'd just said. *Shit. Shit. Shit.*

My.

Mine.

"Tell her the truth," he said finally, his voice firm. "Do it sooner than later. That shit comes back to bite you, you'll have more to worry about than a shit tech."

I paused, the weight of his words settling on my shoulders.

The truth.

Before I could respond, Gabriel continued. "I'm not telling Aidan unless you're serious." A rush of relief escaped me.

"Send me everything Reed has on her."

"Actually, it isn't just Reed..."

14

NISHA

Pick you up at 1?

THE SOFT BUZZ OF MY PHONE ROUSED ME FROM SLEEP.

I reached for it, my hand emerging from the cozy cocoon of my pale pink duvet to look at the text. From Killian.

He didn't waste any time.

I typed a quick reply, my fingers trembling slightly.

Sounds great. See you then.

I added my address, and moments later, he thumbs-upped my response. A smile tugged at my lips, but it faded as I glanced at the time. *11:30. Already?*

How had I slept so late?

Leaping out of bed, I rushed to get ready. Shower, tame my sleep-tousled hair, find something to wear that *wasn't* scrubs.

I think I'm going on a real date.

I twirled my hair up into a claw clip.

Tossed on a cotton blush dress.

I let strands dangle around my face as I fussed with my hair in an up-do one last time, doubts crept in as unwelcome whispers as I smoothed the mini dress down.

Back living with the Graham's I never would've worn anything higher than my ankles in case Eugene liked what he saw. I had learned the lesson really young.

I heard Michelle's voice creeping in.

What a stupid slut. Parading around in her t-shirt. She's just asking for attention.

What kind of a girl wears clothes like that? Cover yourself up.

But it's a sweater.

It's too tight on you. What kind of attention do you plan on attracting.

God had to give me a stupid daughter who tries to seduce my husband.

You're the problem. You're the one nobody likes. You're the one nobody wanted and I took you in.

"Shut up!" I screamed into the empty room, the fiddle leaf fig in the corner shaking a little. "Sorry..." I whispered.

And that was the thing about anxiety...it just happened. It spiraled. And I knew it was there.

I took deep breaths smoothing the fabric over and over again forcing myself to breathe.

It was just Killian. I just breathed in and out. Slowly.

I closed my eyes, remembering the countless times I'd heard those words. After recitals, when I'd dared to hope for praise.

After school, when I'd tried to share my day.

He's just using you.

The memory of Eugene's wandering hands flashed through my mind, making my skin crawl. I pushed it away, focusing on the present, on Killian.

Do you really think a man who looks like that? With money?

Would ever want you?

I glanced around my tiny Brooklyn apartment, taking in the mismatched furniture, the colorful throw pillows, the bits and pieces of the life I'd cobbled together after running away. So different from the sterile, picture-perfect home I'd grown up in.

Nobody wants you.

I'd spent years trying to prove my worth, to be good enough, only to realize that in their eyes, I never would be.

Killian was nothing like my adoptive father.

And I wanted his touch. I wanted him.

But that's what terrified me most.

Killian was like nothing I had ever experienced. Or had known I could want. Sometimes when I'd been a little girl I dreamed of someone saving me. Taking me away and telling me my reality was just a dream.

Maybe I'd wake up and the dream man would tell me it wasn't real.

None of that happened.

But when I was with Killian, I felt like someone starving for him and I couldn't get enough. Everyone said he was dangerous, but he just made me feel safe. In his arms, I felt like I could fall asleep and stay there forever.

And maybe, just maybe—he felt the same. Which was why he kept coming back.

Killian is coming here to pick me up.

In my tiny Brooklyn apartment with my shabby retro decor and too feminine clothes…and what if he didn't like me outside of the hospital?

What if he saw the real me—not the a nurse, but the broken, woman underneath—and decided I wasn't worth the trouble?

Stop. That's not him.

It was my adopted mother's voice.

Michelle Graham voice.

My therapist would tell me to tell Michelle 's voice to fuck off.

To remember how far I'd come, how much I'd overcome.

I took a deep breath, running my hands over the soft fabric of my dress. This was me.

The colors, the softness—this was the person I'd fought to become. The person who'd survived, who'd built a life for herself despite everything.

He did like me. He kissed me.

He brought me lunch. He tried.

I knew the signs of a man who didn't.

But my mother's voice had taken up space in my mind for years.

I shook my head, trying to dispel these thoughts. It wasn't fair to project my past experiences onto Killian.

He hadn't given me any reason to be wary.

Still, the power dynamic made me nervous. He worked for Reed Whittaker, the hospital owner.

Reed Whittaker *owned* Titan Security.

And he was…essentially everyone's boss.

As 1 o'clock approached, I felt my cheeks flush, the heat in my face rivaling the summer warmth outside.

I paced my living room, alternating between checking my reflection and peering out the window like an anxious teenager.

I slid into my sandals, aware I hadn't been on a date in forever. And I was a little unnerved since I was now dating a man twice in the same week. *The next day.*

The knock on my door startled me out of my spiraling thoughts.

He's here.

Killian stood there, tall and imposing, looking impeccable in a crisp white shirt, unbuttoned just enough and tailored slacks.

Devilishly handsome, his dark hair tousled, those eyes of his piercing and bright as he took me in.

He'd always been intense and unsettling but now, it made the butterflies in my stomach lose their minds.

His mismatched eyes widened as they took me in, his lips parting slightly.

I suddenly felt hyper-aware of my dress, how it clung to my curves, how much skin it exposed. The pink fabric against my skin looked nice in the mirror when I tried it on.

But it was my first time not wearing scrubs.

Is it too much? Not enough?

"Should I change?"

"No—" His eyes darkened. "No, you look—"

"It looks good?" I asked, running a hand self-consciously over the dress. The skirting.

"Yes." His voice was gruff.

I tried to bite back a smile as I grabbed my smaller purse, my fingers trembling slightly. "Where are we going?"

"To a farmer's market." His voice was low. "Since you like…food."

Oh...Do not hug him. He is adorable. "Which one?"

"Downtown."

"Oh," I beamed, excitement bubbling up. "I love that one!"

Killian's brow furrowed, confusion flashing across his face. "You already—"

"*No,*" I interjected quickly, heat rising to my cheeks. I didn't want to tell him I went there to take photos for my blog. Because that would be rude. Who wanted to ruin their date like that? "I've just *heard* it's… fantastic…"

As I grabbed my purse hoping he didn't notice how flustered I was. I noticed Killian's gaze had shifted.

His eyes were on the back of my neck since I'd put my hair up with the summer heat. Tendrils had fallen around my face, but I left my neck exposed.

My back. *The tattoo...*

Oh, dear.

"We should go," I said quickly, perhaps too quickly, moving towards the door. "Don't want to miss the best produce, right?"

"You've heard about it." His tone suggested he didn't quite believe me, but he wasn't pushing the issue.

His eyes drifted to my neck, lips parting like he wanted to ask. Messy inky black hair, those eyes on me and his white shirt parted just enough to make me want to lick that spot. My heart was fluttering wildly.

"Should we go? Are we taking the train?" I asked, my voice a little too high.

"No," he replied, his voice a little rougher than before. "I parked two blocks away. I can bring it around—" His eyes drifted over my neck again.

"No, I don't mind walking, it's beautiful outside," I interjected. "When do you have to be back at work?"

His eyes raked over my dress once more, making the butterflies in my stomach lose it. "I don't."

Oh.

15

KILLIAN

I LEARNED TWO THINGS PRETTY QUICKLY WITH NISHA.

One.

Her hips and thighs combined with the way every single bump in the road made her tits jiggle in that goddamn pink *dress* of hers—was going to drive me crazy.

Nisha wasn't petite.

No, she had *curves*. And it drove me *insane*. Lush, full bodied curves, the kind that made me want to tear her scrubs down at the hospital and slide into her heat and stay there.

She was *edible*.

Now? Tanned olive skin glowing in the sun? Combined with her dark hair and smile? I was fucking *gone*.

She kept glancing over at me, doing that little tiny squirming thing she did, biting her lip like she wanted to say something, but she was too nervous. That dress stretched across her tits.

I felt all the blood from my lack of rational thinking rush down to my cock.

And two?

She'd been to the Farmers Market before.

I figured it out when we got to the place I *figured* she'd love.

I'd walked with her to the garage, where she'd stepped into the blacked-out Maserati I'd gotten. The click of her sandals on concrete echoed in the space, matching the rhythm of my heartbeat.

She'd been chewing on her lip, all nervous, the soft flesh reddening under her teeth. My eyes were drawn to that spot, imagining the taste of her, the feel of that plump lip between my own teeth.

She has a tattoo.

I didn't know if it was a musical chord or if she played an instrument or she liked music. I didn't know.

I just knew the sight of dark ink against her skin was surprising. And then my brain wanted to know if she had anymore.

And where...

I couldn't shake the images from Nisha's file, the words Gabriel had passed along burning in my mind. Nisha Graham.

Victim of kidnapping. Unofficially.

Nisha's file flashed through my mind, the words Gabriel had shared seared into my brain. Nisha Graham.

She'd been adopted by a shady agency known for promising poor families a hefty sum in exchange for their kid. Legal trafficking. Sort of. A couple had taken her in.

What followed over the next few years was reports of child abuse, domestic violence, and multiple assaults.

All at the hands of them. My foster mother Michelle, definitely knew. And she let it happen. I read it all.

I figured out Gabriel got the fucking thing from an old friend of his —Lt. Cameron Giroux.

Giroux had been the one to help Nisha as a seventeen year old when she ran down the street screaming for help.

My jaw clenched, a familiar rage simmering in my chest at the image of this girl begging for help. I told myself as my blood boiled reading her file—she would never have to ask again.

I would do it.

I would protect her.

Slaughter her demons. And take care of her. Because this was the woman who took care of me. Done.

I'd already put the wheels in motion. I'd tasked Derek with digging up information. I couldn't just kill Samuel. So, my guys were on it.

Derek had his orders. And I had my information.

Somehow, her adopted mother had avoided jail-time by saying she had no idea. Biggest fucking crock of shit. She definitely knew.

But her adopted father got put away—doing his twenty or whatever it was. It hit close to home, memories of my father's dealings in similar trades.

My father Cormac hadn't been clean since the day he'd been born.

And he'd raised Aidan the same. Not so much for me. I was the outcast. But like recognized like.

I knew the hell Nisha had survived, perhaps better than most.

And he'd brought up Aidan the same way. Not me, though. I was the black sheep and even in my distant memories, black, blood, and my mother's absence reigned. But I recognized the signs.

"You okay?" Her soft question broke me out of my reverie.

How could I tell her that I knew? That I got it? That I wanted to be her protector, her confidant, her everything?

"Yeah," I managed. "I'm perfect."

What wasn't perfect was Nisha lying about not being here before.

The urge to throw her over my shoulder and drag her somewhere private was overwhelming. *In that tiny fucking dress.*

I wanted to pull her to the corner and find out what color her panties were.

Take out my frustrations on that tiny little spot between her legs. Hold onto her throat while listening to her scream.

Stop. I took a deep breath. *Not now. Not here.*

It didn't take me being a fucking detective to know Nisha had been here before.

Was it fair of me to keep my secret from her and expect her to tell me hers? No.

But I didn't play fair.

I didn't win if I did.

I knew it deep down I had to be smarter when it came to how I played my hand. I kept leaning into her, sticking close to her to make sure nobody else got near her.

I felt like an animal around this woman. I couldn't control myself. My body didn't want to fight her. And my mind was losing it.

Because I didn't know why out of everyone she got under my skin the way she did.

Her dark, expressive eyes scanned the market stalls.

Oh, she's fucking been here before. I should've known that.

At The Spice Trail, the ancient vendor smiled at her, greeting her by name over the din of the crowd.

Nisha claimed she'd just passed by before. *Once.* My jaw clenched, but I held my tongue.

Then at the Artisan's Bread Box, they had a bag of apple cider donuts ready for her.

"I may have stopped here as well once."

Once? Again?

Nisha's horrible at lying.

And then she did that adorable squirm she did.

The summer sun must be frying my brain if she thought I'd buy that. As we approached another stall, I made a decision.

I'd give her one more chance to come clean.

The irony wasn't lost on me. Here I was, a man with countless secrets, bristling at a small lie.

"Wanna tell me something?" But before she could answer, another vendor called out.

"Miss Nisha, back again?"

Jeez.

"Umm...uh..." As Nisha's explanation trailed off, she hesitantly reached out and touched my arm. I felt myself drawn closer to her, almost involuntarily.

"You've been here before."

"I'm sorry," she murmured, her eyes wide and sincere, a mixture of guilt and something deeper swirling in their depths.

She's so fucking close right now.

"I just wanted to show you how much I appreciated your idea for the date. I love this place. And I'm happy you suggested it. I come here all the time for my blog. I just didn't want you to think it was a bad idea to bring us here for lunch...I know a good sandwich vendor at the end, or that Greek place," she said, her words tumbling out in a breathless rush. "You'd like it. I didn't want you to be upset. I'd been here before."

And just like that—I wasn't upset. Her breasts, soft and full, pushed against my chest with each rapid breath she took.

She clung to me like she knew me, like I was already hers.

God help me, I wanted to be.

My gaze dropped to her lips, then lower still, taking in the sight of her curves straining against the fabric of her dress. *Pink.* It looked radiant against her skin.

"It's okay," I heard myself say, my voice rougher than I intended, thick with emotions I couldn't quite name.

Some part of me I didn't quite understand yet craved her reassurance, her acceptance.

Nisha pressed closer, whether knowingly or unknowingly, her body fitting against mine like she was made for me. The heat of her skin seeped through our clothes, igniting a fire in my veins.

"I know you're struggling to tell me why you brought me here. But I know you also knew I'd like it. Just like the restaurant you got lunch from, I love it. I don't want to make you think just because I've been here before? That I wouldn't enjoy it."

And then those eyes of her bat up at me. *Oh fuck me. I'm gone.* My thumb traced the curve of her cheekbone, reveling in the softness of her skin.

Nisha smiled softly, getting up on her tip-toes to kiss my nose. My lips. Humming a little. *Kiss her again.*

"I thought you'd like it—" Why did I sound like that?

"I do. I love it here. It's the best first date I could've asked for." She kissed me again. "It's perfect."

A warmth erupted in my chest. My world narrowed to the burning imprint of her lips on my skin. I couldn't quite name the feeling, but I felt my lips curving into a smile without my permission.

"Perfect."

"Mhm. Come on, they have this strawberry shortcake here. You'd like it, I promise."

She kissed me again quickly. And I drew her in for another. Longer.

Loving the soft noises she made when she was pleased, my hands drifting lower down her body until it cupped one of her ass cheeks closer to me.

Nisha moaned low and squirmed. "No."

And I heeled. Except my body remembered that sound. The memory of her coming making those soft adorable noises made my dick harder than a motherfucker. I growled into her kisses hauling her tighter to me.

"Luv—" I murmured. "We gotta stop. Now."

She pulled back licking her lips. "I get carried away when I kiss you."

Yeah. You're telling me, luv.

"Let's go," she smiled up at me again, those dark eyes shimmering with light in them. I pulled her right up on me. And she flushed as she realized I was harder than iron on her.

"I need a second."

Her lips curved a tiny bit as she giggled and next thing I knew I was grinning. "Just say when."

"You think it's funny?"

She giggled. "I think it's cute."

There was nothing cute about my dick.

Nisha bit her lip. "I think you're cute for bringing me here."

Okay...well...I mean...I could be cute.

Yeah.

If that's what she wanted?

I could be cute as *fuck.*

Part of me bristled at ever being called cute but if Nisha wanted to bows in my hair and call me pretty?

I would let this woman do anything to me.

Her eyes refused to meet mine as she covered her face laughing lightly. My cheeks hurt a little from how hard I was smiling around this girl.

But as we approached the strawberry stand where she said they had good cake, my eyes took in this vendor. Manned by a guy about her age. *Younger.*

He looked like he'd stepped right out of a boy band poster—all golden hair and bright blue eyes, with a jawline sharp enough to cut glass.

The backwards baseball cap and casual clothes did nothing to diminish his pretty-boy looks.

I felt my jaw tighten, muscles coiling with tension.A sensation surged through me, hot and violent. *Don't look at my girl.*

"Hey Jesse!"

Is that his dog?

As we stepped closer to the stand, I found myself unconsciously drawing up to my full height, shoulders squaring up like I wanted to fight him.

The vendor—*Jesse*—smile faltered slightly as his gaze shifted from Nisha to me.

"Hey," he grinned easily at her. "Back again, Nisha?"

Don't smile at my girl like that.

"Couldn't stay away," she laughed. "How did your mom like everything?"

"She loved it," he threw her a sheepish grin. "Shamelessly, I ate half of the pan myself."

Her grin was wide, laughter filling the space between them and I watched unable to relate.

I felt the frustration clawing up beneath my skin. I tried to calm myself down but it wasn't working.

Nisha was the only woman I had been around who made me want her eyes on me all the time.

Go find someone else to smile at you, Jesse.

Nisha turned to me effortlessly. "I made a few desserts with the fruit I got from this stand and I started sharing them with Jesse's mom, she's usually at the stand with him...Jesse started Kingston Prep, you know the college beyond Astor?"

I did.

As Nisha explained it to me, I caught his eyes dart over to me and his smile dim just a little.

And I tried—I fucking tried—not to let satisfaction fill me.

"Adam loved them too." But then Nisha spoke again, her voice cutting through the chaos in my mind. "Jess, this is my date Killian. I thought he might love to try a few things...could we get..."

Date.

And just like—it was gone.

Poof. Into thin air.

All my emotions centered on her as I watched her navigate the tent, her eyes shimmering up at me every so often.

What the fuck did she just do...

"Killian likes those. Could we have two of those and the ones next to it? Those look great..." Her smile tipped up at me. And I was stumped. "Is it okay if I grab lemon bars too? I know you said you liked those..."

I did? When? I nodded dumbly watching her cuddle into me and smile at Jesse as he bagged up our snacks.

At one point she tipped her head up and pursed her lips into a little pucker. *Kisses.*

The foreign unfamiliar sensation of my emotions evaporated left me feeling out of place as I bent my head to kiss her. Nisha pulled back too soon and smiled up at me. "See, that's not so bad."

No. Not at all.

I didn't speak as my girl navigated the entire interaction and I just stood there feeling everything I had never felt before.

"Oh, can you add that one in there..." Nisha was talking but her hand was on me.

Her palm flat on my chest soothing my heart. Her arms coming around me tighter. Her head tipping against my arm to lean into me like she was naturally seeking comfort with an easy smile on her lips.

"Thank you, that's great," she smiled at the guy and I realized as long as she was wrapped around me? I didn't give a shit.

I held her tighter to me marveling down at the flutter of pink, her scent all over my body now, and the way she handled herself.

"I promise they're good, Killian. I love them so much, you'll like it too..."

I didn't need to know I would like them.

I liked anything she did.

I was all about Nisha. And I couldn't explain it.

16

NISHA

AFTER THE FARMERS MARKET WHERE HE'D PAID FOR EVERYTHING, HE'D dropped everything off at my apartment for me that day when he'd come over.

Killian carried all the groceries to my little kitchen island. And looked around frowning.

"It's hot as fuck in here."

"The AC doesn't work." His frown deepened like he was mortally offended for me. I explained it to him.

And that afternoon Killian fixed the air conditioner for me, focused entirely on the task at hand. His movements precise and efficient. I'd been a little stumped at how he was doing it.

"Where did you learn to do that?" I peered over and tried not to droll at the six-three shirtless, muscled, hot tattooed man fixing my AC. Any woman would die on him.

He should be illegal.

"Kieran and I took it apart one summer, and Aidan made us put it back together. Said he didn't raise Heathens." He smirked a little as he said it. "But he did."

I felt my lips tip up at the sight of him enjoying himself and utterly focused on helping me.

"He sounds strict." *But he sounds close to his family.*

Something I never had.

"A little..." he motioned for me to pass him a screwdriver. "But he means well."

"And Kieran?" I asked.

A huff of humorless laughter left him as he squinted at the AC.

"Kieran's full of shit most of the time."

But he loved both of them.

I'd quickly whipped together lemonade and some snacks for him keeping them out as he finished covered in a little dirt. I got some wipes for him and helped him clean up.

He'd sat on my island with the AC blasting, looking grateful for the respite despite sweating up a storm. I grabbed extra towels and felt the heat on my face at the sight of him now in my home.

If I thought he'd kiss me I was wrong.

"How do you sleep here when it breaks?"

"I don't sometimes." He hadn't been pleased about that.

Or I slept naked. But I didn't dare say that to him. Not when I could feel his eyes on me tracking my movements, and I still remembered what his fingers felt like in me.

"Tell me if it breaks again."

And that was that. He sat there for a moment longer and pressed his lips to mine before leaving.

During the next few weeks, the man was all over me. Taking me out whenever he could and to wherever he could.

We went to a small Russian restaurant near my place where he thought I might like their pastries. I loved them.

I had Killian try a little bit of everything, and he told me about someone who worked for his older brother Aidan named Alexei, who told him about this kind of stuff.

"Alexei's been Aidan's right-hand man for a long time." Killian took a bite of the pastry I offered him. "That's good."

"Alexei has very good taste."

His gaze softened when he noticed my enjoyment. He bought a dozen of whatever I picked out.

"This will be so good for my blog. This aesthetic is really good right now and I feel like the filter I use will make the pastries pop."

I said it without thinking as I took the photos, muttering about how exciting this was.

When I turned he was blinking a little. "Blog?"

I felt the heat crest my face then.

"Ummm...." And I saw the way he watched me as I squirmed. "Yeah. Uh. I may...I umm...I run a blog."

It was like one big word instead of several words.

IRUNABLOG.

He blinked like he was surprised and a slow smile curved his lips.

"A *food* blog."

I nodded feeling shy all of a sudden at his smile. "Just a little—"

"What's it called? That's why you were excited about the farmer's market?"

"*Nothing*. It's not a big deal. Just a little blog—"

My heart was racing a little and I felt myself squirming, the condensation on the class of water becoming more focused as I felt my anxiety creeping in.

"Nisha."

I swallowed at the way he said my name.

"Well...ummm...do you wanna see it?" I blinked over at him. "It might be easier to explain."

He still wore a little smile as he tipped his head. Scooting closer him I pulled it out on my phone, inhaling his cologne. Killian automatically put his arm around me like he didn't like us to have a centimeter of space between us.

"*Sooo* this is my blog...A Slice of Life...I know it's cheesy—"

"It's not, luv. Go on."

"I started it in college when I realized how much of a food hub everything was...and then I ended up building it up and posting constantly. I would split it up to a post a day...and then I ended up posting recipes. It's a mixture of everything—" I broke off watching Killian observing it.

He moved over to look at it dipping so close to me I think I stopped breathing. His fingers moved over my screen enlarging images and smiling as he scrolled through the first image.

At the bottom it was my logo for the brand. Stories. Comments.

"It's got five thousand comments."

"Some of them are bots...probably...but I have had this since college..."

I rambled about how long I'd been posting photos showing him the progress I'd made over the years when maybe two people saw my post.

I told him about the earlier posts, getting better at taking photo and showing him how I did it.

"That's why you always take photos of our food," he murmured. He was so close I could see the flecks of gold in his amber eyes. "It helps your blog?"

"It's nice to have. Ever since I began at the hospital, I don't get that same time, but yeah..." I nodded, biting my lip unsure of why I felt nervous but Killian watched me carefully. He tracked the movement of my tongue darting out to wet my lips and those eyes of his went dark.

"Show me more, luv."

"You wanna see more...of my blog?" Why? This was so far removed from Titan.

"I do." He nodded as he ate quietly. And so I spent the rest of the time talking. Killian was a good listener...and I liked talking. It worked.

At one point I felt unsure. I could hear my mother's voice in my head fighting Killian's smile.

"Am I talking too much?"

"No."

"And you don't mind?"

"No. Keep going."

He continued eating as I did.

"And then...I ended up making this lemon gnocchi by myself, and it was the best recipe I've ever done. I learned the secret was just to add a little more garlic and lemon than the recipe calls for..."

I didn't even realized Killian hadn't let me go the entire time eating one-handed while listening to me. Occasionally he'd nod and ask a question, but the longer I spoke, the more confident I felt, the less I heard my mother's voice in my head.

The more I felt his eyes instead. One aqua. One amber.

All mine.

This is...really nice.

ONE NIGHT HE TOOK ME OUT TO AN UNDERGROUND BAR, THAT WAS MORE retro than anything else. It was intimate and I curled up in his arms making out with him the entire night.

"I don't think we finished our drink," I whispered into his mouth as the jazz music played around us.

"Do you want to?"

"No." I went right back to kissing him. Hungry for more, gripping his shirt tighter the entire time. His eyes hungry roaming over me but not pushing. "Do you come here all the time?"

"First time," he went right back to kissing me.

"So no dates for you?"

"Not without you."

And I melted.

He didn't push. And I didn't understand why he didn't just go for it. I wanted him but I also felt a little terrified of it.

When he dropped me off that night I was tempted to haul him into my house with my zero seduction skills.

The only thing that stopped me was my anxiety telling me to wait. *Give it some time.*

We just gotten to know each other.

Another time, we went to a Greek restaurant, which he said was a hole-in-the-wall family place a few of the Titans liked.

"Reed likes this place. He singlehandedly supports them. And so most of the Titans come here."

Killian looked devastating in a white t-shirt—the kind of handsome women were peering over at him and his tattoo covered arms for.

But he only inched closer to me as I passed him more pita.

"I can see why. This is delicious." I sat right next to him in the tiny shop he'd closed out. "I love smaller shops like this. It's so nice you looked up so many."

"I know you like it," he murmured watching me with amusement in his eyes. "I found a Thai place for us to check out. I think you'd like the noodles..." And he took me out often.

In between trying new things Killian and I talked about everything until the mango sticky rice came out at the Thai restaurant he had me try. The one I didn't order. But before I could say anything the waiter was gone.

"I didn't get this," I looked at Killian.

"I know," he smirked. "I did. For you?"

I was puzzled. "I didn't ask for it?"

"You stared at it for like ten minutes," he popped another bite of his egg-roll in his mouth.

"And you paid attention?" My heart was doing that flip again.

"I pay attention to everything about you." My heart thumped against my chest in the little family owned shop. He motioned to the sticky rice. "You wanted it. So I got it."

"So you're saying anything I want you'll give me?" I huffed out a breath trying to sound cool as he sipped his boba like he didn't just stun me.

"What if I wanted more Thai tea?" A nod. "And more lumpia?"

A smirk played on his lips. "I can call her over."

"What about if I wanted the entire shop?" I was teasing.

"By tonight?" He raised a brow. Nobody should look that attractive. It should've been illegal.

My smile dipped and my throat worked at the look in his eyes. He was deadly serious. And I got the feeling Killian O'Hara was the kind of man who always got what he wanted.

"You're not joking, are you?"

"I would give you whatever you want. Just tell me." His eyes met mine head on as he said it and I got the feeling the longer this went on the more honest he got.

He's not real.

His tone was direct, but there was a gentleness in his mismatched eyes, one amber and one aqua, that made my pulse race. Butterflies scattering across my stomach.

"Because I'm good to you?" I whispered it unsure of what else to say. "That's it?"

Like it was a matter of fact.

I looked down at the mango sticky rice. "Well, now we have to share it. You ever had it before?"

He shook his head.

"Do you try a lot of new things with me?"

"I do."

"And you like them?"

His smile was subtle but there. "I do." He tipped his head quietly to me and I felt the smile tipping my lips at the sight of his.

"Your brother's aren't like this?"

"We only talk when we need help."

104

Killian began bringing me lunch more often, dropping by during morning shifts with breakfast, or evening shifts with dinner. Sometimes for me and Adam.

When he came to see me injured, I would cuddle him close. Killian was different when you got him alone.

It was like, he could finally relax and calm down.

In those stolen moments, I'd be all over him, recognizing his need for touch, for connection. As much as I needed it.

"Thank you for bringing food for us," I murmured, my heart pounding in my chest. "Adam's really grateful."

Killian didn't say much. He just kept doing it.

Not a man of many words.

The leather seats shifted as Killian adjusted his position, his fingers tightening on the steering wheel, his grip firm.

Killian knew I was paying off student loan debt.

It didn't feel very fair, but I couldn't shake the memory of my parents using their financial support as a means of control.

The scars from those experiences ran deep, and I had vowed never to find myself in that position again.

It became clear that he had money. A lot of it.

Being a Titan meant he was part of the most well-funded ward in the hospital, and it showed.

My therapist's voice echoed in my mind, encouraging me to be honest about my feelings and to take a chance on building a healthy relationship.

"Can I say something?"

Killian's distinctive eyes, one rich amber and one striking aqua, rose to meet mine.

"I know you have money. It's just...I feel off...accepting all these things from you...I don't know..." I turned to face him, my heart pounding so hard I was sure he could hear it. I was struggling. "What are we doing? What is this?"

My fingers played with the hem of my dress, the silky fabric cool against my skin, a welcome distraction.

My mind was racing and I couldn't stop it. I didn't understand what he wanted from me. And Killian wasn't exactly the most talkative.

"I'm sorry—I just don't know what to do. I haven't dated in forever, and I'm not sure what you want."

I glanced up at him, my pulse racing, to find him blinking quietly, his expression unreadable.

"You know Reed Whittaker...he owns the hospital. You've got money. I don't. I know you like me, but I don't get what this is. And I'm a little..."

Killian's voice cut through the stillness, low and rough, like gravel wrapped in silk. "I don't know how to do this either. But I wanted...I wanted to—" he broke off. We were both struggling.

He turned to look at me, his mismatched eyes, one amber and one aqua, piercing me with an intensity that made it hard to breathe.

"I'm figuring it out as I go..."

"Do you...want to be with me?" *Are you my boyfriend?*

"I do." His voice was rough, the words unpolished and honest. "I don't know how to do this. Any of it. You don't have to worry about money," he said, his tone firm. "I have plenty of it. Enough for both of us." He paused, seeming to search for the right words. "Reed is my boss, but it doesn't mean I'd ever...or we'd..."

He was telling me that his financial status and his professional relationships wouldn't define or control our connection.

"I'm not that kind of guy—" he broke off, shaking his head, his hair falling into his eyes. "I don't know—"

Neither of us had much experience with relationships.

The handful of dates I'd been on, the half-hearted attempts at something more, paled in comparison to him. I hadn't dated in years.

But he'd been with...women...naturally.

I didn't need to ask. A man who carried himself with that much confidence? He would have the experience.

I didn't.

Save for the fumbling attempts in high school? I hadn't been with someone in years. And the thought of being with a man like him?

What if I couldn't—be with him? What if I freaked out?

This was a lot for me. And while I didn't know the details of his past, I could sense that he, too, was treading on unfamiliar ground.

We both were.

"I don't know how to do this either," I confessed, my voice trembling slightly, my heart exposed and vulnerable. "But I want to try."

"Do you want to try?" *I can't let you keep buying me things, and for Adam too. I want to do something for you too.*

"Why?"

"Because we're in this together. We're trying."

It was…something.

"Do you want to come over for dinner sometime?"

"Dinner?" His brow rose.

"I can cook. What do you like?"

"Everything. Anything."

I felt my lips tip up. "So dinner? You can't bring groceries for me. They're mine to decide."

"But—"

"No."

He didn't look pleased about this.

Killian paused for a second looking adorably peeved. "Okay."

"And you cannot bring anything."

Now he looked downright angry. I smiled wider.

"See you for dinner then?"

He tipped his head.

KILLIAN

DINNER.

In my world, women who invited me over usually wanted one thing. But Nisha? She was different.

And I was completely out of my depth.

I stood before my closet, rows of tailored suits and silk ties staring back at me, a silent reminder of the roles I'd played for so long—the ruthless enforcer, the calculated businessman, the emotionless lover.

But none of those personas fit the man I wanted to be for Nisha. For a man who could disarm an attacker in seconds, I felt...lost.

If I had been a normal man. With a normal life.

Would I know...

I didn't even know how to feel when I considered it.

Because I had never been...normal. Not when I was beaten to shit by my father for my eyes being fucked up and not normal.

Or not resembling Aidan and Kieran as much as he would've liked.

Or being blamed for everything...it didn't matter what I had done. Nisha...she was the first thing I remember wanting the way I did and I couldn't explain why she made me wish I wasn't...me.

While also making me grateful I was.

What the hell do you wear to a dinner that isn't about business or getting laid?

Aidan and Kieran's ideas of dating was a revolving door of one-night stands.

I didn't even want to consider what Gabriel was into and what his relationship with sex was like. It was a subject even I stayed away from.

And Reed Whittaker?

His exes made *me* look warm and fuzzy.

I sure as fuck wasn't about to turn to Gabriel or him for advice. Especially since I didn't think Reed knew the extent of how deep Gabriel's roots ran with us.

Because I still hadn't told him about her.

Or told Nisha who I really was—a man with a past soaked in blood and secrets, a man who'd never known the kind of love she offered so freely.

After what felt like hours, I ditched the suit idea. My phone pinged in the silence of my room.

Lara.

> I just launched the new lingerie line and it sold out in six minutes.
>
> Six. Fucking. Minutes.
>
> That's a new record.
>
> Alisha says we should do limited releases like exclusive packages from now on.
>
> It'll give us more of a boost.

Nobody did business like Lara. Quick and clever, she'd hired Alisha Malhotra, a social media influencer, a few years back.

The same Alisha that Reed had a crush on.

Her marketing strategy for Teasers had worked wonders. I checked the numbers quickly—we'd doubled our usual sales.

I texted back.

> Good shit. Let me know if you need anything.

Her response was immediate. I stared at the phone, an uncomfortable idea forming.

Could I ask Lara for advice?

No. Fuck no.

I'd faced down armed men without flinching. I could handle a date.

But as I stood there, still undecided on what to wear, doubt crept in. This wasn't just any woman. This was Nisha.

Lara worked for me.

We had a symbiotic relationship, sure, but never like this.

Still, she knew both my world and how to talk to normal people. Maybe I could frame it as gathering intel. Yeah. That's all it was. Tactical.

Before I could talk myself out of it, I hit call.

She picked up quickly. "*Hola.*"

I cleared my throat, keeping my voice neutral. "Hey. About those sales numbers..."

"They're great, right? I told you Alisha was worth every penny," Lara chirped.

"Yeah, good work," I said, then paused. Fuck. How do I do this? "Listen, I need some...intel."

"Intel?" Her voice sharpened with interest. "What kind of intel?"

I gritted my teeth, the admission painful. "It's...personal. I need you to keep this quiet."

"What's up?"

I took a deep breath, bracing myself. "I'm having dinner...with a woman."

Silence stretched on the other end, then Lara shifted.

"A...real one?"

What the fuck.

Motherfucker. It wasn't exactly a secret what I did for Titan.

But I wish people would have a little faith that I wasn't a necrophiliac.

"*Yes, she's real,*" I snapped, irritation masking my uncertainty, my vulnerability. "It's not a big deal. I just need to know if there's anything...specific I should do."

Lara's light laughter floated over the line. "I'm just surprised. I didn't know you were the dating type–"

Yeah. Me either. I wasn't the dating type.

"Where are you taking her?"

"She invited me to her place."

Lara cooed. "That's–"

"Focus." It came out harder than intended but otherwise Lara would lose it. "What do I need to know?"

"Bring flowers or her favorite snacks," she said it like it was a no brainer. For her maybe. Not for me.

"What? Why?"

"Because it's polite, Killian."

"Fine. What else?"

Nisha liked everything. More fresh food, than the fake stuff.

"You wanna be relaxed, you want to look like you're about to get laid, but not like you want to get laid—"

"What the fuck does that even mean?"

"Just trust me! Put on your best white shirt and black slacks. Women love that."

Did they? Women were all over me either way.

They're not Nisha. You can't fuck her on this date.

"Killian? You still there? Did you find the white shirt?"

"Yes. What next?"

"Get her flowers. And her favorite snacks, whatever they are. Do not show up empty-handed and for fuck's sake, no condoms," Lara instructed, her tone firm.

Oh fuck. "I wasn't planning to—"

"I never said you were!"

"You just said I needed to look like I wanted to get laid—"

"No, *don't* show up with condoms. It makes you look like a dick. Just feel her out right now. Kiss her maybe, I don't know—Just don't seem overeager. Look like you're there for dinner and she'll do the rest."

This was *exactly* why I didn't do this shit.

I sighed. "Holy fucking shit—"

"Welcome to the clusterfuck of dating, *Jefe*."

I wasn't built for romance, for the delicate dance of courtship and seduction.

"This is going to be a disaster," I muttered.

"Is she...nice?"

"Very," I answered without hesitation. "Anything else I need to know?"

"Just be yourself," Lara advised, her tone gentle, almost reassuring. "She likes you enough to invite you to her house for dinner. Women don't do that casually. Or if you're weird. And you sound nervous to meet her, so I'd say that's good. Just show up with flowers and the rest of the night will be a success."

"Right. Thanks."

I could hear her smile, could almost see the amusement dancing in her eyes. "I can't believe you're nervous."

"I'm not nervous."

"Suuuuure, you're not."

"Go focus on your sales." She giggled and I bit back a laugh. Dating advice. In my late twenties. From a burlesque dancer.

My relationship with Lara had evolved, had grown from a tentative alliance into something else.

She'd hit twenty-five and built an empire alongside me.

Maybe not what she'd wanted given her background, but she'd made the most of it.

"Let me know if you need anything. Kieran hasn't been back has he?"

"No, thank fuck. I love your family, but I will kill your little brother. I don't understand his deal."

A short, dry chuckle escaped me before I could stop it. "Aidan says the same thing. Have you talked to him lately?"

"No." Her voice was low.

Out of everyone in the family, she talked to me the most.

She tolerated Kieran.

But Aidan...Aidan was the one who'd gotten her out of her situation. And even now, I got why neither one of them knew how to talk to each other.

"Tell me how your date goes," Lara mused. "Nate just hired a dozen guys for security. I have to go meet them."

I grunted an acknowledgment, not committing to anything. But I didn't even know what I was doing.

I ended the call, feeling a tiny bit better, but still acutely aware I was in over my head. This wasn't just another operation I could plan and execute.

Everything else was familiar.

I fucked women.

I protected clients.

I killed people.

And nothing that I was mattered around Nisha.

I grabbed the clothes Lara asked me for looking for shops other than the ones I'd already been to, to grab things for Nisha along the way.

112

All the while Lara's mantra was in my head.
Do not have sex with your girl.

KILLIAN

I was running late.

I glanced at my watch, the hands ticking away with brutal efficiency. *Shit.*

As I drove, the feeling of being out of my depth intensified. I wasn't afraid, not exactly. Just...on high alert. Unsure of myself in a way I hadn't been in years.

I stopped by a local bakery and picked up lemon bars and some cupcakes, remembering how much Nisha talked about baked goods.

She liked that, right?

The florist came next. I asked for a pink bouquet in shades of pastels and vibrant pinks. Nisha's favorite. It fit her. The florist put an enormous pink bow on it and I felt a little wild carrying something so big back to my car.

Lara's checklist, in my mind, was filled with green tick marks now.

Except on the drive to Nisha's, the sky opened up without warning, rain pelting my windshield.

The rhythmic thud of the wipers punctuated my racing thoughts, counting down to an op I wasn't prepared for.

Cursing under my breath, I realized I didn't have an umbrella. I had no idea how to carry everything to Nisha's place without getting soaked, even if I ran.

I let out a frustrated breath and waited until the rain subsided.

By the time I reached her place, I was drenched and on edge. My appearance shot to hell. Hair plastered to my forehead, white shirt clinging like a second skin.

Holy. Fucking. Shit.

Nisha's gonna think I was raised by wolves.

And I was.

I felt like shit now. Not good enough for a woman sweeter than anything I had ever had.

Fuck my life. The doubts crept in, gnawing at my resolve.

What the fuck am I doing?

I raised my hand to knock, hesitated for a split second—like some goddamn teenager—then rapped my knuckles against the wood, steeling myself for whatever lay ahead.

When Nisha opened the door, she saw me, and her eyes went comically wide dressed in a pale pink dress. She looked radiant. And I looked like a drowned wild animal.

"Oh my God! I would've come to the garage! I have an extra umbrella..."

"Sorry, I'm late. The rain..."

I'm a fucking idiot.

"No, don't ever apologize."

Before I could process her words, she was leading me into her bedroom, her touch sending sparks across my skin. "Oh my God, you're soaked."

She tossed a fluffy towel over my head, warmth spreading through me, contrasting the chill of my wet clothes.

"Here, let's get you out of these wet clothes," Nisha said, her tone matter-of-fact but tender.

Her fingers moved to my shirt buttons, and I helped her, feeling like a teenager getting undressed for the first time, my heart racing for an entirely different reason.

She'd helped me so many times and now? Now I felt like I was on fire.

When the cool air hit my exposed flesh, I shivered, but not from the cold. Nisha's eyes flickered over my chest before she quickly looked away, a blush coloring her cheeks.

I'd been undressed around her before. All the time.

But this time…it was different.

"Will you take off your pants?"

This was Nisha's room, Nisha's eyes on me, her scent in my lungs. Amber and warm. Everywhere I looked there were signs of life.

Don't fuck this up. Don't fuck this up. She wrapped something warm around my shoulders, not looking directly at my body.

"Heated blanket," she explained, her voice soft in the cozy space. "I have it for cramps, but it's also nice when it rains outside…"

Her what? What cramps? The words bounced around my head, unfamiliar and slightly alarming.

Nisha disappeared for a moment, her movements quick and light, like a bunny darting through a garden. She returned with a fluffier towel.

"Here," she said, pressing it into my palms. "Dry off while I put these in the washer."

My senses were overwhelmed by the sheer…softness of everything. It smelled like her all over. This was my first time in her bedroom.

A pink comforter dominated the bed, its ruffled edges spilling onto the floor. Soft pink curtains framed the windows, filtering the harsh streetlight. Potted plants along the windowsill with the fairy lights strung around everything. It cast the room in a glow, and I looked around at the occasional books, clothes, and signs of life.

It smelled like her everywhere and I already wanted to lay back in her bed and spend the rest of the night.

Nisha bustled around her compact laundry space, handling my clothes with a care I'd never bothered with. When she rushed back, concern etched on her face, I felt something in my chest tighten.

"Killian, it doesn't say if the shirt is dry clean only. What if it shrinks? I don't want to ruin it for you…"

I watched her eyes widen as she spoke, her genuine worry over something as trivial as laundry catching me off guard.

It was so far removed from my world of life-or-death decisions that, for a moment, I didn't know how to respond.

"I don't know," I admitted, the unfamiliar feeling of being out of my depth settling over me like the damp clothes I'd just shed. "How bad could it get?"

"Killian, if this shrinks to fit a doll, you won't be happy then."

I have a hundred of them.

I couldn't care less what happened to one shirt.

Nisha shrugged and took it back leaving me alone on her bed to dry off. Watching her pert ass and lush hips in that dress she wore was gonna drive me insane for the rest of the night. Because now I was basically naked.

Do not have sex with your girl.

I adjusted the towel around my waist, willing my body to behave. But it wasn't cooperating. I was practically naked, and Nisha was *right there*, filling the space with her presence. Fluffy. Why was my girl so fluffy?

This wasn't part of the plan.

The plan had been simple: *dinner with Nisha.*

Instead, here I was, barely clothed, *in Nisha's apartment.* The reality of it hit me in waves. Over and over.

When she returned, she did that little rushed walk I'd grown accustomed to seeing at the hospital when I brought her food. It was endearing in a way I hadn't expected to find anything.

"Killian, your hair…"

She reached for me again, and I felt myself relax the moment her hands touched me. The heat of the blanket sinking into my skin. She continued to dry my hair and I sat there letting her work.

The scent of amber and vanilla all around me. Nisha.

Her soft voice.

It was *everywhere* like some kind of drug I'd never encountered before.

She was so fucking sweet, so goddamn adorable in her earnestness to take care of me.

Fucking *edible.*

My hands reached for her only to grip the edge of the bed.

The towel in my lap was becoming an increasingly flimsy barrier, and I shifted uncomfortably, trying to ease the growing pressure. But my dick had other plans.

My dick wanted in her so fucking badly.

Nisha's eyes flickered down for a moment, and I saw a faint blush color her cheeks.

Fuck. She'd noticed.

I gritted my teeth, fighting the urge to pull her into my lap to show her exactly what she was doing to me.

117

But this wasn't some random hookup. This was Nisha.

Do not have sex with your girl.

Do not have sex—

Fuck. I don't even have condoms. Lara said I couldn't or shouldn't fuck her. But…I mean…I could kiss her. I always did.

I reached for her.

19

NISHA

Having him in a towel was not the way I saw dinner going down.

His strong hands found my hips, steadying me, but also pulling me closer. The questions left my lips. "Are you warm?"

He nodded. *Not a man of many words at all.*

And my eyes drifted to his lips. I'd kissed Killian before, but always in the context of comfort, of offering solace and support. This was different.

"That's good," I don't know why I was so breathless. "I saw you earlier and I was worried..." I brushed his hair back not missing the contented way he tipped his head to my fingers. *Adorable.* "I thought you might get sick."

"I don't get sick."

"Might."

He smirked. And I brushed my lips over his. Once. Twice. Softly. Until he snapped and kissed me back.

His hands slid up my back and tangled in my hair. The moment he pulled me flush against him, he deepened the kiss with a hunger that matched my own. Over and over.

In one fluid motion, his arm wrapped around me, and suddenly I found myself on my back, the soft mattress cushioning my fall.

"Killian." He dropped down over me, the towel dropping from his hips and I knew, he was gloriously naked.

"Are you all right?"

I nodded, unable to find words.

"Hold onto me."

Then he lowered himself over me, his arms creating a safe little world just for us. I should've felt trapped, but I didn't. His weight anchored me, keeping the memories at bay.

"I brought flowers…"

What…

I almost laughed at his comment. "Did they get soaked?"

"They're in the car."

"Okay." *What else could I say?*

Even when he's awkward he's adorable.

Was he going to leave?

"Did you want to go get them—"

God help me with this man.

"I want to kiss you."

Oh.

Before I could overthink it, I pulled him back down, kissing him with everything I had. All the longing, the fear, the hope—I poured it all into that kiss.

"Just feel me, luv," he whispered, his hips pressing down.

"*Killian.*"

"I know, luv." Those eyes of his watched me low-lidded. Beautiful.

"I love your eyes," I whispered, my fingers threading through his hair. In the low light of my bedroom, the colors in his eyes seemed to shift and change. His brows rose in surprise. "They're one of my favorite things about you."

His lips parted slightly, and I realized he was genuinely shocked by my words. I held his face, suddenly concerned. "What's wrong?"

He shook his head, like he couldn't quite believe what I'd said. "My eyes…"

"They're beautiful," I insisted, nodding. For a moment, he looked at me with such raw vulnerability, like he was seeing me for the first time.

His eyes going wide like he didn't know what to do with me.

Then, without warning, his mouth crashed down on mine.

The kiss was different this time—desperate, hungry.

Each roll of his hips drove me higher, and I found myself clinging to him, afraid I might float away if I let go.

"*Don't stop.*"

"I won't, luv."

I felt a noise leave me—half whimper, half plea—as I gripped his shoulders. "Please."

"I've got you, luv," he murmured against my lips. "We don't have to do anything you're not ready for. Just breathe with me."

"I'm nervous," I admitted, hating how small my voice sounded.

In response, he dipped his head, his lips finding my pulse point.

He pressed soft kisses there, over and over. Long moments passed as he kept going.

"Better?"

I nodded, then gasped as he went lower. Trailing under he was tugging at my dress straps.

Cool air kissed my exposed breasts, and for a moment, panic flared. But then his mouth was on me, his tongue circling one tight peak, and liquid heat rushed through me.

A moan spilled from my lips, louder and more uninhibited than any sound I'd ever made.

God, that felt good. Too good.

"Killian," I gasped, my fingers threading through his hair. I held him to me, afraid he'd stop, afraid I'd wake up and find this was all a dream.

His other hand found my neglected breast, cupping and caressing. The dual sensation was almost too much, hovering right on the edge of overwhelming.

I rocked against him, craving more friction.

The hard ridge of him pressed exactly where I needed, each grind of my hips stoking the fire within me higher. Killian's tongue worked over my nipples and I squealed.

Killian broke away, a growl rumbling from deep in his chest as he pulled me tighter against him. His mouth sucked and bit down gently.

"Keep going, luv," his voice was dark. Velvet. Against my skin.

He alternated between my breasts with a hunger that matched my own, and I marveled at how good it felt to be wanted like this.

Pressure coiled tighter low in my belly, winding me like a spring. I felt like I might snap at any moment, but I didn't want it to stop.

"Let go for me, Nisha. I want to see you come."

Sounds I'd never made before escaped my throat, beyond my control.

Killian didn't stop moving against me as I felt the pressure build to an unbearable peak. Suddenly, pleasure exploded through me, more intense than anything I'd ever experienced.

I felt him moving faster, more urgently.

Then warmth spread across my belly, and Killian's groan of release mingled with my gasps.

And as I drifted in the afterglow, wrapped in Killian's strong arms, one thought crystallized in my mind.

His.

In that moment, I was his. And maybe, just maybe, he was mine too.

And if I thought he was done I was wrong. I felt him trailing his lips over my nipples, down my stomach—

"Killian?"

"Hm?"

The moment I felt his tongue against my clit I stilled. I thought I was going to implode a little. My fingers threaded in his hair and held fast as his tongue explored my body.

I could feel the aftershocks of my orgasm as he groaned.

"Clench on my tongue, luv."

Holy. Hell.

I was going to melt into my bed at this rate.

"*Killian*…don't stop…"

"I don't intend to."

20

KILLIAN

I LAY THERE WITH NISHA, ACUTELY AWARE OF THE MESS I'D MADE OF HER like some fucking teenager.

But she didn't seem to care.

No, she seemed comfortable now that her anxiety had calmed down and I'd eaten her out several times until my cum had absorbed into her fucking skin. And I could taste hers on my tongue.

She just kept kissing me after, those soft whimpers against my mouth driving me crazy.

Nisha did this thing where she hauled me closer and tighter like she wanted me to melt into her. And I wanted that too.

There was something about her that made me want to be a part of her forever. Sink my fangs and teeth into her soul and brand myself into her heart. I wanted more than sex. More than this. I wanted to imprint my heart into hers and live there.

And I couldn't fucking rationalize why I felt so protective of her.

Something in her eyes. In how she held me.

When she looked at me, the chaos and storm of my brain calmed down.

Christ, those sounds she made...for what felt like an eternity, we just made out, our bodies intertwined, our hands exploring each other with a reverence that was unfamiliar to me.

Women used me. I used women. The end.

This?

This was uncharted territory.

And neither one of us seemed to want to stop.

I sure as hell didn't want to let her go.

So much for not ending up in bed with her.

"Luv, I've made a mess of you."

"I don't care."

"I don't have condoms..." I admitted reluctantly, swallowing hard. "That's why—" *I dry fucked you into the bed.* I shook my head a little, closing my eyes. I'd lost all sense of control around Nisha.

"I'm not on anything..."

Well...fuck. She bit her lip, looking conflicted, a war raging behind her eyes.

"We should stop..."

Anything you want.

"We can stop," I murmured, brushing a strand of hair from her face, marveling at the softness of her skin beneath my calloused fingers. "But I'm not going anywhere, luv. I'm here for as long as you'll have me."

I didn't even know where those words came from.

But when we both reached for each other again, my brain short-circuited.

Until my dick pressed hard against her belly and Nisha gasped.

"Killian, we should stop." Nisha's gaze was fixed on my dick, specifically on the piercing that glinted in the low light of her bedroom. *Shit.*

I should've explained.

"I didn't know you had..."

The apadravya was from my wilder days, a remnant of a time when pain and pleasure were often intertwined.

I'd kept it because...well, it didn't matter why now.

Not with *her* looking at me like that, with a mix of curiosity and something else, something darker and more primal.

"Did that hurt?"

"A little. When I got it..." I found myself whispering back, lying there with her in my arms, the intimacy of the moment making my heart race. "Not anymore."

"Does it hurt in me?" Her innocent was in her eyes as she asked.

"If it does, I'll take it off. Promise."

She bit her lip again looking almost shy. "Oh...you should bring condoms next time...Do you want to cuddle while we wait for your clothes to dry?"

As if on cue, my stomach answered with a loud growl, drawing a light, musical laugh from her, the sound warming me from the inside out.

My lips quirked up easily. Something had shifted between us.

"Dinner?"

"Dinner," I agreed, then added because it was on my mind. "Do you really—" My throat worked. *Say it.*

Her eyes lifted to me. "My eyes..."

She smiled softly. "What about them?"

My father used to beat me up and call me a freak of nature. My eyes are my worst trait.

Gabriel valued me and never gave a shit what I looked like.

At whatever she saw in my face her smile fell a little. She moved a little closer. "Your eyes are beautiful, the left one is a shade of amber, I've never seen someone with that color. But your right one is sometimes icy, sometimes aqua blue. It depends. If you're angry, they get darker."

She bit her lip a little and I wanted to bit that spot too. "But right now, they're somewhere in between. A little dark, but I don't think you're angry."

"I'm not."

"I want you to stay tonight." And my nod was immediate.

"I want to stay with you too."

Nisha's grin widened, her eyes sparkling with a joy that held my breath hostage for a nanosecond there.

"Do you want to have dinner and a movie night in bed?"

Shit. I didn't know that was an option.

The thought of lying in bed with Nisha, sharing a meal, watching a movie...

But I knew I had to rein it in, to keep a tight leash on my control. Otherwise, I'd do this shit all night. Go down on her.

On second thought...

"I need to get condoms. Otherwise..."

She nodded, and I didn't miss the way her eyes darted to my dick. I bit back a grin at her innocence.

Fuck, she's so cute.

125

"Nisha—"

"I'm sorry. I keep thinking if it hurts—"

"It doesn't—"

But it was definitely responding to her now.

"I'M GLAD YOU'RE HUNGRY BECAUSE I COOKED *EVERYTHING*," NISHA hummed, floating around the kitchen in a bright yellow dress, the fabric clinging to her curves in a way that made my mouth go dry.

Everything about this woman drove me crazy.

I sat there in my briefs, which had dried the quickest, watching her, my eyes tracking her every move with a hunger that went beyond the physical.

I made a mental note to get her a bigger heated blanket for me too.

And condoms.

Definitely condoms. Even if I wanted her otherwise. Even if I was tempted.

The sounds of her orgasm played on loop in my head, driving me fucking crazy, a sweet torture that I never wanted to end.

I tried to distract myself by looking around her kitchen, taking in the little details that made it hers.

The whole place screamed Nisha. And with the rain outside still coming down, I could fall asleep around her.

"It's coming down hard," Nisha murmured, her gaze fixed on the window, a faraway look in her eyes. "I hate when it's like this and I have to walk from the train."

"You take the train? Is that safe?" I drove her all the time, but there were some nights I didn't. I thought she would've taken a cab.

She smiled. "Yes, I mean...sometimes. Sometimes when there's creeps I just change cars, but for the most part, yeah.It's New York, right?"

"I can drive you."

The thought of her out there, alone and vulnerable, made my skin crawl, a cold sweat breaking out on the back of my neck.

"I couldn't ask that—"

"Why not?" I countered, leaning forward, my hands itching to reach out and pull her to me, to feel the reassuring warmth of her body against mine. "It isn't safe. Walking home in the rain—"

"I have an umbrella," she said softly.

"What about your late-night shifts?"

"Sometimes I walk home with Adam or take a taxi. It's not a big deal."

But it is. To me, it is.

"Text me when you're off work," I said, voice low. "I'll drive you."

"But what about your work?"

"If I'm in the middle of something, I'll come when I can. Or I'll send someone to bring you home safely." The words felt inadequate, but it was the best I could do without revealing too much. Without admitting that the thought of her in danger made me want to tear the city apart.

Her brow furrowed slightly. I wanted to kiss her again, keep her safe, make her mine. But those words...I'd never said them before.

"But I don't want to take you away from your work," she insisted, but her eyes told a different story.

"You won't." I met her gaze, willing her to understand what I couldn't say. *"I'll drive you. I want to."*

I shifted on the stool, hyper-aware of her presence. All I could see was Nisha—flushed cheeks, swollen lips, that hungry look in her eyes that matched my own.

I watched Nisha move around the kitchen, her every gesture stoking the fire within me. The way she reached up to grab something from a higher shelf, her dress riding up to reveal more of her thighs.

"Well, I hope it's not an inconvenience for you—"

"It's not—" I cut in quickly, then caught myself. *"It isn't."* I didn't know how to be smooth. Not around her.

I wasn't at all.

Women didn't come to me for sweet nothings, but with Nisha, I found myself wanting to try.

Her eyes drifted over her shoulder, a hint of a smile playing at her lips.

"Okay, I can let you know when I'm off work—"

"Or your schedule." Shit. Does that make me sound like a creep? I mean...I did know everything about her and she still didn't know.

But Nisha's smile widened, her eyes crinkling in obvious delight that made my heart stutter. "Yeah, you can have my schedule."

As Nisha floated away, I tried to focus on the paper she'd handed me, but my mind kept drifting.

I wanted to take my time with her, to worship every inch of that body.

To trace the line of her collarbone with my tongue, to nip at the soft skin of her inner thighs.

Eat that pussy like a motherfucker.

My hands clenched tighter on the counter as I imagined the sounds she'd make when I finally buried myself inside her.

Nisha bent over to check something in the oven, and I had to bite back a groan. I imagined taking her right there.

I'd take her hard over that counter someday, gripping her hips tight as I pounded into her.

The image was so real I could almost hear our skin slapping together, feel her heat around me. She hadn't held back earlier.

And I loved that. Loved how open and responsive she was, how she trusted me with her pleasure.

"How do you like your steak?"

Nisha's voice cut through my fevered thoughts like a bucket of ice water. I blinked, reality crashing back in.

"Pretty rare," I managed to reply, my voice rougher than I intended.

She nodded, seemingly oblivious to my inner turmoil, grabbing a few items before nudging the door closed with her hip.

"Anything specific you want with your potatoes? I've got sour cream, chives..."

As she turned back towards me, I noticed her eyes, dark and curious, flitting to my chest. To my tattoos.

It wasn't the first time I'd caught her gaze lingering there.

Nisha had her hair up, exposing the tattoo on her neck.

Cello f-chords.

I'd looked it up after noticing it weeks ago, but she usually wore her hair down, obscuring it from view.

Something told me that was deliberate, a carefully constructed facade to hide a part of herself from the world.

Her dresses were tiny, but I didn't know if she had any ink besides the one on her neck.

Curiosity got the better of me, a burning need to know more about the enigma that was Nisha.

"What instrument do you play?" The words left my mouth before I could stop them. Nisha's shoulders tensed, her movements suddenly halted.

Her fingers, gracefully arranging items on the counter, paused. It hadn't been on the file.

No instruments. Weird. *I've struck a nerve. But why? And why do I suddenly care so much?*

"I used to," she said, her voice low, a confession that seemed to cost her something to utter. "I used to play a few."

"You like music."

"I do." Her answer was short, clipped, a wall of defenses I couldn't penetrate.

"I do, too."

Brilliant.

Can you string together more than three words, motherfucker?

At that, Nisha turned, a smile playing on her lips. Something shifted in her eyes. "I used to play the harp."

My eyebrows shot up, surprise momentarily cracking my usual stoic expression, a reaction that I couldn't quite control.

Nisha played the fucking harp.

"I can play the cello and piano, but—" she broke off, a blush creeping up her neck, a hint of vulnerability that made my heart ache. "Unless you want to hear a cat wailing, neither are as good as the harp."

I could see Nisha playing a harp.

A fucking harp.

The image flooded my mind—her delicate fingers plucking at strings, her body swaying with the music, lost in the melody.

"Is that why you like working with your hands?"

"I do. When that didn't work out, I ended up taking up cooking for anxiety, and then I just...became a nurse. Helping people. You know?"

I did know. That's all I ever did.

But this...this was different.

Nisha, as a nurse, I *understood.*

The need to help, to heal, to make a difference.

But Nisha as a musician?

That was something else entirely. Something that didn't fit neatly into the box I'd unconsciously put her in.

"Why did you—"

"And you?" Her eyes sparkled with mischief, but the uneasy smile on her lips cut me off. *She didn't want to talk about it...*" Do you often captain pirate ships?"

I felt a reluctant grin tug at my lips, my hand unconsciously moving to the tattoo on my rib cage. "On occasion."

Nisha mock gasped, her hand flying to her chest in exaggerated surprise. "A joke? What am I going to do?"

That grin stretched wider at her playful response despite my brain being acutely aware she was distracting me.

Sex changed me. But it also changed her.

"Some I was just too drunk to remember."

"I can't imagine you drunk," she said, a hint of amusement in her voice as she reached for a whimsical, floral-patterned oven mitt. "Or losing control."

If only she knew how close I was to losing control right now.

I do it all the time around you.

"It was a long time ago."

Maybe that's why I craved Nisha.

It finally felt like I was waking up out of the darkness for once. Into her. Her light, her warmth, her softness.

"Are you hungry?"

I nodded my mind, musing at what she was doing.

Nisha was keeping a secret from me.

There was nothing in her file about her being a musician. *I'll find out. I always do.*

21

NISHA

I WAS SORE.

Deliciously, achingly sore. And Killian knew it.

Instead of my usual routine of baking or cooking to keep my mind occupied, he'd been wrapped around me until I could barely move.

Until I passed out.

He was insatiable—wilder than I'd ever known he could be.

And I loved every second of it, matching his intensity with a hunger I didn't know I possessed. Hot skin and teeth and tongue and all over him like two wild creatures that couldn't get enough of each other.

He'd taken me to clean up in the shower the first night he had stayed over.

And despite not having any condoms on us, we were all over each other.

His eyes had met mine through the steam, dark and intense.

Water cascaded down his chiseled body, droplets clinging to his eyelashes, his muscles, his pecs.

"You're beautiful," I'd whispered and to his credit he looked almost embarrassed as I said it.

I didn't hesitate to touch him. All over. Feeling more confident in my skin the longer I was with him.

In the shower, I sank to my knees, the warm water beating against my back as I returned the favor.

Taking him into my mouth to his shock. Watching him tip his head back, his throat working as he swallowed—I tasted the metal of his piercing. The hot length of him, thick and stretching my lips.

"That's a good girl," he growled as I kept going and I swear this is why Killian never spoke.

Women would die if he did.

I never felt sexier than watching him like that, taking him deeper until I swallowed around the thick head of him. My lips stretched wider as I struggled a little.

The combination of hot water and my mouth made him even more sensitive and I worked my fist around it, twisting enough to make him groan.

"Just like that, luv," he growled fisting my hair. "You can take more."

I could. I did. Inch by inch. Until he hit the back of my throat and I choked a little.

"Such a good girl. Take me deeper, luv. *There you go.*"

I wanted to come right then at him guiding me.

I moaned around his length remaining still as he drew out and fucked back in with a groan hitting the back of my throat every single time.

I didn't even know I'd like this until him.

Rivulets ran down his tensed abs. Over his tattoos on his chest, his ribs, his arms. He looked like a dark prince for my pleasure. All sin and seductive wrapped in the smoke tendrils of steam.

The power I held over him in that moment was intoxicating. Killian's hips rocking, letting me breathe in between him doing that with the length of him in my mouth.

His hand wrapped around my hair more as he worked himself. I felt my orgasm building as I watched him.

I looked up at him while I took his length, watching me as he pulled all the way back. His teeth sank into his bottom lip.

"Is that all right, luv?"

I nodded, licking my lips, my tongue darting out to take more of him in my mouth again.

"I knew you'd be like this," his voice was gravel over the sound of running water and steam. "So hungry for me, such a greedy girl on her knees for my cock. And you fucking love it, don't you?"

I moaned around him and kept going. Faster. Harder.

I was going to implode if he kept going.

This is why he doesn't ever say anything.

I'd die if he spoke like this all the time.

I didn't know how long I stayed like that his hips thrusting into my mouth, in my throat but he was still hard when he lifted me up and kissed me.

"In bed," he growled. "I want you on my face."

I almost died a little.

We barely made it to the bed, leaving a trail of wet footprints across the floor.

He positioned me over his face, hungry and savage, his hands gripping my thighs with bruising force.

I couldn't resist tasting him again, teasing his piercing with my tongue.

But focusing was *impossible* when he was doing wicked things with his mouth, his tongue, my skin still damp and hypersensitive from the shower.

I still took him deeper until we both came. And I swallowed every bit of him as he pulsed in my throat.

When he finally left in the morning, promising to return to me that night, I was a wreck.

My skin felt electrified, every nerve ending alive and screaming for his touch. Dark. Dangerous. Wickedly handsome and untouchable by anyone else by me.

I needed him, more than I had ever needed anyone or anything in my life. He consumed me completely, leaving me desperate for more.

The *moment* he walked through the door, I was on him kissing him senseless.

"*Condoms*," I gasped.

"Got 'em."

We tore at each other's clothes, the rustle of fabric and the pop of buttons filling the air as he tore into me.

When Killian positioned himself between my thighs in my bed, I could feel the heat radiating from his body, the length of him long and thick and I didn't know how to relax anymore.

Because it was real. It was happening.

"Luv," he rasped, his voice rough. "You all right?"

"Yes."

No. Not really. I was a little nervous.

133

As he pushed inside me, the stretch, the slight burn, the feel of his piercing—it was a sensory overload.

Nevermind.

"Wait—"

Noises left my lips as I felt him. Entirely too much. *Too* big.

I couldn't breathe with him in me. He took up all the space in me. Every single inch.

"Easy, luv," Killian murmured his lips moving over my throat, dipping lower until he sealed over a nipple. "I've got you. Just breathe."

And then he sucked and whimpers left me. My nails dug into his back, feeling the muscles flex under my fingertips as he tugged them with his teeth, alternating until I calmed down. And then he moved again pressing deeper.

I whimpered as he slid in impossibly so. *"Oh...that's a lot."*

His groan mingled with the noises leaving me as he settled painfully deep.

I breathed through my nose as he sucked harder, tugging my other nipple, the sensations going straight between my legs.

"Fuck," he whispered. "I never want to leave." His eyes raked over me and I knew I was squirming to adjust. "I knew you'd be tight as fuck."

"Killian..."

"Let me..." He kissed me steadily. Slowly. Tongue meeting mine hesitating slightly until I sucked. And just like that my body clenched around him. *Hard.* His breath left him in a hiss. *"Nisha..."*

That piercing—with every thrust, it sent sheer ecstasy, coursing through me. I clenched around him despite his size.

His eyes locked on me in concern.

"Don't stop," I pleaded, my fingers digging into his shoulders. "Don't stop, ever."

"I won't," he murmured. "Just warming you up."

I felt a flood of moisture between my legs at that and his lip tipped up. "Do you like that?"

Who is this man?

He was quiet until he got into this place with me.

And once he did? He was *unleashed.*

I got the feeling I was seeing a side of him he kept to himself.

Until he didn't.

134

"Put your arms around me," he bent his head to my neck as he drew out slowly. I obeyed. And then I screamed.

His thrusts were deep, forceful, each one sending tremors through my body.

"*That's it,*" Killian's voice was gravel. "*Let it out. Let me have it.*"

I clung to him, trying to pull him closer, deeper. The stretch, the fullness—it teetered on the edge of something. *Wild.*

Desperate. Maddening delicious.

A cry tore from my throat as he hit particularly deep.

Tears streamed down my eyes with the intensity of it as I sobbed. I could feel myself clenching around him, tighter and tighter—the tension coiling inside me like a spring wound too tight.

I wouldn't survive it.

"*Killian—*"

"*I feel that, luv,*" he growled, his voice dark and rich. "Any minute now, you're gonna come, aren't you?"

"*Yesyesyesyesyes.*"

I was sobbing incoherently.

Every muscle tensed as it slammed into me with no grace.

"Oh God....nggghh."

I pulsed around him, my body gripping him tight as I rode out the aftershocks. I was dying. That was the only thing I could feel.

Every single part of my focus centered down to where he was working inside of me.

"*Baby.*"

"*I've got you, luv.*"

Tears streaming down my cheeks.

Ohgodohgodohgod.

White spots exploded behind my closed eyes. He never relented, turning my orgasm into an endlessly long one.

The thin line between pleasure and pain blurred, heightening every sensation. And just like that, he rose up above me, like a dark prince, his hands moving until one clamped around my throat.

Oh. *God.*

I felt the rush of moisture between my legs and a helpless noise left me at that. I didn't even recognize myself.

"*Come for me.*"

Ohhhhfuccccck.

And just like that my body wasn't my own.

Something flashed in Killian's eyes, his last shred of control snapping. And I belonged to him.

His thrusts became more forceful, deeper, hitting spots inside me that made my vision white out.It was obscene.

And I reveled in it. I could feel my orgasm all over my thighs. On him.

The headboard crashed against the wall with each thrust, the rhythmic banging echoing through the room.

"*OhGodohgodohgodfuckfuckfuck,*" I squealed closing my eyes as starbursts of pleasure exploded in my womb.

"No God will save you from me, luv." His voice was dark velvet. "You're mine now."

And I came even harder from that alone.

I didn't want to be saved.

I wanted to be his.

My entire being sensitized to that one spot he existed in. Over and over.

I was nothing but his. His to use.

To do whatever he wanted to me.

Each thrust felt like it might split me in two, the pleasure bordering on pain in the most exquisite way.

As I came harder this time, his dark growls in my ear coaxed me through it and I shrieked at the white-hot feeling of coming undone.

His hips moved with renewed intensity, almost brutal in their force. Until I felt the hot pulses deep inside me.

I was shaking so hard he dropped his body down on mine holding me steady as I felt wrecked.

I made a noise, cradling his head against my neck. My fingers instinctively threaded through his hair, an act that had become second nature.

It took forever for me to stop trembling.

"It's okay, luv. I gotcha..."

I knew he did. He always had me.

Now more than ever.

22

NISHA

"My periods have always been bad…" I explained to Killian one night as he rubbed my belly while cuddling me.

Over time, the simple dinners turned into long movie nights and conversations that stretched till dawn.

He'd been nothing but attentive to me when I was on my period.

He was curious about everything following me around my apartment asking me questions about things he didn't know.

"That's normal?"

"For me," I murmured. "I think. I don't know. I've never known any differently."

He frowned as he rubbed my belly some more, pressing his lips there.

There was something dangerously adorable about Killian.

He'd grown up with boys. And so he hadn't experienced being with a woman like this. "But I've got it down to a science now."

"If it bothers you at work, you'll let me know? I can bring more heating pads. And those cupcakes you like from *Butterscotch's*."

And this was why I was falling in love with this man.

Any opportunity he found to make my life easier he did it. I didn't grow up with many people in my life, but I had friend's growing up.

A few boyfriends despite what was happening at home. Killian was unlike anything I had ever had.

Something entirely different in my life but wholly safe. He made me feel protected.

"Did you want to go to the immersive art exhibit this weekend?" I asked him, one night, as we lay tangled on the couch. I found myself absentmindedly running my fingers through his hair. "I sent you some photos and it looks wonderful."

Killian was sprawled across me, his weight comforting rather than oppressive. He was becoming my new heated blanket.

"That sounds good. Does it have that room—"

"With all the moving lights? Yeah."

"Mmmh." I chuckled at his noise, massaging his scalp, working out the tension I could feel there. His contented groan made me smile.

"What do you do on your days off when I'm not around?"

"Nothing…" he mumbled into my chest like it was a matter-of-fact. A light laugh left me. "I do nothing without you."

"You just lay there in bed all day? Like a sack of flour?"

His low laugh rumbled through both our bodies. "No, luv. I usually workout…make food…"

"With all that flour?" I teased, delighting in the way his shoulders shook with silent laughter. It didn't take much to make him laugh.

"I bake on my days off, you know?"

He'd been the eager recipient of my baking experiments more times than I could count. He loved my chocolate macarons and the strawberry shortcake trifle I made.

I kept more than enough of it in the fridge for him.

"Sometimes you go out…" he murmured slowly.

"Sometimes I do." I agreed.

"To the Farmer's Market." His tone was light, teasing.

I felt a blush creep up my neck, remembering how I'd tried to keep that little adventure a secret.

"And you don't tell me."

"I have been on a hundred dates with you." I giggled, catching a glimpse of his quick, boyish grin. A happy Killian was devastatingly wickedly handsome. "You won't let me live that down, will you?"

He was beautiful like this.

Everything felt lighter with him now, as if the weight I'd carried for so long had finally lifted.

Killian turned his head on my chest, his lips finding the spot right over my heart, his hair adorably tousled and his smile wide.

My pulse quickened as he pressed soft kisses there, again and again.

"Never." His lips trailed a path through the thin fabric of my night-ie. "In fact...I wanted to do something that day when you did keep your secrets from me..."

"Like w-what?"

I moaned as he trailed lower, his teeth tugging at my panties.

"*Killian.*"

"When that guy smiled at you, I wanted to take you right there in front of him." A bolt of electric lust shot down to my core as his tongue darted out licking between my legs where my pussy was dripping.

"*OhGod.*"

His tongue flicked over my clit and I swore I was going to explode.

"Should I have?"

He could do whatever he wanted to me. I was his.

My fingers tangled in his hair as he chuckled at my lack of response and I felt his fingers playing with me, sliding deep into my body as I gasped.

"*Killian—please—I can't—*"

"I think you can wait, luv."

He dipped down over my clit and *sucked.*

I nearly came off the couch as he curled his fingers in me, his other arm banding around my waist keeping me tight to the couch. "Can't you?"

No. No, I was going to die if I did.

My orgasm was building. Sex with Killian was nothing like I'd ever experience.

For a man of few words, I realized he preferred to use his tongue and fingers.

His hands roaming my body, pinched my nipples as his other hand worked inside of me, rubbing that tender spot that drove me wild.

I cried out with the intensity as he growled. "You are not allowed to come until I say so."

OhGod.

My fingers gripped the couch so tightly, my other hand tangled in his head doing nothing to stop him from sucking on my clit as his fingers moved in me. Harder. Faster.

So fast that I was breathless.

Unable to hold it. Unable to think.

I wasn't going to make it.

"*Killian—please—I'm not gonna—*" I shrieked as he sucked *harder*.

My legs trembled and shook as I screamed into a pillow feeling him pulling my orgasm from me. I screamed even louder knowing I was disobeying him.

It was endless. It went on and on and he didn't relent.

When I finally came down, his mouth was on my hip, those eyes watching me smugly satisfied.

A noise left me unable to formulate words.

"You disobeyed me."

I don't even know why my body clenched at that.

"Y-you m-made it—*impossible*." I couldn't even form words let alone think straight.

"Should we practice?" The look in his eyes was sinfully dark. "Until you get it?"

And then he was turning me around raising my hips up. The first stroke made me scream into the pillows, his length stretching me wide, sinking so deep, so easily from my orgasm.

And even then I still struggled a little.

He settled deep in me sighing as he bottomed out.

"That's my girl." He hauled me up, his arm around my throat. "Let's try this again, luv."

His strokes were so long and deep my eyes rolled back as he growled into my ear.

"Such a good girl, look at you ready to come apart for me again."

I whimpered as his thrusts began so rough, so violent, and I loved it clinging to the couch as much as I could.

"Don't you dare even think about it."

"*Please—*"

"*Fuck, you look so pretty when you beg me.*" My eyes rolled back as his voice like dark silk and velvet sank into my skin. "Deep, isn't it, luv?"

A noise left me. I felt him hitting somewhere I couldn't even speak through but I was so close.

"Never thought I'd take your words from you," his chuckle was wicked as he slammed in and I scrambled to hold on.

It was endless and I was so close and every single time I was he backed off. Again. And again.

Until I was helplessly whimpering, shaking, begging him hoarsely to *let me come.*

"Why?" He was absolutely evil as he crooned into my ear. "You didn't listen to me before—"

"Killian...please...please..." I sobbed. I was going to lose my mind from this. "Right there—*right there...*"

He slowed his hips down and a frustrated noise left me.

Part yelp-part scream. I didn't know he was this playful. *Devious.*

But every single time I was with him I learned more about him.

I felt the tears streaming down my cheeks, my moans soaking into the pillows as I felt my orgasm rushing through me.

I wasn't going to make it. And I cried harder for that.

"No."

A helpless noise left me.

The more he told me not to come, the faster my orgasm bubbled up until I screamed feeling it hit me. It slammed into me like a category five hurricane and I shrieked into the pillows.

His arm around my throat as he held me to him, his lips whispering filthy things in my ear while I came.

"Such a bad girl, coming without my permission again. Is that how sensitive you are?"

I squealed and cried out losing my mind with every brutally vicious thrust.

He groaned low in my ear as I felt warmth flood me as Killian slowed his hips down before burying deep.

Sinking down on me, flattening me out on the couch while his lips pressed into my back, my shoulders, my neck.

"Killian," I whispered. "Sorry."

"For what?" He sounded amused.

"I...came..."

His chuckle shot another bolt of lust through me. "That was the point, luv. I didn't expect you to make it."

"Ohh." I shuddered as his shoulders shook.

"I wouldn't be doing my job if you did make it."

❧

141

On evenings when work kept Killian away, my apartment felt hollow, as if it too missed his presence.

He had become my home. My safe place.

Other nights, he'd slip in late, and I'd stir to the dip of the mattress. He had begun sleeping over with me and staying here.

His mouth would find my pulse, trailing to my collar, between my legs, desire blooming even before I was fully conscious. My body trusted Killian.

His hands seemed to be everywhere at once, turning me this way and that.

Some nights were a frenzy, Killian taking me against the wall, on the kitchen counter, or bent over the couch.

Then there were lazy Sunday mornings in bed, where he'd enter me with agonizing slowness, drawing out my pleasure until I teetered on the edge of sanity.

Please, move.

I will. Just let me hold you.

Please, harder. More.

At work, Killian would surprise me with lunch, always bringing enough to share with Adam.

I marveled at how he managed it, but he simply said he operated on his own time.

How was your morning?

Busy, so many patients today. I think something happened in Brooklyn. How was yours?

I took care of that mess for my boss, luv. It was...a clusterfuck to say the least.

We fell into a rhythm as naturally as breathing, and I quietly attached a set of keys to his keyring when he wasn't paying attention.

I just let him figure it out since he was one of the most observant people I'd come across.

He seemed inherently attuned to my needs and wants.

I knew he paid astute attention since he never said anything but things in my life were definitely easier.

If I so much as said I liked something, hundreds of it appeared or the fridge was always restocked with things I needed.

One night, he came home later than usual while I was asleep.

The dip of the mattress left me momentarily disoriented, the darkness of the room a little overwhelming.

A small sound escaped my lips, when his steel bands of arms wrapped around me, pulling me against his solid chest.

"It's just me, luv. It's just me."

His lips brushed my ear, whispering words I couldn't quite catch, but the low rumble of his voice vibrated through me, chasing away any lingering unease.

As I floated in a drowsy haze, Killian's hands gently roamed, brushing my nightie up. "There you go, relax against me..."

He rolled me partly further on my side, spreading my legs.

In one fluid motion, he slid into me from behind, the sensation so deliciously unexpected that a soft gasp escaped my lips.

Stretching, burning, the piercing hitting somewhere sweeter this time around. I tightened around him moaning his name.

"You take me so well now, luv," he murmured, his voice thick. "I think you can take a little more, hm?"

Oh. God.

I could only moan, the feeling of him filling me coupled with his languid pace intoxicating to my senses.

I panted as his fingers tugged my nipples, dream-like and lazy, moving over to my clit rubbing circles that drove me insane.

"You dream about me, luv?"

Yes.

I whimpered at the sensation, nearly overwhelmed as he held me fast to him.

His arm under my neck, my head tipped back onto him, holding me close as he moved within me, each slow, deep thrust deliberate and measured.

All the while his fingers moving in slow circles over my clit.

"Was I doing this in them?"

This is why he doesn't speak. I'd be beating women off with sticks if he did.

I gripped my pillow. *"God, baby..."*

"You're so wet, luv." His voice was dark velvet against my ear as he pressed down on my clit, making me shiver and clench around him. "Did you want me to fill you up?"

"Yes."

Everything felt more intense like this. I felt like I was going to implode from the pressure building.

"God, that's so good."

"Hmm, better?"

"Yes. More. *Please*."

"I love when you beg me for it..." he trailed off circling faster.

I sobbed as his arm under my neck held me fast, his tongue hot against my neck, his lips brushing my skin with trails of fire. I gasped and arched into him as he bit down gently there.

Ohgodohgodohgod.

Killian's free hand stroked me in time with his thrusts, the dual sensation less like crashing over an edge and more like sinking into a warm bath.

I shuddered in his arms, a moan escaping my lips as I felt my body clenching around him. Pulsing. Losing it for him. Hard.

"Gods, you're beautiful," he whispered reverently. "There you go, luv."

I came so hard I cried out a little as he didn't relent and I trembled violently with the sensation of feeling trapped by his powerful arms. Forced to just take him.

A flood of moisture pooled between my legs and he groaned. "You come so hard. Makes me lose my mind."

I whimpered as he rolled me partially onto my stomach and I gripped the sheets tighter as he rocked into me, sinking even deeper, hitting somewhere sweet.

He shifted and I felt him moving, shuffling under I felt one of my throw pillows under my belly.

And then he rolled me over onto it and shoved deep.

A strangled scream left me as he groaned. "That's it. *That's my girl.* You can take it, can't you?"

Shamelessly, I nodded. I loved this. I loved him like this.

"Fuck me." I moaned surprising myself. "Please." I arched my back up to him. And he went a little wild the way he worked in me. I reveled in it. "*Please.*"

"You love me like this?"

"*Yes.*"

"Stretching you out—"

"Yesyyesyes." I was going crazy with the sensations of him moving like this. I was fuller than I thought possible. "More. Please."

"Using that little pussy until it *hurts.*" *OhGod.*

An animal noise left me as I came. Hard. He fisted my hair impossibly tighter as he worked inside of me, the harder I came, the harder he moved.

Tears filling my eyes with how good that felt to the point of pain.

Killian's groan was guttural as he finished soon after, his grip tightening as he pulsed inside me. Heat filling me.

I let out hard breaths against the pillow as I trembled. His lips moving against my pulse, finding it as he sealed his mouth over it.

These moments became our new normal—hazy, undefined, yet more real than anything I'd ever experienced.

We didn't need words to define what we were becoming.

I cooked, he helped me clean, and he was always by my side, fixing things around my place. I delighted in making Killian's favorite desserts after dinner, and we'd often fall asleep together.

Gradually, almost imperceptibly, my home was becoming our home.

But it struck me as odd that he never talked about his own apartment, though I suspected it was probably nicer than mine.

One night, I gathered the courage to ask about his place.

I was acutely aware that my neighborhood in Brooklyn wasn't the most desirable, but it was affordable and far from my past.

Since the night he'd found me mid-panic attack in the laundry room, Killian had tactfully avoided prying into my history—a kindness I appreciated.

"My place doesn't feel like yours," he said when I asked.

"What do you mean?"

"Your place has you."

Oh.

Beyond his role at Titan, beyond his occasional assistance to his brother, in these quiet moments, I glimpsed the real him.

He offered to show me his apartment if I wished, but assured me he was happiest here.

I didn't press the issue, content knowing that while he occasionally crashed at his place, he considered my apartment home.

I'd come home to find my fridge mysteriously restocked, bags of groceries appearing as if by magic. His clothes in my closet. Us doing skincare routines together.

If someone had told me the hardened man who showed up with a scowl on his face months ago would be sitting on my couch with a vitamin-c sheet mask on his face and neck I wouldn't have believed it.

But he did anything I did, curiously around me taking part in it. He wasn't happy about how slimy it was. He tried new things with me breaking out of his routine.

One lazy morning, as we drifted between sleep and wakefulness, Killian attempted to coax me out of bed. "Wake up, luv."

I burrowed deeper into the covers. Then I heard it—a soft chuckle from Killian.

"It's late," his lips moved over my ear and I shivered burrowing deeper into the covers. I responded with an incoherent grumble, which only made him laugh again.

"I snuck in last night and you didn't even stir. You sleep like the dead."

He frequently teased me about how nothing could wake me up.

Sometimes I'd fall asleep on the couch before he'd come home and he'd pick me up and put me in bed.

I never remembered it.

I just slept through it all with him. After years of running and being alert, I just let go around him.

I turned in his arms, facing him.

His eyes, still heavy with sleep, met mine. In them, I saw a reflection of my own feelings—contentment, desire, and something deeper that neither of us was ready to name yet.

"Five more minutes."

Killian pulled me closer, nuzzling into my neck. "Mm, five more minutes."

"I think I want pancakes today…"

"That sounds nice…"

"With chocolate chips…"

He smiled into my cheek. "And coffee."

"Mmmm, coffee."

His grin met mine as I kissed him. He was my home.

23

KILLIAN

THE LONGER I DATED NISHA, THE MORE THE CONCEPT OF A HOME-cooked meal that used to be so foreign to me that I couldn't pinpoint the last time I'd experienced one—became normal.

Everything became normal.

Years of grab-and-go meals between jobs or hastily consumed protein bars had dulled my palate. But *this* was different.

Nisha didn't allow me to do that shit anymore.

We're having dinner tonight.

And she'd tug me along into the apartment for that lemon-ricotta pasta sauce she had on stock for me with the thicker, chewier egg noodles I fucking loved.

I devoured every single thing Nisha put in front of me. Desserts. Cakes. Hot meals. She'd take photos and I'd help her move things until she got them just right. Nisha had a fucking blog and it did a lot better when she posted all the time.

I saw how much happier it made her. And she saw how much happier it made me to see her like that.

Now, with me to feed and getting her groceries more often? She did cook more often. Waaaay more often.

"How come you don't do this full time?" I asked her one night moving her salt shaker into the frame for her. "You're good at it."

"It doesn't pay the bills," she smiled over her shoulder. "And you're just saying that because you like what I make."

"I love what you make."

I pressed my lips into her neck. But if it did?

Would she do it all the time?

If I paid her bills?

Too much, too soon—back off.

I didn't press it.

I was waking up every Sunday morning in her arms to fucking blueberry lemon muffins. Pancakes with chocolate chips. Strawberry shortcake trifles.

Home.

All with kisses. Lots of them from her peppering my face and I didn't know...this was possible. Not for me. Nisha ran through all my barriers and reached in and yanked me out.

Being with her was different.

One, her food was delicious.

And two, she would sit right across from me, with a soft smile on her face her eyes darting over me every so often.

I entertained the idea of bringing her to my place, but the image of my sterile, museum-like apartment quickly squashed that notion.

No, it was better here, in the warmth of her home.

"...but I thought maybe if it was spicier I'd like it more..." she was saying.

"Do you prefer spicy food?"

Nisha liked spicy food and I was learning the hard way.

I didn't know how to handle it.

But I mean...*I can handle spice, right?*

In my world, details usually meant the difference between life and death, not the perfect ratio of seasoning in lemongrass sauce with enough chili peppers to kill me.

I thought I could handle spice. The truth was—I couldn't. But I tried for her.

This wasn't my usual modus operandi.

Typically, I fucked and left, no strings attached.

But with Nisha...there was something.

Something in those eyes, in her smile, in the way she burst into laughter at my dry jokes.

Her smile came effortlessly, and I found myself grinning in

response. Nisha wasn't trying to play me. And that...that was even more foreign territory.

"You're more relaxed right now."

"Am I?" I managed, the words coming out rougher than I intended.

"It's all right," she said, her voice gentle but steady. "I was just making an observation."

"I'm not used to this."

My throat tightened, memories flooding back—not just of cold, empty rooms and hushed conversations, but of muffled screams, the metallic scent of blood, and the weight of a gun in my hand before I was old enough to drive.

The memory of my mother. A distant dark shadow of her. Aidan blocking my field of vision and tell me to leave.

"Not used to...any of this," I continued, the concept as foreign on my tongue as peace had been in my childhood. "I didn't grow up with people like you."

"My brothers and I, we didn't grow up with a lot of people," I said, the words feeling inadequate. It was the understatement of the fucking century. "We kinda just grew up alone a lot."

She frowned. "How did you guys take care of yourselves?"

The scars on my knuckles seemed to throb with the memory.

I could count on one hand the number of people we'd trusted growing up, and most of them were dead now.

Even Gabriel, who was as close to family as anyone outside my brothers could be, was kept at arm's length. Not like her.

I didn't want to keep her anywhere but with me. I didn't even understand half of what I felt.

And then she looked at me with those eyes of hers, deep and understanding, and I felt the words trapped in my throat, choking me. "We didn't. Aidan scrapped by and did what he could. I think he dropped out of high school, but had a full ride to college somewhere." Aspects of our lives I didn't really think about too much. "I barely got my GED."

I felt a reluctant smile curve my lips. "My father wasn't a nice man or a good man. And he had other plans for his kids that didn't involve schooling."

Nisha looked heartbroken for me so I didn't look at her.

"When was the last time you had dinner with anyone?"

"I can't remember." I did remember Aidan getting us food all the time though. "Aidan took care of us a lot, but most of my memories are fuzzy." I remembered things in bits and pieces from my youth. Some of it was a blackhole, but I had the scars from it.

Nisha's eyes softened, encouraging me to continue. I felt a sudden, irrational urge to tell her everything.

Nisha, I'm mob. I'm sorry I didn't tell you sooner. I promise it won't come back to hurt you.

"Aiden used to make us dinner and we used to live in like this dark apartment," I said, instead of telling Nisha the truth. "Now he works in real estate and owns this house on his own."

On paper, at least.

"You're close to him?"

I wouldn't say that.

"I work with him and Titan. He kept me safe for a long time and when he couldn't do enough he made sure my mentor could. I don't know if you've seen Gabriel, but I'm closer to him. Aidan keeps everyone at a distance for our sake if not his."

He did have Alexei.

The kid he'd picked up years ago when Alexei had tried to rob Aidan —big mistake there—but Aidan had introduced him to us and after Cormac died, Alexei became a part of the family too.

Not quite a brother, not quite a son.

Aidan had done his best but even my brother had his limits.

As I spoke to her Nisha put more food on my plate and refilled my water passing me things throughout the night. Her soft touches, attentive gaze, and warmth in general made it easier to open up. To tell her things I never told anyone.

As she asked me questions, I felt answers leaving my mouth with surprising ease. About me. About my day. About Aidan. Kieran.

"He's so fucking young," I said shaking my head thinking about him. "But you'd like him. Everyone likes him. He's a little shit though."

"How old is he?" Nisha took a bite of her pasta with a smile.

"He's about to be twenty-four in a few months."

Her smile was rueful. "So he'll be my age." She wiggled her brows at me. I didn't mean to wince.

What came out was.

"I forgot that. You're more mature than he ever was so I never thought about it. I always think you're older than me."

"Well, thank you. I love being a cougar."

I winced again to Nisha's laughter.

I was not good at speaking. That's why I never did unless it was work.

"I'm teasing." She giggled at my expression. "I know what you meant."

Nisha's laughter was musical at my discomfort, her cheeks turning pink as she laughed harder while I rubbed my face.

"Did you have your Mom growing up?" She asked that soft smile on her face, taking a bite of her food. Her eyes, soft and understanding, met mine. "You rarely talk about…"

"My mom left when I was a kid. Barely remember her. She had Kieran and she had enough."

My memories of growing up were dark, a blur of survival and nothing else.

Flashes of Aidan and me struggling together to figure it out, neither of us emotional, both of us determined to survive, played through my mind.

The words scraped my throat as I spoke. "My father…he wasn't kind. Or good." I paused, fingers drumming a restless rhythm on the table.

"You said that, I'm sorry, I won't pry about it."

Nisha knew a bit about shit parents since she had them too.

"Aidan's the closest thing we have to a father figure. He is for Alexei…"

"He adopted him?"

"Something like that," Nisha was gonna have to learn about blurring the lines in our world. But her foster father wasn't a good man either. I knew enough about him since he was in jail. And I knew exactly *why* Nisha kept to herself.

I knew why she liked Adam around her. She trusted him.

She trusted me.

Tell Nisha everything.

What did I say?

Hey. I'm in the mafia. But not really in. But not quite out. How did that work?

But if I did tell her everything, and she saw me as the monster I sometimes feared I was?

My entire body revolted at the thought of Nisha not being here.

Of losing her after finding her...*I can't tell her.* I would lose what little I had, this fragile connection that had become more to me.

"I'm sorry," Nisha said softly, her hand inching across the table, not quite touching mine but close enough that I could feel her warmth. "That must have been hard. Do you ever wish you had another life? A different one?"

Did I? No. I never thought about...another life...

"No. I never thought about it. I worked hard for everything I have," I continued, a hint of pride creeping into my voice. "It's all mine and now, being a part of Titan while juggling my brother's work—"I paused, remembering Nisha thought he was in real estate, which wasn't far from the truth.

Just not the whole truth.

She just listened, her attention wholly on me as I found myself opening up, words spilling out that I'd never shared with anyone before.

I told her about starting at a young age, the relentless drive that had pushed me to build myself up to where I was now.

"Money..." I said slowly, choosing my words with care. "It isn't a problem...for me. With you. I don't care. I don't feel used. Not by you."

"But I don't expect that from you."

"But I want to," I said, the words coming easier now. "I want to."

I was horrendous at speaking.

But Nisha's eyes softened at my words, a small smile tugging at her lips.

"Okay" she said simply, her hand reaching out to cover mine on the table. "Then I get to take care of you too."

"What about you?" I asked my brows furrowing. "Do you wish you had another life?" *She didn't say if she did.*

Her hand on mine tensed, fingers curling slightly.

"No," she said, her voice steady but thin. "I'm happy with my life."

Nisha was lying. Just like the Farmers Market. She was telling me what she thought would make me happy.

Not the truth.

24

NISHA

DO YOU WISH YOU HAD ANOTHER LIFE?

My hands trembled, nearly dropping a plate. It happened so fast I couldn't process it.

That was the thing about anxiety, sometimes you were always in a spiral. And when you finally slipped off the hair, thin crack of whatever you were on, you fell harder.

Time fractured within the space that I was standing in because one moment I was in the kitchen and Killian was right there, and in the next—I was gone.

I found out my hands remembered things, and my body recounted emotions quicker than my mind did. My harp strings under my fingers, Eugene's hands all over me, until I plucked the wrong strings.

Eugene sneaking into my room and touching me at night. I wanted to vomit up the food I just had.

You should be grateful we took you in. The girl nobody wanted.

Nobody loved you enough to keep you.

That's how we found you.

Memories flooded in—late nights in practice rooms, the music a desperate shield, early mornings sneaking out, anything to avoid *him*.

My heart raced, panic clawing at my throat at the sensation of feeling Michelle holding my throat.

It was real. It was real. It was real. And it was right there.

"I need—" I needed air. "I need to—"

Did you think you'd bring him home and feed him? To what? Seduce him like you did my husband.

Bile rose in my throat. I could feel Killian's eyes on my back, concerned and curious. It was a tangible force in clear opposition to Michelle's.

He didn't know. He couldn't know.

Michelle's voice was in my head. Again.

Don't make trouble. Don't be dramatic.

Your father didn't do anything to you. Why would your father ever touch you? Don't flatter yourself? You're not that pretty. Why would anyone want you?

Don't spread lies, Nisha. It isn't becoming of you.

We adopted you for a reason. Don't be ungrateful for the life you have. So many girls would kill to have your life.

Oh God. Michelle was in the kitchen with me. With Killian. I needed to run. Everything I had worked so hard to forget came racing back. My breathing quickened, my chest rapidly beating in staccato. The familiar tightening as I felt it happening.

All of it felt *wrong* and distorted.

Sometimes when I was with Killian, I forgot about Eugene and Michelle.And right now? That question sent me into a headspace I couldn't figure out.

I forgot who I was and I just lived in my current state.

Right now? I was back to the past. Back to the girl I had been when everything went wrong.

"Nisha…"

What if I had spoken up sooner? What if I had stayed? What if, what if, what if...

Don't be silly, you stupid girl.

Do you wish you had another life?

No. Sometimes I wish I didn't have this one.

The one where I lived with the shame of what happened to me.

Stumbling to the side to leave, my legs felt like jelly, and I couldn't breathe. I felt like the air was closing in around me as I moved through the apartment.

"Nisha!"

I was moving through my apartment rushing to get somewhere soft. Where I could breathe.

Ungrateful.

I couldn't breathe.

I was in his arms before I could even blink again. Steel banded around me and I felt his scent hit me before I could get any further.

Killian had taken his shirt off and wore his dark slacks. He looked devastatingly handsome earlier and this close to me, I couldn't think straight.

"Don't run," his voice was dark. *"Breathe."*

"I can't—" the words clawed their way out of my throat.

He dipped his head over my neck and held his lips over my pulse for long moments, hugging me so tight I felt like I might shatter.

And yet, I felt like it was the only thing holding me together.

"In and out, luv. I'm not going anywhere, luv. I'm right here. Breathe for me." He pressed his lips to my throat again and again. "Tell me what happened."

"I c-can't." My voice broke on this words. My breathing was harsh and I felt the noises leaving me as I cried softly.

"Why, luv?"

"I'm scared…you won't love me if I do."

There it was. The truth.

"That's all I know…" I told the truth and bad things happened.

Pouring out of my lips as I felt my heart clench as I admitted it.

I didn't know where that came from. But the moment I said the words?

Hot tears burned in my eyes, and I felt them down my cheeks. "I'm a-afraid you won't like me. What if you think…I'm dirty? Or I'm a horrible person…" *Or worse.*

What if I told Killian my adopted father molested me and he didn't like me anymore?

Or thought I was asking for it…

I cried even harder at that aware of how vulnerable I felt. Noises left me as he soothed me and he held me even tighter. "Don't make that sound, luv."

Until I felt like I was going to snap in half, and it was what I needed.

The sheer force of him, the strength in him around me, holding the shattered remains of what was left of me stable.

"That I won't…love you…" the words sounded rough on his tongue. As though he didn't say it often.

I nodded, sniffling and crying harder as I barely whispered it. *"What if I'm fucked up?"*

He was shifting, holding me like I was made of glass as he straightened a little to look into my eyes. He looked stunned.

"That I won't love you?" Disbelief was in his tone, and it confused me. He looked at me like an alien with two heads. I swallowed. "You think I would ever see you as anything other *than you? That anything could keep me from you?"*

Was he surprised by that? I nodded, unable to look at him, focusing on his chest.

Anywhere but his eyes.

Before I could duck my head, he moved quickly, his lips moving over the trails of my tears.

"I love you so much," I whispered. "I'm scared...this is new for me...I don't know what to do—"

I should've known he'd kiss me. But this time, it was different. Hungry. Harder.

Holding me tighter to him, one hand cradling the back of my head, the other pressing me impossibly closer. I tasted the salt from my skin, his tongue thrusting into my mouth seeking dominance.

When he pulled back for a quick second, his eyes were dark and intense. *"Say it again."*

"I love you."

A sound escaped him, something between a groan and a sigh, and then his lips were on mine, stealing every thought but the feeling of him.

I clung to his shoulders, his mouth eating at mine, and this time it changed again. A low noise left me at the sensation that unfurled in my chest.

He didn't stop. And I didn't want him to.

Killian kissed me until I was drowning in his scent.

Until the world narrowed to just us, and then he pulled back for me to see a softness in them that only I got. I recognized it for what it was.

"Nothing will make me see you as less than. Nothing will take me away from you. I've seen darkness. I breathe it in every single day. You have had every right to become just as cruel as me, just as terrible—"

"I don't think you are—"

"And yet you chose otherwise," he finished, those eyes holding me

156

captive. "I liked you the moment I saw you and felt your light. Your peace. I see broken things in the world. You see broken things and you want to fix them. You don't flinch at me. You're not afraid of me."

"I would never be—"

His smile was tight. "I know, luv. But you make me feel like I belong somewhere. My heart feels at peace when I'm with you. You are everything I am not. Everything good I see in the world is through your eyes. And everything I want more for that exact reason."

"I am not going anywhere, Nisha." He held my face in his larger hands and I was forced to meet those eyes head on. *"Nothing will take me away from you.* Not a single fucking thing."

I licked my lips as my heart clenched. "I love you."

"I love you."

The way he said it, as he tipped his head, closed his eyes and pressed his forehead to mine—I felt something seismic happen in my chest. Something uncurling like it had been starving for it.

Something in me shifted almost immediately as he said it, like I had been waiting my entire life for someone to tell me that I wasn't too much, that I wasn't broken—but that I was the right one for them.

"You choose me?"

"I choose you."

"I thought you said you were bad at speaking," I whispered unable to formulate words.

"Turns out when your girlfriend runs away from you, it lights a fire under your ass you suddenly become proficient." His lips quirked a bit without humor. "Don't run from me, luv. Terrifies me."

My chest clenched as I forced out the words. "And you think you're not funny?"

A laugh bubbled into my lips and he smiled a little against them. Our light laughter mingled between us. "I'm sorry, luv. I didn't mean to make you feel like that."

"It's okay."

"If you come back to the kitchen," he murmured against my lips. "I can tell you about my brother Kieran and the fucking cat videos he keeps sending the family..."

A laugh bubbled up from my chest, catching me off guard.

Why is he like this?

"Cat videos?" I felt my smile stretching wider.

"Mhm."

I chuckled harder at Killian's attempts at diffusing the anxiety, but the man also didn't have the best timing for anything.

I felt a smile curving my lips. "I bet it's the ones where it stares at you as it's knocking things over?"

His chuckle was a low rumble. "How'd you know?"

"Lucky guess."

"Kieran is a troublemaker?" Killian nodded, his eyes meeting mine across the kitchen island as he sat down.

"You have no idea."

I reached for the lemon tarts I had out. "Does he work for Titan?"

"Not yet. But he will...in a few months." Killian sighed. "Kieran doesn't want to be anything. Our father...he put a lot of pressure on him to join the family business. None of it in good ways. Now Kieran just...doesn't want to do anything."

I nodded, a wave of understanding washing over me as I reached for the tray of lemon tarts.

"What does he do all day?"

Killian shook his head, a wry smile tugging at his lips. "I can't even tell you half the time."

"I hope you like it," I said, setting the plate of lemon bars in front of him. "I put extra lemon juice in because I think it tastes better...I promise it's good."

"Everything you make is good."

Warmth unfurled in me as he took a bite, and I busied myself with the tea mugs, an idea forming. "Well, now that dessert's settled. Tell me a story about your tattoos. Any of them."

I retrieved the whipped cream from the fridge, adding a dollop to my tart before offering Killian the can.

As he began telling me about the clover tattoo on his wrist, a matching set all three brothers had, I found myself drawn in by the softness in his voice when he spoke of his siblings.

Killian shook the whipped cream can.

Before I could warn him, it malfunctioned. Cream exploded, coating his face, neck, and bare chest in a ridiculous white mask.

For a heartbeat, he stood there, utterly stunned, cream dripping from his chin.

A giggle escaped me, then another, until I was laughing uncontrollably.

The sight of Killian—usually so composed and dangerous—looking like a dessert gone wrong was too much. My laughter cut short when I caught the mischievous glint in Killian's eyes.

"Don't you dare—"

He aimed the can at me and squeezed.

Cool cream hit my skin, and I squealed in surprise ducking out of his way. His laughter lit up the kitchen as I felt his arms wrapped around me.

"*Killian.*"

A light scream left me as he hauled me into his arms. I looked at him grinning—a real, unguarded smile that split his face wide open. I felt my breath catch.

This was a side of him I'd never seen before—playful, almost boyish in his mirth.

But then I caught it—a fleeting look in his eyes.

A tiny flicker of uncertainty was there, and it was gone so fast I almost missed it.

Oh, he should never look like that.

I didn't think. I couldn't think.

In an instant, I was in his arms, my lips crashing against his.

25

KILLIAN

COME HERE, LUV.

I was no better than an animal, starving for her.

She's afraid I don't love her?

Her happiness and laughter. Her anxiety. All of it was mine, too. And if she was upset, my heart didn't like that. Ever.

She's fucking worried I can't love her?

I already do.

I already did.

The whipped cream was cold against my skin, but all I felt was her. Backing up her little body against the counter and pinning her with my lips, I relished the little gasp that left her throat.

She was adorable.

Nipples perked up and peachy for my mouth. Her hands cupped my face closer, and for a moment *nothing* else existed. *"Killian..."*

My throat worked at the sound of my name on her lips.

Those dark eyes of hers watched me closely. I damn near tore off the straps in my rush to get to her body.

"I need you."

It was all the rational thought I had as I palmed one of her tits in my hand and watched the way her eyes lowered a little. Instantly. Nisha was responsive.

I licked my way down her throat, nipping her throat in places I knew made her shiver while playing around with her nipples.

Taking one into my mouth, and playing with the other. Reveling in the soft mewls of pleasure that escaped her lips as she clutched me to her.

"Nisha," I growled, switching my attention to her other nipple. I couldn't get enough of my girl. I kept sucking. Drunk off her taste.

When I reached her soaked baby blue panties, I nearly lost my mind. She was a vision—panting, hair mussed. *Mine.*

How can I not love this woman?

"Fuck me, luv. You're beautiful."

That was an understatement. She had my attention like nobody else. Those lush breasts, tipped with hard nipples, drew me back begging for my attention.

Shit.

As soon as my tongue flicked out and I got that first taste of her, a deep, feral growl rumbled in my chest.

Fuck, I was addicted. I couldn't get enough.

My fingers found her dripping entrance, rubbing, and teasing, driving her wild.

So tight. So wet. I knew she'd feel *incredible* around my cock. I might not fucking survive it, but what a way to go.

She arched her back, a breathless gasp falling from her lips.

So damn responsive to every touch.

I moved up, my tongue over her nipple again, my fingers plunging deeper, curling and searching for that sweet spot.

When I found it, she let out a moan that nearly made me come on the spot. That sound—*fuck*, I could live off that sound alone. I sucked harder, slipping another finger inside her, stretching her, pushing her limits.

Her entire body quaked beneath me, trembling and shaking with need.

"That's it, luv."

The flush on her cheeks intensified, spreading like wildfire down her neck, painting her heaving breasts a deep, rosy hue.

I used my tongue to lick her, while my fingers fucked her harder, faster, deeper—*relentless*. Without any mercy.

I curled my fingers just right, relentlessly targeting that spot deep inside her, applying the perfect amount of pressure with each stroke.

"It's too much, I can't—"

"*Yes, you can,*" I growled, my voice rough with need. "You're so fucking close, baby. I can feel it. Don't fight it." I redoubled my efforts, my fingers pumping faster, harder. Sucking on her nipples. "Give it to me."

I was determined to push her over the edge, to watch her shatter completely in my arms.

"Killian—"

"I know, luv."

She made a noise like a protest. And I didn't take that.

"*Let go,*" I growled rising up a little, holding her by her neck and working my fingers deep.

Her eyes, drowsy with pleasure, met mine and a whimper left her. She clenched tighter and I wondered...for a second...did she—

I switched my hand to grip her throat and squeezed down just enough to feel her clamp down so tight we both groaned.

There you fucking go.

"*Let go for me, luv.*"

I could feel her tightening around my fingers, her walls fluttering wildly, the first tremors of her impending orgasm starting to take hold.

"That's it, luv," I encouraged her, my words muffled against her sensitive flesh. "You're almost there...give it to me. Come for me."

I sealed my mouth around one nipple, biting down hard as I simultaneously curled my fingers inside her, hitting that sweet spot that I knew would drive her over the edge.

Nisha came apart with a raw sob, her entire body convulsing as the force of her orgasm *tore* through her.

Her thighs clamped tight around my body, trembling uncontrollably, holding me in place as she cried out.

There you fucking go, sweet girl.

"Killian...stop..."

I pressed my lips to her chest, breathing with her.

Nisha came *hard.*

"Come here...please." She reached for me with her trembling hands, hauling me up and crashing her lips against mine in a desperate, needy kiss that stole the breath from my lungs. *I got you, luv.*

Nisha clung to me, her fingers tangling in my hair, holding me close as if she never wanted to let go.

"Stay with me tonight. Please."

There was no power on earth—*absolutely nothing* that could have made me leave her. Ever.

"I'm not going anywhere, luv," I promised, sealing my words with another searing kiss. "I'm here for as long as you'll have me."

I will give you anything you want. Everything I am is yours.

26

NISHA

"I want to try something with you," I whispered against his lips. "Can we?"

My heart was racing from my orgasm and the anticipation of treating him the way I dreamed of.

He tipped his head back, curious, a brow rising.

He's so sexy.

And impossibly hard, straining against his briefs, and his breathing hitched as I pressed closer.

I watched him aware of how I must've looked.

Dress tugged down, breasts heaving, and with the way he watched me I never felt sexier.

And I wanted to do something with him. Something I'd fantasized about.

Biting my lip, I watched as his gaze followed the movement, then traveled down the length of my body. A flush crept up his cheeks, mirroring the heat I felt in my own.

I held his hand as I turned around on the island, my back to him and used my hands to adjust. Until I was laying on the counter, looking up at him, my head tipped back. His breathing was hard.

"Luv—"

"Let me...please," I murmured, reaching for his briefs. He'd always taken such good care of me; now it was my turn to reciprocate. I freed his impressive length, my fingers brushing against the metal of his piercing. The contrast of soft skin and hard metal sent a shiver through me.

I scooted back, positioning myself so my head hung off the island. Killian's strong hands reached out to steady me, ever protective.

"*Luv*," he breathed, a note of wonder in his voice.

Without hesitation, I took him into my mouth, moaning at the sensation.

He was enormous in my mouth, lips stretching wide, his length sinking in deep in this position. His groans louder as he sank in and I moaned around him.

"Fuck, luv. Such a good girl taking me like that." He sank in further and I almost gagged. "Relax…relax…luv. There you go."

One of his hands gripped my breast and the other reached for my throat.

I gasped as he drew back and slid back in.

"You can take me deeper, luv. Feel me."

He sank back in deeper and I felt him massage my throat where I almost came from the sensation of him sinking in. Oh God.

This was different.

Overwelhming. Intense. Hot.

He growled holding there as I gagged and choked a little. "Just a little longer, luv. Hold me."

I obeyed feeling myself growing wetter by the second. He sighed as he pulled back and I gasped for air then.

"Oh God," my chest heaved as I drank in a lungful of air. That was still hotter than anything we'd done.

"Keep going?" He murmured.

I nodded.

Killian did it again and again until he was holding for longer every single time.

And I moaned as he gripped my breasts finally, his imposing cock working in and out of my mouth slowly at first. Until I grabbed his hips and pulled him deeper.

He groaned loud then as he sank in. "Such a greedy girl. Did you want more?"

I felt my legs shaking at that.

He always got like this in bed, a shift from his usual calm and controlled self that rarely said much.

165

In bed, he was confident and he knew what he was doing.

In his element. Darker. Ravenous. Precise.

Driving me insane as I panted, my eyes watering as he sank in.

Deeper and then drawing out. Again. And again.

The next thrust would've made me choke, had he not tugged on both my nipples as he fucked in. My legs spread open for him, my pussy was soaking wet as the cool air hit it.

His voice was a dark, deep growl. "You're dripping, luv. Does my girl like that? Fucking her little throat."

I bobbed my head around him wanting more. More.

Thank God he only talked like this in bed.

Killian *in bed?* Was a completely different man. Confident in his ability to drive me insane. Like now.

Until he didn't stop.

He bent over me, hips pumping and I thought I could take him. I thought I could. Until I felt his breath over my clit. I screamed around his length as he flicked his tongue out while twisted my nipples. His tongue and cock sank into me at the same time and I shattered.

There was nothing graceful about my orgasm.

The head of his down my throat, his tongue thrusting into me drawing it out.

His name muffled out of my mouth as he did it over and over and I was coming within seconds.

I felt the head of him swelling inside my throat and if I thought he'd bury deep and come, he moved, straightening, pulling out, his fist.

I gasped as I felt the first spurts of his orgasm on my nipples, my stomach, covering me.

Moving his cock between my breasts covering them in ropes of come. I gasped as pleasure racked through me at the sight.

When he finished, I was lifted, moved, until I was straightened and he was hauling me back against his chest.

"Holy hell, luv."

I felt a light laugh leave me. "I take it that was good—"

His only response was to kiss me.

KILLIAN

That summer, time slipped through my fingers like sand.

Days melted into weeks, weeks into months. My world revolved around Nisha.

She was becoming my home, a concept I'd never truly understood until now. And I didn't know why I didn't fight it.

I didn't even want to. Out of everyone in my life—Nisha was not someone I wanted to fight.

I found myself visiting her at work, bringing food for her and Adam. Reed's brother wasn't a threat, but taking care of him meant something to Nisha, so it mattered to me.

I didn't know what the fuck I was doing. Just that I wanted to do it for her.

Between my work for Aidan, Gabriel, and Titan, and the time I spent with Nisha—my girlfriend, a word that still felt foreign on my tongue—I barely had time to breathe.

Nisha's tiny Brooklyn apartment felt more like home than anywhere I'd ever been.

She took care of me and in turn I took care of her and suddenly we had a little family.

She was my family too.

The way she'd curl into me showing me something on her phone or a new book she was reading on the e-reader I got her, her scent on my pillow all over me when I slept, her laughter echoing through the rooms when she teased me too much—it all became vital to me.

"I talk too much—" she frowned ruefully. "But only around you."

"I like when you talk." I was watching her from across the couch while we watched a movie. "I like listening."

Normally I laid on Nisha but tonight she had cramps and instead of me she had the heated blanket. And sometimes she was uncomfortable.

Nisha had pretty bad cramps she told me. And she laid there looking paler than usual complaining about her bloating.

"You don't think I'm annoying."

"No." I smirked.

"Or awful?"

"No."

"And you love me?"

"I love you."

She pouted at me. "Kisses?"

I obeyed, moving from my side to hers, crawling on top of her and bracing myself a bit to give her what she asked for. Until we both forgot about the movie.

She was the sweetest thing in my life. Since those fucking lemon bars. Or the shortcake trifles. Nisha was the nicest thing I ever had in my life. Even as dark visions of my mother lingered.

My father's past.

Aidan protecting me.

Gabriel warning me to tell Nisha.

Even with all that? With her soft kisses, the way she gripped my hair and shoulders tighter—I forgot about my reality.

With her, I'd found a peace I never knew I needed. Every time I sank into her?

I was gone.

SOME DAYS I RAN LATE AND SHE WAITED FOR ME. I FELT BAD, BUT NISHA smiled at me eagerly, rushing into my arms, kissing me steadily.

"Sorry I was late, luv."

"Don't be, you're here now."

Some days I could see how tired she was. "Rough day?"

"I want to go home and crawl under the heated blanket."

Or other days.

"Killian! You won't believe what happened today."

Tell me, luv.

"Tell me everything."

One evening, as Nisha walked out of the hospital, I could see the weight of the day on her shoulders.

Her eyes were glassy with unshed tears, and my heart clenched at the sight. Without a word, I pulled her into my arms, holding her close and letting her know that whatever she was going through, she wasn't alone.

Not anymore.

"I'm exhausted." She nuzzled into my neck.

I always got you.

And neither was I.

I talked to Nisha about Kieran and Aidan the best I could.

Kieran in turn checked in with me and he was brushing up on everything he needed. Surveillance tech, cybersecurity shit, legal crap, first aid, threat assessment—the whole fucking package.

He couldn't go into Gabriel's operation a half-baked idiot.

"You look different," Kieran mused when he saw me, his amber eyes lighting up like Aidan's did. "You getting laid?"

Only Kieran's looked like that all the time, while Aidan only got that look *after* he killed someone.

Kieran ran a hand through his chocolate brown hair, studying me.

"Who? I don't see you at *De Nuit.*"

"You think I need your club to get laid?"

His eyes went wide and downright mischievous. "You're getting pussy from a *normie*? Who? Is she hot?"

All the time. I might've been a little wild, but Nisha...Nisha liked to try new things with me. And I fucking loved it.

"Fuck off."

He grinned slyly, dimples appearing in his cheeks. "A *lady.* Should've fucking known when you wore heart print bandages. Who is she?" He paused looking at Nisha's bandage on my finger. "*Wait a fucking minute—*"

I made a noise. "Did you get your weapons today?"

"Can I have her?"

"No."

That's all it took. My brother's eyes were taking me in.

"So she's your girlfriend?" Now, he looked intrigued.

"Weapons. Now."

He didn't even look offended, just lounged back in his hammock indoors like some overgrown kid. His long legs dangled off the edge, boots still on.

"Yeah, yeah," Kieran said, finally swinging his legs down and getting up. He moved to a chest in the corner, covered with a ratty blanket. "Come on, just tell me. You got a serious girlfriend? Is that nurse from the hospital? Sean mentioned you smell like a lady."

Jesus fucking Christ. Sean and the guys would yap.

"Focus—"

"I'm focused, I'm focused. Just tell me is she cute? It's serious—"

"Let me see your weapons." Derek should've dropped it off for him.

"—If it wasn't serious you wouldn't be so possessive."

He got that right.

Lifting the lid, he revealed an arsenal that would make most people shit themselves. "Got 'em all right here, big bro."

Kieran grinned, running his fingers over the hoard of weapons like it was a toy.

"You're seeing *the nurse?* I never took you for the—"

"I will shoot you." I could feel heat creeping up my neck.

"You have a girlfriend! You didn't think about telling us? Does Aidan know?"

I rubbed my eyes with my hands.

This was the problem with having a little brother.

I loved him.

But I also wanted to kill him with every sentence.

Fuck. Since when did I blush?

I opened my eyes to find him grinning. All wicked and wide.

Amber eyes dancing with mischief.

He'd caught the tell, the *fucker.* "Holy shit, you're squirming. Is she alive at the *minimum?* Tell me you don't have any intention of killing her like the other girls."

"I don't wanna talk about other girls. And I never killed them—"

"Unless they begged."

"No."

I just choked them out the way they asked. Begged.

If they wanted rougher I gave it to them.

Part of why women came to me and Kieran was because I knew how to deal with my needs and theirs.

"Don't act like you're not vicious with women," I muttered. I'd seen him.

I would never even ever dream of doing half of that violent shit to Nisha. Unless she asked. But even then?

What the fuck was wrong with everyone?

This idiot.

Even as kids Kieran had been the most playful, driving me and Aidan crazy, but he kept the spirit up.

Now he was using those powers of observation to make me uncomfortable as hell. I let out a breath trying to control myself around this kid I raised.

"Fuck off."

He grinned. The asshole who sent me and Aidan cat videos to fuck with us. I was fully allergic to cats, couldn't be in the same room with the fuckers without sneezing my brains out.

Aidan was only semi-allergic, but I think he just didn't like 'em.

He preferred enormous dogs, but we never had the time for pets as kids.

Kieran, though?

He'd been obsessed with cats since he was five.

Probably why he tortured us with those videos now.

It was his way of getting the pet he never had, even if it was just to annoy the shit out of his brothers.

"She's gotta be patient as fuck with you. Get it. Patient? Ha!" Kieran looked like it was Christmas morning.

I didn't want to laugh.

I didn't want to laugh.

I was not going to laugh. Not with him.

"Come on, I won't say a word—"

"Shut up," I growled, but there was no real heat in it.

And that just made Kieran's grin grow even wider.

I rolled my eyes, turning to walk away from him as he laughed.

"Make sure you don't fuck up with Gabriel."

"I would never—"

"Yes, you would—"

"I'm not that dumb—"

"Yes, you are—"

"I'm hurt, seriously."

I rolled my eyes. "Gabriel will kill you."

"Oh, come on! *You've* never been in a relationship. I didn't even think you liked people like that. Tell me if she's hot! Is she hot?" Kieran's voice was full of that annoying glee. He'd been like this since we were kids. "Give me a hint. Anything. I can see the fucking bandaid. Sean says your nurse is hot but you never talk about her. She's at the Titan hospital?"

She is hot.

And she's mine.

I flipped him off without looking back, but I couldn't help the small smile tugging at my lips.

"Should I go after her?"

I never reacted so fast. "I will rip your intestines out and string you up to the fucking Empire State building if you so much as look at her wrong."

All I heard was Kieran's laughter letting me know he successfully provoked me. Asshole. Little. Brother's.

I stared down at Nisha's bandaids. Today they had hearts on them.

I fucking *loved* Nisha's bandaids. I despised anyone asking me about my girl though. That shit was for me. Every little pink bow, soft kiss, and cuddle was for me. I wanted to keep her home and lock her up to me forever. Brand myself into her soul.

Fucking Kieran.

He was a pain in the ass, but he was my pain in the ass. And as much as I hated to admit it, his stupid jokes and cat videos kept things from getting too dark.

Not that I'd ever tell him that.

I only talked to Nisha. About everything.

Save for one thing.

The whole, I'm in the mob...not really. But kind of. My family definitely was. Aidan wanted to let Kieran out.

But me? I was...in between.

I wondered what Nisha would think of all this, of Kieran. Of the life I was trying to keep separate from her. Darkness and light.

War and peace.

Every part of me the complete anti-thesis of her.

The image of her soft smile next to Kieran's arsenal made my stomach twist. But then again, this wasn't just Kieran.

This was my life at Titan.

Two worlds that didn't belong together, and me, stuck in the fucking middle.

Trying to push those thoughts away, I focused on Nisha. And our impending lunches. More kisses. On my way through the city I found a pink coffee table piece and picked that up for her. I got her flowers.

I was out here in the city collecting pink colored shit like it was my business.

One quiet afternoon when I had off, I finally asked her about her career as a musician.

I held her close, savoring the warmth of her body against mine. Nisha's voice was soft, almost wistful as she spoke.

"I actually played the harp growing up. We had one in the house..." She trailed off for a moment, and I knew she was thinking about her adopted family.

Nisha didn't talk about them much, so I stayed quiet, not wanting to interrupt this rare moment of openness. I didn't tell her I knew. I knew a lot of things.

I rarely operated off my moral compass. Especially with her.

"I learned to play really young," she continued, her voice soft with memory. "I was drawn to it. The harp, the cello, a little piano too."

As Nisha unfolded her past, I hung on every word. I propped myself up on an elbow, gazing down at her.

I knew *what* had happened.

Her father was in jail now...and I knew why.

Derek had reported a few findings to me. Her father was supposed to be let out. I had him stall it. Figure out any legal loophole needed to make sure it didn't happen. I didn't know if Nisha knew. If she cared. I just knew if that fucker got let out, I would do whatever it took to protect her.

As of right now, I had Derek handle it. He was competent and capable.

My worst nightmare was him getting out on any kind of good behavior.

And coming after Nisha.

"That was a long time ago. I haven't touched a harp in years."

"Would you?" I dipped my face lower to hers, loving the way her breath caught.

Her eyes flickered to me.

"Would I?" I nodded. She considered it, her expression unreadable.

I chose my words carefully. "You miss playing, luv. I can tell."

I can tell everything.

Her delicate hand on my arm flexed a tiny bit. Just enough for me to know...Nisha had loved music. Still did, maybe.

And fuck if I didn't want to give that back to her, to see her eyes light up the way they must have when she played.

I thought about Kieran's stupid cat videos and Aidan's rare smiles.

Maybe, just maybe, I could show her the good parts first.

Ease her into it.

Because if I was going to keep her—and fuck, did I want to keep her —she'd need to know all of me.

My little brother, always running from something—or towards something he could never catch.

I saw a reflection of my past self in his restless eyes.

Kieran needed stability. The same way Aidan and I had. And he had a way to go.

He didn't have Gabriel to mentor him and I wasn't sure that was what he needed.

I didn't share Kieran and Aidan's humor, but I made up for it with strategy, and for that Aidan was thankfully one of us was functional after the piece of work our father was.

Still, the more time I spent around Kieran, the more I knew something had to change.

And he wanted to work for Titan. Gabriel had his own requirements and if Kieran met them, we could try for something.

If Kieran felt a fraction of what I felt with Nisha, he might settle down. Find some fucking peace. But he was too busy running, too scared to face his own shit. Watching him, I realized how much he was missing out on.

As kids, as teenagers, I'd always made the smarter plays.

That's why Gabriel zeroed in on me to run the chapter he knew would help us most. Aidan was coming to the city to talk to Gabriel.

Most people had no clue how tight Aidan and Gabriel were, how much they leaned on each other.

Sometimes I wondered if even they knew each other, with all the secrets. But it worked for them.

I knew Reed Whittaker had no fucking idea how deep Gabriel's loyalty to Aidan ran. All for one thing—*Lara*. If there was one word Gabriel believed in? It was loyalty.

And his loyalty to that woman was unmatched.

Aidan was the fucking underworld—the darkness in my life. And I was part of it too, whether I liked it or not.

I wondered if, after introducing her to him, I'd finally have the balls to tell Nisha the truth about my family.

Because if Aidan knew about Nisha, if he accepted her, it would mean everything to me. She would be as good as mine. A part of my world in every fucking sense.

But the thought of telling Nisha who I really was? Scared the shit out of me.

Would she still look at me the same way once she knew about the mob? Could she handle the darkness that came with my family?

I'd never had to worry about someone else's perception of me like this before. And the summer passed with her, fading into the fall chill. I spent more and more time with her. Our lunch dates became regular or I tried to make it regular.

And she'd rush up to me with kisses and a smile on her face.

I noticed Adam shooting her knowing looks as she rushed off to meet me.His raised eyebrows and sly grins said it all.

Our lunches weren't just at the hospital. On her days off, I'd take her out to explore the city's food scene.

Hole-in-the-wall joints, fancy bistros—I was always on the hunt for new spots where we could try different shit.

Growing up in Chicago, I hadn't experienced much and the little I had, Nisha when she found out, was determined for me to experience everything.

She grinned over me trying things all the time, wrinkling her nose, kissing my nose, everywhere she could.

When she found out, we got into this whole debate about pizza. She swore by New York's thin crust, while I defended Chicago's deep dish like it was my fucking job.

I watched Nisha grinning at me, her eyes sparkling with mischief as she got up to sit next to me, feigning outrage over my love of Chicago style pizza.

"It's a casserole, Killian."

"It's good if you try it, luv," I'd insist, unable to keep the smile off my face. I didn't know where that part of me came from. "Just a bite."

"Gosh, where do I even start on it?"

The more she teased me about my "casserole" pizza, the more I found myself grinning like an idiot.

I'd never had someone to argue with about stupid shit like this before. Not without losing it.

It was a side of me I didn't even know existed. I watched her lips move and her eyes light up as she defended her slice and I grinned wider until she kissed me.

"What was that for?"

"I feel like I don't even know you right now," she laughed, and I'd grin wider, drinking in her joy. Something unfamiliar in me blossoming.

"Do you like this better?"

I didn't know why I asked.

Her smile dipped a fraction. "Not better. I like all of you. For every part of you." She leaned in and kissed me. "You're so cute."

Heat crawled up my neck into my face.

Nobody had ever called me cute before.

She kissed me again and again. And again. Until we were making out. At the fucking pizzeria.

When we were home, Nisha would laugh and throw her arms around me like it was the most natural thing in the world, rushing out of the shower.

Throughout the apartment, she'd kiss me, all quick and spontaneous, like she'd forgotten to do it earlier and suddenly remembered.

"Baby, did you try the gnocchi I made?"

"I did, that was good..." I watched her walking around in her towel. Just a towel getting ready for her everything shower as she called it.

She kissed me in passing as she said it doing her hair up.

And fuck if I didn't find myself chasing after her.

I'd never been like this before.

Never wanted more of someone just…being them.

But with Nisha, I was different.

Softer, maybe. Still me, but a version of me I didn't know existed. She'd rush off to do something, and I'd find myself following, just to be near her. It was like she was pulling me into her orbit, and I didn't want to break free.

I didn't know what it was, but her hands landed on me and I was cozier than a motherfucker.

One particularly shitty day, after someone bailed on her shift, Nisha gave me this look that said it all.

"Home?"

She nodded, and I had her in my arms a second later, holding her close as she made this soft, content noise. "Missed you."

"I miss you too, luv." Every fucking day. She pointed at the bandaid on my finger. "You wore this all day?"

I grinned at her expression. She just snuggled deeper into my arms.

As things got more serious, I started crashing at her place all the time.

I hated my own place, but I don't know why I kept it. It was still a part of my life.

And maybe, I was tempted to just move Nisha's entire apartment into that space.

2 8

KILLIAN

BUT BECAUSE OUR PASTS WERE VIOLENT—ONE NIGHT, I WOKE UP thrashing from a nightmare. Unable to catch my breath. Unable to do anything but focus.

Cormac's face loomed in my mind, threatening Nisha, threatening everything good I had found.

She's not yours. I can sell her just like everyone else.

"*No!*"

Nisha's voice and hands were all over me. "*Killian, it's okay. I'm here. I'm here—*"

"*Nisha...run...he's coming—*" I grabbed her until she was flush against me. "*No.*"

"*Who?*" She smoothed my hair back, her touch grounding me in the present. "Nobody's here, *Killian. Wake up, baby.*"

As I came to, I realized we were in bed, my legs tangled in the sheets, the comforter stripped away.

I was breathing so hard like my father was back. Trying to take Nisha away. Trying to turn her into another whore for his enterprise.

No. Not my girl.

Lara. Help her.

When Aidan came into power, he released every single woman under our father's name but it didn't mean I wasn't haunted by some of what I did know.

And I had a dream my father was branding Nisha. Turning her into *that*.

Nisha was laying on top of me like a blanket now. Her eyes watching me as she tapped on my bedside table lamp.

Warm light flooded the room and I blinked a little as she slowly came into focus, illuminating her doe eyes, raven hair around me, her brushing my hair back from my head as she kissed me over and over.

"It's okay, you're okay. You got home from work a few hours ago, I know it was stressful, but you're okay. I promise. You're safe." She kissed me until I calmed down. "I take it something happened at work today?"

I shook my head. I couldn't talk about it.

I heard Cormac's voice in my head.

You'll never make it, boy. You'll never be happy. That girl of yours? I can take her away from you.

Everything you touch turns to shit fucking scum.

"Breathe, Killian. I can feel your heart racing."

I hadn't heard his voice in my head in a while. "Luv, I'm afraid."

I was shaking, the words hitting too close to home. I knew what happened to Nisha growing up.

"Of what?"

"Losing you."

The abuse she'd endured. She didn't know the extent of what I knew, of what I had done to protect her.

My father had trafficked girls, and even though Aidan had cut ties with that business, the knowledge of what could have happened to Nisha in *that* world made me sick.

And Nisha had been a *child*.

I couldn't tell her how much I knew about her past. I'd let her share when she was ready, keeping my own secrets in the meantime. It wasn't fair, but fairness had never been part of my world.

Instead of responding she kissed me slowly, steadily, soft enough to make me forget where I was, who I was.

I couldn't breathe.

"I'm right here, nothing is wrong. Nothing is happening." Her lips moved over mine as she kissed me.

"I saw him...come after you." It left my lips as my heart raced, her hands moved over my chest.

"Breathe, baby." Her hands rubbed my chest, over my tattoos. My heart. "Breathe. Nothings happening. I have you."

I could hear the concern in her voice.

"Talk to me, Killian. What's going on?" She brushed my hair back.

I swallowed around my fears, my anxiety—everything.

"I don't want to lose you. Not like everyone else. My mom...I felt...I thought I saw her..."

She was...on the ceiling...I didn't understand.

"Aidan's blocking me," I whispered. "I can see her. She's coming from the ceiling. It's dark in the room. Aidan...he blocked me."

Nisha froze above me like she wondered what I did.

What I suspected.

Mom had killed herself in that home leaving her sons. Leaving me and Aidan to figure it out. Mostly Aidan.

I wondered what my brother felt in those moments. Did he feel alone? Did he feel devastation?

"Did she..."

"I don't even know...Aidan's the last thing I remember." Distant memories filled me. Vague ones that felt more like a dream. A story. "My father...was a monster."

And I was his son. I was a monster too. By default.

"I got my tattoos over the scars just like Aidan did." I moved Nisha's hand over my pec. Over the raised ridges there from being whipped. Nisha made a noise.

"He did that to you?" Her eyes welled up in front of me. "I thought your back felt off too. I can feel the bumps sometimes and I didn't know what that was."

"You were so soft and concerned about my shoulder," I didn't feel the smile I put on. There was no humor in it. "But the truth was, I had so much worse done to me—"

"That doesn't make it okay—"

"But that was my life."

And I never wanted to see a fucking scar on Nisha. Ever.

The words poured out of me as I told Nisha about it. The beatings. The whippings.

The way Aidan and I had gotten treated like dogs.

Worse than that. I thought Aidan had it worse but he could argue for me.

"You were nothing familiar to me. And yet the moment I tasted you I knew you were mine."

My throat worked as it left me.

I never opened my mouth very much around Nisha. I let her talk to me, her voice soothing me as I listened. I didn't like talking. I wasn't important enough and I was good at two things—fighting and fucking and that was it.

But Nisha made me feel like—I was worth more.

I didn't know what I was feeling.

I just knew since the day I met her? It was her eyes, her soft reassurances, her gentle hands and kisses had all gotten under my skin. And stayed there.

I liked this woman and I was *terrified* of losing her.

"You aren't anything I am used to, and everything I can't get enough of. I can't go a day without thinking about you. Your voice in my head all the time. Your scent all over me."

As she held me, I kept talking, revealing parts of my past I'd kept locked away.

"I'm shit," I whispered. "I was thrilled. Relieved when he died."

He had trained his sons as his legacy. To be warriors. Something all three of us knew which was why nothing fucking phased us anymore.

She nodded wiping her eyes. Wiping mine.

"Aidan took over being in charge of the family."

"He sounds like a rock," Nisha whispered. "Holding you guys together." If she only knew what the fuck Aidan was holding together.

Now Aidan had an empire he built up. Without half of the problematic shit my father did. No prostitutes. No drugs.

"Sounds like he went through a lot with both of your parents," she murmured. "He sounds good to you. When you talk about him, I can hear it in your voice."

Could she?

"You'd like him, you're a lot like him in some ways." Her ability to give me shit and stand her ground. He'd appreciate that. And on that note. "Would you want to meet him?"

Her eyes went wide as she drew closer to me. I got that it was kind of serious now. But it had been for a while.

I was trying not to freak the fuck out.

"He can bitch to you about Kieran's cat videos." I huffed it out determined to diffuse the moment.

Nisha's laughter was light as she kissed me again, those dark eyes of her soft with understanding.

"I'd love to." Her fingers threaded through my hair as she cuddled me to her. "Come here, get some rest. You're always up so early."

She ran her fingers through my scalp and rubbed and I groaned into her chest. "I fucking love this."

I felt her chest shake as she laughed quietly. "Are you okay?"

"I am now." *I am with you.* "When I'm with you, I don't feel like I'm theirs. I feel like—"

I'm yours. I was hers. Nisha felt like coming home after years of searching and wandering for a place to live. Her heart was my home. And I wanted it forever.

Any threat to Nisha would have to be taken out.

"You feel loved?"

I nodded. "Yours." I finished. "I'm happy with you."

As I said it, my chest clenched tightly despite Nisha trying to calm me down.

"I'm happy with you," she whispered in the darkness and I held fast to her drifting in her arms. "I love you too."

When I woke up, Nisha was still fast asleep. I didn't have anything today until the evening. I was breathing to calm the fuck down.

Because keeping secrets from Nisha about who I was while confiding in her my truth felt fucked up.

But I was scared.

I was scared if she knew I came out of the Underworld. Out of shadows and death—Nisha might not see me as her hero anymore.

But a monster.

So I turned off my alarm to curl back in her arms, pulling the blanket over both of us.

In my home.

NISHA

TODAY WHEN KILLIAN PICKED ME UP FROM WORK, THERE WAS A TINY smile on his face as he glanced at him.

The mischievous glint in his eyes had me curious. "Everything okay?"

He just reached out and squeezed my hand. "You'll see."

"I feel like you're up to something."

His chuckle was low and warm as it caressed my skin. He didn't say a word and instead murmured. "Tell me about your day."

I chattered all the way home with him grinning every so often about my stories.

Nothing was off when we got to the apartment. Or at least until he opened the door and I stepped inside halting like I ran into a wall.

I should've guessed after our conversation about instruments, Killian would show not tell.

His *surprise* dominated my living room—six feet of gleaming golden strings and intricate design. A harp. It stood like a work of art, one of the more high-end models.

Its curved neck gracefully arched towards the ceiling, the sound-board catching the soft light from the sunlight going down outside. The string seemed to shimmer in that lighting and I felt my hand go over my mouth.

How did he get it in the apartment?

The room seemed to spin as hot tears pricked at my eyes. Through my misty vision, the golden harp shimmered.

He didn't know I had gotten accepted to a prestigious school for this. He didn't know how badly I wanted it. My chest tightened, breath catching in my throat.

How much I wanted to perform on a stage. Live a different life. How I worked through my emotions and how even if being a nurse was fulfilling—it wasn't the life I wanted.

That's when Killian motioned to something I had almost missed—a large, familiar-shaped case resting against the wall.

"Is that a cello?"

My heart was pounding out of my chest. I didn't even see it.

"I put the case in my car," he said softly. "Figured you'd play it so no need..."

I was speechless. Dizzy with the memories that flooded back.

"I only got those two because the piano wouldn't fit..." Killian's voice held a hint of uncertainty, pulling me back to the present. *Hang on a second—*

"The piano..." My eyes met his in question. *"You got a piano too?"*

I just told him the other day.

He looked a little embarrassed. "You've never been to my place, but I had it delivered there..." He trailed off as I gaped at the thousands of dollars in front of me. He motioned to the cello. "Figured you'd test out how rusty you were."

I couldn't breathe right now. My head was spinning, and everything felt like it was over-welhming.

"You got me..." He got me my instruments. My old life was staring back at me in my apartment, with Killian at my back taking me in.

"What am I going to do with you?"

I turned back searching those eyes of his, watching me a little wide now. There were these moments when I looked at Killian—and he was the man in bed with me making me scream.

And then there were these moments I looked at him and I saw something else behind those eyes. Something less confident and more unsure of himself. I threw myself at him.

His arms wrapped around me, lips against my pulse feeling it out until it landed where the erratic flutter was.

"You like it?" His voice was gruff. He pressed his lips there again.

"*Like* it? I *love* it…" My heart pounded in my chest. "This is insane…I can't believe you did all this…that's a concert grand pedal harp." I liked this man so much. The way he comforted me. Took care of me. Kept me safe. Made my heart happier than it had been in forever. It all felt like a dream.

He felt like a dream. One, I didn't want to wake up from.

"I'm guessing that's good?" Killian asked quietly. I didn't even know how to speak as I nodded.

This was so much work.

He had thought of everything.

I swallowed, the memories like broken shards of glass in my throat as I felt the emotion bubble up. It was. But the hesitancy didn't come from anything he had done. No. It came from me. From a past I had locked away so tightly I wasn't sure where to begin.

"I never wanted to talk about my past," I whispered. The words formed slowly. Like I was underwater. "I was adopted when I was a baby." I didn't look at him. "I started playing music at a young age. I loved it. My adopted parents encouraged it saying it was a good hobby to have. My adopted dad—Eugene—he introduced me to the cello and we would go on these drives to my afterschool programs."

I didn't look at him.

"I felt special. Like it was our secret world."

I couldn't. I just held him tight to me.

Because I was admitting it. Out-loud. To Killian.

"I was eight when he touched me for the first time. It was my chest, but I remember him watching to see my reactions. And it went on. But it was almost like he hated himself—I didn't know what it was called as a girl—but he hated himself and hated me. And then my adopted mother hated me. She said I was stealing her husband…"

I still remembered those days I spent my existence more confused about why I existed.

How…my reality was…warped.

He was holding me tight to him I could feel his heat. His arms banded around me. Tight. Stable.

Unmoving.

Solid. It gave me the strength to keep going.

"I was sixteen…" I kept my voice down. "It was…getting worse. And I stayed out avoiding him. Music class was long and sometimes it ran so late. It was nice." Music class had been my only escape from him.

From everything. When I played I forgot anything else existed.

"It was the summer I turned seventeen all the…touching and *every-thing*…" I couldn't even form the words, the humiliation and shame washed over me as I did. "I came home."

I would never forget that day.

He had been drunk.

And I knew.

I just *knew*. I was in danger. I was trembling as a shiver racked down my spine reliving the moment everything changed for me.

And I ran.

"I ran as fast as I could. Bumped into a cop." I shook my head feeling my eyes close. The shame. The humiliation. The fear.

The way my adopted mother said I was crazy. Killian's body stiffened as I said it.

And I didn't know what to do at the time. I cried and cried and cried. For a long time. Before I knew I needed to do something with my life.

"I spent a year in foster care. And thankfully got into a decent school. Put myself through nursing school to maybe help other girls…" I felt his lips against my pulse over and over.

"You're the first man in my life I've felt this way for…"

I felt the hot splash on my cheeks as I looked at the harp. He must've spent a fortune on this. I knew he had money. He mentioned it wasn't a problem. But this had brought everything—every single memory back —and I was drowning in them.

"I've never felt this much hope before in me that maybe my life didn't have to be all that."

I took a deep breath as I felt his lips at my neck again. "She didn't believe me. She said I was being dramatic, seeking attention. And he had been drinking…" I still remembered it like it was yesterday. "I thought love like yours was a dream…not for me…when I met you I was so afraid of you. Of letting you in."

I felt my lips quirk even as I cried harder and harder silently.

"And when you'd kiss me I'd forget why I ever thought that in the first place."

I turned to him a little, his eyes guarded as he met mine but his fingers digging into my hips. "Thank you. You're one of the best things thats ever happened to me."

His Adam's apple bobbed as he watched me and I saw—I saw him fighting—his emotions written all over his face more than before as his eyes softened.

"I promised you I wasn't ever going to think less of you. Wasn't ever gonna leave you." It was a growl over my lips as he kissed me harder. "You have my word. Tell me want you want. What you need."

His voice was gruff. I inhaled his cologne and the feel of him as he held me rubbing my back.

"Tell me *whatever*. I'll get it to you."

The room faded away until there was only me, the harp, and Killian's steady presence.

I moved to it, my fingers feeling it gently.

"I do want to play it." I looked at him. "Would you like me to?"

"I do."

And so that night after dinner, I felt my nerves kick in as I stepped out of the bedroom in my nightie and I sat by the harp. I couldn't even look at Killian I was so emotional.

My hands were out of practice as I found a good seat for myself and I began to play. And just like that years of it came back to me.

My fingers over the chords, my heart in tune with the music pounding as I was aware of Killian's presence watching me.

Those eyes on me as I played. I felt like I was in peace for once doing this around someone I loved, someone who loved me enough to give me my dreams.

When I hit the last note, I took a breath and I didn't even get a chance to turn before he was on me, his mouth over mine. He was saying something in Gaelic.

"What are you saying?"

"You looked like something out of a fairytale, luv." His lips brushed over mine as he kneeled in front of me. "Like magic, like fairies, everything unreal."

His eyes met mine as my heart swelled.

"Thank you for giving me the opportunity to do this—" I broke off motioning towards the harp.

His smile was wide. "You can play whenever you like. I'd love that."

187

"You would?"

"Mhm."

I was in his arms a second later.

3 0

NISHA

"Baby—"

Sometime during the night, he'd licked his way down to my pussy and stayed there.

I was writhing, thrashing my head side to side as he didn't relent.

Something was in his eyes as he rose up above me. I barely saw him put on the condom before he was driving into me, arms bracketed my ears.

His voice gruff and dark as he growled. "I know, luv. You can take me, can't you?"

A whimper left my lips as the stretch of him filled all my senses. His beautiful sculpted features watched me with soft eyes as he sank in further.

I wanted him to kiss me and I felt my lips pout a little at him.

Even though he looked like he was holding back—dark and sinful above me—his lips quirked a bit.

Dropping down over my lips like he knew. And the moment he did I sighed feeling him sink in all the way.

My fingers tangled in his hair as I moaned around his tongue. Legs trembling, body aching as he stretched me so deep I wanted to scream.

It always took a second to adjust to him. Always.

"Just a second," I murmured. "Just a second…"

His smile against my lips made me clench tighter.

The dull pain deep in me had faded a long time and he kissed me until I felt languid and pliant for him.

My inhibitions calming down until it could only focus the place where he was inside me.

His hand drifted down to my hip, adjusting, and he slid in the last inch and I whimpered into his mouth.

"That's better," his voice was low, his eyes dark right before he closed them. "I haven't even done anything and you're already losing it."

I was. I could feel it. But he didn't move.

To my surprise, he slowly hooked his arm under my knee, drawing my leg up, higher. I whimpered as he calmed me down a bit more until my leg was resting on his shoulder.

"Should we try this?"

A helpless noise left me at the angle as he drew back.

The first drive into me had me squealing.

"Oh, this is different—"

"Good or bad different?"

Why did he sound like that?

"Good."

I opened my eyes again to find his expression dark as he reached down to my other leg. With both of my legs on his shoulders folding me in half he ground deep.

"OhGodohGod—" I broke off already beginning to shake as stars exploded in my vision.

His smile was devious. I didn't recognize him in bed like this. Like a dark prince taking me somewhere sweeter than I could understand.

Or when he drew back and thrust back into me.

A strangled cry left me as I felt my orgasm rapidly approaching and he hadn't even gotten one thrust in. My legs rapidly shook as he worked in me.

"You're so fucking close, aren't you?"

"I am—" my voice sounded like a whine as I squeezed my eyes shut. Every single drive of his hips was making me lose it. Closer and closer so fast. *"Right there, baby. Right there."*

He didn't another word in as I screamed losing it, my orgasm slamming into me with the grace of a tsunami having built from my previous one.

I screamed a little as I came even harder.

Killian's groans filled my ears as I struggled under him as he drove into me. And my orgasm felt like it was taking me under.

I held onto the sheets tighter feeling like they would rip with how hard I was gripping them. I sobbed as I came and came this time in this position.

Every drive of his hips prolonged my orgasm and I squealed as the pleasure grew and grew and grew.

I screamed his name as he did something with his hips and his piercing he drove in. And I *heard* my orgasm.

"Ohhh, fuck."

Through my slitted vision, I saw something in Killian changed and his eyes widened a little as he felt it and I cried out at the sensation.

I felt it soaking the bed, between us, the obscene noises bringing heat to my cheeks as it made him wilder.

"That's a good girl, squirt all over me."

I thrashed under him, a sweaty mess, held together by those drives of his hips and I felt it prolong my orgasm, every drive of his hips making me gush.

"Fuck, fuck, fuck," Killian growled. "Not gonna make it, luv." He groaned as he worked.

I could only feel.

I felt like he was drawing out every pulse of my orgasm from me. It was endless.

Above me he groaned as I felt him finish. I was shaking, crying out and clamping down on him as he did and he sank down on me with a groan, grinding deep. Driving me wild.

For long moments I felt my legs shake, noises left me as he gently lowered my legs and kissing me steady.

"I didn't think you'd squirt in that position," he murmured. "I knew how wet you'd get but nothing like that. You did so good, luv."

I could only tremble as he kissed me.

31

KILLIAN

THE MORNING I LEFT FOR CHICAGO, I TOOK NISHA WITH A DESPERATE hunger in me.

I usually held back in bed with Nisha. I didn't want to lay into her and hurt her in any way.

But after I'd found out she could squirt in one particular position? I lost my mind a little.

I had her ankles to her ears on my shoulders and *driving* into her needing to be deeper than I normally got.

Nisha. Lost. Her. Mind.

Naturally, my inner monsters did a double take and smiled deviously. I coaxed Nisha into a few more orgasms and learned how wet she got.

Until she was limp and shaking in my arms. I made out with her for what felt like forever. Nisha had grabbed my hair then and held me tight to her and my entire body shuddered.

"Luv," I whispered into her kisses. "Wanna try something?"

"Hm?"

"Can I show you?"

Nisha nodded lazily into my lips.

At some point in the night I made restraints out of my ties and tied her calves up to her arms—and then to the headboard.

Now, I had her up with her wrists and ankles tied while I pounded into her. Hard. *Ruthless.*

Brutal.

The kind of fucking that I only gave when I was feeling righteously ticked off or afraid. And I took it all out on her pussy.

Leaving her so gloriously exposed to me. Pretty and pink. Wet.

Lush.

Nisha was gone.

I didn't want her neighbors to think I was killing her even if Nisha wasn't loud all the time.

I gagged her with another tie, and she'd looked so pretty as I slid into her, eyes rolling back in pleasure as I worked my hips in.

My piercing sliding inside of her, the little vibrator in my hand over her clit driving her to insanity.

"Sensitive, luv?"

She nodded weakly already shaking.

Nisha was insanely sensitive after she came. Something that had driven me a little crazy as much as her. She was so fucking perfect for me.

The moment I laid the vibrator on that swollen bud of hers, Nisha had come so hard I groaned louder.

Without me moving. And then I'd felt something dark swirling in my vision.

Fuck the damn neighbors.

Some part of me was rearing up. And it only did when I was completely unhinged. I felt her pussy clamping and her first scream erupting, muffled and gagged—and I was losing my mind.

If I took her to *De Nuit*—I could fuck her however I wanted.

I'd lost all composure then slamming into her with zero restraint working at her as she came over and over.

"You're so fucking beautiful when you scream. So. *Fucking.* Pretty." I was gone. "There you fucking go, luv. Let go."

I lost count of how many times Nisha orgasmed after the third one she'd had. I held her throat, holding her down as I fucked deep, my other hand holding the vibrator at her pussy.

I growled into her lips. "You're gonna come again, aren't you?"

I had taken her all night with a violence, a need that Nisha met time and time again as I held her down.

Now, the suns rays crept up into the bedroom as I drove in deeper and harder, hearing the sound of me fucking her would never *not* get me off.

I held the vibrator on her clit knowing it drove her over the edge over and over so easily.

She was coming so much it left a mess between us.

Something in me was brewing. A storm inside of me lashing out at everything in its path. Her.

I wanted to rip off the condom I wore and fuck her until we were one person.

Ditching the vibrator, I moved over her the angle changing and Nisha went wild for the first time as I braced my arms on either side of her head, tearing off the gag.

My thumb running along her eyes, her lips.

And then she did that little thing she did when she wanted me to kiss her.

She pursed her lips a tiny bit just enough to let me know and my heart cracked open. "Baby," she licked her lips. "Too much."

"You can take it. You're gonna be a good girl and take it, aren't you?"

She whimpered as those dark, tear-stained eyes watched me.

I was hers. Utterly hers. I kissed her steadily breathing through the sensations. She felt like heaven and I didn't want to lose myself yet.

"I don't wanna break you yet, luv." I growled. "I still want more."

So fucking pretty. Those eyes. Fuck.

They were soft and pliant as she sobbed my name.

I know, luv.

"Look at you, pretty baby," I whispered grinding down loving the animal noise that left her as I sank deeper, grinding into her driving her insane. Moving my hips lazily loving how slick she was. "It feels good, doesn't it? And I'm nowhere near done with you."

Nisha was about to find out just how much I held back as she nodded.

"You fucking love this too," I smiled into her skin as she whimpered running my nose along her throat. Where I knew she was sensitive. I bit down gently loving how her pussy clamped down on me tighter as I did.

"You're gonna come for me a few more times, won't you?"

My fingers brushed over her tight nipples lower down to her clit.

"Should I play with you again? You can't fight me, can you? *No*, you don't want to. Are you gonna be my good girl and come for me agai—"

I groaned breaking off as she came again, her orgasm soaking my dick, as I said it, the sound leaving her hoarse.

She didn't even scream anymore, just little adorable noises letting me know she was getting tired.

"Fuuckk, I will never get used to that."

Because she *liked* it.

I plunged into her and out like a barely held together man.

Fucking her with a savagery I only saved for the nights I needed one time with whoever was in front of me.

I fucking loved it growling filth in her ears I didn't usually dare.

But I felt safer now.

And I knew she did too.

"You take my cock so well," I growled pummeling into her still quivering pussy. "Like that pussy was made for me. And it was wasn't it? *My. Fucking. Pussy."*

I punctuated my words with every hard thrust.

Nisha's sobs became my motivation to *keep* going.

"OhGodbaby...Killian."

"That's my girl. Say my fucking name. You're gonna spend days remembering me. And when I'm back I'm gonna fuck it some more until it remembers me again. Remember who *owns* it."

I groaned at how bad I needed it. Needed her like this.

Shitshitshit. That was so good.

I felt her thighs start to shake as her cries turned into sobs. She was shaking so hard, the headboard creaked.

"You're going to come again, and again, and again, until I *say you're fucking finished."*

It felt too good and I couldn't stop driven by something deep in me to watch her like this.

"There you fucking go. Such a good girl. Keep going for me." My voice automatically darker.

She bucked up, almost fighting it. A wilder muffled scream leaving her.

"That's useless in trying, luv. I don't intend to let you escape."

I wasn't letting her go.

I knew her better than she knew herself like this.

195

"It's my personal fucking mission to see you come until you pass out," I growled into her ear like I was confessing. "Wanna ruin that pussy a little. Keep you tied up and taking it and you'd fucking love it."

The noise that left her was music to my ears as I felt her warmth flood all around me. I could hear her orgasm and that shit drove me insane.

"That's my fucking girl. Come all over me."

I *knew* it was right there. I angled my hips, hitting that spot I knew would make her lose it, grinding down as I did.

"There you go."

When she came, she came hard. Even harder like this.

An animal noise left her as her entire body shook in the restraints, the headboard creaking.

And finally. Fucking. *Finally.*

It had taken every single thing in me to not come with her. My demons demanding orgasm after orgasm from her.

But *finally.* I broke off, following her over the edge with a guttural groan.

For long moments I stayed buried deep, savoring every moment of her sobs while I kissed her.

"Shh. You're okay. I promise, you're okay."

"Baby." She mouthed it against my lips as she trembled around me. "Oh God."

I unclasped her arms from the headboard slowly, letting the fabric dangle on her wrist as she wrapped her hands around my head and I practically sighed burying myself in her neck.

"I got you, luv."

I *always* had her.

Untying her with a quick snap of my wrists she immediately groaned curling into me. *Sweet.*

My hands instinctively went to her thighs massaging them, as her legs dropped around me. Noises left her. Soft whimpers.

"Not too bad, luv?"

"I love you," she gasped sounding weak. Shit. I had to take care of that. *"I love you."*

That was easier to stomach now.

"Love you." My throat worked as my heart raced even after calming down. I hadn't gone easy. On either of us. "Love you more than anything." *More than everything.*

But Nisha knew me too. Too well.

"It's *just* Chicago," she whispered against my temple, her breath warm on my skin. "You'll be back soon..."

Because that's why I was losing my mind. At the idea of leaving her. At all. Losing her for a bit. I would be back soon.

Not soon enough.

I hadn't ever been apart from her and the idea of leaving sent a riot of panic through my system. How could I walk away from her?

I didn't know how to.

"In a few days, luv." I nodded, knowing it was just Chicago, but it felt different this time.

Everything felt different with her.

Her fingers threaded into my hair, tugging gently, and I leaned into her touch. I buried my face in her neck, breathing her in.

"You don't want to go..."

I shook my head, grumbling into her neck.

I never wanted to leave Nisha. "You'll come home sooner than later. It'll be okay. I promise."

I kissed her softly, over and over, pouring my love, my devotion into each press of my lips.

Until I felt myself stirring again, my body responded to her as it always did. Nisha gasped.

"We should change the sheets."

"After." I bit her lip tugging gently. A noise left her.

"Again?"

I was a monster.

I nodded into her neck. "Need you." Nisha clenched internally. "Not too sore?"

She shook her head. "Just need a minute."

I could do that. I had to deal with the condom first.

"Give me a second, luv."

I looked down at the condom suddenly, aware of why Nisha had felt so good. *Shit.*

"Fuck," I swore softly. *Of course, it would break.*

My piercing had done its job, snapping it in half.

It was basically useless and had been for some time. No wonder she felt like fucking heaven around my dick. *No wonder I hadn't stopped.*

"What is it?" Nisha rose up slowly, and when she saw it, her mouth dropped. "Tell me that happened just now."

I shook my head, emotions rolling through me. My eyes met hers. "I thought you felt different."

Her cheeks flushed. "I can take Plan B or something. I'll be okay. I'm nowhere close to getting my period. It'll be okay…"

But I couldn't think. Nisha…*pregnant.*

Nisha and me…having a life outside of ours.

"Baby, are you okay…"

I should've been afraid. Terrified even. And I wasn't. I saw something other than her in front of me.

I saw Nisha curled into me, her stomach slightly rounded. My eyes traced her soft curves, her full hips.

Someone with her eyes, not mine.

Even if Nisha loved them. Soft dark hair. I could imagine that person. A part of me and Nisha…

I didn't know how to process my feelings as Nisha rose to her knees, her hands on my face, eyes worried.

I'd never allowed myself to ever consider putting Nisha in that spot. But the moment, the fucking moment, it appeared in my vision, it didn't leave. Nisha.

Pregnant.

Leaning on me for the world.

Mine.

And *everyone* knew it.

I should've been afraid. Should've been *terrified.*

But staring into her dark eyes, from day one, this woman, had *me* ensnared. My heart began racing.

"*Killian!*"

I snapped back to reality, suddenly aware I was holding her closer, tighter than before.

"It's going to be okay," she lowered her voice. "There are options. I'll get Plan B. It'll be fine."

But I couldn't tell her that I didn't care if she was pregnant.

Because suddenly, the idea of Nisha carrying my child was… everything.

What the fucking fuck was happening to me around this woman?

Why did I want her so fucking badly?

Unable to speak, I poured everything into kissing her. Just like the first day I met her, I communicated what words couldn't.

I was shit at talking.

I tried to tell her everything was okay. That I was just...*overwhelmed* by the possibility of us.

She pulled back, her eyes searching mine. "Killian." Her lips brushed over mine again and again.

"Tell me if you—" I swallowed hard, my voice rough. "If we—"I couldn't finish, but I had to make her understand.

Why couldn't I fucking talk around her?

"Okay." She nodded, and I knew she understood what I was really asking. What I was offering. "Are you okay?"

My throat worked. "I am."

I will be.

"I'm solid."

I would be.

A promise, unspoken but as solid as my bones.

My word is my life. She is my life.

And it was hard not to feel like a part of me slid into place the moment I considered a possibility of a life beyond what I knew.

Because I didn't hate it.

32

KILLIAN

It was the end of summer when I had to go see Aidan.

Nisha worked as a nurse so she never doubted that I was busy with Titan. Both of us had hectic schedules.

Her job was to keep other patients' secrets and my job was to protect Titans assets and in turn, neither one of us doubted each other.

Which was why I didn't think twice about never telling Nisha. It never occurred to me I had to. Every so often she'd talk about work. And I'd mention something vague about my job for that day.

I washed the blood off my hands whenever I got to my penthouse and made it home in time to get Nisha or have dinner with her.

Chicago was a familiar trip, but now, leaving Nisha felt like tearing away a part of myself. And the possibility of someone else between us… a potential baby.

Something I had never in a million fucking years considered. I wasn't father material.

Not after the nightmare I'd lived through with my own father. Vague faint memories of a mother who cried too much and didn't love Kieran enough. She held me though. Sometimes. Not Aidan. Not Kieran. Me.

Someone who took care of me until she didn't.

But without Nisha? What did I have?

An empty apartment I rarely went back to.

A house that wasn't a home.

Moments in between I didn't feel like myself.

With Nisha…I healed. I could feel parts of myself aching in places I didn't know I could. I lived with her, in her smaller apartment and didn't leave.

Without her, there was no one to come home to. I had gone back to my own place, feeling like a stranger in my colder space.

Neither one of us had good parents, and decent homes. I'd never had a home and Aidan and I created a space for Kieran, but not for ourselves.

The lack of parenting, the lack of warmth meant Nisha and I practically huddled in bed sometimes curled into each other soaking in each other.

No fingers running through my hair, melting away the day's tension.

No silly skincare routines with that bandana she made me wear to keep the hair out of my eyes. Her laughter at me scowling while she put a mud mask on me. I hated the sensation, but damn it was calming and cold.

"You look like a greaser," she'd giggle fixing my hair back. "From the movie…you know?"

I didn't.

"Or like one of the *Outsiders?*" She quipped. "You know? The middle brother?" I had no idea.

I was pop culture illiterate but Nisha wasn't. She introduced me to new things, foods, movies. All the time. My free time was now in her arms.

Without her? No more soft whispers as she fussed over me, insisting on under-eye masks during our murder mystery marathons. Or any masks. Nisha was big into skincare.

She was my home.

And I was determined to keep her and protect her. My hands were stained with blood, my world built on violence and secrets. And yet I went home to…*her.*

I was Titan's weapon, the shadow that cleaned up messes and eliminated threats.

And now, with these mysterious kill cards showing up, shit was about to hit the fan.

But for the first time, I found myself wanting something different. Something more. Something I never thought I deserved.

But I wanted now. The moment I did, a whisper of another thought drifted into my mind. Blue eyes. Dark hair.

Mom.

She floated into my brain.

Her face above mine as she was crying. Wiping my eyes for some reason. I didn't have many memories of her. I was too young. But that one...that was right before she left me. Left us. Left my brothers.

And suddenly the ice in my chest hardened again. I pushed her out of my mind.

As I dressed, my mind drifted to the job, a welcome distraction from the whirlwind of emotions.

Someone in New York was leaving kill cards, markers for their hits. In our world, people had ways of claiming their work, but these were different. I hadn't seen anything like it in years.

Nisha doesn't know who you are.

And there was that.

I didn't know how to tell Nisha about Aidan, about the real depth of my involvement with Titan.

Some fucked up part of me wanted her to think I was just a Titan employee working in the city for a security firm and not...me.

Not the man with blood on his hands and secrets in his heart. As I finished dressing, I lingered, inhaling her scent on me, drawing strength from her presence even in her absence.

I flew to Chicago to brief Aidan, my mind torn between the job and the woman I'd left behind.

I ignored the flight attendant trying to run her hands down my arm. Or her fingers down my shirt. Or her friend eyeing me as well.

Stepping out of O'Hare, the crisp autumn air nipped at my face as I looked at my phone.

Text me if you need me, luv. Make sure to eat more when I'm gone.

As if, make sure you text me and eat when I'm not there. No protein bars unless their snacks.

I grinned like an idiot, having texted her the entire time.

> Miss you already.

Miss you too, luv.

And fuck, did I miss her. I sent her a photo of her bandaid on my finger which was becoming my way of keeping her close to me.

We'd been together long enough now for me to know this was the most serious relationship I'd had in years, maybe ever.

Kieran and I used to run wild through some of the worst streets. We had more in common back then. I pulled out the black card with gold bird claw marks, its surface cool against my fingertips. They'd been popping up on bodies all over the East Coast.

My guys noticed patterns. That's what we did.

Aidan had Feds in his pocket, Gabriel knew politicians.

This didn't look good for either one of them.

But all I could think about was keeping this shit away from Nisha, protecting her from the darkness that had always been my world.

The taxi pulled up to Aidan's towering house.

At nine million dollars worth of solitude and space, he had enough to breathe in now instead of our cramped living situation as kids.

I stepped out, gravel crunching beneath my feet.

Wrought-iron fence, manicured garden, gleaming brass fixtures—everything screamed success and power. His place was silent, save for the distant hum of the city and rustling leaves. I rang the doorbell.

Alexei Markovik, my brother's enforcer and ever-present guard, opened the door, his familiar face welcoming in the setting.

At six-one, he was a little shorter than me, platinum blonde hair catching the chandelier light. His piercing blue eyes, set in distinctly Eastern European features, looked pleased to see me.

"Killian," he greeted me his accent thick but a smile on his face. Alexei seemed leaner. Sometimes I forgot he was just a kid, barely twenty-one.

"What are you eating around here?" I asked him with a frown.

A trafficking victim turned loyal enforcer, his eyes held the weight of someone much older.

I stepped into the opulent hallway.

"You don't look so good, kid."

He rubbed the back of his head embarrassed. "I eat everything."

"Right."

The crystal chandelier cast shadows on the hardwood floors, a far cry from our childhood's flickering fluorescents. Everything about Aidan's manor was dark.

A king of hell needed an apt kingdom. This entire city was his. Aidan appeared at the hall's end like he'd been summoned by the doorbell. Aidan was an inch shorter than me and Kieran, but broader, more imposing. Black hair. Bright amber eyes.

Where Kieran and I were built for speed, Aidan was a force of nature.

His presence filled the space, eyes sharp beneath a furrowed brow. "I thought you'd come earlier."

"I got delayed."

"I need to run in a bit, but I got twenty, come on."

Plain and simple, Aidan could be an asshole.

Not nice. Not polite. As head of the organization, he couldn't afford to be. And sometimes he made choices that pissed everyone off.

"Alexei, make sure we're not disturbed." The young man nodded, his eyes meeting mine briefly, a flicker of understanding passing between us.

Aidan gestured for me to sit, his movements sharp and controlled. "How are things in New York?"

I pulled out the black card in my pocket, placing it on his polished mahogany desk. Black. With distinct gold claw marks.

"Sean said a few of the guys found these along the coast. I talked to Gabriel. He doesn't know. Neither did I. Nobody on the street knows what the fuck it is."

Aidan's amber eyes, brighter than Kieran's, glowered as he examined the card. "They're showing up all over the East Coast. On bodies."

Aidan's gaze snapped back to me, amber eyes glinting in the fading sunlight that filtered through the heavy curtains.

"Assassinations?" he murmured, voice matching the low rumble of distant traffic.

I nodded, watching his jaw muscles tighten beneath his stubbled skin.

For a moment, I glimpsed the boy who'd once shielded me from our father's rage. But that boy was gone, replaced by the hard man before me.

"Headshots. All of them," I continued, leaning forward in the leather chair. "Arrowhead bullets. Designed to cut through anything."

Even bone. It was a little too precise.

Something was in the country since these didn't pop up until now.

Aidan leaned back, his frame dominating the space.

The city sprawled behind him through the floor-to-ceiling windows, his iron-fisted kingdom bathed in the orange glow of sunset. "Who's turning up dead?"

"A mix. High-level businessmen, board members, a judge, a city councilman. Plus some random civilians."

"Any connection to our operations?"

I shook my head, the scent of leather and old books filling my nostrils. "Not that we can see. It seems random, but…"

Because random wasn't random.

"Names, dates, locations. I'll send Alexei and a few of the guys out here to take a look."

Out of everyone, Aidan mattered the most to me.

He was the oldest, but he was in charge. Kieran would like Nisha easily.

"Kieran's doing better," I commented, breaking the silence.

I thought of Kieran then, how easy it would be to introduce them. Nisha would have charmed him with her warmth.

His easy smile and laid-back attitude would welcome her immediately. But Aidan? He was a different beast. But he was the most important person to introduce her to.

"Killian." Aidan's voice cut through my thoughts, sharp as a blade. "You good?" I didn't realize he'd been talking to me.

Shit. I blinked, forcing myself back to the present. "Yeah, just thinking. Go on."

Aidan's eyes narrowed, his gaze sharp as a blade. "You've been distracted lately."

I hesitated, the weight of my secrets heavy on my tongue.

Aidan's lip tipped up, a hint of amusement in his amber eyes. "Is it your girlfriend?"

Shit. Kieran talked. "No." *Too fast.*

His brow rose. *Oh motherfucker.*

I looked away, feeling trapped in the opulent office. I could feel Aidan's gaze boring into me, waiting for the truth he knew I was hiding.

Did he know?

"No," I repeated, my voice steadier this time.

He didn't say anything, but his amusement was palpable. "That why you got Derek to spy on her father?"

"It's nothing," I lied, the words tasting like ash in my mouth. Even I knew it sounded weak.

"He molested his teenage daughter. What did you think Derek's gonna do?" *Aidan. Knew. He knew about Nisha.*

I kept my voice calm not liking where this conversation was going. "I keep it open ended. My guys have free will. Are you spying on me?"

"You go digging in prison and I'm not supposed to know?"

Derek wouldn't say a word but Aidan would have eyes and ears everywhere. Whereas Nisha was none the wiser.

Aidan's eyes were bright. "Free will."

The irony of that never escaped me.

I kept my voice low. "It's nothing."

"Derek found a few ways to keep him in jail because you were worried if he got out he'd come after Nisha." Aidan was quiet. "Still nothing?"

I breathed through my nose. Her name didn't sit right in Aidan's mouth. Not with me.

"So you have Derek pulling strings for you?" Aidan's eyes were narrowed. "And if it pisses off the wrong people—"

"I don't give a shit." My throat worked. "I don't wanna go into this right now. That's not why I came. You had twenty minutes, you're reaching it."

He leaned back in his chair letting out a breath. Looking surprised with me. And I felt unease.

I never griped about anything with Aidan. Never got upset with him. We were partners. He lifted me up.

I supported his six. Easy.

"Derek said he's found enough to make sure they delay his release."

"And if he's released?" Aidan's voice was low. "If he gets out?"

I take him out. Easy.

Before I could stop myself, I found myself asking. " Do you remember Mom?"

As soon as the question left my lips Aidan's entire face went blank.

"I just remember—"

"She left us," Aidan's words were clipped. "She left her family. She ran out. Couldn't handle it."

But I remember her hanging from the ceiling. Hanging. The darkest part of me still saw the black. And then Aidan. I just saw Aidan. It had always been him protecting me.

His eyes watched me. "You remember something?"

"No," I cleared my throat. "Nothing."

His entire demeanor shifted, and the energy in the room was…it was bleak. He never spoke of her but now I wondered. With Nisha in my life, visions were unlocking in my head and I kept seeing her.

"Why now? Your nurse?" His eyes couldn't meet mine.

I looked at him. "Curious. No." He already knew. No point in denying Nisha totally.

His amber eyes flickered over to me. "About her? Or your memories?"

Something about the way he said it made me wonder. It did.

I didn't know how to ask him.

Did our mother kill herself because of Cormac's abuse?

I hadn't cared until now. I didn't even remember until now.

Why around Nisha memories of her swirled in my head.

Why I thought about her eyes. Blue. Dark hair. In my eyes.

Why it bothered me.

I shook my head. "Just curious."

"Why the fuck does it matter?" I saw the hardness in his eyes. He remembered her better than anybody. "She's gone. She's not coming back. You have me and Kieran. And worst case—if you need us over Nisha, let us know."

That was surprising. I hadn't expected Aidan to factor her into the situation at all.

Aidan's phone went off, cutting through the tension. He swore lightly as he looked down.

"Who is it?"

He sighed. "Chief of police."

I snorted. Gotta love a cop you could have in your pocket.

As Aidan stepped away to take the call, I took in Alexei's form again outside the door.

He didn't look good at all.

Nisha's influence had me noticing things I never used to.

Her voice echoed in my head.

Killian, he doesn't look good. Has he eaten today?

"He doesn't look good," I said quietly when Aidan returned.

Aidan's mouth turned down, a flicker of concern passing over his features. "He's got a few cockroaches in town he needs to kill and he eats like a teenager for a twenty-one year old."

I understood what Aidan was saying.

Competition. Even with Aidan running the show, and Titan's backing, we still had flare-ups. Little shits wanting to test the limits of Aidan's patience. And Alexei's, apparently.

"Why's Alexei stressed this time?"

"Some dumb fuckers who don't know when to quit." Aidan explained how gangs were trying to step into the city, inspire fear, leave their marks. "Bunch of idiots I need to hang from the FDR if they get rowdy."

He rolled his eyes, but I knew better.

Only Aidan could talk about murder so casually.

I remembered the day he handed Gabriel a gun, telling him to do whatever it took to make Aidan king.

Nobody had anything on us. Not the cops, not the Feds. *Nobody.*

Aidan was ruthless, and he made sure everyone knew it.

Suddenly, I was reminded of the life I lived. Second-in-command to an empire...and I didn't mind it. I didn't because it was all I had ever known.

Until her.

Until I remembered who I had at home.

Nisha, with her soft pink dresses, amber scent, pale greens. All over me, all over my life.

And the potential for more.

Would Nisha care? Would she accept me?

I knew Aidan's legacy would eventually be mine.

He was destined to die somehow, someday. None of us had wanted kids before. But now…that fucking broken condom haunted me. What if Nisha was pregnant?

What if I had a son? Would he be my legacy?

And if it was a girl?

With Nisha's hair, a love for pink, and she thought I wasn't a good father?

My chest tightened with an unfamiliar sensation.

As Aidan quickly wrapped up our conversation, I realized how little time we'd actually spent together.

We only get together for work or help.

Not for real.

Not as a family.

I had a few more things to polish up in Chicago before seeing my girl, but Aidan was already leaving.

The older I got, the more I realized—I only saw my brothers when shit hit the fan.

Otherwise, it was like I had nobody at all.

Nobody except Nisha.

My phone pinged.

> Baby, did you eat today?
>
> I miss you.

My lips quirked up. I missed her too.

> Not yet, luv. Been busy.
>
> Home safe?

> Yes. It's so late.
>
> What do you mean not yet? It's LATE.
>
> Killian.
>
> Protein bars do not count as real REAL food.

I smirked down at her texts. Technically it was a substitute.

But without Nisha I didn't feel comfortable eating normally. Besides, eating took too much of my time.

I wanted to spend it with her.

My phone pinged again to a photo of Nisha curled into a pillow in bed. Her smile evident, her hair waving wildly into her eyes.

Damn.

Miss you.

Love you 😘

Love you.

33

KILLIAN

I HAD ONE MORE STOP BEFORE I COULD SEE NISHA.

Gabriel.

I drove to the imposing Titan Manor tucked away in Greenwich.

The place was a fortress of security and grandeur, a testament to Gabriel's wealth and power now.

The money was built from a hodgepodge of my father's wealth, Gabriel's connections—and his ability to pull strings enough to land this home.

And since Aidan had the cash? A couple of million later—Gabriel was the owner of this place. The headquarters of Titan.

Gabriel lived there with his baby sister, Evie Monroe.

The Manor loomed before me, its white walls stark against the late summer sky.

The landscaped green lawns, a singular bust of a woman around the foundation that I drove around parking my car upfront were the constants.

Everything inside changed all the time.

Inside, there were all types of houseplants everywhere.

Evie liked all things green. I knew little about Evie.

There were so many secrets at Titan; unraveling one led me to the ball of knots at the center.

The one whose office I was about to go into.

The reason behind everything. Gabriel.

I walked up to the second floor, the temperature dropping with each step. Reaching the heavy oak door at the end of the hall, I knocked and entered.

Gabriel's pale blue eyes were already fixed on me as if he'd been expecting me all along.

The room temperature plummeted several degrees like it always did around Gabriel.

He made ice look friendly with that stare of his.

Closing the door behind me, I got straight to the point. "Aidan's in the dark, but he's putting Alexei on it.

It's definitely a black-ops unit—they've popped up all over the city. And all over the East Coast. All my guys are on the lookout. How quiet do you want this?"

Gabriel didn't like to talk about shit. "Not a fucking whisper."

"Do you know who this unit is?" I held up the black card with the gold claw marks.

He shook his head.

"But you've seen them before?" I had to ask.

The soft glow of his computer screen cast eerie shadows across his face, accentuating the sharp angles of his features.

"I have. I've heard of them through the years."

"Who are they with?"

"I don't know for certain."

I knew little about him. But I saw the way he looked at me. Steady. He was lying.

You fucking know.

He smirked, eyes colder than usual.

"I have a hunch. That isn't enough."

The first time I saw Gabriel, he'd been intense. Over the years, I thought it would soften, but it didn't. If anything, time had only sharpened his edges, honing him into the formidable man he was today.

His pale blue eyes remained sharp and calculating, always several steps ahead of everyone else.

I took a breath. "A black ops unit in the city is wandering around for what? Why are they killing execs and randoms?"

"Are they random?" He raised a brow. "These three," he pointed at a folder. "Were supposed to be arrested by the Fed's for racketeering in a week." He motioned to the seven folders stacked up in front of him.

"This set was supposed to be on trial. Notice how it's not ending up on the news?"

"They're connected."

"They've got connections to keep people quiet."

Who the fuck had the power to do that?

"But you have a hunch?"

"I do, but I'm digging into it. In the meantime, keep me posted if you find anything else."

We tracked everything happening in the city.

Every single thing. Anomalies didn't do well in our world. And this one was clearly skilled.

"Did you get one of the bullets?" Gabriel asked, leaning back in his chair, his posture relaxed but his eyes never losing their icy focus. "It's the fucking arrowheads, isn't it?"

I nodded, reaching into my pocket. "Sean picked it up."

I passed Gabriel what I'd shown Aidan. An arrowhead bullet was designed from a material I couldn't identify.

Gabriel frowned, turning the bullet over in his hands, his expression darkening like a gathering storm.

"We need to get copies of these made downtown and send them to Landon to test them out. See what the impact is on these." His frown deepened at the material. "These aren't normal bullets either. Anything else?" His eyes flickered over to me.

I filled him in on Kieran's well-being, knowing Gabriel would need to know. Aidan planned to come down in a few days to talk to Gabriel in person about a few things.

It was best for Aidan to come here; they could check in with Kieran together.

"Reed won't be thrilled about taking Kieran in," Gabriel said, his voice as cold as the room. "I can ask him, but he's more worried about Aidan losing it if anything happens to him."

"Aidan won't be upset about Kieran's choices. Better him getting shot on the job than overdosing over another hooker."

He nodded slowly, taking in the information and analyzing it from every angle.

Something was going on, and I wondered if Gabriel had more information than he was letting on.

"Keep me in touch, send Landon to get this work done. I need a man on Congressman Young."

"Kill him?"

Gabriel shook his head. "Make 'em squirm." He smirked. "And then kill him." He paused. "No, kill his dog first. He loves it more than his wife."

"Anyone else?"

Gabriel thought about it quietly and sighed, looking bored. "Take out the entire family. Discreetly. I don't want any blowback, and if I so much as catch a whiff of this on paper, I'll just blow the building up."

That was Gabriel.

"Nate already fucked his wife, some annoying sorority sister from a low-tier college with a hard-on for bikers." Gabriel rolled his eyes as they went positively glacial. "Get rid of them. Given that there's only three of them left, I'd say killing them now is the best bet."

Gabriel had switched out all of Congressman Young's detail with Titan operatives. The nail on his coffin was coming.

Gabriel didn't like politicians. And so, in turn, he played politics. Specifically, he didn't like the Young family. Something about them from the jump.

He'd been after the entire family over the last few years with a vengeance. Another secret he wouldn't tell me.

"Clear?"

"Yes, sir."

∼

"Hey, baby."

Nisha's voice washed over me soothing every inch of the knives and thorns I felt inside of me.

"Luv, I'll be home soon." I left the Manor, and I was a few minutes away from entering the city when Nisha called me.

"Are you still bringing dinner?" She asked me, a tremor in her voice. Immediately, the back of my neck prickled. There was an edge of *something* in her voice.

"What's wrong?"

She continued, her voice unnaturally cheerful.

"I was just taking a cab home off Lexington and 5th, and I remem-

214

bered when I passed that Italian restaurant you like so much that you mentioned you'd wanted some?"

I looked at the street I was in. I was ten minutes from her without traffic. But it was the city so twenty with traffic. Not if I rushed.

This conversation didn't make sense to me.

Something was wrong.

"Are you safe?"

"*No*, I'm starving." She wasn't safe. "Oh, you're inside, Tony's already?"

"Is that where you are? What's happening? Is someone listening?"

"Yes. Yes. I understand."

My mind raced, piecing together what she couldn't say. My grip tightened on the steering wheel as I realized she wasn't alone, and whoever was with her was a threat.

I heard her voice again, this time clearly not directed at me. "Sir, hi, my husband's on the phone. He says he wants us to stop right here. Yes, thank you. Right here is fine..."

She was in a cab. She was in danger.

"No, he's here. Thank you. I'd like to get off here."

My heart rate sped up tenfold.

I was going to rush.

Fuck.

"You're in trouble."

"Yes, baby."

"You're by Tony's?"

"Mhm."

"I'm ten minutes away," I said, already calculating the fastest route in my head. "Go straight to the back. Tell Maria I'm coming to get you. Scream. Anything. I'm staying on the phone with you until you tell me you're safe."

Maria was Tony's wife and an old-school Italian. She would shoot someone if she could.

"I love you," Nisha whispered, her voice trembling slightly.

And my blood was boiling.

"Yes, he's right there...he's outside." Her voice was shaking. "No, he's outside...hey, Oliver!" Oliver Hart was Tony's son.

"Miss Nisha..." Oliver was a solid guy.

"Hey, I was waiting for you—"

I heard the little noise she made. I knew every single fucking thing about my girl.

Oh, I'm gonna kill this motherfucker.

And now, this time, there would be no Nisha to stop me.

"Give the phone to Oliver, luv," I instructed, trying to keep her calm. "If you can, get the plates. I love you too."

I will move heaven and hell to make sure you are okay.

I floored the accelerator, the engine roaring as I weaved through traffic like a man possessed while barking orders to Oliver.

Who the fuck was after her? Was this connected to the kill cards? I was ready to tear out of the car and run to her.

Had my world, the one I'd tried so desperately to keep her from, finally caught up with us?

Shitshitshit.

I was back in the city for five minutes, and my girl was already in danger. We didn't have enemies in the city.

Nobody should be coming after Nisha. If they did...

Oh, fuck...*heads will roll if anyone lays a hand on her.*

34

NISHA

"It's all good."

Oliver Hart, the tall blonde had been outside the shop talking to a blonde woman when I'd burst onto them.

"I'll stay with you until Mr. O'Hara get's here—"

"So sorry that happened to you," the elegant blonde was a woman named Caroline who had been with Oliver. With how close he stood to her, I took it they were together.

"Miss Nisha, does Mr. O'Hara know—"

He broke off when the door slammed open, the sudden noise making me flinch as Oliver moved in front of me and Caroline who wrapped her arms around me.

"Ollie, I think that's him," Caroline murmured looking down at me. "Killian's here."

Oliver's massive shoulders blocked me from view, but I peered around him and saw Killian standing there, brows drawn, eyes a little wild on me.

"Oliver." His voice was clipped.

"Sorry, sir. She's right here." He got out of the way and quickly hauling Caroline with an arm around her. "Come on, *cara.*"

In his black suit and tie, his hair rumpled, Killian looked like my dreams, but right now, the look on his face was terrifying.

One I hadn't ever experienced.

He took me in immediately. And he took in Oliver Hart next to me who scrambled out of the way. "I'll leave you two it."

Out of all the ways to welcome him home, this was not one of them.

Perched on a rickety wooden chair, clutching a chipped mug of chamomile tea that Maria, Tony's kind-eyed wife, had pressed into my hands, I watched him move towards me.

The warmth seeped into my palms, but did little to stop their shaking.

Killian loved the pasta here, but food was the last thing on my mind right now. My stomach churned over and over again, the anxiety overwhelming.

"Luv."

In an instant, I was in Killian's arms, my body melting into his as I inhaled his scent, letting it fill my lungs.

"That was terrifying," I whispered my heart pounding out of my chest.

"Tell me you got the plates. Tell me everything."

"I did. I left work and hailed a cab to go home. Everything seemed fine at first, but then..." I trailed off, the fear creeping back in, constricting my throat.

Killian's arms tightened around me, solid and reassuring. "Go on, luv."

He didn't let me open the windows, the backseat smelled strange, and he kept slowing down around the same street. Twice.

I felt Killian's body go rigid, tension coiling in his muscles, but he stayed quiet, letting me get it all out.

My voice shook as I continued, the words spilling from my lips in a rush. I swallowed hard, my throat dry despite the tea.

"He asked if I had a boyfriend, and I thought to call you—"I couldn't finish the sentence, but I knew Killian understood.

"I was originally going home," I whispered, my fingers digging into Killian's shirt, feeling the warmth of his skin beneath.

"But then...my gut was screaming at me. I knew I had to do something..."

"You did the right thing, luv." Killian's voice was fierce, protective. "Tell me the plate numbers." I rattled them off to him.

"He let me out when I told him Tony's son was you," I rushed to add, the words tumbling out in a desperate need to reassure both Killian and myself. I could still feel the burn in my legs, the way my lungs screamed for air as I fled.

Killian was eerily silent for a moment, the only sound his measured breathing and the distant clatter from the kitchen. His face, his body language—everything had shifted.

His mismatched eyes—one amber, one aqua—were blazing with a fury I'd never seen before.

I'd seen a glimpse of this side when Eugene had threatened me, but this...this was something else entirely. He was coiled in tension, a predator ready to strike.

"Killian?"

He pulled me to him again, his lips finding that spot on my neck. Over and over against my pulse. I felt the tension in his shoulders as he held me tighter.

"Let's go home," he murmured, his breath hot against my skin.

"You okay?"

He nodded, but his eyes told a different story.

They were dark, stormy. Killian was seething. I didn't know what he'd do. What being a Titan really meant. I just knew he was...ready to explode.

His fingers gripped the steering wheel, knuckles bone-white. His jaw worked, grinding teeth. But when he glanced at me, his gaze softened. "I missed you."

"I missed you." I kissed him. "One way to welcome you home."

He didn't smile as he held my face for a long moment staring into my eyes. Like he was reassuringly himself at the light.

"Home?"

"Home."

On the way out, Killian opened to Oliver and Caroline wrapped around each other in a hug. He looked embarrassed as they pulled apart. "Sorry, guys. Mom says you two can have dinner, after that," he looked apologetic as he handed us some takeout bags. "Glad I was outside for ya."

I think he knew better than to address Killian and I shook my head, but he insisted with kind dark eyes. Caroline, red faced behind Oliver smiled at us reassuringly.

I reluctantly took dinner as Killian stood there looking ready to fight someone but he shook his head at something. Oliver looked uneasily at him and then me and I could see now how Killian scared people.

"Thank you," I murmured.

Once we got home, my body reacted strangely to the stress and Killian's silence. He was usually quiet.

He never said much as a whole.

Killian's absence had given me time for Plan B. The doctor had warned me my hormones would be off for a while.

I reached for him as soon as we were inside, peeling off my clothes and kissing him hard. I needed to feel safe, to feel him.

The apartment's cool air pebbled my skin as I pressed against him.

"Talk to me," I whispered. "You seem upset."

He returned my kiss, firm, and grounding. "I am." He held my face, something in his eyes I had never seen until then. "Nobody's going to hurt you. Ever."

Before I could ask, I was in his arms, with him picking me up and kissing me soundly. "I need you."

I wrapped my arms around his neck. "Whatever you want, just talk to me so I know you're okay. Are you—" The insidious sensations in me were back. "Do you feel like I—"

"No." He cut me off watching me. "No, it's not a bother. You are not a problem. You weren't asking for it. He's just a fucking monster and I'll handle him."

I didn't even have a second to respond as he lifted me into his arms.

Taking me into the bedroom, where I felt the desperation running through him.

His hands tearing at my clothes, until I was fully naked and he was moving over me with an intensity that left me breathless.

His hips moved in me when they did, with a frightening intensity that made my eyes water. I couldn't stop crying as he took me.

Demanding more.

Pulling out orgasm after orgasm until I was breathless and ready to black out. Like he was cementing himself into my body. Like if he didn't move this way—I would vanish. But I wasn't going anywhere.

"Killian," I pleaded. "I'm okay."

But I got the feeling nothing was going to satisfy him, as he licked my throat, his hips relentless and brutal.

35

KILLIAN

Vicious.

That was one way of putting what I was turning into with her.

I moved inside of her with enough force to make me groan. I was taking Nisha harder than I ever had. Noises left me.

I was an animal. Teeth. Tongue. Biting. Fucking.

My. Fucking. Girl.

Nothing was going to stop me from loving her. The way I needed right *now*.

To become so infused into her, I would never leave. "Such a good girl coming for me," I growled. "Look at how fucking wet you are for me."

Hot, wet and incredible, I slid into Nisha feeling the head of my dick deep in her, the piercing against that spot that drove her insane.

Over sensitized and soaked for me—Nisha's cries were muffled into my shoulders, wild and untamed as I fucked deeper.

I could hear her orgasm and lost count of what number she was on.

But *fuuuuuccck*, she sounded so sweet.

Nisha didn't always come loudly. Sometimes she came like this. All sweet and sexy as she held onto me. She never let me go far.

And I just knew I had to stay and love her. Fuck her. Bury myself in her.

Her ankles at her ears as I ground deep, gripping the headboard until I felt her come.

"*Oh God, baby—*" she whimpered as she held onto the sheets. "*OhGodOhGodOhGod.*" It ended in a little scream.

"*That's my fucking girl.*" I growled, punctuating each word with a powerful thrust of my hips that made her sob and scream.

I couldn't help the way my lips tipped up at her quivering.

"*Baby—*"

"*I know, luv. Let go.*"

This position drove Nisha over the edge so easily I loved it. She bit down on her lip hard as she quivered around me making an adorable noise as she came.

I stamped my lips over hers grinding down. Whatever she wanted, I was hers.

I knew she'd be sore. I knew it would ache. I didn't care. I wanted to brand her, myself into her skin. Live there for good.

Nisha let out a muffled noise as her pussy rippled around me. I drove further into her, relishing all of it. I said completely fuck it to condoms right now. I couldn't even think about anything other than taking her.

Only then, after what felt like an eternity, did I feel my orgasm rush through me. I spilled myself in her not giving a shit about anything.

Consequences be damned.

I wanted to plant myself so deep in Nisha I was a part of her forever.

My orgasm was the hardest it had ever been at the thought of that.

She'd taken Plan B after I'd come in her and I knew while I'd been gone? Nothing out of the ordinary had come up with her.

But part of me wanted to be so deep in her—I couldn't find my way back out of her.

I pressed my lips to the erratic flutter finding it against the column of her throat.

Over and over. I knew if I stopped feeling it one day—I would stop existing.

Initially, I just found Nisha hot as shit and sweeter than cotton candy. Now?

Nisha was in my blood. She was everything. She was a part of me. And I couldn't lose her to anything.

I ran my tongue along her pulse before sinking my teeth into her soft flesh, marking her as mine.

A strangled noise left her as she went wild under me.

Nisha fucking loved when I was rougher. I couldn't hurt her. Not enough to draw blood, but enough for her to clench down onto me tighter than before as I came.

It took me long, long minutes to calm down.

"I love you," she whispered against my skin. "I love you." My head snapped up. Those eyes looking at me were soft and wet. Tears flowing down her cheeks. "I love you."

She kept saying it in between kisses, rubbing my back, holding me to her.

The heat of her pulsing around me wildly as I felt my heart race. And it was only then as I dropped her legs down I heard it.

That tiny little noise she made when she was in distress.

"*Nisha—*" I cupped her face with my hand in horror, washing over me. Her eyes opened, wet and tearing up. "I'm sorry..." I made a move to slip out of her, but she held me then.

"I'm okay," she whispered but she didn't look it. "I love you so much."

"I'm sor—" *I love you too.*

"Kiss me." *Anything for you, luv.*

I did slowly, hesitantly, as she cried as I did, even as my heart began to race and ache at the idea of hurting her

"Luv, did I—"

"No." Her words were weak, her voice hoarse from screaming. "No, just really intense." Her eyes were shy, as she admitted. " It's okay, I just need kisses now."

After care, you punk bitch. It's called aftercare.

I heard Kieran's voice in my head telling me to cuddle her now and get her that heated blanket she loved and chocolate things she liked. "I didn't hurt you?"

She shook her head. A sigh of relief escaped, the weight lifting off my chest at the idea of making her hurt.

Because of my fucked up feelings.

I kissed her over and over, and slowly, Nisha calmed down, and her eyes opened.

"It's okay," she whispered, her voice soothing. "I'm okay." I pressed my forehead against hers, our breaths mingling.

"You're okay."

She nodded, but as I shifted, I caught the slight wince that crossed her features.

Shit.

Her hand moved to cup my face, her touch gentle and comforting.

"Don't," she whispered. "I wanted you. Okay? I love you." She wrapped her legs around me tighter, pulling me closer. "I loved it." Her eyes met mine, a flicker of heat dancing within their depths.

"You always hold back...sometimes I like when you don't." She paused, considering her words. "Sometimes I love it when you're gentle. But sometimes, this is nice too."

And at that, she looked up at me. Dark pools meeting mine with soft sincerity. Her hand reached for mine, moving it over her heart.

"Stay with me? Just like this?"

I nodded, aware of what she was asking. She knew I wasn't wearing anything.

I didn't say a word. Just kissed her over and over.

If I stopped kissing her, I thought about the ninety ways I was going to make that motherfucker bleed out for trying to ever come near my girl.

Even now, I had quickly fired off a text to my team. To find who it was that had threatened my peace.

Even now, as I lay with her letting her soothe me after what the fuck I did.

"Killian," she whispered, her voice cutting through the shadows in my mind. She was crying again. "Come back to me."

Shit. She knew me too well, could sense when I was slipping into that dark place inside myself.

"I can't lose you."

"You won't lose me," she promised, her fingers tracing soothing patterns on my skin.

"Ever."

"To anything, baby."

36

KILLIAN

The sound of someone awful dying always brought me peace.

I did believe in justice.

A different kind of justice than normal folks.

"He really shouldn't have scared my girl."

I finished wiping the blood off my hands in the stark-lit bathroom of my satellite office.

The metallic scent mingled with the harsh sting of industrial cleaner, creating a nauseating cocktail that filled my nostrils.

But it was a familiar scent that usually brought a sense of grim satisfaction.

Not today.

Today, all I could see was Nisha's terrified face. All I heard is that noise. She didn't even know she made it when she was afraid.

But I did.

I knew everything about her.

Her panicked voice on the phone, pleading for help.

The thought of what could have happened if I hadn't answered, if I'd been a minute too late, made my blood run cold.

Seth Torres.

The name tasted like ash on my tongue. Third-generation scum, dishonorably discharged from the military for sexual assault. A real piece of work.

But he isn't anything anymore.

Not a threat, not a man, not even a memory.

I'd made sure of that.

The room was little more than a box, save for a chair and a drain in the center of the floor.

Torres was slumped in the chair, his face a bloody, unrecognizable mess. I'd lost count of how many times I'd hit him, my knuckles raw and throbbing. But it wasn't enough.

It would never be enough.

I lashed out again, my fist connecting with a sick crunch. Torres' head snapped back, a noise escaping his ruined throat.

I didn't stop. I couldn't stop.

"Boss, he's dead." Sean's voice cut through the haze. Barely.

Torres was slumped over, held up only by the zip ties binding him to the chair and I took a step back.

He'd stopped making noises a while ago. I turned to Sean, meeting his gaze. "Get rid of this trash for me."

I watched Sean work to clean it up and, I felt a new weight settle on my shoulders.

This wasn't just another job, another nameless target. This was personal.

This was about Nisha.

The image of her terrified face flashed through my mind, fueling my rage anew. Nisha didn't scare easy. She genuinely didn't.

The fact that he had frightened her enough to make that panicked call...Not with Nisha, though. *Never with Nisha.*

I stepped under the scalding spray, letting the water cascade over me in the shower.

As I scrubbed my hands raw, trying to get rid of the last traces of filth, my mind kept circling back to my girl. I leaned against the shower wall, my forehead pressed against the cool tiles.

I saw the security camera of her running to Tony's.

I saw the way he circled back. And I had been there with her.

Oh. Motherfucker.

I felt the grin stretch my lips the moment he realized he was a dead man.

The moment he knew whose world he was threatening.

Not her. *Mine.*

As I stepped out of the shower, wrapping a towel around my waist, I caught a glimpse of myself in the now-cleared mirror.

This man. Versus. The man who went home, ate dinner, and listened to her play her instruments.

My Nisha.

The thought of her in the hands of that piece of shit made my blood boil.

I'd tear apart anyone who tried, burn the whole fucking world down if I had to.

Because a world without her smile, her laugh, her touch?

That wasn't a world worth living in.

And because it was Nisha, I didn't just go straight to her.

No, she deserved more than that. And I needed to get rid of the sensation of touching his filth before I made it home to her.

I picked up an enormous bouquet of her favorites—sunflowers, lilies, and wildflowers—a riot of colors that I knew would make her eyes light up with that childlike wonder I loved so much.

Her eyes got huge whenever I showed up with flowers. And I knew she loved it when I did.

But flowers weren't enough. I grabbed a bunch of basil plants too, their pungent aroma filling the car.

I could already imagine her delight, knew she'd love them for her homemade pesto that she insisted on making from scratch.

I got groceries ordered to her place, making sure she had everything she needed—and those fancy chocolate-covered berries she thought I didn't know about.

And when I did see her, when she grinned and squealed, running up to me like I was her whole world...nothing else mattered.

The blood, violence, and darkness all faded away in the light of her smile.

Her arms around me felt like coming home.

Nisha tilted her head back to look up at me, her eyes shining with joy. "You just cleaned up? Your hair looks longer now."

I nodded, pressing my lips to the top of her head. My hands cupped her face, reminding me of how tiny she was compared to me.

I kissed her hard. Steadily, soothing myself through her like I always fucking had. Taking until I got my fill. Knowing full well I'd destroy her at home.

227

"Baby, do you wanna know what happened today?"

No, tell me, luv. "Tell me." I kissed her again, quickly grinning at her wide smile.

"Adam met this girl in his neighborhood. He won't tell me her name but apparently, his wallet was stolen…and she stole it back for him…"

I smirked. "A reverse pick-pocket?"

Nisha squealed and I grinned down at her. "And he says he can't stop thinking about her…" Nisha told me about Adam's new crush while we walked to car.

Did he? Good for him.

I smiled, listening to Nisha talk to me on the ride home.

And I knew I'd do it all again.

I'd face any threat and cross any line to keep her safe. I'd spend the rest of my life making sure she never had reason to be afraid again.

Even if it meant Nisha was in bed with me, a monster, I didn't give a fuck. Because I had her.

I was going to do whatever it took to keep her sunshine in my life.

By any means necessary.

NISHA

I'M PREGNANT.

Plan B wasn't foolproof.

I knew that.

And those first pregnancy tests that came back negative?

They weren't always reliable, either. Apparently.

But was reliable was a missed period, sore breasts, mood swings, and nausea—and then the pregnancy test I took in the hospital this morning.

The two lines stared back at me and I thought I was hallucinating since there was no way I could get pregnant that fast. No.

But then there had been the day Killian had left for Chicago…and I still turned beet red thinking about it.

I waited for the nerves to kick in, but it didn't. Instead a strange soft sensation came over me. From Killian's reaction to the broken condom. To my own…*it just felt like it was a part of him. And me.*

I wasn't scared at all.

I had another test hidden in my bag that I planned on taking. I needed to get a blood test done, but I didn't want to do it at work.

But I felt it in my body, and my period was *late.*

I thought it might've been the Plan B, but my breasts were swollen and tender, and even the softest bra felt like a crime. And the *nausea.* It was awful.

Only when Killian came home did it seem to settle, as if his presence alone could calm me down.

I was at least seven weeks along if I did the math correctly, but I didn't know for certain.

Between Killian's demanding work at Titan and our relentless hospital schedules, we barely had time to breathe, let alone discuss life-changing news.

Killian had been busier at work.

When he did swing by, I ended up trying to tell him once, but he'd gotten a call and had to leave in the middle of it. I told myself I'd tell him once I took the blood test.

Today, I found a moment of peace in a quiet corner of the hospital with Adam.

"And she kissed me," Adam finished his story. "She fucking kissed me."

His eyes widened on mine like the story was more shocking for him than me. In all the times I'd known him? I hadn't seen a woman capture his interest even though people liked him.

"She kissed you?" Adam had bumped into this girl over and over, which was driving him crazy since she refused to tell him her name.

"On the train," he admitted, a flush creeping up his neck. "I bumped into her when I was leaving the other night…"

It was rare for Adam to be so smitten with someone, although plenty of girls at the hospital had crushes on him.

With his tousled, dirty blond hair and charming smile, it was easy to see why. The way he blushed while telling me how adorable she was— just a bit shorter than me—his eyes lit up.

Adam rarely looked like that.

"She sounds like a guardian angel."

But then he said something that made my chest tighten. "…she doesn't care that I'm me—"

"What?" I interrupted my brow furrowing. "There's nothing wrong with you, Adam. You're fantastic." The self-doubt in his voice pained me, reminding me of my own insecurities. "I don't see why any woman wouldn't be all over you."

I couldn't resist adding with a playful nudge. "I'd be all over you if I didn't have…" My words trailed off as my hand unconsciously drifted to my abdomen, my thoughts momentarily consumed by the possibility of what might be...

Adam shot me a look of amused disbelief. "Nish, I'm not dumb enough to believe I'd be your type."

When Adam asked what I'd said to Killian when we first met, I felt heat rise to my cheeks.

At the memories of how he'd just kissed me.

It wasn't conventional, but it was ours. I didn't tell Adam.

Adam's brow furrowed slightly. "Does it matter to you that Killian's a Titan? His life...it can't be easy."

I paused, considering his question as thoughts of my recent physical changes flooded my mind.

I wanted to tell Adam eventually I was having a baby. And that Killian would no doubt be happy.

I knew him.

And I knew how he'd reacted. For both of us, I saw the baby as just family.

And I felt a little giddy and lightheaded at the thought of telling him...I was having a baby. I felt a smile tip my lips at the thought.

Killian's job never bothered me. What mattered was the man beneath the title, the Killian I knew when we were alone.

Pushing aside my own worries, I finally said. "I just care if he's honest with me. Killian comes over all the time, and we talk about everything, including his family. He has a life outside of Titan, you know. His older brother, Aidan, visits from Chicago sometimes. Killian wants me to meet him."

Adam's eyebrows rose in surprise. "Killian has an older brother?"

Nodding, I shared a small smile as I told him about Killian's family dynamics, including how their other brother, Kieran, loved to tease them both with cat videos despite their allergies.

I hadn't met Kieran yet, but Killian wanted me to. I longed to be a part of Killian's world in every way possible.

As I spoke about Killian's family, I felt a warmth spread through me, reminding me of the intimate moments we shared.

"Sometimes," I whispered, feeling heat creep into my cheeks. "He wonders why I...you know...I told him I liked him for who he was, not who he was pretending to be." I saw the real Killian, the one hidden beneath the tough exterior.

Adam pointed out. "You're also not afraid of him."

But I had never understood why everyone found him scary.

When he kissed me, the world fell away, and it was just us, lost in each other.

How could I fear someone who made me feel so safe?

"I don't think he's scary. I see him for who he is at heart, not what the world wants me to see. I just treated him like he was human. People said things about him, but I didn't care. I think he just needed someone to give him a chance."

"And now he can't let you go."

"I don't want him to," I admitted, my voice softening as I rubbed my stomach a little. "With me, Killian doesn't have to be the Titan everyone expects. He can just...be." And that's why I knew he'd be okay with the baby.

It was the same for me. I could just exist with Killian. Just be myself.

No pretenses, no expectations, just two people in love.

"I don't judge him," I said softly. "In turn, I think he feels safe with me. Because he can be himself."

I moved closer, and my thighs touched his.

"I think your guardian angel sees you for who you are, not what you think you are. Isn't that what matters the most?"

I raised a brow. Part of me wanted to reassure him, to tell him about the moments when Killian, stripped of his public persona, came to me. For comfort.

Part of me knew it was best to keep it to myself because Killian was super private. But I trusted Adam enough to tell him this.

"But she never told me her name," he murmured.

"I think you'll see her again. You've got it bad."

"So does Killian," Adam replied with a knowing grin.

Heat rose to my cheeks as I turned away, my hand unconsciously drifting to my stomach.

"So do I," I whispered, knowing full well I was freaking *pregnant* and I didn't know how to say the words. "And so does she..."

As Adam and I talked, my thoughts wandered.

Killian had always encouraged me to be open with him, to share my thoughts and feelings.

But now, the words wouldn't form.

I knew our child's life would be filled with safety and happiness.

Something neither one of us had. Neither one of us were criminals like our parents and our baby would be loved.

I was so happy when I thought about it like that.

I was only a few weeks along but I'd be going to get an ultrasound soon. I told myself I would tell him then.

With the photos.

I'd surprise him, and it would be fine. I could bake cupcakes, put the photo under it,, and hide the color of the baby's gender in them. That would be cute.

At work, as Adam's relationship with his mystery woman progressed, he began seeking my advice more often.

I didn't mind; it was a welcome distraction from the growing tension within me.

Once, Adam brought up what Killian and I had in common.

I found myself telling him about the little things Killian enjoyed, like our shared taste in music, food, and movies.

But then I mentioned the harp, how I played it for Killian on quieter days, and how he loved watching and listening to me.

Recently, though, Killian had been busy.

He'd been handling something for Lucas Devereaux and a few real estate tycoons around him. Whatever he was working on it was helping his brother Aidan and Titan.

"I don't play it anymore, but Killian got me one when he found out..." I told Adam, my voice trailing off as I remembered the day he surprised me with a cello, too.

Adam's eyebrows raised. "He encourages you...Why not go to school for that?" I felt a pang in my chest.

"It wasn't in the cards..." I mumbled, trying to push away the memories of the past away. I was pregnant. That's all that I cared. The future. My family. Killian.

Killian had been so busy he hadn't come home in a few days.

He texted me all the time, dropped by with food when he could, but I saw the exhaustion etched on his face.

Something was happening weighing on him, but I couldn't bring myself to add to his stress.

So I went to my ultrasound appointment at a smaller clinic alone three weeks later. My breasts, already large, had grown even more, but we rarely had time together like we did in the summer.

Killian wouldn't know the signs of a woman's pregnancy.

As I laid there on the table, the ultrasound wand on my belly, I wished Killian were with me.

I wished he knew about the life we had created.

I had to tell him.

38

KILLIAN

Weeks had passed and I couldn't remember the last time Nisha and I had sat down for dinner.

If at all.

I saw her with quick kisses, bandaids wrapped around my finger. Quick bursts of love-you's in between our rushed schedule.

I was dealing with a mess.

Reed's girlfriend—Alisha, and her little sister, Avani—had been the victims of an attack by a stalker/serial killer.

Selena Tavares, one of the Titan operatives had been attacked as well.

Kieran had joined the Titans and was now babysitting Avani, and out of all people—Reed might've been a better mentor to him than Gabriel.

Nisha was now in the hospital taking care of Tavares and I was babysitting Tavares's hot headed boyfriend—Kellan Watts.

I was juggling that fallout and clean up.

Watts was the poster-child for private school with the way he looked.

Or he would be. Had he not almost killed a man in the hospital a week ago.

Specifically Nathan Wyatt.

Idiots.

Now, I had a student under me courtesy of Gabriel's orders to make sure Watts didn't do anything stupid, and Nisha was under orders to make sure Selena healed.

With the two of us baby-sitting the couple, Gabriel wanted them to heal in their own ways.

I didn't know what the fuck all happened, just that Watts wasn't allowed anywhere near her.

And she had yet to ask for him.

In the meantime, Gabriel and I were dealing with a black-ops unit was turning the underworld upside down.

New guys weren't exactly handled well in my line of work. Being who we were, rival gangs and issues were always a thing. But that was where being a Titan came in.

With Titan I didn't have to worry about it because when smaller groups tried anything with us? We had the backing to shut them down.

But this was something nobody had any clue about.

"Get a fucking haircut," Gabriel grumbled, eyeing me like I was some delinquent teenager. *Fuck that.* Nisha liked my hair longer.

The way she tugged on it...*That shit felt amazing.*

I'd come to him to give him updates after the insanity that had ensued, and to fill him in on what information I did have.

I cut straight to the chase.

"I'll worry about my hair after you tell me why these fuckers are after your *necklace*. They're trying to kill Lucas Devereaux over some jewelry?" Shit better be worth its weight. "Lucy Devereaux stole something from Marcus Hagen. You know that shit is messy at best."

At the *mention* of Marcus Hagen? His face went blank.

I knew bits and pieces about my mentor. But I didn't know where he came from. His past. His old life.

I just knew Gabriel Monroe. *And his alias, Raphael Santos.*

I didn't know who he was before this. Or where he came from. Neither did Aidan. For all we knew, he trusted a ghost.

"On paper, he's dead. My guess is someone eventually got to him and offed him since you said he double crossed someone."

"Lucas's father wanted something from them and now he's offing anyone who might have a connection to him?"

"Potentially."

Reed had something this black-ops crew wanted. Bad. And someone was gunning for both Lucas and his sister, but for different reasons.

"I've been on their trail for years. Last time they surfaced in the city was seven years ago."

Seven years ago.

When Gabriel walked into my life and flipped my world on its axis.

When everything changed, mostly for the better.

"But then why does the necklace matter so much? Lucas is just collateral for his father? Why would they think Lucas would be after them?" I frowned at him.

The only reason he'd be chasing after a fucking necklace is because it meant something to him.

Something more than he was letting on.

"I don't give a shit about Lucas Devereaux," Gabriel made a noise. "As long as he stays away from anything under my roof, I don't give a fuck what happens to him. I want the necklace and I want my family. That is it."

Dismissed.

I made a mental note to sync up with Liam Sullivan about Lucy and Lucas's case. It wasn't just about following orders; I had a soft spot for Lucas Devereaux.

And then a week later, Sean dropped a bombshell.

"Boss, Devereaux's got a girlfriend. I had my eyes on him for a few weeks now. Same girl."

He slid over a photo of Lucas entering Lucy's building, not emerging until dawn. Several shots of Lucas with a woman—I paused.

"But it's not who we expected."

It was Evie Monroe.

Dark mahogany colored hair, dark eyes beaming up at Lucas.

Shots of them together, him kissing her on the street—*Holy. Fucking. Shit.*

Evie Monroe is dating Lucas Devereaux.

"What's our next move?" Sean asked, watching me carefully.

Telling Gabriel was the logical choice, but given his hatred for Lucas, that powder keg could explode in our faces.

Yet Evie wasn't just anyone—she was Gabriel's whole world.

He's going to kill Lucas if he finds out.

And Evie had the same eyes Nisha did, soft and sweet. The kind I never wanted to see hurt. Seeing this eyes hurt would gut me. I didn't care to see that.

I made my decision.

"We keep this under wraps," I said. "Shadow them discreetly. Report directly to me. Make sure not a single fucking thing happens to her."

I didn't give a shit who Lucas fucked as long as Nisha wasn't in the picture.

Most people didn't understand how I operated. The truth was—as long as nothing touched my family? I was fine.

Even if Gabriel did try and kill him, Aidan and I would step in.

Sean nodded grimly, understanding the weight of the situation.

With that settled, I shifted gears to Derek's investigation into Charles Devereaux down in North Carolina.

I fiddled with my bandaid on my finger—this one had these adorable pink bows on it—as Sean and I worked on what the fuck was happening at Titan.

> Are you coming home tonight, baby?

Not tonight, luv. Working late on the Devereaux case.

> Did you eat dinner yet?

I hid the protein bar in my pocket like Nisha could tell.

> Please tell me you had real dinner with that protein bar.

I felt a light laugh leave me at that.

Are you spying on me, luv?

> No, I can feel your eyes from here.

> Miss you. It's been a long day.

Tell me about it. I can't talk but I'll text you until you fall asleep.

Hmm, Adam's dating someone, a cute girl he met near his neighborhood.

No shit?

Yeah she kissed him on the train and everything 😏

I spent the rest of the night texting my girl between working until she fell asleep.

39

KILLIAN

By the end of the week, I found myself at Teasers.

Seven years ago, Teaser's was a rundown dump where my father pimped out girls like Lara. I didn't know how bad it was.

While I was relegated to Chicago with Kieran, Aidan had been in New York. And when we switched places?

Gabriel had let me meet Lara Ford.

Well…not Lara at the time. I forgot her real name to be fair.

But she had stayed and turned Teaser's around to what it was today with no one any wiser.

Teaser's old clientele had been stripped apart and eliminated.

The new clientele was mostly women.

Lara had thought about catering to the image of sexy women, stronger ladies themed bars and nights—and a safe space for women.

The occasional idiot did show up—but they were carted out quickly by security.

As I stepped inside, the flapper-era style decor stood silent—multicolored parasol umbrellas hung motionless from the ceiling, and the warm lighting cast long shadows across the room.

Vines dangled near the plush velvet barstools, untouched by the usual crowd. Flowers everywhere.

Once…a long time ago it had been an empty building filled with blood and violence. That was the life I remembered.

The scent of white sage in the air. Without the performers and guests, the place felt almost eerie though like a cavern.

As I walked through two of the girls walked by me, both of them topless with stars covering their nipples and one of them wearing a pair of blue wings.

"Hey, boss," Gianna May was a blonde country girl we'd rescued a few years ago. She was sharper than she looked and Lara's understudy.

She was still learning, but she showed the most spark.

I'd caught her wrapped around Nate Wyatt once or twice and I didn't judge how the girls got around if they needed it.

I just didn't want anyone thinking I was holing up with prostitutes again. Aidan would kill anyone who dared to think so.

The redhead next her eyed me up and down and I tipped my head to her despite her eyes wandering over my chest. I ignored it.

"Ginger."

"Mr. O'Hara."

"Ladies." I moved past them. At least they knew I was somewhat in charge. Lara owned it in name.

Everything in New York was mine. The clubs. The shops.

The merchandise. Everything. Technically the cut that went to Lara was hefty—but I was the owner.

Nobody knew any better which was for the best.

Ginger stopped me before I walked past them, in a breathy voice. "Say...I don't see much of you round here often. You plan on coming by more often or..."

"Ginger," I addressed her calmly peeling her hands off me as Gianna blinked at her friend awestruck at how bold she was. "I have a lady. I'd like to not be felt up."

"Dammnit Ginger!" Gianna grabbed her friend and I bit back a laugh. "I told you he's taken. Man like that's not gonna stay single for long. I'm so sorry, Mr. O'Hara. Some of us are feral and horny."

I tipped my head knowing full well the girls would flirt with a tree if they could.

As I approached Lara's office, an unexpected sound brought me to a halt. Laughter. But not just any laughter—it was Lara's, intertwined with a deep, masculine chuckle.

"Come on, *muneca*."

"*Liam*—"

"You say my first name like I'm in trouble. We have a few—" Liam's response was cut short by a soft giggle from Lara.

"We do not. We can't—"

But she laughed outright at something he did.

I hadn't heard Lara laugh like that ever.

"One more."

"Liam—"

"*Muneca.*"

Lara's laughter was loud and musical as I heard them making out.

I knew that name because Nate used that for Selena. His doll.

Because Selena Tavares according to Nate Wyatt was hot as fuck.

Lara wasn't officially an O'Hara, but she might as well have been—unofficially I'd taken her in like a little sister all those years ago.

The woman behind that door was a far cry from the broken girl that Gabriel had rescued years ago. The one I met over a kitchen table making me breakfast with that brand on her arm. The one my father's men gave her.

She was the reason why I was here. If Gabriel hadn't been invested in saving Lara? None of us would have the life we do.

To the world, she was Lara Ford—strong, independent, and untouchable. But I knew the truth. I remembered the haunted look in her eyes when Gabriel first brought her in.

Gabriel offered her our name as a shield, a new identity to protect her from the ghosts of her past. My father's guys had done a number on her, leaving scars both visible and hidden.

And slowly, as she realized we were nothing like the monsters from her past, she began to trust us. To trust me. Aidan—not so much—but he looked like our father.

In turn, I felt fiercely protective of her since I'd made Teaser's with her and I still remembered the eighteen year old who had wanted to stay in the pile of shit and make something better out of it.

She hadn't wanted to go home.

I didn't have a place to go.

I found myself hesitating, my hand raised to knock. The unfamiliar action set my teeth on edge. This wasn't me. I didn't hesitate. I rapped my knuckles against the door.

The shuffling of feet was followed by the door flying open to reveal a glittering Lara in her sequins and shorts.

"Killian, you made it!" Her smile was radiant. "It's good to have you here. Liam came earlier."

I heard.

"Hey," I managed. I felt oddly out of place.

I opened my mouth to ask Lara about her day, but the words didn't form as my gaze locked onto a figure rising from behind her desk.

Tall and lean, he filled the room with an undeniable darkness.

As he stood, a cane appeared in his grip, each movement deliberate. Measured. Controlled.

But it wasn't the cane that made my skin prickle.

It was his eyes.

Dark green eyes, that should have been bright, alive, but held, shadows in their depths—a darkness I recognized all too well.

It was like looking into a warped mirror, a silent acknowledgment passing between us. Two predators sizing each other up, recognizing the caged monsters we both carried within.

I knew the moment he looked at me, something was wrong with him. Not just the physical disability.

Liam Sullivan.

Oh, he's a little fucked up.

The man who had coaxed laughter from Lara like I'd never heard before. He stood before me now, leaning on his cane, yet radiating a coiled energy that set every instinct I had on high alert. I knew he was taller than me by an inch or two. Enormous, like Reed, but disabled.

Lara's *boyfriend.*

Liam sized me up quietly, his eyes trekking over me, his messy inky hair falling over his eyes.

"Killian, this is Liam."

Liam's fingers moved over the frame of his glasses, adjusting them slightly as his gaze swept over me.

"O'Hara," he said, his voice smooth as polished steel. He extended his hand. "Lara's told me a lot about you."

Has she? That wasn't like her.

There was something about him I couldn't put my finger on.

As we shook, his sleeve rode up slightly, revealing glimpses of corded muscle and the edges of blacked out tattoos.

"I'm so excited for you guys to meet," Lara gushed, her eyes shining with an enthusiasm I'd rarely seen from her naturally in her private life.

"I've told Liam so much about you. Let me go get you both some coffee and tea and cookies and I'll be back!"

Liam's gaze never wavered, studying me with unconcealed curiosity. As Lara slipped out, his eyes softened momentarily, tracking her movements.

"You work security now." He was also the one tracking Lucy Devereaux. And I was pretty sure he was handling the other half of Reed's technical job while Reed kept his family at K2.

A flash of two silver tongue piercings darted out as he talked. I was clocking every single thing about this guy.

"That I am."

"You're working with the Lucas Devereaux case."

"I am." He looked me over and I knew—I fucking knew—he was Agency or he was military. "Lara said good things about you. You guys work together long?"

I tipped my head, not wanting to give Liam anything. I didn't know who he was on paper or how and why Lara finally let herself into another man.

Not since whatever she had with Gabriel's brother.

The door opened, and both of us turned as Lara poked her head in.

"Killian, I ran out of whole milk. Do you want your coffee with cream?"

"Black is fine."

She smiled and ducked back inside. I caught Liam's mouth tipping up at her. Heat in his eyes for her with that mischievous glint.

"You're dating her." I couldn't stop myself. "How's that work?"

He shrugged slightly, turning back to me, and I was aware neither of us had sat down. "The same way you and your nurse work."

Intelligent green eyes peered at me through his glasses.

So he is keeping tabs.

"Lara told me." He said it quietly. "I'm not here to fuck up what you've got with your nurse. I want to take care of Lara just as much as you have… even if she didn't want this life." As he said it, his eyes drifted to mine.

What did he know?

Did Lara tell him?

I didn't know what to say to that. Lara hadn't been with anyone save for Gabriel's brother years ago.

And now she was with Liam?

And turns out I didn't have to as Lara burst back. I would've gone to help her get the door, but Liam moved to her holding it open for her, smiling down at her as he did.

Something about his comfort with her...if he'd just met her, he wouldn't have gotten cozy so fast. Would he?

You kissed Nisha. On day one.

"Liam wanted to go over some security protocols. But I thought we could do both the updates and that together."

Liam turned to Lara, the hard edges of his expression melting away. "*Muñeca*, why don't you share your recent news?"

Lara's cheeks flushed as she straightened, her sequined outfit catching the light. "I'd love to," she said, suddenly eye-level with us despite her petite frame.

Lara's enthusiasm was infectious, her hands painting pictures in the air as she spoke. With each word out of her mouthLiam's eyes tracked her movements, smiling at her not giving a shit I was there.

This was no fling.

But he knows more than he's letting on.

And he's lying to me.

And that cane isn't just a cane.

Lara's voice lilted with excitement as she spoke about her latest project. She'd never been this animated before, not even during her most daring aerial performances.

"Liam said it would be great," she said, a note of uncertainty in her voice. I didn't like how much she relied on Liam. Not because I was jealous. But because the three of us—Aidan and, Kieran, and me—considered her something of a baby sister. She was a little older than Kieran, but it didn't matter.

Lara was five foot nothing and weighed maybe one-ten soaking wet. To us, she was an O'Hara who decently tolerated Kieran.

"You did a great job, *muneca*." He said something in a quick flash of Spanish, and I heard it in his inflections.

Even if I didn't understand, he sounded like...a native. A natural.

Liam reached for a cookie, popping it into his mouth with casual ease, looking out of place in her plush office filled with sex toys and lingerie, but I could tell he was comfortable.

My phone pinged at that moment and I knew it was Nisha going to work.

Another day without my girl.

Around me, I dimly heard Lara talking to Liam.

"Do you want your tea again with honey today?" Lara looked at him with a bright smile. He nodded as she floated around her desk to pour him his tea with his eyes on her while I texted Nisha. "You eat too much sugar, *amor.*"

"Not enough apparently..." he murmured, and Lara turned a bright shade of red.

"Liam—"

"*Muneca.*"

"Eat your cookies."

Liam put his hand on her back, saying something that made her cover her face. She batted his hands away, and it made him grin. Both of them lightly teasing each other again like *I wasn't even fucking there.*

Liam's grin was wide as she laughed at him swiping another cookie.

I caught a flash of ink on his wrist. A name before his sleeve covered it up again.

And even as she said it, I saw he only grabbed the chocolate ones.

The rest were different colors, and fewer of them.

"I got you the chocolate ones because I knew you liked them..."

"I do, muneca. Thank you."

Oh fuck, she's his Nisha.

Despite my lingering suspicions about Liam Sullivan, one thing was clear—whatever Liam was playing at, his feelings for Lara were real.

40

NISHA

KILLIAN AND I BOTH HAD BUSY SCHEDULES.

The hospital nights stretched endlessly, each shift blending into the next as my pregnancy progressed. I couldn't tell Killian much about my job because of HIPAA and Killian, because of his job.

Although in this case. There was something I had to tell him.

At fourteen weeks along, I was just starting to show a tiny bit. Which I took as a good sign. Morning sickness? Was not.

I don't even know how I kept it hidden from everyone when I had to rush into the bathroom so often.

I should've told Killian.

But Killian had told me the extent of what he was juggling, and I couldn't bring myself to add to it.

I knew I should've said something. But...I didn't know why the words didn't form in my mouth. I didn't want to worry him. Stress him out. Make him think I was in a bad way. I wasn't.

Me and the baby were fine which felt a little strange to say, but I wasn't nervous. With Killian as the father? I felt more secure than I ever had. I felt safe and stable.

This wasn't my old life and I could give my future son or daughter a life I only dreamed of.

I just didn't know how to tell him so I kept baking these cupcakes telling myself I would fill it with the color of the baby's gender. Even if we hadn't been together for long?

I deeply trusted Killian to react well. I knew he liked me and everything I wanted just appeared. A man of few words, major actions, and enough love between us for me to feel secure in my relationship.

I saw him *sometimes* and most of the time he had his phone going off. Killian to stay at his place so he could run around in the middle of the night, which made him miserable. As nocturnal as he thought he was, he really liked falling asleep on me.

Right now he was running to Chicago for his brother and juggling Titan here in the city. It had been hectic to say the least.

We hadn't had dinner in forever and it was getting to me. It was eating at my insecurities and while Michelle's voice was quiet?

I still felt anxiety over my pregnancy. The morning sickness didn't help. But neither did my shifts.

Killian wasn't there the days I got sick which was all right with me.

And so his visits became less frequent as his job kept him away, but he made sure I was taken care of every so often he did appear.

Killian had been working a lot with Lucas Devereaux, the real estate tycoon Aidan worked with, and in turn, I got to cope with my nausea and pregnancy symptoms alone.

I was going to find out the gender of the baby soon. I practiced— *I'm pregnant. I'm pregnant. I'm pregnant.*

Over the weeks, Selena's quiet hospital room became my second home.

With her staying in the hospital, our days fell into a rhythm of exercises and rest.

Selena was striking. Magazine-cover beautiful, with dark hair framing her face perfectly and vivid green eyes, slightly tilted and framed by long lashes. Her Cuban accent added a musical lilt to her words.

One afternoon, as I was helping Selena with her exercises, she paused and looked at me intently with her green eyes. "Your skin is pretty. What do you do?"

I blushed, knowing ever since I knew about the baby my skin had indeed changed.

But I still kept up my skincare routine so I didn't think twice about introducing her to it.

I missed the nights with Killian where we both did this together, me sitting on his lap while he grumbled about how cold it felt. And then moments later about how nice it felt.

I missed him.

"Your hair would look great in a bob," I said combing it out for her one day.

Despite her various bruises and injuries, she started recovering solidly once I got her protein shakes in all the time.

And we ate everything Killian and one of Selena's team mates Agent Garrett Fuller brought.

Neither one of us brought up the elephant in the room that upset her. Her husband Agent Watts.

He wasn't allowed to see her after nearly shooting someone over her a few weeks back.

We were all ordered to keep that from her.

Mr. Monroe, Selena's boss, worried about her fragile state, had been clear—*don't discuss anything that would stress her out.*

Killian and Garrett became regulars, bringing foods that unknowingly eased my morning sickness.

I knew Killian didn't know about the baby. But part of him was attuned to me somehow. And I really was dying to tell him.

We're having a girl.

Someone Killian might adore, spoiling her with musical toys, letting her sleep on his chest. I hoped.

Part of me felt anxious. My boyfriend was saving CEOs, juggling Titan projects, helping his brother with real estate.

There was so much on his plate.

He didn't need to know yet he was having a baby right this second.

We were having a baby. *And speaking of babies...*

It was during one of his visits that Killian brought his baby brother, Kieran, to meet me. But this wasn't just a social call; he was requesting a favor with his charge.

A young woman named Avani Malhotra—Alisha's sister—and technically? Reed and Adam's family by extension.

"I'm sorry, luv," Killian gruffly whispered in my ear as he pulled me in front of him to show me the pair standing with pleading eyes. "Kieran's guarding Avani. She wants to know if she can meet Selena."

I blinked, caught off guard.

"You want to see Selena?" I was looking at them incredulously. "Gabriel forbid anyone but me and Adam from seeing her."

"Garrett sees her," Kieran told me.

"Garrett is a gentle giant," I argued quietly crossing my arms over my chest. "The man is six-feet-six on the outside and a mouse on the inside."

"Please, Nisha," Kieran looked at me with his hands clasped. "Avani was with her when the incident happened. It would mean a lot. She's even more mousy than Garrett."

He motioned to Avani standing here with her chestnut hair and dark doe eyes blinking back at me. She was eagerly nodding at that.

Behind me I felt Killian shift and I turned to look over my shoulder. He was shaking his head at Kieran.

Mismatched eyes flickered to me. "Your choice, luv."

My throat worked as I turned back to Kieran and Avani. As adorable as Kieran was—I was protective of Selena. "She's very fragile right now. I can't her being upset by her memories. She's not doing well and she's healing. If either one of you two upset her—"

"I won't," Avani murmured in a thicker English accent, holding up an e-reader. "I want to give her some books and see her." Her eyes were wet. "I promise to be quick."

The duo stood in front of me looking like guilty children asking me for a cookie.

Kieran's amber eyes widened adorably as he pleaded. "Please, Nisha. I won't ask you for anything ever again."

And he looked so much like Killian. This was my first time meeting him. Kieran was absolutely the troublemaker of the brothers. But right now both of them wanted a quick second with Selena. I knew that was how they saw it.

I knew it was deeper than that. Selena was shaken up by her attack.

"Yes, you would," I whispered. "I just don't want Selena being upset."

"She won't be—" Avani broke off looking at me and Killian. "Just once."

And rather than looked ashamed Kieran grinned slowly. "Please? Just a few minutes. Gabriel will never know."

That's what I was afraid of. Gabriel Monroe was not the kind of man you kept things from.

I blew out a breath and looked at Killian who watched me.

"Now I see why he's a troublemaker."

My boyfriend pressed his lips together to stop himself from laughing as he ducked his head. "It's your call, luv."

Combined with his chocolate hair was in contrast to Killian's exhausted expression and darker features.

Though handsome like his brother, Kieran was Killian's opposite in demeanor. And he knew I was heisting only because the last time Selena was triggered she screamed bloody murder and wouldn't relax without medication.

It was part of the reason why Gabriel kept her boyfriend Kellan Watts away from her.

"Nisha, I will do *anything* you want me to do—"

"You're terrible," I laughed, and Kieran's grin only widened.

Killian closed his eyes, rubbing his temples but I caught his smile.

I felt a wave of sympathy for Killian.

How could I say no to them?"

"She's very delicate," I added with caution. "But I understand why you want to see her. No riling her up. No comments about what happened to her even if she asks. Just positive self-talk and good things. Mr. Monroe wants Selena to heal. Not be hurt over and over. Is that clear with both of you?"

Avani nodded, her mocha eyes wide with sincerity. "I understand."

I was weak in the face of their pleading looks. Meeting Killian's baby brother for the first time since he'd arrived in the city added an extra layer of pressure, and Avani's genuine worry was palpable.

I chewed my lip as Killian stood beside me not saying a word but frowning at Kieran. Who was absolutely adorable as he looked at both of us.

"You cannot go inside the room with Avani," I told Kieran.

"But Garrett—"

"Garrett and Adam are different—"

"Why?" And then he flashed me a smile.

Ohhhh, he was definitely the baby.

"Does any woman resist your smile?" I had to ask wryly.

He grinned wider motioning to Avani who turned a bright pink fidgeting with her charm bracelet on her wrist.

I glanced at Killian, who sighed at his brother's persistence. He shook his head at me and we shared a look.

"All right," I conceded, my resolve crumbling. "I'll give you thirty minutes, not a second more."

At that, Avani squealed and enveloped me in a tight hug, her perfume surrounding me and for a moment throwing me off. I instantly felt Killian at my back steadying me.

Kieran flashed another grin, his amber eyes twinkling. "Thanks, sis." My heart flipped as he said the words to me.

"Wait outside her door I'll meet you guys there," I was struggling to keep my composure as Avani grinned.

"Good to finally meet you," Kieran said with a wink, catching me off guard. "My brother's ape shit about you and I can see why. Hot as fuccck."

Killian all but growled as Kieran hauled Avani out, the two of them darting off with laughter. I laughed up at Killian's scowl.

"He asked me to finesse," he admitted, running a hand through his hair. "Sorry, luv."

"Don't think you're getting off as easy as them," I teased, my heart quickening at our proximity. "I have a price for my favors."

"Oh?" Killian dipped his head, hovering tantalizingly close to my lips. "Name it, luv."

I pretended to think about it as he smiled wider, his eyes tired but amused on me. I pursed my lips at him.

"Kisses."

"Hmm," he murmured pretending to consider it, leaning in to brush his lips softly against mine. He said the words against my lips. "How many?"

"As many as you have," I breathed, laughing into his kisses.

"I don't know, luv. I got plenty."

When he kissed me, everything calmed down inside of me. The effect he had on me was instant as he brushed his tongue over mine over and over until I tipped my head back.

His groan was low as he ate at my mouth all hot and heady.

My heart stopped racing, my entire body eased and I sighed leaning into him.

I forgot how relaxing it was to be in his arms, strong and like iron holding me to him. I could sleep forever in his arms.

Right now, kissing him, every rational thought in my head faded and I wanted to stay here forever.

"It feels like I haven't seen you in forever," I gasped. "I wish you could stay."

"Me too," he murmured gruffly, kissing me softer this time. I could feel his arousal against my stomach.

I laughed low at his dark eyes. "No," I shook my head. "We have to go find out where those two ran off too."

He sighed loudly and I laughed harder.

His mouth dropped over mine in the quiet moment. "Saw you had the clinic on the calendar, are you good? You got cramps, luv? You need anything from me for real?"

And there it was. That was why I loved him. He did pay attention, he did know things—and I felt like a horrible girlfriend for not letting him know. But telling your significant other you were pregnant was not the same as telling him you need parmesan cheese picked up from the supermarket.

I wanted to go home with a pregnancy test, cupcakes, and maybe a little onesie. I wanted the moment to be special because it was important to me. But I also wanted it to be special for him.

I was planning.

Just then Killian's fingers brushed over my abdomen and I swear I felt our daughter move. I swear. But it was too early I was just imagining it.

"Luv? Are you okay?" Those eyes of his watched me. "Tell me if anything is wrong."

"No, just a regular checkup." I breathed out quickly. "Not cramping just normal. Let's talk about it when you're home, yeah?"

My chest twisted at lying to him, but I knew him and I could already see him rushing off to get what he needed.

Killian's dark brows drew down on his face. "Luv."

"I know, you worry. But you're working really hard, and I don't want to be the reason why you worry."

His lips brushed my pulse. "You'll let me know if you need anything? Don't want anything happening to you."

"I will," I whispered, my hands gripping his shoulders to steady myself against the wave of emotions and sensations.

"I'm sorry, luv. I'm drowning. Otherwise I'd stay longer."

I know. And I have to go home and bake cupcakes.

Because we're having a girl.

"It's okay. I'm okay." *We're okay.* "Let's go make sure the kids follow my rules."

He chuckled softly. "Mhm."

I told myself I'd just tell Killian later.

Right now, I kissed him with everything I had.

It's not like I could tell a man he was having a baby and have him run off.

41

KILLIAN

Lucas Devereaux had been shot.

The attacks had finally gotten to him.

Gabriel had been with him which meant I fucking knew Gabriel would find out Lucas was dating his sister.

Lucas had been hit in the arm and Reed called me to tell Aidan. Who called me. Both of us had shown up to the hospital and I sent Derek and Landon to scope out the area.

Through the glass of Lucas's room, I could see Reed, phone pressed to his ear, his face a mask of controlled urgency.

Evie lay curled into Lucas's side crying like she had for a long time.

She looked so much like Nisha it ached a little to watch her broken. Gabriel knew and he wasn't anywhere near her for once processing his own emotions.

And I felt more for Lucas then. Him and his shit situation. The whole someone wanting to kill him for something he didn't do. Gabriel hating him for things he couldn't control. And the list went on for the guy.

Gabriel had discovered their relationship on his own, and his reaction had been as volatile as expected.

Reed had managed to corral Gabriel into a separate room where he could be pissed off without attacking everyone else.

Lucas was nothing like his father, but Gabriel's rage was going to mow over everyone.

I stuck by whoever needed me.

It only got worse if Aidan appeared. Whenever the three of them stood in the same room, I felt the energy turn dark, murky, and get harder to breathe around them.

Even for me, it was a lot.

The first night had been chaos, with Reed and Adam fully engaged in Lucas's care. Now, a fragile calm had settled over the ward. I saw my chance.

Nisha.

Aidan was here. I could introduce her to him.

And then tell her who I was. I would after she met him. Aidan would love her. I knew he would.

I approached Adam, noting the weariness etched into his features. His usually pristine appearance was disheveled, mirroring my own state.

"I know this isn't ideal," I said, choosing my words carefully. "But I'd like Aidan to meet Nisha. He's not here for long, and with her looking after Tavares…"

"You want Nisha to meet Aidan?"

Adam's eyes flickered towards Aidan, then back to me.

"Yes."

He nodded. "Let me go get her."

Relief washed over me. *Good man.*

Both Reed and his brother shared that trait—always stepping up, always doing what needed to be done.

I followed Adam and through the window in Tavares's room I caught sight of Nisha. She was curled up in a chair, her face bathed in the glow of her e-reader—the one I'd given her after she'd mentioned Tavares's love for books. She was reading tonight. And she looked cozy.

I waited outside as Adam went to talk to her. I didn't wanna scare Tavares. Nisha was out a second later and in my arms.

"I'm sorry," I blurted out, the words escaping before I could rein them in.

I'm sorry, luv.

"Missed you," she murmured, her voice soft against my chest. "Don't be sorry, I didn't know you were working tonight. I thought something happened to you."

I drew back, gently framing her face with my hands. "Missed you too, luv. I know the timing's not great, but—"

"It's okay," she said, her eyes full of understanding. "I get it. Adam told me Aidan is here?"

I nodded feeling myself take a deep breath and steel myself.

I took her to the hallway where Aidan was. And of course, he found us instantly. Even from a distance, the intensity of his stare was unmistakable.

My brother's presence was a force unto itself, worlds apart from Gabriel's. Aidan radiated raw power. Right now in Chicago, I knew he was juggling a few problems of his own.

I knew all about Aidan's empire he built from the shadows. I had been there until he pawned me off to Gabriel.

Something I'd always be grateful for.

My older brother was something else—he always had been. Sometimes I thought he resembled our father if Cormac had any soul left in him. Aidan still had heart and I thought he secretly got along with Lucas because they were both closet nerds.

The hospital lights accentuated the hard planes of his face right now and I knew he was tired.

He looked like a mean regal motherfucker. A knot of worry formed in my gut at introducing Nisha to him.

Putting Nisha next to him was like a hummingbird and a jaguar in the same space. One of them did not fit in.

And I was worried now.

Her small frame appeared even more delicate next to his imposing presence.

I stepped forward, protective instinct kicking in, as Nisha looked up at him.

"Hi, you must be Aidan," Nisha's voice was steady despite the subtle tension in her shoulders. She held out her hand.

"Aidan, this is—"

"*Nisha.*" Aidan's voice was a low rumble.

His eyes never left her face as a half-smile played at the corners of his mouth. He extended his hand, the movement deliberate and graceful despite his size. "I've heard a lot about you. Never a good time, is it?"

"All good things, I hope," Nisha murmured, her smaller hand disappearing into his as they shook. "I don't mind."

She never did mind.

My fucking sweetheart. A wave of tenderness washed over me at my girl holding her own.

It had been ages since I had her. Since I could stop. Since dinner. Nighttime movies.

Where the fuck had my summer gone?

Standing there, Aidan and I flanking Nisha, the top of her head barely reached my chest, and next to Aidan's broad frame, she seemed almost fragile.

I was in unfamiliar ground wanting to hold her tight to me and protect her from the world while simultaneously introducing her to *my* world.

"How'd my brother land you?" Aidan smiled, his tone playful as he looked at her. An unfamiliar sensation burned in my chest. I wasn't jealous of Aidan? Was I? Why? Nisha wouldn't—

"I can assure you, I landed him." Nisha's laugh, low and warm, cut through the tension as she leaned into me. "He's been wonderful." And just like that, just like she'd done the Farmer's Market, Nisha diffused everything in me. Her hand flattened on my chest as she smiled up at Aidan.

"Is that so?" He glanced at her, a newfound respect in his eyes. He had caught the way she touched me. "I don't think Killian fought back once—"

Nisha laughed. "No, he didn't. Killian's great. He's told me so much about you…" As she talked I watched her, the ends of her waves curling a bit more, she instinctively reached for my arm, lacing her arm through mine as she held me listening to Aidan.

Who I knew didn't miss *anything*.

"Has he?" Aidan kept his voice low as he drew closer. "You should take my number down. If Killian ever decides to not be great, you can call me. I'll straighten him out."

"I'm not sure that's necessary," I interjected feeling defensive. Like I would ever hurt Nisha. "She's fine—"

"No truly—" Nisha murmured breaking off. "It's all right." She looked embarrassed too.

"I need to borrow him for a few days," Aidan said, his eyes still fixed on Nisha as she saved his number. "You can have my brother back then. Text me if you ever need anything."

The worry I felt ebbed into cautious hope that Aidan liked her. I knew my brother. He never gave his information out to anyone.

And he was passing Nisha his info like they'd known each other for years. I saw the way he watched her. Reading into her. Aidan was one of those people who knew people from a mile away.

He read into everyone.

And he liked Nisha.

I felt my entire body sigh in relief as I played with the ends of her hair while she talked to Aidan softly.

42

NISHA

While I was helping Selena Tavares, Adam had begun working for Titan officially with his brother.

He'd texted me someone's info, named Sonya Amin, and he said she wouldn't mind me messaging her for a potential job offer.

He explained Sonya worked at a women's shelter and he thought I might want to check it out.

> Her name is Sonya Amin. She's good friends with Alisha, Reed's girlfriend, and she's starting a new project.

> I think you'd be perfect for it.

When I had, Sonya had agreed to meet with me at a Turkish coffee shop.

Intrigued, I found myself agreeing to meet her. Even if I wasn't actively looking for a new opportunity, Adam wasn't wrong about the importance of networking.

Unlike the Titans, who seemed to have wealth at their fingertips, I didn't have much to fall back on.

As I got ready for the meeting, my phone buzzed with a message from Killian.

> The coffee shops name is 'A Steamy Dream'...

> Sonya thought it would be funny. She said influencers love it.

> Luv, you're meeting Sonya Devereaux?

> I thought it was Amin. Adam said she was finalizing her divorce.

I sent Killian the location, and he thumbed it up, adding.

> Let me know if you need anything, luv.

But he was busy as always.

I found Sonya inside the eclectic little cafe in one of the cozy nooks.

I knew it was her since nobody else had a designer bag set on the table, her hair luxuriously deep brown, and the way she carried herself —Sonya came from money. I knew that much.

As if sensing my arrival, she looked up, and I found myself caught in the intensity of her darker green eyes.

"Nisha," she said, her voice warm and tinged with an accent I couldn't quite place. "I'm so glad you could make it. Would you like anything to eat?"

"Your accent is beautiful."

She blushed then and her smile was breathtaking. "Thank you. I'm Turkish. My parents live there, but I moved to the States with—" she broke off abruptly, something flickering across her face too quickly for me to read as she ducked her head almost embarrassed. "I live here now."

Her ex.

I'd looked Sonya up online before our meeting and knew about her recent divorce, but it felt invasive to bring it up. I didn't want to make her feel uncomfortable.

Instead, I opened my mouth to ask about the project, but before I could speak, a waiter approached a nearby table with a tray of food.

The scent of spices and olive oil hit me and my nose.

My stomach, which had been relatively calm until now, suddenly lurched uncomfortably. I felt the color drain from my face as I fought against a rising tide of nausea.

Oh no, I thought desperately, *not now. Please, not now.*

But as Sonya's concerned gaze met mine, I knew it was already too late. "Nisha? Are you alright?"

I pressed a hand to my mouth, desperately trying to hold back the rising tide of nausea.

"I'm sorry," I managed to gasp. "I need to..."

I didn't finish the sentence. Baby girl did not like anything.

The thought flashed through my mind as I stumbled to my feet, nearly knocking over my chair in my haste.

I caught a glimpse of Sonya's worried face as I rushed towards the restroom sign I'd noticed earlier.

Behind me, I heard Sonya's voice, tinged with worry, but I couldn't make out the words over the roaring in my ears.

The world narrowed to a tunnel as I focused on reaching the bathroom before I embarrassed myself further. I threw up everything I had eaten that morning into the trash can, not even making it to the toilet.

A gentle knock on the door startled me.

"Nisha?"

Before I could respond, I felt Sonya's warmth beside me, her arm steadying me as she gently held my hair back.

The kindness of the gesture made my throat tighten with unexpected emotion. I shook my head weakly as another wave of nausea hit.

My morning sickness had been relentless lately, exacerbated by anxiety and the growing weight of my secret.

The longer I went without telling anyone, especially Killian, the harder it became to say the words.

As the nausea subsided to a dull roil, I became acutely aware of the awkwardness of the situation.

Here I was, throwing up in front of a woman I'd just met for a potential job opportunity.

Embarrassment flooded through me.

"I haven't told anyone..."

"It's okay—"

"I'm so sorry," I started, mortification coloring my voice. "This was not how I wanted to meet you—"

"No, don't apologize," Sonya interrupted. "You're fine. There are worse ways to meet people, believe me." The sound of the paper towel dispenser filled the small space as she handed me some.

"Are you...ill?" Sonya murmured, concern evident in her tone. "Or do you need anything?"

I shook my head, trying to steady myself against the cool tile wall. "I'm not sick..." I trailed off, unsure how to continue.

In that moment, looking into Sonya's concerned green eyes, I felt a sudden, overwhelming urge to confide in someone.

With jarring realization, I understood that Sonya would be the first person I told who wasn't a medical professional.

Even though Adam had introduced me to Alisha Malhotra, Reed's girlfriend, she had been away with Reed for the last few weeks.

I didn't know who to tell or who to turn to and the loneliness of my position hit me. A lifetime of being alone had taught me to be alone.

Maybe I didn't have to be though...

"I'm pregnant," I whispered. I watched Sonya's face, searching for her reaction, half-expecting shock or judgment.

Instead, her expression softened, a small smile tugging at the corners of her mouth.

"Ah. Morning sickness?"

"Although it seems to have missed the memo about sticking to mornings," I added with a watery smile. I was grateful her reaction was one of empathy and nothing but warmth.

Sonya's smile widened, her eyes crinkling with warmth. "I have heard," she said, a hint of knowing in her voice. "How far along are you?"

"About sixteen weeks going on seventeen," I replied, marveling at how natural it felt to share this with her. "I haven't told anyone else yet."

Sonya's emerald eyes softened. "Is he—"

"He's in my life," I answered. "He's wonderful."

"Your husband?" She looked at my ring finger.

"No," I hadn't thought that far and I just felt embarrassed.

He worked for Titan and his job was crazy and he didn't...

"I'm not one to judge you. Lord knows I have enough complications in my own life." She smiled a little rubbing my back. "Are you going to be all right?"

I nodded. "Just disgusted now. Sorry, I tried to be perfect—"

"You don't ever have to be perfect—"

"But I met you for a job interview," I protested weakly. "and here I am, throwing up in the bathroom—"

Sonya made a dismissive noise, waving her hand. "You're all right," she assured me, her grin widening. "I'm not too concerned with the perception of perfection these days. I'm learning to let that go."

Her eyes met mine, a shared understanding passing between us.

"Perhaps it's something we both could work on, hmm?"

Sonya was infinitely kind to me then as she stood there helping me.

In that moment, surrounded by the lingering scent of Turkish coffee and the cool tile of the bathroom, I felt a weight lift from my shoulders.

Sonya's acceptance, her easy dismissal of the need for perfection—it felt like something I didn't even know I needed.

I didn't have many women in my life that were close to me. Some wounds ran too deep and I didn't like letting people in.

But Sonya felt different.

At one point as we were talking, she straightened her shoulders back all of a sudden, adjusting her posture like someone lifted her like a marionette puppet. *Wait a minute...*

Now I knew why Sonya felt familiar to me.

"Were you a dancer?"

Her eyes widened in surprise, a flash of recognition passing between us. "Are you—"

"No, I'm a musician—or I was now I run a blog—I just noticed the way you stood just now, your shoulders, your back...I went to school with ballerinas."

Her smile turned wistful. Her eyes becoming guarded and I caught a shadow of pain in them. "I was...I did ballroom dancing after I couldn't do ballet. Too hippy..."

"If *you're* too hippy, I'm a hippo." I had always had comments about my weight despite being at a normal weight for my height.

Sonya laughed, blushing and waving that comment off. *"Nonsense."*

In that moment, I realized Sonya was...just like me.

"Why did you stop?"

She shrugged slightly, the movement looking almost out of character on her elegant frame.

"Life," she said simply, her gaze drifting around the tiny restroom. "I got married." Her eyes met mine again, a world of unspoken history in them. "I got divorced."

I nodded, understanding all too well how life could derail our plans.

The familiarity of her story struck a chord deep within me, reminding me of the choices and compromises I'd made in my own journey.

"Your ex-husband didn't like your dancing?" I was curious now.

There was a darkness in her eyes as she shook her head. "No. He did not." She tucked her hair behind her ear. "My ex-husband didn't like anything about me...and I spent a long time trying to be perfect. You don't ever have to be perfect with me."

Relief coursed through me.

Her eyes met mine and I knew she was trying to connect with me. To let me in after she'd seen me going through this.

But Killian encouraged me.

I'm going to tell him.

And we just stood there as Sonya told me a bit about Haven.

"You'd still hire me even if I was pregnant?"

She nodded. "Yes, I'm not in the business of shaming women for wanting a family."

As she said it her eyes went dark again for some reason but she pressed on.

"Nor would I not cover your maternity leave. It's hard finding the right people and I'm not an employer who would hurt you at a vulnerable moment. You can think about it..." she motioned to my stomach. "And for now, maybe some lemonade might help?"

"That sounds amazing." My heart was pounding now but for another reason. "But I don't know if I want to work at Haven full time. I actually have been debating other avenues for myself, but I thought I'd come meet you. I'm sorry—Was that silly of me?"

"No, you can tell me all about it since I am free." Sonya's eyes were bright. "Come, I think they have something sour and tart here which should help with the baby."

"Do you have children?" She knew a lot about pregnancy like me.

Something crossed her features as I asked the question.

"No," she shook her head. "I don't have any children. But I know enough. Shall we?"

I let Sonya lead me out of the bathroom aware I had just made a friend. And it felt really good.

We talked every so often, but Sonya was easy to get along with despite her social background.

At thirty, she had experience I didn't and leaving her husband behind had given her a newfound confidence.

We did talk about Haven, but mostly, Sonya and I talked like we had been friends for years. Maybe me being vulnerable and letting her in made her feel comfortable.

When I left her? I didn't want to go.

I felt so hungry for connection with a woman who I had so much in common with I didn't want to lose it.

"In my culture we don't always say goodbye, sometimes we say to go happily or I trust your God will take care of you—" Sonya broke off. "I trust we will meet again in the future whether you choose to work at Haven or we just stay friends. I could use more girlfriends. Besides Alisha always likes us to get together. Maybe your future husband can babysit your daughter and you can come out with us."

I beamed at the thought. "It's date."

43

KILLIAN

Training Watts was a challenge.

But not an insurmountable one.

He was six-feet-two inches of muscle and pretty boy blonde hair and blue eyes. And a naivety that came from a decent upbringing.

Parents were Fed's. Sister was a lawyer. Do-gooders all around.

That was the irony about Titan, they didn't give a damn where they hired from so long as everyone kept their mouths shut.

Watt's mother was in the BAU, behavioral analysis unit of the FBI and so Watts had a lot of skills an average civilian wouldn't have.

And he had one weakness.

Selena Tavares. Who had been injured when she'd gotten caught up by a serial killer.

That *one* weakness was why he was my pet project.

Get me a better operative, Killian. He's pissing me off.

That had been Gabriel's words. Not mine.

But he was pissing me off too.

Watts was softer than most people in his own ways. Probably why Tavares liked him. The goodness in his eyes was still there. Or it had been. The last few weeks of training had reshaped it. Now they were harder and darker.

The kid had potential but needed to learn fast in our world.

Today, we were in my car waiting outside a local dive bar to get to an informant gone rogue. Selling information he shouldn't have been. Gabriel wanted him taken care of.

"You know the plan?"

"Go in, ID the target, distract him—you'll do the rest."

"And if something goes wrong?"

"Kill him."

Watts and I went in, plain clothes and casual my tattoos completely covered in all black. I spotted the target already.

Hector Valencia. Third-rate criminal. At best. Short-motherfucker with an ego that needed to be scraped off with his skin. I grimaced. I could already tell he was a piece of shit with his beady eyes and reddish hair.

Watts made his way to the pool table and I planted myself at the bar keeping a casual eye on the target when one of the female bartenders walked up to me.

"Anything I can do for her?" She raked her eyes up and down my body.

I leaned in, feeling none of it since her eyes were too bright telling she was on something. And she smelled like cheap perfume. For a moment, I swore I felt Nisha's voice in my head, but I quickly pushed her out of the way. Thinking about Nisha was going to get me killed in a time like this.

I loved her too much to focus on anything.

"Whatever's on tap," I tipped her a fifty. Her eyes widened a bit, and she quickly hustled over. Money always made people move.

I casually glanced over at Valencia. He hadn't moved. But when my eyes moved over to Watts casually hanging out, I stopped. That was the thing about working with Watts.

You couldn't send every operative into every situation.

Some operatives were suited for places like this.

Watts wasn't. And he was attracting some attention. And not the good kind. I needed to speed this up.

The bartender came back with the beer, but I caught the bikers eyeing Watts. Fuck my life with this pretty boy. Watts was a poster child for some Ivy League colleges. *Motherfucker.* That was why he was Tavares's partner and not mine.

I bit back a sigh as the lady bartender leaned in trying to flash her tits at me and I look at her larger pupils of blue.

"Anything else I can do for you, baby?"

Mentally? I grimaced. But my poker face was solid.

"Yeah, you can go over to College Football back there and get him a drink." That should help. She eyed Watts then.

"Bit clean up for this place," she said casually.

"Looks like it, better help him out." I slid a hundred on the table, and she was off. Thank fuck. Five minutes. I needed five minutes.

My attention moved back to Valencia. I needed to go. He was getting antsy, his eyes darting towards the door.

I needed to move now.

Whatever deal he had was happening and soon, and he wanted to get the fuck out of here. I didn't touch the beer, and I made my way over to him.

"Hey, is that sedan outside yours?" I kept my voice light. "Man, I think someone slashed your tires. Just a heads up, man." And I clapped him on the back and moved away just a little, keeping it casual.

He swore as he threw some bills on the table. "Fucking kids—"

"Every time." I smirked. "College kids don't know when to quit."

And as he moved to get up I made it look like I was leaving from the back. I caught Watts with the woman trying to wrap herself around him. As he caught me leaving, I figured he could untangle himself. Better her than the bikers who were now looking away.

Couples made people uncomfortable. I learned that in my line of work. You put a couple together and nobody bat an eyelash. Probably why the Titan teams were paired. People saw what they wanted to see. Single guy flirting with a bartender was one of them.

I followed Valencia out the back door, and I saw him frowning as he walked over to his car. Someone had slashed his tire. Me.

"Hey! You found it," I called, injecting some of Kieran's humor into my voice. "Need a hand?"

Valencia looked over at me, suspicion warring with the desperation he felt. Some people just weren't meant to be criminals. But I was.

And I was trained by the best.

"You got anything in your car?"

"Sure do," I grinned. "It's over here. Let me go get it, you don't gotta follow me—"

"Nah, I need to get the fuck home—" That he did. Too bad he wasn't gonna make it.

He followed me. Hook, line, and sinker.

"It's around the corner." I walked ahead of him so he wouldn't be afraid, and the moment he was close enough? I was on him.

Years of training kicked in, and he didn't have a fucking chance.

Before he could react, I had my fist in his face, his solar plexus driving the air from his lungs in two hits.

He doubled over, gasping like a fish out of water.

"Sup, Hector." I shifted to my natural voice, getting tired of playing the good boy. "You've been selling intel to the wrong folks. *Playing both sides—*"

"*You're a—*"

"*I'm your worst fucking nightmare—*" I growled. "*That's what I fucking am.*" I took out my gun and shoved it into his throat. "And you so much as scream, I will fucking blow your brains out."

His eyes were terrified.

"You're gonna tell me who you're selling information to." I grinned shoving the gun into his throat deeper. "There's a start."

44

KILLIAN

"Did you have to kill him?"

Watt's was holding a frozen bag of peas to his bloody lip and swollen cheeks. Turns out, the bikers had decided to go after him.

And I didn't know Watts could fight dirty.

Once I knocked out Valencia into the trunk of our nondescript sedan, I had gone back for Watts.

Who had between in the middle of a fucking brawl with three guys.

And then I saw what he was hiding underneath that fucking pretty-boy exterior. Watts was lethal. No wonder they paired him with Tavares. Or they had. Gabriel still had a ban on Watts going anywhere near her.

I didn't realize where that hot-headed temper came from.

Now? I saw it in action.

"How many did you kill?" I glanced his way driving down the dimly lit road. I had to bury Valencia currently dead.

"None. I broke the first idiots arm though." And he almost stabbed one of them. Not too bad. He'd held his own.

"Where'd you learn to fight?"

He smirked at me through his cut lip. "The college brochure I came out of."

My lips stretched into a wider grin. "I need to dump Valencia and then we have another tasker tonight."

Watts and I moved on to short tasks, kill requests, and interrogations. Watts struggled with the last one.

Torture wasn't his forte, but in our line of work, it was sometimes a necessary evil. I counted Watts' mistakes, shaking my head.

Finally, I stepped in and shot the motherfucker in the hand until he confessed. And when he did, I just shot him in the head.

Watts stared at me, mouth open, as Derek and Landon cleaned up. A harsh lesson, but a vital one.

To his credit, Watts improved.

Our next extraction went smoother—him on perimeter, me on the asset. In and out, clean and quick. No casualties. Progress.

This week's target was a slippery bastard.

Three countries, five identities, selling Titan secrets to the highest bidder. Gabriel's orders were clear: no extraction, no interrogation. Too risky. I tracked him down in 24 hours.

The objective was simple—take him out from two hundred yards.

As Watts and I set up on the rooftop, my mind wandered to my next problem—Kieran's latest bender.

I thought he had gotten better.

But I figured withdrawal was a bitch to go through.

I was going through Nisha withdrawal.

The long hours, the longer days—combined with not seeing her? Made a cranky son-of-a-bitch.

If Watts hadn't lost his temper, I'd be with her now instead of babysitting this hothead who couldn't get within ten feet of Tavares. Still, he was my responsibility.

I was training him the way Gabriel had trained me, hoping he'd learn to think before acting.

In our world, that difference could mean life or death.

After the chaos at Titan manor, with Talon emerging as a new threat, everything had shifted.

Aidan's intel from Alexei painted a grim picture—Talon, a unit created by Malcolm Nash now potentially run by his daughters.

Their targets?

Reed. Lucy Devereaux.

And Gabriel wasn't say shit.

I had to take a deep breath. Because Aidan, while he cared, wanted to know how big of a threat this was to us.

To his empire. That was it.

Gabriel's secrets be damned. He wanted to know if we could protect ourselves.

Once we got the information, we knew the unit's name was Talon.

And we knew they weren't as much of a threat to the O'Hara name. But Reed? Reed and Lucy were in danger.

Because this was all about Lucy and *a fucking necklace.* In other words. Not my concern. No, that was all Liam's now.

In the middle of all this chaos, Gabriel did something unprecedented—he left the manor.

In seven years of working with him, I'd never seen Gabriel step foot outside those walls haunting the damn place.

A few days later, Reed took his place at the manor.

For about three weeks, I'd been juggling his training with everything else.

And there I was, stuck in the middle, missing Nisha like a physical ache and dealing with Watts' bullshit.

Then Aidan called, his voice tight with concern.

Kieran hadn't checked in with Gabriel or him.

And it wasn't like him to renege on his deal to Aidan.

I glanced at Watts beside me. Even here, in this grimy underground garage, he looked like he'd stepped out of an Ivy League brochure.

Blonde surfer hair combed back, bright blue eyes alert, his navy suit crisp and pristine.

"Where exactly are we?"

"This place runs on discretion. Members pay for it, and Kieran's rules are strict. Unlike Teo's."

The keycard slid into the slot with a soft click, a sound that seemed to echo in the tense silence.

"Do not speak. Do not say a word. Not a fucking move against my orders, clear?"

"Crystal."

White plush carpet swallowed our footsteps.

Colorful doors lined the corridor, each one hiding stories I'd rather forget.

Muffled sounds leaked through the walls. Moans, cries, laughter— the soundtrack of depravity.

We stopped at the Topaz Suite. My fingers hovered over the keypad, a moment of hesitation.

"If it doesn't open, I'm shooting it," I growled, the weight of my gun suddenly very present. "It'll alert the guards, but if Kieran's dead on the other side, I'm killing everyone in this place. *Starting with Teo.*"

The keypad beeped green. Thank fuck.

My stomach turned, but my face remained impassive. I'd seen worse.

I turned to Watts, his blue eyes wide in his pale face.

"Not a word," I mouthed.

We stepped inside, and the smoke enveloped us.

Half-naked, sprawled in a chair, a shell of the man I knew. *Kieran.*

Watts coughed beside me, his eyes watering. I barely noticed. All I could see was Kieran, his tattoos stark against his too-pale skin, ribs visible as he took a shaky drag from whatever he was smoking.

The ropes, the restraints, the passed-out women—one still bound to the bed. I'd been here before, in more ways than one. But seeing Kieran like this...it was like looking in a fucked-up mirror.

"Shut the door, Watts," I growled, not taking my eyes off Kieran.

The beep of the door closing echoed in the quiet room. I moved on autopilot, opening windows, pulling back curtains. Kieran spat curses in Gaelic. I ignored him, tossing a wad of bills on the bed.

My eyes swept over the scene.

Blood on the sheets, on the girls.

The table was a pharmacy's wet dream—lines of powder, pills in every color of the rainbow.

Knives glinted next to long-barreled guns. I knew exactly what Kieran did with those.

I looked at my brother, really looked at him. His eyes were glazed, unfocused. Alive, but barely there. Something in my chest tightened. I'd worn that look before.

Never thought I'd see it on Kieran. I tried in Gaelic. No response. Switching to English, I asked. "How fucked up are you?"

Kieran slurred something unintelligible, desperation leaking through the haze. I glanced at the drugs and motioned for Watts to clear them.

Kieran's head lifted slowly, his eyes finding Watts. I'd never seen them so cold, so empty.

"I wasn't finished," he mumbled, voice thick.

I held up a hand, stopping Watts in his tracks. This was delicate. Push too hard, and Kieran might snap. Not enough, and we'd lose him to whatever hell he was trying to drown in.

"You're finished, little brother," I growled, shoving my shoulder under Kieran's arm. I motioned for Watts to take the other side. The kid hesitated for a split second, then moved. *Good.*

"We need to get out of here, take him to Adam. He's tracking this already," I said, keeping my voice low. Watts nodded, remembering my earlier warning.

As we dragged Kieran's dead weight out of the suite, I caught Watts taking in the surroundings. The elegant walls, the color-coded doors.

I decided to fill in the blanks. "That is one of the Topaz Suite rooms. This place uses a color code system. You have to know someone to get in. Topaz is Kieran's." I paused, meeting Watts' eyes. "The colors signify people. One floor above us, the Sapphire on the doors? Dupont. Go down this way, we'll get back to the car quicker," I motioned to a different elevator. "No guards. Easier."

Kieran slumped against Watts in the backseat, gulping down the electrolyte drink like a man dying of thirst.

In the harsh light of the car, the evidence of his night was written all over his body—bruises, scratches. Rope burns.

Watts helped Kieran with the window.

"Didn't Reed just give him his break after Avani?" Watts blurted out.

I watched Kieran in the rearview mirror. At the mention of her name, something flickered in his eyes.

"*Avani...*" he murmured.

Watts, trying to be helpful, said softly. "Avani's safe. Remember?"

Kieran's reply is what made me frown. "*Not from me...*"

Fuck.

The pieces fell into place. Weeks on the job. The women on the bed —brunettes.

Kieran lost his mind over a girl he was supposed to protect.

I caught Watts' eye in the mirror.

He'd figured it out too. I shook my head, warning him off. This wasn't the time or place.

"You need to text Gabriel, now. Tell him, Eros is cleared," I said, cutting through the tension.

But I couldn't tell Gabriel, my little brother was bent out of shape over a girl he couldn't have—little Avani Malhotra would never belong to Kieran and it was a hard reality he'd have to get used to.

45

NISHA

"He's coming down hard," Killian's jaw clenched tight. "I'll stay with you."

Out of all the ways to see Killian to tell him I was pregnant, bringing his little brother in for a drug overdose, had not been one of them.

I'd seen addicts before, but never someone I *knew*. Never family.

Because that's what Kieran was now—family.

Or he would be, once Killian and I...the thought trailed off as I focused the problem at hand. We weren't getting married or anything but I felt this desperation in Killian whenever he looked at me ever since he'd left for Chicago.

And he hadn't wanted to leave since.

Adam and Killian maneuvered him onto the bed, working in sync while I prepared an IV. My hands moved on autopilot, years of training taking over.

That's when Kieran's eyes found me.

As I brushed his sweat-soaked hair back from his forehead, something in his gaze shifted, a spark of recognition that wasn't quite right.

"*Avani...*" Kieran whispered, his voice raw and desperate.

Before I could react, he yanked me against his chest.

A startled yelp escaped my lips as his muscular arms enveloped me, surprisingly strong for someone in his state.

Oh no...

The room erupted into motion. Footsteps, a sharp intake of breath, Killian behind me—

"*Whoa, Kieran.*" Adam's voice, tense but controlled broke through the silence.

Killian's hands were on me in an instant, trying to pull me away.

"No, this one isn't yours," he growled, a dangerous edge to his voice that I rarely heard.

Kieran's grip only tightened, a low rumble building in his chest. His fingers threaded through my hair, gentle despite his state.

His breath was hot against my neck as he mumbled a string of desperate apologies. "I'm sorry, I'm so sorry, Avani. I didn't mean to…"

"He doesn't know." Adam's calm voice cut through the tension, a lifeline of reason. "Kieran, did you want Avani to stay with you?"

Kieran's arms tightened around me in response.

I could feel the rapid, erratic beat of his heart, smell the acrid mix of sweat and chemicals on his skin.

Adam spoke again, his voice low and careful. "It's okay, Killian and I are going to make sure nothing happens to her."

I heard movement, then Adam's steady tone once more. "She isn't going *anywhere*, Kieran. Isn't that right, Killian? You'll keep Ni— *Avani* safe. Come on, let me get her comfortable for you."

Time seemed to stretch as Kieran held me. I could feel the violent tremors running through his body, the desperation in his touch.

His grip was tight but not painful—as if he was clinging to a lifeline.

Slowly, with agonizing reluctance, his arms began to loosen as Adam swapped me out for a pillow.

I felt Killian's hands on me again, gently but firmly pulling me away. My hand moved instinctively to my abdomen.

Adam, ever the professional, turned his focus back to Kieran while Killian ran his hands over me gripping me tight to him.

His voice was low and soothing as he spoke, coaxing Kieran to lie back, to breathe deeply. Adam was soothing Kieran.

When Adam finally turned to us his brows were furrowed. I couldn't stay with Kieran, given his obvious state of being.

"I'll stay. I'll tell Gabriel he's stable." There was a look in Adam's eyes I didn't recognize. "Nothing I did for you today is out of the ordinary. I would've done it for your brother and you *regardless* of *who you are*, yeah?"

I was confused. What was he talking about? *Who Killian was?*

But whatever Adam was saying, Killian seemed to understand.

"Thank you." Killian's voice for once was softer with Adam. Just like it was with me. "If you need anything, *ever*, tell me. My word is iron-clad." As he said it, I tucked myself into his side, aware of what he was saying. Adam was doing Killian a favor by not telling anyone about Kieran's spiral with Avani. Which was a big deal to Killian, who did everything he could to protect his brother.

"I'll keep that in mind." Adam smiled despite looking more tired ever since he started working for his brother. "Let me go talk to him while you two lovebirds escape."

I felt myself warming and ducking my face into Killian despite Kieran watching me with confused eyes.

"Was he with anyone else?" Adam kept his voice low, recounting the disconcerting evidence.

Killian frowned, the crease between his brows deepening and he quietly moved me behind him. Discreetly. What was happening?

"I found him with..." Killian trailed off watching Kieran. He shok his head at Adam.

"People don't typically reach this state alone," Adam said, his voice low and clinical. "If we knew who Kieran was with when this began, it might explain his emotional state, why he's mistaking Nisha for..."

He trailed off, his eyes moving to Kieran's wrists. "These rope burns. Someone restrained him. Who was he with?"

Killian's eyes settled on his brother. "I'm going to kill Teo."

Adam's head snapped up, confusion clear on his face. "*Teo?*"

"You know Teo?"

Now, I was completely lost. *Who was Teo?*

Adam's eyes flicked towards me for a fleeting second before returning to Killian.

"We've...talked."

Killian's frown deepened, his brow furrowing. "You can ask him what happened then."

"Are they close?" Adam glanced between Kieran and Killian, clearly trying to piece together this puzzle.

I gripped Killian's shirt tighter, feeling overwhelmed by all I didn't understand. His eyes darted to me, softening slightly. "I'll explain everything at home, luv."

I listened to them talking quietly and realized even if I saw Killian.

There had never been the proper moment to sit him down and tell him I was pregnant. His brother just had a drug overdose.

One of his clients was shot earlier.

He'd rescued Alisha, Reed's girlfriend out of her stalker situation weeks ago. She was safe and sound now.

And even with Agent Tavares in the hospital, there was no quiet for Titan.

In this world, there never seemed to be the right time to do anything.

I understood thats why he quickly introduced me to his brother the way he had.

Every time I did, he had to race off. It wasn't obvious. But now I felt the nagging sensations of would I ever get a chance to?

When? How?

46

KILLIAN

I USHERED NISHA OUT OF THE ROOM, GRATEFUL FOR ADAM'S DISTRACTION of Kieran.

The moment the door closed behind us, Nisha pulled us into a private room.

Before I could even process it, she was in my arms, dark hair, the scene of amber around me.

Motherfucker, I missed her so much.

"What happened to Kieran?" Nisha's voice was mumbled into my chest.

I let out a breath. "Think his crush with Avani went south, luv—"

"But they were so good—"

Were they? I didn't know.

"I don't know if they were dating." I thought about it and even if they seemed close...Alisha and Avani Malhotra were...nice girls. And a little like mine. I got why Kieran would be attracted to her—but unlike Nisha who was mine?

Hitting on Avani was a one way ticket to hell. Of Reed's making. I knew how protective Reed was of her. And Alisha.

I explained to Nisha how unlike the women Kieran was with. "Avani's kinda like you. But—"

"Squishy—"

I bit back a laugh at that. Nisha had a way of softening things. But she wasn't wrong. Avani wasn't exactly Kieran's type.

I told Nisha that.

Nisha blinked up at me. "She is now."

Yeah. I think it had something to do with Nisha. I did. Because my brother's knew about Nisha and up until her? None of us had a steady woman in our lives, but once I met her? I latched on.

It made sense Kieran—who wanted everything I did—would find Avani and think that was his.

"I think he got close to her family. He was with Reed and them for the last few weeks…" I trailed off explaining to Nisha that knowing my brother? He probably found a home with them. "He's not used to a home and Alisha's warm. He probably felt like he was a part of it."

"And then something happened?" Nisha made a noise. "Poor thing, you think he missed them? Or he wanted her and didn't know how to tell her?"

"I think something happened but I'll talk to him when he's sobered up. All of it, luv. We're not exactly civilized."

"You're civilized."

"Barely."

Even I knew I was insane for kissing the first time I saw her. But I knew what I wanted and I wasn't a man who deviated from what I liked.

"I feel bad for Kieran. Avani seemed sweet." Nisha's fingers found their way into my hair. "Are you taking care of yourself? I know you've been running around with Kellan lately."

When I wasn't off getting shot at or shooting others? Maybe.

"Sometimes."

I couldn't lie to Nisha outright. *Right?*

"Liar." There was no bite to her tone.

I smiled softly leaning into her cheek. "I miss you, luv. I'm fucking exhausted," I murmured into her hair, the admission feeling like a surrender. "I have to run and go back to Watts. He's in the car right now. And I can't stay away for too long."

She hummed. "He's better?"

"He is."

"I have to talk to you too when we get home."

At that I paused drawing back to look at her. And saw her squirming. Her cheeks looked fuller than usual and she looked adorable.

"Are you all right?" I asked, concern creeping in.

Had I missed something? Been too caught up in my own chaos to notice if she was struggling?

"Everything okay, luv?"

"I'm fine, it's just…" she trailed off, biting her lip in that way she did when she was anxious about something.

Her hand drifted to her stomach for a split second before dropping away.

The gesture was so quick, I almost missed it. I held her face in my hands.

"Tell me." *Did she not feel good?*

"No, I'm all right—" But she didn't look at me and I felt guilty.

"I haven't taken care of you recently," I said, the admission tasting bitter. It was true—I'd been so wrapped up in everything else, I'd neglected the one person who mattered most. "I'm sorry, luv. I've been all over the place."

I cupped her face in my hands, really looking at her.

There was something different, her skin glowing in a way I couldn't quite place.

Had she always had those little freckles across her nose? Her hair was longer now and I wanted to just hug her.

"You look beautiful," I whispered. "You smell different too."

I felt the pang of guilt increase for not noticing these small changes earlier. Her skin felt warmer than usual under my lips.

"I've been at work forever," she whispered back like it was our secret.

"I'll wrap things up with Watts as quick as I can and come home. We'll talk then. Dinner?" I asked, wanting to make up for lost time. "Anywhere you want to go."

Nisha's answer was to kiss me as I held her tight for long moments. When she pulled back, there was a hesitancy in her eyes. "I forgot to tell you. Selena is gone…"

"Gone?"

Watts wouldn't take any of this well.

She nodded, her fingers playing with the fabric of my shirt and I took her fingers in my hands kissing them as she talked. Brushing her hair back. I couldn't take my hands off her.

"She left recently. Mr. Monroe came and gave her a choice…"

Watts…*Christ*. He was already a powder keg waiting to explode. Fuck my life.

"I'll have to tell him." I resisted the urge to growl. Not with her.

"How is he doing?" Nisha frequently asked me about him since she felt bad for him after those first few nights she saw him sitting outside Tavares's room. My girl and her big heart. "Is he still hurting? I feel so bad for the two of them, she didn't even talk about him when she left…"

And something told me nobody told Tavares her man almost shot Nate Wyatt for threatening his relationship. Jeez.

"I don't know what happened—" I broke off. I kinda did. But also I didn't. "I think they might've gotten into a fight. They won't talk to each other, but he's obsessed with her."

Nisha sighed. "It's romantic in a really tragic way. I hope it works out for them. But if Selena left for Miami, what is Watts doing?"

Then again, I'd do the same for Nisha. Shit. I'd go after Kieran if he spoke to her wrong.

"I think Gabriel is gonna send him after her—"

Nisha frowned. "Why?"

I shrugged. Maybe he wanted to fix their relationship?

"I don't know exactly, but I suspect he's close to Tavares and he doesn't want her to be mad at Watts forever." But I didn't know. "He's a pain in my ass. If he wasn't so fucking trigger happy, I'd be with you."

Nisha smiled ruefully up at me, her dark eyes twinkling. "You miss me, baby?"

Yes.

I smiled down at her. "I miss you, luv."

"You're helping him now, he's doing better though?"

"Mm."

"And you two aren't eating those gross protein bars?"

I grinned. "I need protein, luv—"

"You can get it with real food—"

"It's not the same—" I grinned at her laughter. "C'mere."

"Wait—" she held me back. "Are you working for the next few days?"

"Mmm, Gabriel asked me to hang back at the manor to make sure Reed and Lucas were good. But I was gonna bring you food after dropping off Watts, yeah?"

She beamed. "For me and Kieran?"

I sighed looking at the ceiling. "Yes. I will bring food for my brother. But I swear to God if he touches you again—"

"He didn't think it was me—"

"No, but somehow that makes it worse."

She smiled up at me. "Promise me you'll take care of yourself. I haven't seen you in ages."

I kissed her.

"I'll handle it," I assured her, pressing a kiss to her forehead. Her nose. Her lips. "Thank you for telling me, luv. I'll take you out this weekend, once I clean everything up."

GABRIEL TEXTED BACK, INSTRUCTING ME TO INFORM WATTS BEFORE I even reached the parking garage.

After breaking the news to Watts about Selena Tavares leaving the city, I made a quick call to Gabriel.

Initially, I wasn't sure how Watts would handle it. He almost hadn't taken it well.

I understood Watts's feelings, but I knew he needed to be in better shape if Gabriel was going to assign him a task.

I'd been given permission to send him on his way.

"Hang on…" Gabriel answered, his voice muffled. There was a rustling sound, as if Gabriel was moving to a different room. "Kieran's solid?"

"He is," I confirmed, thrown off by the lightness in Gabriel's tone.

I had to double-check my phone to make sure I was talking to the right Gabriel.

"Watts is too. I told him, and he handled it better."

When Gabriel spoke again, his voice had lost some of its earlier lightness. "I'll have Reed send him on his next assignment."

To Tavares.

"He's good to go to Miami?" I didn't know, but he better fucking behave.

Gabriel let out a breath. "Reed and I think so, you pushed him enough. If he isn't, Lena still knows how to shoot him."

I didn't know why Gabriel was helping the two of them, but then again, Gabriel operated in a way I didn't always understand.

I took a breath, my thoughts drifting to Nisha.

I needed to tell her who I was. I wanted to. But then Kieran happened. Then Watts. Now, this weekend, I had no more excuses.

I was going to take her out and tell her the truth.

47

NISHA

"Do you want to talk about what happened?"

I was sitting with Kieran in his room, talking to him after he'd woken up.

A day later, Kieran had recovered fairly quickly letting Adam off the hook. Now he was sitting upright in his bed watching cartoons with me while I sat next to him on the pullout couch.

His eyes, usually bright amber and brilliant went dark. "Nothing to talk about."

But there was.

It had been written all over his face when I had seen them.

"My brother wants to marry you," Kieran said, a hint of a smile tugging at his lips despite his own turmoil. "He loves you."

"Does he?" I teased him ignoring the way my heart flipped in my chest.

I didn't know *if* Killian did.

I didn't know what we'd do about the baby but from the sound of it, things had calmed down enough and we would go out to dinner. I could tell him then.

"I love him too."

"Yeah," he said quietly his eyes holding something warmer. "I can see that."

Maybe with the recent breakup or whatever it was he'd been through with Avani, he was more heartbroken.

He paused, studying me for a moment, his expression turning thoughtful. "You know, you're good for him. For all of us, really."

He leaned back, running a hand through his tousled hair.

"At first, I didn't know how to feel about you two. Killian's not one for..." He motioned vaguely in my direction, searching for words. "Relationships, I guess. Or feelings. But now?"

I frowned. "He has feelings...he's just quiet about them."

"He hardly speaks unless it's about work, Nisha," Kieran said dryly. "I'm surprised you get a sentence out of him. When were growing up, he didn't talk for weeks."

My chest tightened at that.

He did speak more with me, but I understood with their father and their mother being who they were.

Her walking out on his family, and the way Killian mentioned his dad had been a criminal? It couldn't have been easy.

"I think given who you were father was, anyone would shut down about him."

Kieran's eyes went dark for a moment as he watched me. "He told you about Cormac?"

I swallowed feeling a little uneasy talking about this without Killian. "He told me enough to paint a picture."

I didn't know Cormac O'Hara was his name though.

Kieran's nod was grim. "He was a piece of shit, but I'm surprised Killian talked about him. He never talks about anything related other than that. He's always been work focused."

"He has been a work a lot," I mentioned.

And I worried the impact it had on him since he looked much more haggard.

It was why I didn't say anything about the baby.

The Killian I knew would be out and about stressing about the baby and me all the time. He didn't need that in his head.

I would tell him when he was back.

"He's better with you though," Kieran said quietly. "He's got that fucking bow print bandaid on his finger? I fucking knew that shit was yours."

I blushed. "It's nothing—"

"Once he introduced you to Aidan, I should've fucking known. And you're so fucking chill about this," Kieran said conversationally, reaching for another pudding cup. "Marrying into the mob isn't for everyone. Drove our mother insane. I feel like she's why he likes you."

Kieran turned to me as I processed what he said.

"Is that why he kept it from everyone for this long? Wanted you to get used to us so we don't scare you off? I get he told you about Cormac..."

I didn't really hear what else Kieran said as my ears focused on 'marrying into the mob' bit.

What?

Used to...what?

Wait...what?

I laughed. "What do you mean mob?" I swallowed a spoonful of pudding. "Is that slang for Titan?"

Maybe they had codenames. Killian mentioned his was Ares.

The god of war.

Which suited him if it was a bit violent.

Kieran's smile dipped a fraction as he looked at me.

His arm hung halfway to grabbing a new pudding cup.

"What do you mean slang for Titan?"

I smiled reassuringly repeating my question. "Is mob slang for Titan?" I grinned. "You guys all speak in code and I'm not fluent in your lingo."

His smile vanished off his face as his mouth opened in shock a tiny bit. Enough for me to know mob was *not* in fact slang for Titan.

"Nisha..." he looked like he was struggling for words. He looked around the room for a moment before back at me. "What—How—Who—"

I laughed lightly, even as my nerves crept in. "*W-what is it?*"

Kieran's smile vanished, his expression shifting to one of dawning horror. His eyes, moments ago warm and playful, now went blank. "Mob..."

With trembling hands, I reached for the remote.

"Kieran, you're freaking me out a little, what's going on?"

Marrying into what mob? I muted the cartoons, plunging the room into a suffocating silence.

"What do you mean...if mob is code for Titan?" His Adam's apple bobbed a little. "Nisha...what do you think Killian...who do you think he works for?"

"He works for a security firm," I swallowed hard, trying to keep the nausea at bay. "He works for Titan. In Midtown." *Right?*

"*Oh, shit,*" he muttered, running a shaky hand through his hair. "He... Killian never...But he told you about our father, you met Aidan, you know...you live with him..."

His eyes darted around the room, as if searching for an escape. "*Oh, motherfucker.*"

"*Kieran, what are you talking about?*" My stomach was going crazy right now. "Killian works for Aidan," I finished, grasping at the familiar narrative. I knew that much. Killian and I talked about everything. Almost. "And Titan sometimes."

Kieran's jaw dropped. "*...Who is mafia. Nisha...my family is mob. We have been for a hundred years.*"

"What?" I breathed. "Are you..."

Was he being serious right now?

"Nisha, you met Aidan the other night," Kieran pressed, his eyes searching mine desperately, his head shaking. "You've been with Killian for *months...*"

We had. We had been together for *months...*

I am pregnant. I'm having his baby. Our baby.

"He works for Titan. That's all."

"He does work for Titan," Kieran confirmed, speaking slowly. "And Aidan...*Nisha, my family is mafia.*"

"What?"

He was out of his mind.

"*You're lying and you're on meds—*"

"*Nisha—*"

"You're trying to freak me out because of what happened to you—I don't know what's going on right now..." the feeble words left my mouth. "I don't *understand* because if this is a joke this isn't funny."

His eyes went wide and I felt my vision blurring, hot tears running down my face.

"Nisha, nonono, don't cry, don't cry love, I thought you knew," Kieran pleaded, his hands hovering uncertainly. "*When he introduced you to Aidan—*"

I felt the panic overwhelming me then and I couldn't keep myself steady. Kieran's arms were around me suddenly, steadying me, but his touch felt alien now.

"Nisha, I swear I thought you knew. I never imagined he would keep this from you."

"Aidan works in real estate," I mumbled, the words hollow and meaningless. *I thought he worked in real estate.*

"Oh, fuck, *nonononono*, no don't cry Nisha. Please, he's gonna kill me. *Shitshitshit*," Kieran's voice was thick with regret. But I was spiraling. I couldn't even look at him. I was *horrified*, the fluttering in my stomach wild.

I'm pregnant.

Oh my God.

"Nisha, I'm so sorry. I didn't think he meant it—"

"He meant it." *He never...he never wanted to tell me.* He had deliberately kept this secret. "Your family is...full of criminals..."

Just like my father.

"We aren't criminals. Not technically anyway," Kieran pleaded, his hands fluttering around me helplessly. "Aidan's not half the bastard our dad was. But he still kills enough—*nonono* not like that. Oh *shitshitshit*, where's Killian when you need him?"

The sound of his name should've brought me comfort but for the first time since I met him, I felt terror.

I was beyond hearing. Beyond comfort.

I felt myself spiraling, unable to stop the flood of emotions overwhelming me. *How could I have been so blind?*

My hand pressed against my belly, instinctively protective of the tiny life growing inside me.

The baby. Our baby.

I wanted to vomit.

I could feel it in my stomach. The low grade nausea bubbling up in me.

A sob left me and then another as a noise left my mouth and Kieran's face fell his lips at my cheek, my ear.

"Please Nisha, don't freak out—" I was gone though. "Oh shitshitshit, Killian's gonna kill me."

A noise left me.

I felt *completely* shattered. *I'm pregnant...with a stranger's child.*

I never even knew him. The man I loved was a facade, a carefully constructed lie.

And he had known it the entire time.

I have to get out of here. I have to protect my baby. I have to run.

And with the understanding that my entire life felt uprooted—I threw up.

4 8

KILLIAN

After I dropped off Watts, the plan was simple: go home and shower, pick up Nisha from her shift, check on Kieran. Routine.

Except my phone rang after my shower and I had just finished packing up a bag to take over to Nisha's.

"Derek."

"We got a problem, boss." Derek's deep voice cut through my rush to get to my girl as I listened to what he was saying. He barely got through it before I stopped him. My blood ran cold.

"What the fuck do you mean they let him off? What technicality?"

Derek's voice was grim. "His scum lawyer argued that new evidence had come to light, evidence that the original defense failed to present. Combined with overcrowding at the facility, the judge saw fit to release him pending a new trial."

"On what grounds?"

Nisha.

I gotta get my girl.

"Technicalities, boss. They're claiming procedural errors during the initial investigation, potential witness tampering.It's all bullshit, but it was enough to create reasonable doubt." Derek swore a bit and he said the words before I did. "I can't take him out."

I swore violently. "What about the restraining order?"

"Still in place, but you know as well as I do how much that's worth if he decides to ignore it."

"Fuck," I breathed, my heart pounding. "Is he free?"

"He is."

I let out a breath resisting the urge to throw my phone across the room. "I gotta get Nisha. Keep your eyes on the case. If he so much as moves an inch to her—"

"I got 'em."

I texted Nisha en route. No response.

I would've brushed it off. Normally I imagined her absorbed in some show with Kieran, lost in banter.

Nisha could make me laugh and no doubt, she'd get along with Kieran.

It was the only thought keeping me sane as I gripped the steering wheel tightly all the way to the hospital.

The first hint of wrongness hit when I didn't see Nisha waiting outside Kieran's room.

I pushed open the door, expecting to see them both. Instead, there was only Kieran.

The look in his eyes made my stomach plummet.

I knew instantly *something* was wrong.

"*What* happened?"

Where is she?

Kieran's face drained of color, his mouth working silently. In an instant, I was across the room, looming over him.

"*Don't be angry.*"

"What. Happened." Each word was clipped. The worry in me was a storm brewing.

And then it poured out of him. Word after word. My jaw slackened, the world tilting as the weight of his confession hit me.

Nisha *knew*.

She knew *everything*.

Or Kieran's version of it.

And she was *gone*.

"I thought she knew," Kieran whispered, his voice cracking.

"What do you mean you told Nisha about our family?"

His eyes, usually brimming with mischief, now held only fear and regret. "I thought you'd told her *everything*. We were just talking. And I brought up how good it was she was...like Mom but better, and I

294

mentioned our family, and she..." He swallowed hard, Adam's apple bobbing. *What the fuck...*

My blood turned to ice.

"What about Mom?"

My control snapped.

My hands shot out, fisting in Kieran's hospital gown. The flimsy fabric twisted as I leaned in, my face inches from his.

"You told Nisha what!"

The rational part of my brain screamed that this wasn't Kieran's fault, that I had no right to be angry with him.

But rationality was drowning right now. I was ready to kill my brother.

And now her father was out of jail?

Holy. Fucking. Shit.

"I didn't know!" he choked out, his eyes wild, words tumbling over each other in his haste to explain. "She just...left. Said she needed air. I tried to stop her, but—"

"She left the hospital?" And she was out God only knew where? Did she go home? Why didn't I just go there? Every single fucking minute I spent with Kieran—fucking Kieran—was a second wasted without her.

My eyes narrowed on him.

"I can't fucking believe you right now."

I had never snapped like this.

"You fucking told her about some shit you had no right!"

"I thought she knew! How were you fucking her—"

I was on him in a second machines beeping like crazy as he growled back.

I knew, somewhere deep down, that this wasn't entirely his fault.

That I was being irrational, unfair. But I couldn't stop the torrent of words, years of pent-up frustration finally finding release.

I grabbed his throat pinning him to the bed aware I was still older. Bigger. Stronger.

"I cleaned up after you for years! I have picked up all your dirty laundry. Switched places with you! Kept you from hurting yourself."

The words came faster now, each one a dagger I knew I'd regret.

"I would never have opened my fucking mouth to tell Reed—

Amber eyes flashed at me enraged. *"It's not the same—"*

295

"Yes it is!" I was a fucking savage right now. "We both know if Reed found out about your little fucking crush he could kill you."

I knew my eyes were terrifying as he looked at me.

"You think he'd let you near Avani if he knew what you did to the girls at De Nuit?"

"I didn't know—"

"Why the fuck would you bring it up!" I was in his face, voice rising to a level I'd never allowed before. Years of control shattered in an instant. "Why the fuck did it even come up! I was going to tell—"

"I never meant to—"

"You fuck up every single thing!"

And my hand was around his throat faster than I could stop.

I shouldn't have said it. It slipped from my lips one after the other.

"Now you've fucked up my life too! My girl ran from me? Because of you!"

Kieran's face went blank. I felt it erupting with the panic of losing my girl.

"I spent my whole life, cleaning up after you. Covering. Protecting you. I left her with you because I thought I could trust you!"

I was beyond caring now.

"I gave up *everything* for this family. For you. And the one time, the *one* time I find something for myself, *you fuck it up!*"

The silence was deafening.

The rapid beep of Kieran's heart monitor filled the room. My own ragged breathing. He stared at me, wide-eyed, pale. Like he was seeing me for the first time.

I shoved him back into his bed taking in his hospital gown. Going after Kieran wasn't fair.

And I didn't care.

"Don't call me next time you need help. I don't give a fuck anymore."

The door slammed behind me, the sound echoing in the sterile hallway.

If anything happened to Nisha…*because of me…*

I had to find her.

I didn't even want to think about it. I yanked out my phone.

My mind raced, desperately searching for a solution.

There was only one person I knew with the resources to find anyone, anywhere.

It took Liam a few rings to pick up. When he did, his voice was thick with sleep. *"I swear to God—"*

"Nisha's gone. Help me find her."

49

NISHA

Devastation was an understatement.

Sonya's arms wrapped around me as I broke down—I couldn't stop crying since I'd gone to my apartment, packed up a bag and ran to Sonya terrified out of my mind at what was happening in my life.

The irony wasn't lost on me—I'd spent so long building walls, only to have them torn down by the one person I thought I could trust.

My world was a sand-castle on the beach swept away by the water.

I couldn't stop freaking out.

"I just...I can't think straight."

"No, I don't expect you to," Sonya's voice was quiet as I cried into her arms.

It felt like my entire world crumbled at my feet.

The same way I knew my parents hadn't loved me.

The same way I knew my adopted parents had abused me.

The same way I knew my life...was...solitary.

I couldn't stop crying. I felt so alone and like my entire existence was a lie and the shame that swallowed me whole was one I brutally recognized.

You stupid girl.

You seduced my husband.

Don't you have any shame?

You're so fucking fat and ugly.

Nobody will ever love you.

And I broke.

"I feel so stupid," I whispered. "I feel like an idiot."

I did. For falling for a man who had done nothing but lie from the start. I hated him, I didn't trust him—I didn't know him. Was it all a lie?

"I didn't know him."

I didn't *know* Killian. I thought I did.

But if he had lied about something so big? What else had he lied about? Killian being in the mafia was the last thing I expected.

Images of Killian flashed before me—his smile, his touch, all tainted now by the knowledge of his true identity.

Sonya murmured, her hand making soothing circles on my back.

"It's all right. Everyone has human moments...especially since..."

She paused, and in that silence, I felt the weight of my decisions pressing down on me.

I broke down and told Sonya feeling like I was betraying him and even if I felt the urge to protect him? I was terrified and I couldn't enter her home and not make her aware of it.

I was shaking so hard I didn't know what to do.

Since I had started dating someone in the mafia...without knowing.

"I'm stupid."

I'd run from the hospital, from Killian, from the life I thought I knew. My hand drifted to my stomach, still flat but holding so many secrets.

"I don't know what to do," I whispered, more to myself than to Sonya.

The future I'd imagined—a life with Killian, our child, a normal family—crumbled around me.

In its place, fear and uncertainty loomed large.

Was anything he told me real?

How could I have been so blind?

My fingers traced the slight swell of my stomach.

"And I'm pregnant." I broke down harder unable to stop the emotions ripping through me. "Sonya, I don't know what to do and I'm scared."

"I know, darling."

She held me tighter and I cried. I sounded like a wounded animal.

And Sonya wiped her own eyes making small noise as she held me.

"It's all right, I promise. It's gonna be okay. These moment's don't last forever, darling."

"It feels like it's never going to get better."

"I know," she kissed my head again, her lips warm brushing over my temples. "I know, it feels like that, but that's okay. I'm here for you."

It took me hours if not days to stop crying. I felt out of it completely. Sonya was surprisingly calm as I broke down and told her what I knew. She said she knew Alisha who was dating Reed Whittaker—the owner of Titan.

Sonya was trying to stay calm to talk to the people in her circle.

To figure it out with me. For me.

The nausea had become all over worse and I felt sicker than ever before. I couldn't smell anything off without wanting to vomit and my anxiety raced.

The fear in my body was trapped inside of it.

Sonya insisted on having her female doctor from Haven, a pretty blonde woman named Vera Sinclaire come over.

She held an air of quiet competence as she came with a bag and a little boy with dark hair and glasses.

"Simon, stay with Miss Amin, while I go to see Miss Graham."

"Yes, Mama." Simon dutifully followed Sonya who beamed down at him.

"So sorry," Vera's dark brown eyes met mine. "His babysitter had something come up today so I brought him to work."

"It's perfectly all right," I shook my head as Sonya chatted with Simon. "He's tall."

"He's eight," Vera's eyes widened in mock shock. I bit back my laughter at her expression. And he was no doubt growing faster.

"I'm guessing his father's tall?"

An indecipherable expression went through Vera's eyes as she nodded. "He is. Would you like to find a comfortable place for me to assist you, Miss Graham?" Her tone was light and calm.

I just went into a private room with her where she did some pre-natal checks.

"Do you know if nausea is common to this extent?" I asked her quietly laying back while she moved over me.

She tucked her ear length blonde hair behind her eyes her expression warm. "It can be but it depends. Every pregnancy is different. Even medical science can't explain why some mother's have higher stress levels or even elevated nausea…but given the fact that he isn't here and you're with Miss Amin, I gather that might be a factor."

I didn't know what to tell Vera. Her features were sharp despite her height being mine, she was thinner with pixie-like features.

Her eyes, darker brown like mine were warm though.

"I'm really sorry Miss Graham. But I think my professional advice would be to do things that bring your stress down a bit…taking a bath or doing something that cultivates a tiny bit of relief. I'm not saying it will fix everything but even if you can reduce it temporarily will be good for the baby. In the meantime, I can prescribe some anti-nausea pills but I can't promise it'll work given how far along you are."

Vera and I talked for a bit and I realized she was the doctor who worked over the woman at Haven. She smiled. "Are you working with us?"

I didn't know. I didn't know anything. But Sonya's words came back to me.

You don't have to know the answer to everything. Sometimes it's okay to take a break. A breather.

That's what this is. We all need one.

Sonya had gotten her with her friends Gemma and Lucas she spoke fondly of.

"I'm sorry—" Vera started. "I shouldn't have asked—"

"No!" I stopped her. "No, it's fine…I'm just somewhere in the middle right now."

Her eyes held a wealth of unspoken knowledge in them as she nodded at me. "Everyone at Haven is. You'd fit right in."

I smiled at her for the first time that day. "Thank you."

"Don't mention it. Pleasure to meet you."

When Sonya came back for us with Simon she was red in the face and he was beaming ear to ear. He was tall for his age and I could tell he'd surpass all of us in a matter of years if not months.

"Better?" Sonya asked me with a smile.

"Better." Sort of. There was something healing about being around the women in Sonya's life. Like they had all gone through enough of their own shit to relate to mine.

And that made me feel less alone. Less distrust.

Less nauseous.

"I'm sorry for bringing this to your door," I whispered when Vera and Simon left.

"Not at all," Sonya winked. "I could use some excitement after the rather boring life I've had. I can take a little mafia man any day."

"You're handling this better than I am."

Sonya's laughter filled the room. "I can assure I am not. I'm just really good at wearing my mask."

50

KILLIAN

"I found Nisha," Liam said, his voice low as he ushered me into his living space with discomfort in his entire expression. "Only one catch. You can't see her."

What?

"The fuck do you mean—"

"You cannot see Nisha." Liam said flat out repeating himself. I caught a whiff of something in the room. White sage. Something floral and feminine. He had someone over?

Lara. He has Lara over.

My vision tinged red, the world narrowing to Liam's impassive face as he crossed his arms over his chest. I clenched my fists, fingernails digging into my palms, using the pain to anchor myself.

"Why the fuck—"

"She's with Sonya," Liam interrupted, his calm demeanor only fueling my rage. "Not my orders. It's all Reeds."

"Sonya *Devereaux?"*

"Amin now," Liam corrected, his tone carefully neutral. He gestured towards the couch, but I remained standing.

"Reed set up her security. His rules are strict. No one gets through. If Nisha went to her…well, you can't just storm in and take her back."

Watch me.

The urge to act, to do *something*, was almost overwhelming.

"You didn't tell Nisha about you," Liam said quietly. "Sonya didn't know either. She was afraid for her, so instead of calling the cops, she reached out to Alisha."

Sonya had done right by us, asking questions instead of immediately involving law enforcement.

"Reed is going to settle this—"

"I need to talk to Nisha. Now."

Liam hissed, his voice razor-sharp and low, his entire profile contorting with simmering rage at me. "You need to *breathe*. Lara's *asleep*, so keep your voice down. Or I will kick you the fuck out myself." And it was then I caught little bits of life around his sparse utilitarian space. Little tiny things that hinted at a woman living there, the feather fucking boa for one thing—but it was the scents, the candles.

"What the fuck is your problem?" I advanced on him, my body coiled tight with tension. To my surprise, Liam stood up straighter, and his chin tipped up like he knew what was coming.

Gone was the hunched figure I was used to seeing. He was always slouched. So I never realized how fucking tall he was.

His build was...familiar. Like a fighter's.

Lean, powerful, dangerous.

Where the fuck had I seen him before?

"Who the fuck are you?" I growled. "You can't keep me from Nisha. You think you can hold my girl fucking hostage—"

"Nobody is holding her hostage you moron—"

And I was itching for a fight. I was. Fighting Kieran hadn't been enough and I didn't care if Liam was on a crutch. He wasn't now.

I was on him with a growl grabbing him by his collar. Or I tried to. I didn't see him move.

Not once.

One moment, I was reaching for him. The next, I was spinning—he moved fast, and I was upside down, flipped onto the couch. The impact against my back, with the air rushing out of my lungs, made me gasp.

Liam stood over me, his green eyes glazing with a colder fury than I'd seen in someone else. I still couldn't rationalize it. That move...

"Still got it, motherfucker." His voice was still low, and he looked slightly off, grimacing like it had cost him to move like that. "Now shut the fuck up and sit down. Because if *she* so much as wakes up, I will fucking kill you."

I was staring at him like I didn't know who he was. Because I definitely knew him, but I didn't know who Liam Sullivan was.

Liam's voice was iron. *"I know enough to know you fucked up, and your girl ran from you—"* He cut himself off, jaw clenching. The slip, small as it was, didn't escape my notice.

"Sonya's got her hands full. She runs Haven, a domestic violence shelter. Her husband's family is giving her grief and bad press. She doesn't need more heat with him looking for ways to tear her apart. Any association with the mob? Would destroy her. Reed's handling it. And your brother...well, he's stepping in too. Reed figures keeping you out of the picture might help—"

"If I can't talk to her—"

"Reed knows you're ghosting everyone but me. But he wants to smooth it out. We're juggling too much right now. We can't afford this—"

"I can't see my own goddamn girlfriend?" I couldn't stop myself. *"What if it was Lara?"*

"I wouldn't lie to Lara about *a goddamn thing*. You know why? *Because I fucking love her.* You've lost your *fucking* mind. *Nisha just found out you're in the fucking mob."*

"That's not the whole truth—"

"It doesn't matter. Lara had to break it to me gently about you, and that was after years of worrying about her. Even then, I was worried sick. If she hadn't worked with you..."

"Sonya's trying to handle this without it blowing back on her. We're keeping it quiet, keeping the O'Hara name out of it. Reed doesn't want this getting any bigger. Neither does your brother. She's terrified, Killian. She ran to Sonya for *protection*. From *you. Why the hell did you keep her in the dark?"*

And suddenly, the door opened to the bedroom was a snick.

The soft feminine voice that drifted out made Liam's face go dark at me.

"Amor..." Lara sounded sleepy. *"Ta bien?"*

Liam looked at me disgusted like I was bug under his shoe. "I'm not finished," his hiss was vicious as he shot me the finger as he shuffled off to her.

I barely heard the murmur of his voice.

"Muñeca..." His voice completely changed from the drill sergeant

305

type who was ripping me a new one to someone softer as he spoke to her completely in Spanish.

Why was he so—

He reminds me of someone.

Who?

And for some reason, an ice cold chill rattled down my spine at the thought of who. *He reminds me of Gabriel.*

Because that's who it was. The way he shifted and moved. That move was *Kyokushin* karate. *What were the odds?*

But Liam is a new hire. He never worked for Titan. He doesn't know Gabriel. Does he? He's Reed's team.

My eyes drifted over his space, searching for anything. Clues. Something to tell me who the fuck he was. And there wasn't much.

There was nothing in it save for the couch I was on, a simple coffee table, a TV.

It looked more like a hotel room with nothing personal in it. There were a few photos Liam's TV frame but that was about it.

One of him as a teenager no doubt wearing a scowl, an older gentleman who was looking at him with a smile, and a dark-haired woman between them grinning ear to ear.

Had I seen her before?

Her expression looked a little familiar to me I just couldn't place how.

His family?

I didn't know much about Liam but I absorbed it all trying to focus on anything but the panic I felt about Nisha.

I lost my girl. I closed my eyes then as the ache built in me. And now I was getting my ass handed to me by him.

Because I'm a fucking idiot.

It didn't long for Liam to come back and he was furious with me.

"Get out of my house—" he growled. "You woke her up."

"Not until you get me, Nisha—" I stood ready to take him, and his face was dark fury, but I cut him off. "I don't give a fuck if you're disabled, I'll make sure you don't want anymore—"

A growl left Liam's throat, as he barred his teeth. "You came into my home begging for help and you pissed me off—"

"If it was Lara, you'd break down my fucking door to get her back

—" I could meet him toe to toe. "If she bolted because of some misunderstanding—"

Liam's eyes were crazed. That was the only way to explain it. The darkness in them came out in full force. And he all but hissed at me with the words. *That if would never happen—I would never hurt her.*

I had him by the throat and this time when he tried to maneuver me, I held on. "What is that? Kyokushin?" His eyes widened. I went for kill. "And yet if it did, you'd kill for her—"

"Don't bring Lara into this."

His eyes were wild and I saw a bit of something in there I recognized in my own youth. Something familiar.

"You can't keep Nisha from me." I knew where Sonya lived. I could fucking do it. I could get Nisha back. "I don't care what Reed's orders are— I will get my girl back. We both know you'd kill me if I held Lara from you. The only reason I haven't put a bullet in you yet is because *she loves you.*"

I saw the crack in Liam's armor then. The mention of Lara got him going. His eyes softened immediately the moment I said she loved him. Something passed through his face.

"Who are you to her?" I dared to ask. "Who are you *period?*" Because I didn't know who he was to make her this way. But I was going to find out.

"*If* it was Lara," Liam said finally not looking at me as I let him go, each word measured and deliberate. "I would do whatever it took to get to my girl."

"And you don't expect me to do the same?"

I leveled with Liam.

"You don't think I'd break down Sonya's apartment to get to my girl?"

That was my girl.

And she didn't know the truth.

It was burning through me to get her back. The rush of adrenaline in me had me itching for a fight.

"Fine." He let out a breath looking grumpier than normal at the mention of Lara. "I'll help you get Nisha back. On one condition…"

"Anything—"

He smirked. "Careful what you agree to."

I didn't care. I would make a deal with the devil to get Nisha back.

51

NISHA

I MISSED HIM.

God, I missed him so much it physically hurt.

Time lost all meaning in Sonya's guest room.

I had been staying with her for maybe a week and a half now. I couldn't stop crying and freaking out. Laying there even more emotional over the baby.

She was all I had. She was my family.

Days blurred together, marked only by the shifting sunlight filtering through the sheer curtains.

At four months, my pregnancy was making itself known in ways I couldn't ignore.

The nausea returned with a vengeance, rolling waves that left me dizzy and hollow. But I thought it was more the anxiety than anything else—and that wasn't my friend.

My clothes fit differently, my body no longer feeling entirely my own.

In the wake of Killian's lies, those old wounds felt raw, gaping and exposed. I found myself spiraling, utterly losing my grip on the life I'd worked so hard to build.

Michelle's voice haunted me.

I kept thinking I saw Eugene everywhere, shadows of him at night outside my window. His silhouette, but it couldn't be true because I hadn't heard anything about him being let out.

And it had been quiet for months now.

The only thing I did think about…

Killian.

He had been my hope, my chance at a different life. With him, I had felt loved and *understood*. For the first time, I had begun to believe that I could have a family, a home untainted by the shadows of my past. A new legacy. For both of us.

And now? I felt completely. Shattered.

When he had said his father had been a criminal—I had never imagined this.

Now, that fragile dream lay on the floor, pieces cutting deep into my heart and aching every single day. I didn't know how to not freak out.

If I closed my eyes, I felt his hands holding my face. Asking me if I was all right. I had kept her from him, and now I feared she, too, might inherit a legacy of uncertainty and heartache.

The thought was unbearable.

I didn't call out sick. I quit. Call it rash. But I didn't know what to do. The fear that gripped my throat was crippling as I'd curled into Sonya crying harder into her arms.

She became my lifeline.

The everyday sounds of her existence—footsteps, rustling papers, clinking china—formed a backdrop, a reminder that life continued. But she was there.

Even now, she was holding me tight to her.

Her dark brown hair was pulled back into a loose bun, a few stray wisps framing her pale face. The crisp white blouse she wore only emphasized the weariness that seemed to cling to her like a second skin.

"Darling."

I wiped my eyes, my skin sensitive and raw from crying.

"I know you're feeling sick, but I was curious. Would you want to speak to…Aidan?"

I blinked, confused. "What?" *Aidan?* Killian's brother? Why?

I struggled to sit up, my body protesting with every movement. The room spun slightly, a reminder of my constant nausea.

"Aidan?"

Sonya nodded, a flush coloring her cheeks. She perched on the edge of the bed, her fingers twisting in her lap.

"Yes. He says he wants to help." Her eyes held something in them, a darker shadow of unease and nerves. "That's all he told me, but...there's something about him, Nisha. I can't quite put my finger on it."

"*You* talked to Aidan?" I'd dragged her into this mess, and now...

"Well...Gabriel spoke to him. And directed him to me. I've met him once...or twice," Sonya confirmed, her expression quiet as she focused her eyes on her lap, twisting the fabric of her skirt. "He doesn't seem... like a bad man or malicious. If anything, he seemed genuinely concerned. He was more concerned about your well-being than anything else. He wanted to talk to you privately—"

"Because I know?" I asked.

"Because I know." Darker green eyes held a wealth of unspoken emotions as she watched me. "I am struggling to come to terms with this new reality, but I spoke with Aidan. And he wants to know if you're comfortable meeting with him." There was a flush to her cheeks as she continued. "He said if you're comfortable, he can come to you?"

"He wants to come to your place?"

She nodded. "I know it's a lot to process, but I do think he's trying."

I closed my eyes, taking a deep, shuddering breath. My hand drifted to my stomach. Aidan wanted to see me? The walls around me seemed to close in around me a bit more. But why?

The last time I met him? He told me if I needed him, if his brother messed up—

"He told me to call him," I whispered. "If Killian was ever...not great." And a tiny spark of my sadness felt curiosity. Because...I wanted to know. I didn't know why Killian didn't do it himself but I didn't understand many things. "But I feel stupid."

Sonya's entire expression was one of sympathy. "No, don't feel stupid—it's not every day you find out these things, I can't imagine anyone reacting to her appropriately." Her eyes went mock wide.

I felt a reluctant smile tugging at my lips.

But I made my decision too.

"I'll see him here if you're all right with that," I said, my voice quiet but determined as I opened my eyes to look at Sonya. "I'll speak to him..." But I didn't feel confident. I felt afraid. Not of him.

"I am all right with it. He's already been here before."

"What?" My eyes were saucers, I knew that and Sonya grinned easily.

"He was quiet about it." Her smile was light. "I know you're scared… I understand fear all too well. But sometimes, we need to face our fears head-on. Talking to someone close to Killian might give you the clarity you need. When I left Michael, I was terrified. He was all I had known. But I learned on the other side of my fear I found freedom."

"Did you have help?" I swallowed hard, my throat tight. I didn't know much about the ins and outs of Sonya's divorce. "What is there on the other side of my fears?"

"I did. My friend Andrei and his friend Lucas stepped in. I have my girlfriend's Gemma, Alisha…" Sonya's smile was soft and sad. "I know you don't have much. And while I don't know the exact answer for you, but I'm going to help you figure it out. I know you're afraid. I do. I know all too well how fear can control our lives…"

Her eyes met mine. "But if you live forever afraid of the things you don't know, you will miss out on so many more opportunities."

"You sound wise."

Sonya smiled at me with a twinkle in her eyes. "I feel ancient compared to you—"

"You're only thirty—"

"But you're twenty-four? Turning twenty-five? Give yourself some grace. You're young—"

"You don't judge me for being pregnant and—"

She made a noise like that was a ridiculous thing to say. "Not at all! Your life choices might not reflect mine, but it isn't my place." And her eyes turned down at the comforter, something unfamiliar lurking in them. "Besides…having children with Michael was never a possibility for me…but your child with Killian, albeit his criminal activities…is your choice. I would never judge you or your child or your decisions. It isn't my place."

And my chest expanded with something unfamiliar at the sensation of being so wholly accepted by this woman. I didn't keep many close relationships given my upbringing, but maybe I could start to expand it. For my sake.

"Sonya—" I broke off. "You're wonderful."

Her smile was delighted. "Thank you, it's been a long time since I've had good company in my home. Let's get some food in you and we can discuss meeting Aidan."

52

NISHA

THE DAY I MET AIDAN, I PUT ON A COZY SWEATER THAT HID MY BUMP AND I walked into Sonya's living room where Aidan was waiting for me.

The scent of Sonya's home—a mix of vanilla and cardamom with elegant magazines strewn about—usually calmed me, but today it did little to quell the storm of anxiety brewing in my chest.

As Aidan O'Hara rose to greet me, the air seemed to thicken, pressing against my skin. He looked even more imposing than I remembered in his dark suit with a hint of tattoos peeking out.

Unlike Killian who I knew was tattooed the moment I saw him, Aidan's crept up a tiny bit. Kieran's was completely hidden.

But the moment I saw him?

My eyes immediately began to water, and I didn't know why.

Sonya was somewhere in the house sitting with Aidan's assistant, a young man named Alexei, who seemed reluctant to leave him alone until Marta had fed him.

Then he'd stayed put with Sonya.

The moment he saw me, his eyes went wider and he reached for me.

"I'm sorry." It was the first words he said to my surprise.

He cut an impressive figure in a crisp white dress shirt and dark slacks, the top button undone and sleeves rolled to his elbows revealing double arms full of tattoos.

Aidan was the kind of man you knew held presence. People bowed before him. *And he ran the mob.* I knew that now.

Except…I didn't see him like that once I looked at him.

Aidan wasn't the kind of man who visited people for tea. So the fact that he was here, I knew—it meant *something* to him

I stood there a little jarred as he approached me, getting really close. "I'm sorry, Nisha. I shouldn't have let that happen—"

"You didn't do anything—"

"I did—" he broke off looking uneasy. "I did."

He let out a breath like he was the one who should be sorry, and I didn't think of him as the type to speak this way. To anyone.

His inky black hair so much like his brother's looked a little wind-blown. "I know this isn't easy for you. But I appreciate you giving me a chance to explain."

I swallowed hard, trying to find my voice. "I'm not sure what there is to explain," I said, surprised by the steadiness in my tone. "Killian lied to me. For months. Kieran told me by accident—"

"I think you deserve to know why." His eyes were grim despite being a shade brighter than Kieran's on his tanned face. They were a little scarier.

I paused. "Why?"

His smile was humorless. "Because my brother loves you, and he's losing his mind without you."

"You've seen him?"

"No, I don't have to. But I raised him and I know him. He's not the type to take things lightly."

My heart began to do that thing it had when Killian had brought me the harp. Like it was aware of being faced with something that was going to make it question it's very reality.

His eyes drifted over the sage green candles in Sonya's living space. The lush plants around us, and elegant backdrop made it calmer to have this conversation in her townhouse.

I waited for the feeling of unease at being around him, but it never came. Which…was odd.

Shouldn't I have been afraid?

Once I sat down and got a moment to study Aidan, I saw the resemblance between the brothers. *Maybe that's why I trust him.*

313

The arch of their brows, the straight line of their noses, the way they carried themselves with an inherent authority.

Adam had always compared Killian to a dark prince, but Aidan... Aidan was a king.

Even in Sonya's tastefully decorated living room, all whites and pinks, Aidan looked like a dark king holding court.

"I don't think my brother intended to deceive you..." he began. A flicker of unease crossed his face, so brief I almost missed it. "Killian, he's...not good at talking." A humorless chuckle escaped him, the sound rough and unexpected. "But you probably knew that already."

I shifted a little putting a blanket over my lap to hide my stomach more and once it was I felt comfortable. Aidan didn't know, and I didn't want him to.

"He's always been closed off, especially compared to Kieran," Aidan continued. I felt pinned by those amber eyes, unable to look away.

"He didn't tell me anything about you for months. I only recently realized just how serious he was about you. He wasn't always meant to be who he is now. For a long time, he was an outcast. Our father...He didn't like Killian."

I swallowed. "He mentioned that to me..." Aidan paused as I spoke. "He told me months ago that your father was...he wasn't a good man."

Aidan nodded, the shadows in his eyes evident. "That's a polite way of putting it."

There was a darkness in his expression I didn't think could exist. It made him a tiny bit terrifying. "Our father didn't like the way Killian looked."

"Because of his eyes?" I breathed, remembering the shock that had flickered across Killian's face months ago when I'd expressed my love for his unique gaze.

"More because he reminded my father of my mother."

At that something shifted in his expression. His gaze turned distant, focused on Sonya's coffee table.

"She left the family—"

His throat worked. "Something like that."

Aidan's eyes were darker now.

Bottomless and pools that reflected back deep pain and something even more haunted than Killian's. *This is his family.*

"I didn't know—"

Aidan nodded, his expression softening slightly. "Seems like you and Killian have a lot to say to each other."

Now, it seemed like we had more than that. How had I slept next to him and not known these things?

"Killian's always been the one helping everyone else. Always there for others as a way to not be there for himself. He doesn't know how to treat himself...until you."

Aidan's words, carefully chosen, were bridging the communication gap his brother couldn't seem to cross.

"My brother isn't eloquent," Aidan continued, his smile turning wry, a hint of affection softening the edges of his expression. "He doesn't know how to tell you that when Kieran left the family business, he stepped up. Took over."

He was giving voice to the struggles Killian had likely grappled with for years, the things he didn't—couldn't—say.

His eyes grew serious, the warm amber darkening to a deep, rich bronze, the color of secrets. I got that now.

For every single thing Aidan said, there was a wealth he wasn't telling me.

"I didn't know if he knew what he wanted. I just knew...it was what he did. We've changed, Nisha. Stopped most of what our father did. Now, our family is mostly just that—a network within Titan. We don't always participate in..."

"Killian, he deals with real estate, legitimate ventures. He helps Titan, runs his own industry. Now, the only real criminal in the family is me. I can't say my brother doesn't do things for Titan that on paper are...morally bankrupt. But the only member of the mafia in the family is me. What Killian does for everyone else? That's sanctioned. I'm not saying he's a good man—but I'm trying to tell you—he isn't a bad one."

In all the time I'd been around Killian, he'd never given off the aura that Aidan was emanating right now, the weight of a life lived in the shadows. Darkness.

"I know he messed up," Aidan continued softly, running a hand through his hair, the gesture so human, so at odds with the power he exuded. "I messed up too. I should've sat down with you guys, but I was too busy. I should've talked to you."

"I..." I began, my voice shaking, the words sticking in my throat like honey, thick and cloying. "I don't know what to do. I ran away from home…after my life…I never wanted to run again. And…I'm angry with him."

"That's fine, you can be." Aidan nodded, his expression softening slightly, those eyes of his brighter than Kieran's but somehow…different, holding a depth of understanding that belied his years.

"But I think the longer it went on, the harder it was for him to tell you. But I'm not here to convince you to go back to him. I only wanted you to understand his point of view. Not that I do…"

He paused, a hint of frustration creeping into his voice, the first crack in his composure.

"Killian hasn't said a word to me."

"How can I trust anything he says now?" I whispered, more to myself than to Aidan.

"I can't make that decision for you," Aidan said, his voice softening. "But I know he's doing everything in his power to make sure nothing happens to you."

His eyes met mine, and I was struck by how much brighter they seemed now, like molten amber catching the light.

"I know it would help if you at least spoke to him," Aidan continued, his words careful, measured. "If you choose to."

"I…I don't know if I'm ready," I admitted. "I just found out you're in the mafia…"

Aidan opened his mouth as if to say something more, but hesitated.

"I can't explain the entire thing to you, all I can tell you is, Killian isn't fully in or out. He's been in the middle of everything for a long time. But it's up to you what you want to do—"

A muffled thud came from somewhere in the house, followed by raised voices. Aidan's eyes changed instantly.

The sound of shattering glass and a woman's cry—Sonya's voice—followed. And then a volley of Russian from a man. Aidan's eyes widened as he swore.

I didn't think, we both moved towards the kitchen.

Sonya stood near the marble island, her usual poise lacking. Her eyes darting towards Aidan.

Her dark brown hair, typically immaculate, fell in disarray around her ashen face.

In front of her, the housekeeper Marta stood protectively.

She was speaking to a young man dressed similarly to Aidan, who seemed startlingly out of place in Sonya's elegant kitchen.

Alexei.

His platinum blonde hair framed a youthful face that contrasted sharply with the cold intensity in his piercing blue eyes.

What made my breath catch in my throat was the gun gripped tightly in his hand, its metal gleaming under the soft kitchen lights.

"What the fuck is this Sonya?" Came the voice from in front of them.

Alexei bared his teeth at a a figure I recognized instantly from news reports—Michael Devereaux, Sonya's *ex*-husband.

The one she had a clear restraining order against.

His face was contorted with a rage that seemed to radiate off him in waves.

"You have men in this house holding a weapon to me? Are you fucking kidding me right now? My parents will hear about—"

Alexei swore at him in Russian going off on him.

I flinched at the sound of Michael's voice.

"It is none of your business who I have in my house," Sonya shouted her voice quivering and her body shaking. "You are violating your restraining order. And you need to leave."

Back in the living room, Aidan been caged and leashed.

Darkness cloaked in silk. But now? Those amber eyes were eerily bright watching Michael, his mouth almost tipping up in humor, except there was nothing funny here.

And suddenly, I understood *why* Killian yielded to Aidan.

He was dangerous. Unholy. Danger. Because Aidan thought this was amusing.

Which meant his average day was worse.

I felt my heart race, my hands moving over my belly protectively.

Michael's eyes darted to me, then Aidan, who moved in front of me, a wall of muscle and iron and black.

"This is why you won't take my calls?" Michael spat at Sonya, his voice dripping with venom. "Who the fuck is he? Why do you have men over in this house?"

At that moment, I saw who Sonya had been with during her marriage.

And it was a little more than terrifying. I couldn't have imagined someone like her with that man.

I glanced at Aidan, watching as his eyes flicked to Sonya as he must've realized the same thing.

Something shifted in their amber depths. "I suggest you watch your fucking mouth, Devereaux—"

"*Don't tell me what the fuck to do—*"

Alexei spat something at him in Russian, moving in front of Sonya. He said something rapidly to Aidan, who nodded.

Sonya's voice shook as she spoke, a far cry from her usual measured tones. "*You're* not allowed here. And I am allowed to have *whoever* I went in my home."

And if the rumors about Michael Devereux were any indication of how he treated Sonya in his personal life his expression clouded over.

"*Allowed?*" Michael's gaze snapped to Aidan, his body language aggressive as he seemed to swell with indignation. "Who the fuck are you?"

Aidan tipped his head back like a predator, as he slowly unbuttoned his shirt by a few buttons, then reaching for his cufflinks.

"I suggest you listen to your ex-wife. Because if you don't, I'm the man who's gonna be escorting you off the fucking property." He turned to Alexei. "How the fuck did he get in?"

Marta held up a shaking hand. "I'm sorry sir, I thought he was the mailman."

Aidan nodded, his jaw granite tight. "*Don't* let it happen again."

Marta looked like she wanted to crawl into herself as Sonya watched Aidan with wide eyes.

Aidan said something back in clipped words before Alexei's eyes landed on me. Alexei's jaw clenched as he moved to me, motioning for me to follow him.

"I don't want to leave her," I whispered about Sonya who Aidan was watching.

"We have to," he murmured coming closer to me and ushering me out. "His orders, Killian's wife, not mine. And I have to obey him."

53

KILLIAN

I SAT IN MY PENTHOUSE, A GLASS OF WHISKEY CLUTCHED IN MY HAND, THE amber liquid swirling as I stared into its depths.

The room had one lamp lit because I couldn't tolerate anything else. Since I'd come back to my place ready to tear into anything and everything? I knew Aidan had stepped in doing damage control.

It had been two fucking weeks.

I'd checked out.

Too fucking angry at the world. My chest feeling like it had been ripped into pieces.

Nisha had ran from me.

I lost my girl.

And me?

I hadn't said a word to anyone or tried not to. Liam had found Nisha with Sonya. He had surveillance set up on the street cameras to see if Nisha was good. But otherwise?

He was just watching.

I couldn't go get her.

Because Aidan stepped in realizing how badly I'd fucked up.

And didn't that make me feel like a fucking child.

I was ready to break into Sonya's home if I knew Gabriel and Reed wouldn't murder me.

On top of all that? Derek had said Nisha's father, Eugene had gone back to his wife. In his old neighborhood. Derek had eyes on him. And

319

he wasn't coming anywhere near Nisha's apartment...my apartment with her. Our home.

Empty. *A void without my girl.* So I stayed in my penthouse.

I'd lost count of how many I'd had, the alcohol doing little to numb the ache in my chest. Aidan was on his way, and I knew he was coming to my place after meeting with Nisha.

I hadn't spoken to Kieran since the hospital, the weight of our last conversation hanging heavy on my shoulders.

The anger I'd felt then, the resentment that had bubbled up from somewhere deep inside me, had been a revelation.

I needed to fight something. Someone.

The fact that Aidan got to see Nisha, to figure this out so she wouldn't be even more afraid, while I was stuck here, drowning my sorrows...it was a bitter pill to swallow.

I'd always been the one to handle things, to keep everyone else together.

But now, when it mattered most, I was helpless.

The whiskey burned my throat as I took another swig, the alcohol doing little to dull the ache in my chest.

When my door opened to the apartment, I knew it was Aidan.

"I'm not in the fucking mood." I bit back anything else. I wanted to light someone up, but instead I was corralled into my fucking penthouse like a wild animal.

"Well you're about to be," Aidan stalked up to me, Alexei right behind him shutting my penthouse doors, his expression unreadable. "I talked to Nisha."

That got me listening.

"What the fuck were you thinking?" His face contorted with rage. "You didn't tell her! She's out of her mind scared. She quit her fucking job!"

"I know." I stood abruptly the glass shattering.

A fight. I need to fight someone.

"You don't think I know I fucked up!" I was losing it. "You came in here to tell me how much I did after you got to see my girl? You know what the fuck it costs me to hold back?"

He grabbed me by my throat. *"...you should've told her the moment you knew about your fucking kid."*

I froze, every muscle in my body turning to stone.

320

The world around me faded away, Aidan's voice becoming a distant echo as a roaring filled my ears.

Slowly, I turned to face him, my movements mechanical, my mind struggling to process what he was saying.

"You think I'm a moron! The way she hides it from me! She's pregnant and she's fucking terrified! I don't know why you didn't say a word to me or at least Gabriel–"

"My kid…" The words felt foreign on my tongue.

She's pregnant and she's fucking terrified.

"Bringing a fucking kid into our world without even considering telling the mom what the fuck she was getting into—" Aidan was in my face.

"What kid?" I managed to choke out, my voice rough with confusion and growing dread.

My heart was racing for another reason now.

I felt it pounding in my ears.

The way my stomach bottomed out the taste of alcohol gone. Alexei shifted behind Aidan to watch me.

"What fucking kid?"

Aidan stopped mid-sentence.

His amber eyes met mine, a haunting look dawning in them. He closed them, pain etched across his features.

"Oh, fuck me." He rubbed his eyes, looking more out of it than me. "Both of you…fucking *kids."*

But I was processing what he didn't say.

"What. Kid?"

I advanced on him, my heart pounding so hard I could feel it in my throat.

"What the fuck did you just say?"

She's pregnant and she's terrified.

Because Nisha wouldn't run and quit her job willy nilly.

No. I know my girl. She had given in to me since the day we met. Nisha wouldn't fight me just like I didn't fight her.

She'd been spooked.

Not just by Kieran.

"She's pregnant."

He shook his head, his expression a mix of sympathy and shock. "You didn't know—"

The broken condom.

Nisha had to tell me something. She stopped me that day with Kieran. She didn't look good. She said it *several* times. My mind was spinning with every single thing I knew. Her skin. Her hair. Her body.

Her clothing fitting differently, her breasts were bigger, her *entire* body looked different.

She hadn't been eating as much.

She hadn't been feeling good.

She was going to tell me over dinner.

"She's pregnant." I whispered, horror coursing through my veins like ice. Devastation. Shards of absolute pain sliced through my insides at the realization that—"*Nisha's pregnant.*"

Aidan's entire expression softened, those amber eyes of his realizing at the same time I did that I just found out I was going to be a dad.

"Killian—"

"*And I fucked it up?*" I could tell I wore my horror on my face.

"Killian, breathe—she's four months pregnant," Aidan said his voice uneasy.

Four months?

"That's why Sonya got involved. She knew—" *Was that why everyone was tiptoeing around me?*

"She knew and she was worried about Nisha and the baby—"

I couldn't breathe.

Nisha. And the *baby.*

"*Four months.*"

"Nisha found out and didn't say anything—"

"She was going to tell me."

"She was scared—"

"*She was going to tell me that night!*"

Because I was going to tell her about my life. My truth. My secrets.

Oh.

Fuck.

Me.

I was losing it. My breathing had shifted and for once, I felt like I'd been cold cocked with a gun instead of finding out I was—there was—a *baby.*

In an instant, every moment with Nisha flashed through my mind. Every smile, every laugh, every gentle touch. I was drowning.

She was out there, alone and scared, carrying *our* child.

I couldn't breathe.

I couldn't think anymore.

She had an appointment at the clinic a few times.

She said it was routine, that we would talk. I had been so busy—I didn't stop and think because I had other things to figure out.

Nisha had been with Selena and I thought she would be fine.

Aidan's voice cut through the haze of my self-loathing. *"Killian, listen to me—"*

"No, you listen to me," I growled in his face grabbing his jacket and his eyes went wide.

My brother looked at me like he'd seen me for the first time.

"You had me sitting tight thinking she didn't want to see me. She needs to see me. I'm the fucking—"

Oh. Shit. I was about to be a *father.*

Something painful twisted in my gut at the thought of being a…dad. A fucking dad. Nisha was *pregnant.*

And this is how I found out?

"She needs me. I am hers. Do you understand me? You won't keep me away from her. *Not anymore.*"

I was in his face for once.

I saw my brother's expression shift and change. Something coming over his eyes. I could break into anything if I chose to. I would.

"Nothing is going to keep me away from her. Not anymore."

I set the glass down grabbing my jacket.

Sonya Amin's townhouse be damned.

Stay with me?

Nothing will keep me from you, luv.

Nothing in this world would stop me from finding her. From keeping her.

Whether she liked it or not.

She was mine. And now, so was our *child.*

Goddamn, I fucking knew Nisha would've talked to me.

Had it not been for the fact that she was fucking *pregnant.*

She was having a baby.

And I'd be damned if I let anything or anyone keep them from me.

Not even Nisha herself. I didn't even bother saying anything other than calling Liam.

He sounded out of breath when he picked up. A feminine oomph

sounded and I couldn't feel guilty about Lara's personal life being interrupted while mine was going up in flames.

Because nothing was going to stop me from getting my girl.

"*What?*"

"I need you to disable all the alarms in Sonya's apartment."

5 4

NISHA

ALEXEI HAD BROUGHT ME TO MY ROOM AND SAT WITH ME QUIETLY looking all of sixteen.

There was no way he was an adult.

It wasn't until he sat down that he'd taken out a sandwich from his pocket he'd snuck in there when he'd left the kitchen.

And I didn't know why I burst into tears at that.

"You are so adorable," I whispered in the quiet room. "What are you fifteen?"

He blinked a little at me looking confused. "I am not a baby." He had an Eastern European accent. "I am twenty-one."

Yes, you all are big babies.

I sniffled and didn't say anything. He'd been a little alarmed but I sat there quietly with him eating and me crying over the sandwich. Everything made me cry it seemed.

But also, it had been a little surreal.

"What do you do for Aidan?" I'd wiped my eyes profusely.

"Do you understand the word Enforcer?"

I shook my head.

He offered me his sandwich.

"Is that from Butterscotch's?"

"Killian likes this place." And I cried a little more because it was our place. "Miss Sonya took us there too and she brought me these."

No freaking way he was twenty-one.

325

"Did she buy you cookies?"

He thought about it and a little smile came to his lips. "Yes."

Oh my god he's adorable. All that messy platinum blonde hair and bright eyes made me forget I was sitting with a mafia enforcer with a gun. And a sandwich.

He looked too hungry and I did want to feed him cookies.

If we were back in my home I wouldn't let him leave until he was full. I just cried silently feeling for him.

He chewed quietly as he said. "I kill people for Aidan."

"That was very straightforward." His lips quirked. "Where are you from originally?"

"Belarus." His voice was low like he didn't want to startle me. "I was picked up by Aidan when I was much younger. He trained me. Now I am his soldier. Make sense?"

I wiped my eyes listening to him. "You...work for him?"

"Yes." He paused like he was unsure of how to ask me anything. "And you are Killian's wife."

A statement.

"Erm...not exactly." I didn't know how to tell him where I was at emotionally. I was a little worried about Sonya. But I got the feeling if anyone could handle it—it was Aidan.

"But you are..." he motioned to my stomach. My heart stopped a little.

"Is it obvious?"

The cat was out of the bag. And I wondered how long it would take for them to tell Killian.

Oh, he might be pissed.

But I was angry with him too.

"You have," he said again, his blue eyes brighter now watching me. "When you are back with Killian."

He said it like it was bound to happen and inevitable. Maybe it was. But right now I felt nausea stirring at the idea of Killian finding out like this. Did he already know? What did he think?

Aidan was here. That was good or bad?

I didn't understand any of his life.

I just knew—the idea of making my daughter relive any kind of hell of my own? Gave me chills. At this point my entire being wanted to protect my baby. And that was it.

"I'm new to this whole..." I motioned to him. He'd set his gun down next to us like he was ready to strike at any moment. "This is your life?"

He nodded quietly. "Always." After a moment Alexei spoke. "Killian is not doing well."

At the mention of him my chest tightened and I felt a low cramp in my stomach. Baby girl was not happy. I rubbed it gently soothing her as I said.

"Neither am I."

It was a whisper. But I think Alexei got it.

He finished his sandwich as a knock at the door came.

Alexei moved so fast my heart began pounding as he grabbed his gun, until Sonya walked in, her eyes rimmed red with Aidan behind her.

Sonya's smile was watery.

Both of the men had left Aidan bidding me goodbye as he looked at Sonya one last time something passing in his eyes as he did.

~

Now, hours later, with a pizza and gummy worms between us, Sonya lay next to me on the bed, her usual poise gone.

She was in her silk pajamas and I was in a nightie stretched over my belly as I rubbed my girl slowly.

My stomach had dull cramps that just felt like I was getting my period. But I knew I wasn't.

Probably stress or anxiety leading up to it.

Sonya suggested getting pizza and having a girls night.

Something to alleviate the fact that...one of us was pregnant with a mafia prince's baby and the other one was combating her ex-husband violating his restraining order.

With said mafia prince's older brother.

"Aidan is helping you with Michael?"

Her dark hair, usually so immaculate, was disheveled, and her green eyes were rimmed with red.

"Yes." As she spoke about her marriage in hushed tones, I saw a side of her I'd never imagined existed beneath her polished exterior.

"He wasn't supposed to be here," she whispered, her gaze fixed on some distant point. "I filed for a restraining order against him…but the paperwork is taking forever. Aidan offered to assist."

Sonya's elegant lines of her face filled with worry.

"Why does he…" I trailed off. "I don't know how to ask about your ex."

"Michael is from the Devereaux family? Do you know who they are?"

"Lucas Devereaux, Killian says he worked with him—"

"That is Michael's cousin. I believe Lucas is connected to the Whittaker's somehow." Sonya's brows rose, her fingers nervously plucked at the silky fabric of her blouse. "They are distant cousins. Lucas does not like his family. Especially Michael. They're all some variation and shade of madness. Michael is a product of his parents, spoiled rotten from birth. He's never had his mother say no to him. She's so proud of her son and who he is, he routinely breaks the rules and his mother bails him out of everything. Whereas Lucas's mother died and his father sent him to boarding school at maybe thirteen? Not sure. But Lucas is friends with the DuPont's who were much better."

Sonya explained the DuPont family had much more rigid standards and so Lucas had been raised like them. Which was how Andrei the eldest DuPont, and head of his family's conglomerate had saved Sonya with Lucas.

"That sounds like a nightmare. A long one."

She gave me a look that told me that I had no idea.

"When I was married to him, the first time he…" she motioned to her lip. "It split my lip…and his mother told me to put more gloss on so nobody could tell. My mother said I should've been flattered my husband thought of me so highly he would hit me."

"That's insane." And yet something about it struck a chord in me. "My adoptive mother, Michelle , she told me not to flatter myself when Eugene, her husband molested me. For years." It was the easiest it left my lips. I told Sonya how whenever I tried to tell Michelle , she told me girls only make up stories to get men in trouble.

"She said women make up everything."

Sonya paled as she let out a shuddering breath. "It's always insanity coming from the families we do, to know women in our own culture perpetuate the nightmare." She was clutching the comforter more now but I knew how she felt.

Both of us had been trapped in prisons designed from us by our parents. Both of us had been victims.

And now survivors. Maybe that's what I saw in Sonya that day I met her. Someone who was a kindred spirit in many ways.

I wanted to murder Michael Devereaux's family and his mother in that moment. At the haunted look in Sonya's eyes.

"She knew what he was doing and she asked me who else did I think he was going to do it too? She said it was my duty as his wife for him to take his anger out on me."

She couldn't be serious. At the expression on my face her smile was bitter. "I tolerated it for years because I didn't know who else to go to. And then we were at a party, and Lucas and Andrei happened to see." She seemed to shrink into the blanket more and more. "I thought Andrei was going to kill him. If not Lucas." Sonya looked even more haunted than before.

And suddenly it all made sense.

"He's why you started Haven."

She nodded. As messed up as it was, I realized I wasn't the only one trying to put myself together.

"Michael's relative, his grandmother for lack of a better word. Eleanor Kennedy Devereaux was a wealthy woman. When she died, I had her wealth. And everything that came with it. I decided to use my money for good."

Sonya explained with the money Eleanor gave her that Michael was after—she had set out to create a better life.

"I didn't realize how much of myself I'd lost until I left," Sonya continued, her voice gaining strength. "It is why I started Haven. I couldn't bear the thought of other women going through what I did, feeling as alone as I felt."

As she spoke, I began to understand why Sonya had been so supportive of me, why she seemed to intuitively grasp my conflicted feelings about Killian and his world.

She'd lived through her own version of it. Even though Sonya and I were worlds apart, she was reaching out to me because she saw the same things in me I saw in her.

"And you trust Aidan to help you?"

It was surprising but not surprising at all. Killian had been abused at the hands-of his father. Now I knew why he had all those scars on his body. His memories were dark as he told me about some events. Some brutal. Some painful.

He told me he didn't feel hunger the same way or the cold because it was used against them so much. All three brother's were scarred in their own ways. And now one of them wanted to make amends.

"I've stopped believing in simple notions of good and evil after watching what Michael got away with in broad daylight. Everyone watched me be abused. Nobody told me it was wrong. They let it happen."

Same with me.

For years I thought I was alone and crazy, but after seeing patients coming in day and night, I realized it would've taken one person to reach out. Just one. For me to see it sooner. For someone to save me.

I waited my entire life to be rescued and then just like Sonya—I ended up rescuing myself. Until Killian.

Killian's secrets, his family, his reasons for lying...they all tangled together in my head until I could barely think straight. But even with all those emotions—I knew I loved him. I was angry with him.

But I loved him.

"I don't think people operate in right and wrong," Sonya whispered. "And I think today was the first day someone stood up for me in my eyes to Michael...my own family didn't even do that."

Her eyes met mine, a mix of gratitude and irony in their depths. "And he isn't even on the right side of the law and he defended me."

No, he wasn't. I nodded in understanding because I didn't think it would matter.

"I was twenty-one...my parents wanted connections. My parents thought marrying a Devereaux would be great. They didn't care which one. Michael's cousin Lucas was in the military and so Michael was... my only choice." Her smile was tight. "Sometimes we do not get a say in our lives."

"And now Michael doesn't leave me alone and he's been dragging the divorce out. Something Aidan does not take lightly," she murmured. "I think perhaps if his younger brother is anything like the older, he would not take lightly to losing you as well." Her eyes met mine. "Killian sounds lovely. And might I remind you, since you have been here... you've not said a bad word about him."

"I have nothing bad to say about him." It was the truth.

"But you are afraid."

"I'm terrified of bringing a daughter into his world."

Sonya's smile dipped a little. "Maybe he might be too." Her eyes were a little downcast. "Aidan knows about the baby...so I'm guessing at some point Killian will too."

"I'm not upset if he knows—"

"I'm saying *he* might be."

We both paused as Sonya traced patterns next to her pizza, untouched and probably cold. She had a hard time eating like I did. Only hers I got was from years of training.

"Are you going to talk to him when he comes to see you?"

"When?"

Sonya nodded.

Almost unconsciously, my hand drifted to my stomach, resting on the small bump that was just beginning to show. Our baby.

I had to tell him. Had to talk to him.

But even as I grappled with these fears, I couldn't ignore the fact that I'd had opportunities to tell him.

Moments when the words were right there on the tip of my tongue, but I'd swallowed them back.

Hot tears stung my eyes as the weight of my own secrets crashed over me.

How could I condemn Killian for keeping things from me when I'd done the same?

We'd both been trying, in our own ways, to protect each other. Killian, by shielding me from the darker aspects of his life, and me, by... what?

Protecting myself? Our baby?

The life I thought we could have?

But even in the midst of these conflicting emotions, one thing became painfully clear—no matter how much he'd hurt me, no matter how scared I was of his world...I still loved him.

And if Sonya could see Aidan for who he was...I needed to do the same for Killian. Because I did love him.

Completely and irrevocably.

"I am."

55

NISHA

After Sonya left I went to sleep feeling out of it. I was restless, tossing and turning.

The dull ache in my stomach had spread and I couldn't stop having nightmares.

Nightmares where my feet pounded the pavement, each step a desperate attempt to escape. My heart thundered in my chest, threatening to burst.

The terror was a living thing, nipping at my heels, its hot breath on my neck. I was prey, hunted, cornered.

I had a horrific nightmare with Eugene and Michelle , trying to hold me down.

Trying to take my baby away from me. My daughter.

Then, with a violent jerk, I was awake, every muscle taut with fear and noises left my lips as I trembled.

My stomach was aching violently now.

"Oh gosh," I moaned low as I gripped my belly. I focused on breathing. A noise left me in distress. *"Oh..."*

I felt the panic before arms circled me. Like steel bands hauling me to something. My heart raced as I was pulled back against a solid chest, the warmth of his body a stark contrast to the cold fear that gripped me. I knew *that* scent.

"Luv—"

"Killian—"

Was I still dreaming?

Only this time, he felt *outrageously* real.

"I got you, luv. Breathe for me. I gotcha..." Killian's voice pierced through the drowsiness. "I gotcha...Tell me what's wrong?"

"Something's wrong with the baby. It hurts...it hurts really bad."

My mind struggled to process what was happening. His voice was in my ear, his hands moving to my stomach.

"Cramping," I gasped, my hands clutching desperately at my stomach. "Killian, please...I'm scared...call Sonya...hospital. I need to go to the hospital."

I didn't know if I was still dreaming or not. How was he here?

"Put your arms around me, luv."

I felt myself being lifted, wrapped in something soft. I couldn't stop crying.

I buried my face in the crook of his neck, clinging to him like a lifeline. His pulse throbbed steadily against my cheek.

"I'm scared." I whispered. "She's been upset for hours."

I rubbed my belly as he carried me out of the room.

"I gotcha," he whispered fiercely, his breath warm against my ear. His voice cracked slightly as he added. "I got both of you."

Through the haze of pain and fear, a single coherent thought formed. It couldn't be *real*.

"How...how are you here?" I mumbled, the words slurring together. "Sonya..."

Killian replied tersely. "Couldn't stay away from you."

The journey to the hospital passed in a blur of motion and light. I clung to Killian's hand so tight I wanted to scream.

I thought I was dreaming. Even now.

The fluorescent lights assaulted my eyes and I clung to him, squeezing them shut, turning my face back into Killian's chest. I made a noise in distress.

"Oh God. That hurt's—"

"I know, luv." As another contraction gripped me, I tightened my hold on Killian.

I answered questions of the nurse, my responses punctuated by waves of pain. Gasping I clung to him.

Through it all, Killian's arms stayed around me. Part of me processing he was here. Physically. But also the pain.

A young doctor approached, his eyes barely lifting from the chart in his hands.

"It's probably just Braxton Hicks," he said dismissively. "Common in first-time mothers. Nothing to worry about."

God, spare me from men in the medical profession making light of women's care.

Anger flared hot and bright, cutting through the haze of pain.

"*This isn't Braxton Hicks,*" I snapped, my voice stronger than I felt. "I've had those before. This is different. Something's wrong."

A noise left me then.

"*Get me someone else.*"

I felt Killian tense beside me, his body coiled like a spring ready to release. His jaw clenched, eyes flashing dangerously as he addressed the doctor. "*You heard her.*"

The doctor's eyebrows shot up, clearly taken aback. "Sir, I don't see how—"

"*Now.* I know you fucking heard her. Get me someone else. Before I start tearing this hospital apart."

The young doctor paled, beating a hasty retreat.

In the tense silence that followed, I found myself studying Killian's profile, tracing the sharp line of his jaw, the furrow between his brows. "Thank you."

His gaze drifted to my belly, and I winced as his hand gently covered the swell. "*This* is why you ran from me."

"I was terrified," I admitted, my voice breaking as I trembled. "I wish you'd told me the truth…about everything."

I held my stomach grimacing. He didn't say a word holding me closer to him as I shook. A low noise left me as I sat up unable to sit still. I bent over breathing harder.

"I just want her to be okay."

My voice sounded weak to my own ears as an older female doctor entered, her face lined with experience and kindness.

"I'm Dr. Patel," she introduced herself, her voice calm and reassuring. "Let's run some tests and see what's going on. Better safe than sorry, especially when it comes to your little one."

She looked at Killian. "Will you put her on the bed again? I need to check a few things."

He moved me over to the hospital bed slowly, helping me lay me down. The sensation only increased and grew unbearable.

Another low noise left me as she felt around. "Sorry," she apologized. "So sorry, this will be quick."

I whimpered while Dr. Patel murmured a few things, checking over my stomach as Killian stood by. I felt the anxiety radiating off of him.

"How long have you had these?" Dr. Patel's eyes were concerned.

"Is everything okay? Is she okay?"

"I think so, I just wanted to know."

"Just tonight," I whispered. "But she hasn't been happy the last few weeks." Neither had I.

"Let me go grab a few things for you," Dr. Patel murmured as she finished. "I'll be right back."

I nodded as she left, drawing my nightie over my stomach again leaving me there hauling the blanket around me.

I didn't even know how to look at Killian.

This was one hell of a way for him to find out about the baby. That he was having a daughter.

The thought brought a fresh wave of guilt and confusion.

Part of me wanted to lose myself in his comfort, while another part remained wary, remembering the lies that had driven us apart.

"Aidan told me," Killian's voice was lower than usual, tightly controlled as if he was holding back a torrent of emotions. "She…"

He was standing watching over me and I dared to look at him. His eyes were on my stomach, an expression on his face I had never seen before.

Inky black hair, disheveled from worry, fell across his forehead in a way that softened his usually imposing presence.

He looked younger. Tired.

"She…" he whispered. "You kept saying it earlier and it didn't hit me until now."

His mismatched eyes—one a stormy blue-grey, the other a warm amber—locked onto mine, filled with an intensity that made my breath catch.

"We're having a little girl," I whispered, unable to stem the flow of tears as I wiped my eyes. "I b-b-aked cupcakes with pink filling inside… to tell you. I wanted to make sure she was…healthy."

My voice broke on the last word, a fresh wave of tears blurring my vision.

"But you didn't tell me about your secrets."

I wiped my eyes over and over, lying there as he moved. I felt him closer, his lips finding my temple, my cheeks, and I didn't know who grabbed who, but he was in my arms in another second.

"She's gonna be all right," his voice was so thick with emotion it made me break down even more. "We're...you're having a girl..."

He looked downright stunned and horrified.

"I've had a r-r-really h-hard pregnancy." My cheeks were burning from how much I was crying. "Why did you keep it from me?" I croaked. "Why didn't you just tell me who you were?"

"I didn't tell you because I thought you'd run." His voice was gruff. "You'd hate me...see me as..."

He didn't finish. I knew. From what Aidan had said.

And I had run, hadn't I?

I'd confirmed his worst fears. Except it wasn't for the reason he thought it was for. It was for her.

But the mixture of pain, anger, confusion warred within me, and it sent spasms into my stomach.

"I was afraid for her. I trusted you," As the words sank in, another cramp seized me. I winced and held onto him tighter, my fingers gripping the fabric of his shirt. "I trusted you with my life. With my body. It meant everything to me that you were honest—" I winced again.

"Tell me where it hurts," he said gruffly, concern evident in his voice. "Tell me, I'll try to help."

I moved his hands to where it was cramping.

His fingers, deft and strong rubbed the spots where it ached.

"I was afraid. Afraid of what your world meant to her, to me..." I drifted off at his expression.

"Her," he repeated. His eyes watched me and then my stomach. I nodded, understanding all that single word. *"Her."*

A shuddering breath left me as I nodded, my vision blurring again. "You're having a girl..." A *daughter.* "We're having a girl."

I couldn't have imagined it until his eyes moved over me then.

Eyes haunted and wide on my stomach as he rubbed the spot I asked him.

Before he could respond, the doctor returned. Her face bearing a reassuring smile at us holding each other.

"I have good news." Her voice was tinged with warmth and kindness. "I reviewed all the test results, and she's healthy. She's more than healthy, she's wonderful. Do you both want to see her?"

I felt Killian's body relax slightly against mine, his breath catching in his throat as I nodded.

"Yes." I couldn't stop myself from crying. "She's good?"

The doctor continued with a smile. "I can get all that set up for you. What you experienced was most likely round ligament pain. It's caused by the stretching of the ligaments that support your growing uterus. While it can be quite severe and alarming, I want to assure you that it's not dangerous to you or your baby."

Relief washed over me in waves, bringing with it a flood of emotions I couldn't contain. "Thank you."

Gathering myself, I asked Dr. Patel a few more questions about precautions and what to expect in the coming weeks.

"Is your husband comfortable with staying in the room with us?" she asked after a beat.

I looked up at him, watching as a light shade of pink crept up his neck and into his cheeks.

"I'm not going anywhere."

56

KILLIAN

My heart was going to explode.

I could see my daughter moving on the ultrasound screen.

My daughter...

I didn't even process the good Doc calling me Nisha's husband.

Of fucking course I was.

I was *hers* from the day I met her.

Nothing would keep me from her. The fact that I hadn't seen her in weeks? Didn't even matter.

I had missed out on so fucking much.

Now all I could see was the tiny black and white image. Of her. Tiny. Moving. All mine and Nisha's.

"She's so big," Nisha whispered. "She's gotten much bigger."

Because Nisha had seen her weeks ago.

When Aidan came and told me Nisha was pregnant, I knew I had to go to her. Nothing was going to keep from Nisha.

I didn't even think straight the moment I knew.

With Liam getting me into Sonya's place, me finding Nisha in pain —timing, fate, luck all of it hitting me then. I promised Liam two solid favors in the future no questions asked.

I knew what I was trading.

But none of it compared to this moment looking at my daughter moving in her mom's belly.

Pride, the sheer joy and horror of imagining Nisha going through her pregnancy without me—without me ever knowing?

I felt the agony ripping through me. My inner turmoil ratcheting up to a nine hundred out of ten on the scale of hurt.

I was having a *girl*.

A little girl whose existence I'd been *oblivious* to hours ago.

A little girl who would love pink bows, strawberry shortcake trifles her mother made, and gnocchi. A little girl who needed me to protect her from the world.

And now she was the center of my fucking world.

Fuck me, I would've missed out on her.

On both of them. Because I decided to keep secrets from Nisha.

I glanced at Nisha, her eyes fixed on the screen, tears streaming down her face. In that moment, I saw our future reflected in those eyes of hers.

Our daughter would have those eyes—eyes that saw the best in people. Who was soft and wrapped in her pink bows. Her instruments.

The urge to wrap them both in my arms, to shield them from the world, was overwhelming.

I didn't want to let her go ever again. But she ran from me because she was terrified of something happened to her and that girl.

"Strong heartbeat, good size for her gestational age. Everything looks good."

The doctor smiled at both of us, but I barely registered her presence.

"She hasn't been happy lately," Nisha whispered. "And my morning sickness has been terrible."

"She can feel everything you feel," Dr. Patel made a noise as she gave Nisha and me suggestions on how to help keep it down. "Has your anxiety been bad for the last few weeks?"

Nisha nodded almost shy as she answered. I hung my head a little unable to even face my shame.

Nisha and my daughter were uneasy because of me. And my vision blurred a little.

I couldn't even breathe as Nisha told her how she could only stomach smaller amounts of food. How she'd barely been eating.

Because of me.

My kid isn't even in the world right now.

And I'm already fucking up her life.

"Sometimes it helps to reduce stressors and take it easy. I know you said you've been a little tense lately, it doesn't help the baby…"

My fault. That was my fault.

I'd been the thing causing Nisha stress. I couldn't focus.

If I had hated myself before? I fucking *hated* myself now. I felt it burning through a hole in my stomach. In my chest. Eating me alive.

"You okay?" Nisha's soft voice pulled me from my thoughts. Her eyes, still glistening with tears, her hand had been in mine and I didn't realize how I was shaking.

No. I wasn't okay.

My throat was tight. I felt like a fucking failure as my chest rose and fell rapidly.

Words failed me as I stared at the screen, watching our daughter's tiny form move. The memory of walking into Sonya's and finding Nisha in that much pain flashed through my mind.

Timing had been everything, and for once in my life, I'd been exactly where I needed to be. Always with her.

As the doctor left to get the printouts, Nisha turned to me, her eyes wet and red-rimmed.

My vision blurred, and I felt something inside me crack open. I couldn't hold it back.

"*I'm sorry.*" The words felt inadequate, but I pushed on. "I fucked up."

That was an *understatement.*

I couldn't see straight as I looked at the swell of Nisha's body and bent my head to her. Resting it right there and the words left me. "I'm sorry to you too."

She wasn't even five months yet and I fucking failed her.

I couldn't stop losing it. They were both in a bad place. And it was my fault. I felt soft fingers in my hair, tugging gently. I'd missed that.

Fuuuccck.

"Look at me," she whispered and I turned my head unable to even face Nisha. Her voice was small and uncertain as she wiped her eyes over and over again. "Don't lie to me again. I love you. I do. But I can't have her and listen to you lie to me ever again."

Nisha's words hit me harder than any injury or wound I had. Like a hot knife slicing through me.

"I don't ever want to take her away from you. But I don't want to be with you right now. I don't want it because my father put me in danger. And my parents let me down." Her voice was broken. "And I didn't wanna do that to my—to my baby." Her face crumpled. "I was terrified the last few days—"

Fuck. She was cutting me open.

"*Everything* is all I ever wanted with you. From day one. You have been my home—" I heard myself say not recognizing my voice. I was choked up. "You are all I have ever wanted—"

"Then why didn't you say so?" Nisha's whimpers were going to cut their way down to my skin. *"Why didn't you say that? Why didn't you tell me about your father or your brother? Your entire life was a lie—"*

"No, Nisha, it was the truth, the entire time, I swear—"

"No, it *wasn't.*"

She winced and I felt nothing but shame fill me as my hand moved to her stomach. I pressed my lips to the spot Nisha told me.

Over and over until apologizing to her was the only thing on my mind.

I couldn't breathe around my feelings. It was bubbling up to the surface. I was good at work. Good at talking about anything other than my emotions.

"I fucked up—I stressed you out. I'm sorry, luv. I'm so fucking sorry. You were pregnant this entire time. I'm *sorry.*"

I was holding her face in my hands in another second.

"I swear, the only thing I never told you was my position in the family—"

"That was a big deal though—" she was crying harder. "That was such a big deal!"

I knew. I fucking knew.

"I'm sorry."

I hung my head, pressing my forehead into hers.

Whatever legacy I thought I'd have...it had been completely obliterated.

To her. For her. For...our girl.

"Nothing I am matters without you."

And that was the fucking truth isn't it?

I recognized that when I was in Chicago.

Or anywhere without her.

I'd spent the last few days in my penthouse unable to even exist in Nisha's place because it was our home.

Without her it was empty. There was no home.

Her eyes searched the room before coming back to me, her eyes watery and her face in pain.

"All my life, I have dreamed of someone like you. Not a knight coming to save me, but someone who would do anything for me. Anything to keep me safe. You gave me that...when you lied to me I felt like that entire world shattered...and I didn't know how to forgive you."

Her voice broke and I didn't know who reached for each other but I was in her arms then.

I never thought I'd lose my shit.

But it wasn't every day your runaway girlfriend told you about your *daughter*.

"...Aidan said...you're clean. But how can you be both."

"I'm not gonna lie to you. My family is mob. We are." I felt my entire being shaking. "I'm a backup if he dies. And I still am involved. I tiptoe a middle ground but I'm as clean as I can be. You were never in any danger. I swear it. Titan stands over the O'Hara's and it makes us stronger. Nothing was ever going to happen to you." I softly explained to her still holding onto her, rising up to find her wiping my eyes, my cheeks. "I promise I would've told you. That's why I wanted to take you out. I swear I was gonna say something—"

"Before or after I told you about her—" she broke. "What if I told you about the baby? Would you have told me?"

Her entire face crumpled at my expression.

No. I don't know if I would've. A shuddering breath left me.

Because if Nisha told me about our girl?

I would rather die than ever run the risk of losing Nisha. She wiped her eyes sobbing quietly.

And it was like nails ripping through my chest.

It hurt more than anything else in the world to know Nisha was crying over me. Because of me.

I stressed out my pregnant girlfriend.

"I need space—" she murmured. "I thought I could forgive you but I need space. I need time—"

Nonononono.

"Nisha—"

342

"*No,*" she whimpered a little. "No, you had no...intention of letting me in...you kept your secret this entire time...I thought you were a—" she grimaced rubbing her belly. Oh. Fuck. "I thought you were a *Titan.*"

Panic. It was like a gunshot in my body.

Finding out about my daughter and then finding out Nisha needed space from me?

Panic.

It ripped through my body with little grace, tearing my heart into shreds.

"*Luv—*"

"No." Her voice was breaking. "I didn't care who you were. I cared that when you didn't tell me it felt like you were keeping a dangerous secret from me. What if something happened to her—"

"She wasn't—*nobody* is going to touch her. Not under me. Ever. I swear, baby, I swear." I was feeling the desperation clawing at my throat to hug her, to hold her. "I promise our daughter was never in danger."

Words. I *never.* Expected. To. Say.

You're losing your child. And your wife.

No. Nonononono.

"I can't do this," she whispered. "I thought I could, but now the reality of it is really scary. I'm terrified."

Her eyes met mine and I felt myself shatter.

"I love you so much. I do. But I cannot do this with you. I won't stop you from being a part of her life—"

Nononono.

"Nisha, luv, *don't—*"

Don't push me away.

Please, just love me.

I was reaching for her and she whimpered drawing back. And just like that. My heart shattered. It splintered into pieces.

"No," she shook her head. "I cannot be with you. I thought I could but you never were going to tell me."

"*I love you,*" the words felt raw coming out of me and my heart fucking *broke.* "Fuck, I love you so much. I never want you to leave me ever again. I'll do anything. I swear. Just tell me what you want from me and I'll give it to you. To her."

For her.

Holy fucking shit—I thought getting shot hurt.

Nothing compared to this. Nothing hurt more than watching the love of your life tell you she wanted nothing to do with you.

I looked at her lying there, her eyes soft and wet as she whimpered a little.

"Just tell me what you want," I croaked, feeling my eyes blur. "Nisha, please. Don't do this. I promise I'll fix it. I will."

I would do anything to fix it.

She wiped her face with the backs of her hands. "I would never keep you from her life," she whispered. "I would *never* do such a thing to you. I couldn't tell you because you were busy, you've been keeping it from me from—"

And just like that my heart dropped to my stomach.

Because I knew what she was going to say.

Even if everything in my body was snapping as she did.,

"I don't know how to trust you again after you kept something from me that was so big. I was scared for me. For her. And you acted like it was fine—"

"Nisha—"

"No, I need time to…" she rubbed her stomach. "I don't feel good. I can't think straight and I've had weeks to think about you. This was a start." And my heart twisted as she said the words. "But I need time too."

"Does that mean—"

"It means I want to go back to old life without fearing my new one. It means I want to be a Mom really badly because it feels like I can change my future even if my entire past was awful. She doesn't have to be a bad legacy. For either of us."

Her eyes met mine. I never thought I'd be the reason those softer dark eyes would be in this much pain.

"That's why you wanted to have kids with me," she whispered crying harder now. "Because you saw a future outside of your life. I know you did. But I wish you had told me the truth. That isn't a tiny secret. That's really scary for me to hear from your brother."

"I will *always* be here," I added, my voice cracking with the weight of my emotions as I felt my vision blur several times and I couldn't stop. "Whatever you—she—whatever you two need I'm here. What do you want? Tell me, luv. I'll get it for you."

Always.

344

"I think I'd like to go home…" she hiccuped wiping her eyes crying quietly now. "I think it's going to take me time to forgive you…"

But we could go home together?

I'd take that. I'd take her.

One step at a time.

A faint burst of relief filled me even if I knew my entire relationship with her was in jeopardy.

NISHA

He brought me back to my place.

My apartment in Brooklyn out of all things and the sheer comfort of my bed had me passing out after the ER visit.

It felt so good to be home my entire being sighed and my stomach finally calmed down enough to let me sleep.

When I woke up in the late afternoon the next day, Killian was wrapped around me in my bed, shirtless and beautiful as his palm pressed into my abdomen. I could feel the heat coming off his hand rubbing gentle circles into my skin.

Wherever he moved I calmed down.

I blinked slowly at him. "You stayed?"

He tipped his head slowly. "Do you need anything today?"

I swallowed around my dry throat, and before I could ask he had water in my hands. I slowly sat up with his help and I had to admit—he was all around me gently rubbing as I sipped my water.

"Sonya, she must be worried," I murmured.

"Liam let her know. He didn't want her to be worried." Killian set my water down and wrapped the blanket around me. He didn't look like he'd slept a wink, his eyes normally calm were rimmed red. And I felt a bit of guilt and unease at putting it there.

He'd turned the heated blanket on and wrapped that on me too. "It's cozy in here."

"I took care of your plants and kitchen," he murmured. "The cupcakes on the counter were pink…for her?"

I nodded slowly. Her. I had an idea of a name picked out for her.

When he'd been a Titan, I didn't understand the extent of who he was.

I just knew he had resources and funds to get what he needed in life. I had no idea those resources came from blood money, that he had the ability to break into people's home—and take what he wanted.

That reality? Was a little unsettling. To say the least.

My heart felt fragile at that moment then.

"Do you have plans, luv?" He murmured. "Today?"

"No," I'd been so freaked out I left the hospital, a fact that made me cry a little. "I quit…the hospital."

My voice wobbled again as I wiped my eyes.

And here we went again.

Maybe I was hormonal. Maybe it had been a stressful few weeks.

Everything made me cry a little but I needed my own headspace to heal. I didn't hate Killian. No, I was angry. Upset. Coping with my new reality.

"I feel afraid for our daughter, I don't ever want her to grow up like me," I wiped my eyes feeling him make a small noise. His lips found his way to the column of my throat as I cried again. "I don't want her to live her life afraid of her every step. Being vigilant. I didn't know. I feel like I wasn't giving a proper choice at knowing if I wanted this life with you or not."

That wasn't fair to her.

"I'm sorry…I didn't mean to scare you. She's not in any danger. I promise, she wouldn't be, I'm not just saying that. I swear—" he broke off. "I swear."

I wiped my eyes frantically as I felt his lips pressing into my pulse on my neck trying to find it and hold me steady.

That only made me cry more.

And the fact that if I had told him about her—our girl—he never would've told me who he was. *Why?*

Because he'd been afraid to lose me? Or her?

"Nisha, I know you don't know much about my family. But I swear when Titan built their empire around ours, Gabriel he did his best to make sure my family was safe-guarded—"

"How?"

"It's a long story and no, don't cry. I promise I wanna tell you. Let me get you something to eat first. Let me help you."

"You don't have work?"

"I have Landon covering for me."

I didn't even know who that was.

"I'm starving…but my nausea flares up at everything."

The intimacy of the moment aside, we were in a weird place.

Not quite there. Not quite where we both wanted.

I didn't know what I wanted. I just knew I didn't want lies between us to take up the space that it had.

"You like those sandwiches I got you before, have you tried those?"

"I completely forgot about *Butterscotch's*," I yawned. "Those sound so good."

"I can go get them for you." I was turning to him stunned at how quickly he decided that as he was up and moving around the room. Just like that.

I gaped at how quickly he had done that.

"You-you can't just—" I watched him sputtering as he stretched and got ready. "I want to go with you."

I don't know where it came from but he motioned to my stomach with his eyes holding all of the darkness from the night before. Like he couldn't stop thinking about us and our conversation. But neither could I.

"You're going to be okay?"

I nodded. And so off we went. He brought the car around and double checked my seat-belt before getting us lunch.

At the tiny cafe, I found the smells comforting as Killian stood behind me, my back against his chest as I stared up at the drinks menu.

I couldn't ignore how good his heat felt and after we'd gotten the food he and I sat down in the back corner in a booth and munched on our brunch.

"Tell me about your life," I murmured while having some soup and ginger ale.

He looked around. There was nobody here, but I realized it wasn't the best place to talk. The overhead lighting emphasized the shadows underneath his eyes. For a moment I caught a glimpse of the person he'd been worried about me and afraid when I'd left him.

"Let me move next to you so I can talk to you."

I blinked a little surprised as I shifted and he sat next to me, cornering me a little in the booth, the size of him so much bigger than me I almost forgot how much space he took up.

But I did check in and realize I felt instantly comforted and my stomach calmed down with his scent in my lungs. His hand wrapped around my waist over my little bump.

As he told me about it, I sat there a little light-headed and stunned.

"Are you for real?"

He nodded looking unsure of himself slightly as he spoke low to me dipping his head down while motioning for me to eat something. "That all happened to you?"

He tipped his head. "I've done a lot of shit. Been through a lot."

And my heart ached for that boy that he had been. Was that why... because of his Mom? Did she kill herself?

Is that what Aidan was protecting him from?

"Gabriel..." I swallowed. "He's...the head of Titan..."

Killian nodded dipping his head lower to my ear. "You're not supposed to know. Not technically. But...given the circumstance." He motioned to my stomach. "You wanted to know."

I nodded, taking a deep breath.

"Did you think I would end up like your mother if you told me who you were?"

A silence passed between us. One beat. Another.

Before he tipped his head not having touched his food.

"She had us..." his voice was so low I couldn't hear him properly without straining over the elevator music. "It didn't matter."

But I wasn't her and deep down I knew why he felt the way he did. I knew. But I wished he had more faith in us. In me.

"A long time ago, I remember my mother always crying. She was always crying," he murmured. "She didn't like Kieran. She tolerated Aidan, but me...she...I have fuzzy memories of her rubbing my hair back. Everything is fuzzy." I held him tighter as he spoke. "I can see her the one afternoon, the sun is in her room and it's the only light. She's on the ceiling. Aidan wouldn't tell me...he wouldn't say a word to me. He just blocked me from coming in the room. He was crying. He called for help and shoved me outside into Kieran."

"You were a baby."

Killian was quiet.

"She hung herself," I whispered horrified.

"It was her only way out."

"Aidan won't—"

Killian shook his head quickly. "He began working with Gabriel years ago. To get us both out. That's why me and Kieran are in New York. Working with Titan. It absorbed the gang, got rid of the old guard, and replaced us as something better. My mom was perpetually upset. Always crying and Aidan got the worst of it and he became who he is today from that. He won't say a word about any secrets he has."

Because Aidan protected his family.

And Killian protected me.

"I'm sorry," I murmured. "I'm upset because I knew you weren't like Eugene or Michelle. I wasn't afraid of you. I never have been. I know what you are and I don't care. I only cared that you didn't tell me. And when you didn't? It made me feel like I was in danger. Like you kept it from me afraid for me—not that I was okay. But that if I knew? Something would happen to me."

His eyes met mine with burning determination in them. And something else. Love.

"I would *never* let anything happen to you. You are never in danger because of me. Everyone thinks twice before they come after me. Because it's not just Titan backing us, it's every single branch of Titan. There's a team in Chicago that works with Aidan, their boss, Cade—he makes Reed look nice. We have systems in place. Aidan wanted me and Kieran to leave. He did. But I stayed because I belong here—this is my life. Or it was...until you. Until you I knew what I wanted."

And at that...something in his expression shifted.

"There's something else," he reached for my stomach and I didn't draw back. Drawing me almost closer as he said it, those eyes of his meeting mine. "I do have to say this. But my timing is shit."

I felt a reluctant smile curve my lips.

"Eugene...he got out of jail." My heart dropped to my stomach. "I've been keeping tabs on him. On you. I've been trying to protect you this entire time."

What? At my expression he quickly explained.

"When I first started dating you, I didn't want you in danger. So I looked into you worried if something might put you there. Nothing would hurt you," his palm flattened on my stomach. "Ever. But I found out about his prison time..."

And just like that a newfound horror filled me. "You found out..."

"I don't care," he reached for face, the little bit of food I ate turning to rot in my stomach. "Not a single fucking time did I care. It was all to take care of you—I will never let anything happen to you under me. Ever. You said you didn't trust me. But you are still mine." His lips brushed over mine as I felt my heart race. Pounding with the information he had. "I don't care about your past, the way you don't care mine. My love for you has never changed, will never change, do you understand me? I'm sorry I wasn't honest with you, but I swear I had a plan to tell you as soon as my life calmed down."

And then he proceeded to explain his reach to me and how someone named Derek was watching my adopted father.

"I'd like to take you to my penthouse. It's not the same as your home, but it's more secure. It's safer than Sonya's and I'd like you close to me...you can have your own space if you'd like, or we can stay together."

I was a little overwhelmed.

"I never realized how much you knew," I whispered unsure of how to feel. "This is intense."

He brushed his lips over mine again, drawing back a little to look at me.

"None of it mattered. I was on him the moment I knew. Nothing was ever going to hurt you." His eyes dropped to my stomach. "Or her. Ever."

And in that moment I realized something. Something that I didn't factor in. He may have kept the truth from me, but that had been because of his upbringing.

"Please, luv. Please, listen to me."

Not because of me. Killian was still coping. Just like I was sometimes.

I didn't know how to process who he was.

But I was taking a page out of Sonya's book. She was just going with it.

They weren't bad guys. Not Aidan. Not Killian.

He'd been nothing but good to me. Minus, the whole...he'd left out who he was. But…when I thought about it, I didn't think I cared now that he'd explained what he had.

I also didn't really understand what his role was. It seemed multi-faceted. Flexible. And larger than I could comprehend.

And one of the first things I did was tell Sonya about Killian and that I had, in fact, spoken to him.

"I'm processing this," I whispered. "I don't know what to do."

"I can't leave you out in your place without me," he'd said quietly rubbing my stomach. He couldn't take his hands off me, like he had to reassure himself I was here. "I don't want to. Do you want to stay with me? I know you need time. But will you take that time with me?"

It was still a little much to process for me.

"Okay." I whispered realizing how close we were. Those eyes of his met mine, his hair a little messy and unruly as always.

"Okay."

I nodded feeling his palm on my stomach.

"Is she hurting? Are you in pain?" He looked like it made him uneasy to even ask.

"No, she's okay." The heat of his hand felt blissfully nice. I don't know why the words left my mouth. "When I was at the clinic the first time, I imagined you buying her her first toys too…"

"I would, luv," he murmured. I blinked back emotions at imagining how much of a supportive father he'd be. "Whatever she wants." He wiped my eyes.

"I'm sorry," I sniffled. "I'm just emotional now."

He dipped his head lower and I saw the heated look in his eyes and I swallowed a little, his eyes dropping to my pulse at my throat.

"We should pack to get you to my place tonight."

AND SO OVER THE WEEK I MOVED INTO KILLIAN'S PENTHOUSE WHICH WAS clearly made for a man or a fancy hotel.

Nothing personal in it but everything was state of the art including the locks on his doors and the security code.

He wasn't kidding.

Nothing was getting through his doors. He made space for me and helped me with moving everything. Someone named Sean stepped in

352

and helped me, his blonde hair tied back in a ponytail and his all black on. A little menacing and imposing but I recognized him from the hospital. And then it occurred to me I didn't know the difference between the Titans and the O'Hara.

Killian smiled as I said slowly. "That's the point, luv. You aren't supposed to."

"Sean was so nice," I murmured to him as Killian helped me around the house. "He brought in all my stuff."

Within forty-eight hours my entire apartment in Brooklyn was now in Killian's. He told me not to stress out and he could handle it or he'd find someone else to handle it.

Now at his disposal I was adjusting to the fact that he was capable of this. And how he wasn't letting me go.

And over the next few weeks I acclimated to him.

Sonya didn't expect me to do anything for her and instead told me to take it easy.

"Your brother is spending time with Sonya," I told him one night over dinner. My stomach had calmed down so much after being around Killian. "I didn't know Aidan had relationships."

Killian simply frowned. "He doesn't."

He didn't let me cook—opting to hire someone to bring us prepped food or using this meal service he said Reed Whittaker used. They were friends. Hence, how he was connected.

Killian's expression was curious. "My brother's helping her with her divorce?" He raised a dark elegant brow at me.

I told him about the incident at Sonya's house and his expression turned contemplative.

"What do you think?"

"Do you want my safe answer or my real answer?"

"Your real answer."

He didn't even blink as he said. "Michael Devereaux is a dead man. The moment he got in my brother's way? Aidan won't let him walk away."

"Like...he'll kill Michael?" I was surprised to find there was no love lost for me to hear that. Because Michael Devereaux was the worst kind of man.

Killian nodded watching me, that look back in his eyes. The one I had seen him wear sometimes when he was dealing with his demons.

"Does that bother you?"

"No," I answered honestly. "Michael...he hurt Sonya." I explained what I knew about Michael Devereaux and Killian's face turned dark.

"Aidan's not going to let him off his hook."

"Your brother is a little dark and terrifying."

That made Killian grin. "Kieran can piss him off."

I adjusted on the couch I was sitting on. Shifting little in my nightie smoothing my hands over my ever shifting body watching his eyes track the movements as I did. He was there adjusting a pillow under my back and moving the blanket over me.

"Sonya told me some of the things Michael did to her..." I told Killian all of it. I did genuinely trust nothing left him and with Sonya accepting Aidan's help? I realized she saw something in them too.

"Aidan hasn't said anything to me, I'm not surprised. He won't answer to me." Because Aidan was the head of their family. "He won't tell me anything unless I need to know."

Which meant Michael was...well...Michael was now the prey.

"I'm not upset," I surprised myself. "I can't imagine hurting someone like Sonya like that. She's barely a hundred and fifteen pounds if that. She just started gaining a little more weight..." Probably because of Aidan. "Is she why he's staying in the city?"

He nodded looking like he was piecing it together now. "He said he would be here for a bit with Alexei."

I swallowed around my emotions.

"Maybe your daughter is turning me into something blood thirsty but I would pay to see Aidan torturing Michael," the words leaving my lips stunned me. Especially as a health care worker.

But I knew what Sonya had been through and what no woman should ever have had to deal with.

Killian's grin was wide and wicked as his eyes softened on my belly.

"She's getting bigger now."

"She's the size of a medium banana."

I laughed softly at the way his eyes widened.

"Can I?" He motioned to my stomach.

I don't know why Killian made me feel shy all of a sudden.

My throat worked as his hands moved to my stomach and he came impossibly closer.

"Luv," his breath was shaky. "I would do anything for you and her."

I knew.

Which is also why I knew he was breaking down my resolve.

⟿

"I like my job, but Haven is smaller and more concentrated. I can have it a little easier there."

"Is that what you want to do?"

Killian and I were lying on my bed. Reed had officially granted him paternity leave and he was determined to spend it with me sampling things that did not make me sick.

He passed me some sour candy which seemed to help. As I took it, his lips pressed to my growing bump.

"I don't know," I admitted. "I've done everything. I love working with my hands and I love being a nurse."

"But is that what you wanna do?" I could feel the heat from his lips on my belly button. "Is that what you would do if you could?"

"No," I admitted honestly thinking about it. "If I could I'd do my blog full time."

"So then do that."

"What?"

His eyes met mine as he spoke into my stomach. "So then do that."

I swore I felt my body releasing so much tension the moment he said that words.

"I can support you and her. I can stay on paternity leave. Landon's more than qualified and pretty sure he's taking after Nate Wyatt. You haven't met Wyatt besides that idiot's hospital visit."

"When he almost killed—"

"Watts."

I did remember Nathan. "Landon is replacing him?"

"Probably. Reed won't pull from anywhere else and I think Gabriel wants to replace that position. Nate is guarding Gemma Marchand but I think he left the Titans so once his contract is up? He's out. But Landon is taking my spot temporarily too which isn't too bad. It all works out. By the time Nate leaves, Landon will replace him—"

"And you'll go back." I paused. "I don't like the idea of you being in danger all the time."

Killian looked at my stomach and pressed his lips to it. "Funny,

355

Gabriel moved my job a little so I wouldn't be going out. I'd function as a trainer from now on so I can come home to you, but I still have to coordinate with a team."

"Home to me?" My heart pounded in my chest now.

He didn't look at me. He just tipped his head pressing his lips into the spot I had told him ached nights ago.

"I want you to do what makes you happy," he said after a long moment. "I want you to do what you love. What makes you feel contented at the end of the day. Not just as her mother, but as you, Nisha. Whatever makes you feel good inside."

My hands stilled over the candy as I slowly wiped them off.

"You don't have to live in survival mode," his eyes met mine. One aqua. One amber. Watching me with quiet strength.

58

NISHA

My stomach gave a growl midway and I felt his eyes turn to it.

"Dinner?" Killian asked, his voice low.

I nodded, feeling a blush creep across my cheeks. "Mhmm."

His eyes traveled slowly up my nightie, lingering on my chest.

I shifted uncomfortably, still getting used to how my body had changed.

When I glanced down, I noticed the wet spots on my nightie and gasped, mortified.

"I'm—"I stammered, trying to pull away. Killian's grip on me tightened gently. "C-can you get me a towel?" I asked, covering my chest with my hands. "I didn't even feel it! Is this normal? I thought I wasn't supposed to start lactating until after the baby came..." I was floundering.

This was different.

I looked up at him, wide-eyed, caught off guard by the raw hunger in his expression. He remained silent, his eyes flickering back to my chest. The heat in his gaze was unmistakable.

"You can't be serious," I murmured, but the unwavering want in his eyes told me he absolutely was. "I didn't even think this was a kink."

"You look beautiful." He held my gaze as his finger traced my nipples. It was *electric*.

I felt it shoot bolts of lust straight to my core. My lips parting in a gasp as I closed my eyes.

"I haven't had you in forever." Because we were still...adjusting.

It had been a long time since we'd been together.

And now my body was responding in all sorts of ways to him.

"Are you sensitive?"

Gosh, his voice should be illegal.

I nodded unable to look at him over the heat in his eyes.

"How sensitive?"

He drew me closer on his lap, his fingers tugging down the fabric of my nightie. The moment I felt the cool air hit my nipples, I let out a sigh.

"They're a little uncomfortable."

I could feel how hot my face was and how I looked right then and he made a soft noise tracing my swollen nipples.

They weren't leaking per se but they had been.

My hair flowed all around me, even longer now than before and over my shoulders. Swirling over my breasts.

I dared to peek at him watching me. His cheeks were flushed deep red as he watched me and I could feel his arousal digging into my side.

"You have no idea how beautiful you look." His voice dropped another octave. "The moment I saw you I thought you were beautiful, but now?" His voice was a whisper in my ear and I wanted to melt into him. "Luv...please...let me..."

I nodded desperately my brain short circuiting even if I didn't know where to start.

His hand cupped one of my breasts and I pressed my lips together at the sensation as he squeezed gently.

A noise left me as I felt a trickle of moisture leave and I squirmed as he dipped his head.

"Killian—" I gasped his name as he sealed his mouth over my nipple. And bit down gentle. I almost came out of his arms with how sensitive I was. "*Ohgodplease.*"

I moaned as I held him to me as he alternated for long moments tugging and playing with me as I felt my orgasm building.

"*Killian.*"

He growled around my nipples as he played with them and shifted me on his lap so I was straddling him.

I held his head to me as he sucked harder.

I screamed a little at how quickly my orgasm came over me. It hit hard and fast, until I was shaking in his arms. Riding it out as his hands undid his pants.

His eyes meeting mine as he let my nipples go. "Are you sure?"

I nodded desperate to feel him. Anything to be close to him.

I was so wet for him, I took him easily. That piercing sliding against me felt like heaven now as I held him.

"We don't have to use anything," I whispered.

"No," his lips moved over mine. "And you feel…incredible."

I panted as I took him deeper, sinking down, until I felt stretched to my limits like this. I didn't remember the last time I'd been with him. It had been so long ago.

"Love me," I whispered. The words leaving my lips unbidden. "Love me, please." My vision blurred as I held him to me.

"I love you." It was a guttural sound from him as he brought me so close it felt like we were one person. "It's been forever since I had you."

It had been. And everything felt different.

"It feels different."

He paused. "In a bad way?"

"No." I whispered it against his lips. "I feel so sensitive. Like I'm gonna come again." I bit down on my lip at the look in his eyes as my hips rocked a bit. "*Ohhh*."

I closed my eyes.

I was ready to explode. When I opened my eyes, his eyes, held a dangerous glint in them as I squeezed helplessly as my eyes watered from the intensity of everything. *"God, baby."*

"Too much?"

I shook my head rocking my hips a tiny bit more. God, pregnancy was going to ruin me. "Kiss me."

He did. Without question as he pressed up into me and I came just like that.

I screamed a little as I did. I felt him groaning into my mouth, deep in his chest, as he rocked up.

"Fuck," he murmured. "This is gonna be nice."

～

ONE NIGHT, I WOKE WITH MILD INDIGESTION. BABY GIRL WAS uncomfortable most of the time.

Before I could fully register my discomfort, Killian was up, nuzzling into my neck. Helping me up. Easing me onto my side.

"I gotcha, I gotcha." Everything I went through he was there.

He was attuned to everything I did. And in a way this was our break.

As we walked around my living room, his arms encircled me from behind, his quiet murmurs of comfort in Gaelic mixing with my measured breaths as he rubbed my belly.

"I don't understand why I can't have one of those easy pregnancies," I was frustrated. To say the least. "I feel like she's ready to leave me right *now*."

I felt his smile against my cheek as he held me.

"Breathe for me, luv."

He just cuddled me tight to him.

It was a moment of quiet even if it was late for us, we had to adjust to parenthood. "It's all good, I don't mind ever."

His hands splayed over my stomach as he said it. I breathed out harder with him calming down as he rubbed circles.

"You feel different," he murmured.

"My nausea is a lot better," I commented after it passed. One night I sat savoring hot pepper flavored pickles as I ate them straight from the jar. "I just want sour food though. Gummy worms, pickles…"

He swallowed in a grimace at the jar. I giggled and his lips curled up at me pulling me on his lap. "As long as you're eating something."

"Pizza sounds good right now—don't you dare get deep dish anything."

He did get one for himself and I sat across from him eyeing it with suspicion. Because I wanted some now.

He silently moved his paper-plate over to me and handed me silverware with a smirk.

I took a bite of it and moaned. And then I added hot pickles to it to Killian's dismay.

"Oh my gosh, she's your daughter for sure. I can't believe I'm eating this…" As I munched I caught him eyeing me again with a soft expression. "You're never going to get used to that."

He shook his head quietly with a small smile on his face, and just passed me more pizza.

Tugging my chair closer until I was practically on his lap, his hand on my belly while we ate. Killian couldn't stop touching me since I'd come back.

A man of action.

Amidst these moments, I kept in touch with Sonya, updating her about Killian. And that I would be joining her team at Haven.

Even Sonya and Aidan wanted both of us to respectively take a breather after the last few weeks we'd both had.

In the meantime I finally got back to Adam noting it had been a few weeks since his last text. He texted me saying he was happy I was doing good and he'd be back from vacation soon.

Adam was on vacation?

"Adam said he also works at Haven now. So we'll be working together. What happened while we've been out of it?" I asked Killian. "How's Kieran? I feel stupid for not asking sooner."

His eyes went dark. "I haven't spoken to him since…" Since he found out Kieran accidentally spilled the beans?

I was a little thrown. "At all?"

He tipped his head back. "I don't know what to say to him." He paused. "After everything…"

I paused in what I was doing. "I think you should go talk to him, even if it's difficult. I'll go with you. He didn't do anything wrong."

"It's not just that—" he broke off, his eyes darting elsewhere. "I didn't think I'd be so angry with him."

Chewing my lip I moved to him. "Are you upset at him still?"

Killian nodded slowly. "I don't know why."

I thought about it for a moment. "When you're ready to talk to him," I paused. "I was thinking…I think you should invite Aidan and Kieran over for dinner one day…here. Even Alexei. Since he's always with Aidan."

He blinked looking up at me confused a bit.

"I'm serious. I've heard family dinners are important and Aidan knows about the baby…Kieran should too."

His eyes were guarded and I knew he didn't want to. If he could he'd keep her all to himself.

"Just one dinner? It'll be nice to have all of you sitting around a table. When was the last time you boys did that?" I smiled at his expression. "You can't keep her from them."

I swore I heard him mutter, 'watch me' before he nodded looking adorably grumpy. I grinned at his possessiveness. He had known about her for a few days now and he was attached.

"Just one?" I asked drifting closer to him. His eyes flared a little as I did. "One little dinner."

He looked defenseless as I sat on his lap, letting him cuddle me to him. His pout was out.

"One…" he said gruffly.

"Just one." I moved my lips over his whispering. "For me?"

He tipped his head, closing his eyes. "Just one."

One evening Killian had stepped out to get us sandwiches from Butterscotch. Leaving me in his apartment as he went to grab hot cocoa and a few other items I'd been craving.

My phone pinged maybe twenty minutes after he left to get dinner.

"Nisha," Sonya's voice sounded shaky, almost unrecognizable. "Do you have a second?"

"What's wrong?" My stomach clenched. She sounded like she'd been crying.

"I—I fell down the stairs." She sounded robotic almost, her words too measured. "I think I broke my arm…"

"I'm coming!"

I was up in an instant, ignoring the twinge in my lower back. I threw on a hoodie and sweats, texting Killian as I rushed out.

I shot text to Killian as I rushed out the door.

He'd understand. It was Sonya after all and her place was safe.

Sonya has also helped you and supported you. Go to her now.

It took me fifteen minutes to get there by cab and when I did, I rushed upstairs.

Her door was wide open already and a chill ran down my spine for some reason. A cold seeped into my skin.

Don't go in there.

It was like a warning in me, my instincts screaming. But it was Sonya. I had to help her.

"Sonya?" I whispered, approaching the door with caution, my hand covering my belly.

As I swung the door open, I froze, the world tilting on its axis.

The metallic scent of blood hit me first.

"Nisha," a voice from my nightmares rasped.

Standing there was Eugene, more terrifying than I remembered. His eyes, cold and lifeless, bore into me with predatory intent.

"*Eugene.*"

He tsked, casually kicking something on the floor. My eyes dropped, and my heart stopped.

"*Sonya.*" She lay motionless, blood pooling from her temple, her skin ghostly pale. The room spun, and I gripped the doorframe to stay upright.

"What did you do to her?" I choked out, bile rising in my throat.

This was a trap. Why didn't I think that?

Because it's Sonya.

Eugene's lips curved into a cruel smile, and I felt the last vestiges of hope drain away.

"To her? Not even close to what I'm gonna do to you."

And then he smiled, a sight that turned my blood to ice. I screamed as I felt something come over my head, rough fabric scratching my face.

He wasn't alone.

And I felt a searing pain in my head before my vision faded to black.

59

NISHA

My head was throbbing. Everything hurt.

Slowly, I straightened. Nausea overwhelmed me like I was in a moving car. Shifting.

A groan escaped as the fog cleared. Another wave of nausea hit. Not the baby this time. My surroundings.

It was something out of every nightmare I could've imagined. But worse.

Because this was no nightmare.

This was real.

The dining room of my childhood home stretched before me. Unchanged. Frozen in time. Floral wallpaper. Heavy curtains.

Even the china cabinet with all the tea sets we never touched.

I blinked, awareness creeping in.

Ropes bound me to the chair, my swollen belly evident even under my hoodie. My heart began to race.

And then my mother walked in.

My eyes went wide.

Michelle.

Her mousy brown hair. Her sickly sweet voice. Those dark eyes. Terror filled me. Those dark eyes of her watched me with a manic look in them.

I'm going to die.

"You're up, you lazy stupid bitch." She glided across from me, perfectly coiffed, smiling vacantly. Set down a plate. The smell of garlic turned my stomach. "Life without us made you fat and lazy."

I was having a nightmare.

What the fuck was happening?

And then the person of my nightmares walked in as if this wasn't bad enough. Eugene. But he looked…worse. Prison had not looked good on him. At all.

His face was gaunt, cheekbones jutting sharply. Deep-set eyes gleamed with a manic light. Skin sallow, almost yellow. Hair greyed and thinning.

He'd lost weight. But not in a healthy way.

This wasn't the Eugene I remembered. This was something far more terrifying. *He's going to kill me.*

But not before he does worse.

My throat worked as I realized I could move my hands but I was tied to the chair.

"Eat up," Eugene said, his tone deceptively light. "You know how your mother hates to see food go to waste."

I'm going crazy.

I'm losing it.

"H-how did I get here?" I managed, my voice hoarse and trembling.

"Don't be silly," Michelle said. "You've always been here. Now, tell us about your day at school."

The surreal normalcy of the conversation chilled me more than any outright threat. My mind was racing. "What did you do to Sonya?" The last thing I'd seen was Sonya

Eyes darting, searching for escape. But everything was just as it had always been—neat, orderly, unreachable. A perfect prison of normalcy.

"You've been away for a while, haven't you? Meeting new people?" Eugene's words slithered across the table.

Was he for real?

"I asked you a question." Eugene.

His voice cut into my head and I felt something hot, like rage bursting through me. No. He wasn't going to hurt me or my child ever again.

The moment I thought about the baby? It sent something through me. Rage like no other.

"You're a fucking monster."

365

"Do not curse at your father." Michelle's hand shot at me rapidly then. I felt the hit coming from a mile away but the moment her hand connected with my face, hot fire exploded on my cheek.

I spit out blood and a noise left me.

"Stupid little bitch," she hissed. "You ruined my life."

"Easy, Michelle."

I barely heard Eugene's voice.

I was surrounded by crazy. Drowning in it.

These people were insane.

Panic clawed at my insides. Anxiety stretched me thin.

"You're a fucking coward," I spat at her. "You only came after me when I was at my weakest! You're a bitch—"

"That's enough!" Eugene's voice was a roar. "You've been nothing but disrespectful and ungrateful since the day we brought you into this house—"

"I was fucking child!" I shrieked. And I felt Michelle coming over with a vicious growl ripping my hair back. I felt an animal noise rip from my throat at the taste of copper filling my mouth.

Killian.

Eugene's eyes flashed, dangerous. "Nisha's been learning nothing but bad things. From that man she's been seeing."

Michelle grabbed my hair and ripped it back bringing her face, wild eyes close to mine. "We're going to do what we should've done years ago to you, you stupid bitch. I never should've had you—"

"You are not my mother—" I spit in her face a savage growl leaving me. "You're a fucking coward—"

A cramp seized me, fiercer this time. I bit down, tasting blood.

"Shut up." Michelle yelled.

I felt searing pain in my scalp and I screamed in her face.

"What the fuck is wrong with you people?" I screamed. Losing it. Losing my mind now. "You're just going to sit here! Let me out!"

I didn't care. I screamed and shoved the chair back dragging myself up with her in my face and her fist came into contact with my face again. I shrieked as she did it two more times. The impact was explosive. Until I was spitting it out.

"Enough, Michelle. I think Nisha's learned her lesson, haven't you?"

Not their puppet. Not their prisoner. Not again.

"Go fuck yourself."

Without warning, Eugene closed the distance and his hand came down hard across my face.

The force of the blow sent my head snapping to the side, pain exploding across my cheek.

I tasted blood as I fell over from Michelle letting me go and crashing to the floor.

Eugene reared his foot back. *"You stupid fucking bitch, you did this to me—"*

And then I heard the shot go off.

I was screaming. Michelle was screaming for another reason.

I didn't recognize who it was. I just saw Eugene drop and Michelle screaming and throwing herself to the floor as I saw two figures darting around them. I didn't hear anything.

Someone reached for me. I sobbed as I met a pair of blazing amber eyes. Chocolate hair disheveled, face set with fury.

Kieran.

"*Sis*, oh holy fucking shit, Nisha." I was dragged into his arms a second later, a broken sob leaving my lips.

A loud vicious *snap* echoed and my face would have contorted had it not felt like I was on fire, followed by Eugene's howl of pain.

Kieran helped me up, steadying me his expression grim.

For a moment I didn't know who else was there and my head turned to the scream.

And I froze at the figure over Eugene.

Killian.

I had never seen that look on his face. I nearly retched at the unnatural angle of Eugene's arms. A sound escaped Eugene—something that was pure animal as I watched.

Kieran's hand moved over my eyes but not before I caught a dark-haired man stood grimly to the side, gun trained on Michelle who was shrieking.

Kieran's chest suddenly blocked my view of Killian's face.

My...Killian. Looking like *that*.

"He wouldn't want you to see him like that," he murmured in my ear. "Put your arms around me, Nisha."

I obeyed, overwhelmed and shaking in fear, my eyes blurring with tears.

Michelle's shrieks pierced the air. A sickening crunch. A strangled noise left my throat.

Killian was—

"I gotta get you out of here." Kieran moved fast. Men and women in black materialized like wraiths. *"Face in my neck. Close your eyes. Now."*

Animal screams echoed from inside. I made a noise feeling Kieran's shaking. *Or was it me?*

"I'm sorry, Nisha. But I need to take you to a hospital. I can't stop him. Nobody will."

60

KILLIAN

A FEW HOURS EARLIER

I MISSED HER CALL IN THE PARKING GARAGE.

I missed.

One.

Call.

But I got her text.

That's all it took. I lost service for a minute. Just enough to miss her call.

And when I did? Something was wrong.

I fucking knew it.

Because while my girl was sweet and loyal.

I wasn't.

Not one bit of me was a good man. But I was *her* man.

If Sonya fell down a flight of stairs, why call Nisha?

Why didn't she call an ambulance? *Why'd she call Nisha?*

But my girl is loyal to a fault. And a fucking sweetheart.

I knew Nisha would've gone.

Instinct kicked in, overriding everything else. I forgot about the sandwiches, texting Nisha to stay put.

Her phone went straight to voicemail when I called.

"Damnit, pick up, luv." I fired off another text, my fingers already dialing Aidan. He was at K2, closer to Sonya's.

He could get there faster.

"*Aidan—*" I blurted out the situation as soon as he answered. He'd be there in ten.

I was already in my car, tearing out of the garage, when traffic hit. Fucking New York.

Derek's call came through, his voice strained.

"*Boss— I got jumped—*"

"*What the fuck do you mean you got jumped?*" My knuckles went white on the steering wheel.

"I was watching the Grahams' old place...Thought I saw Eugene leave. When I went to investigate, someone blindsided me..."

Dread coiled in my gut. "*Who?*"

"*I think it was his wife.*"

"Fuck." Everything in my stomach soured. I left her alone for a second. A fucking second.

The pieces were falling into place, a nightmare scenario unfolding. I rattled off Sonya's address.

"Go to the hospital. Send the address to Landon. Now."

"Yes, sir."

I hung up, my mind racing. Something was very wrong at Sonya's.

Every instinct screamed at me to abandon my car, to run there on foot.

By the time I reached Sonya's, I was out of the car before it fully stopped. I burst through the open door, the scene before me confirming my worst fears.

Aidan knelt on the floor, cradling an unconscious Sonya. The look in his eyes was unholy. My brother was in a killing mood.

Alexei was on the phone, his voice low and urgent.

And then I saw him—Kieran his amber eyes dark with worry.

Any lingering animosity evaporated as he spoke the words that turned my world upside down.

"Nisha's been kidnapped."

And he wasn't finished as my world tilted.

"I'm gonna help you get her back."

∿

NOW STANDING OVER EUGENE'S BROKEN AND BLEEDING BODY, I WASN'T anywhere near finished with him.

Not one bit.

"You kidnapped my girls."

My voice sounded alien, even to me. Michelle's shrieking grated on my last nerve.

I sneered in disgust as Eugene pissed himself, his arms bent at unnatural angles. I'd taken care of those first.

"I should've waited," I heard myself say, distant and cold. "Should've broken each bone slowly. But Eugene, what I'm going to do to you now—"

Michelle's cursing cut me off. Each scream like nails on a chalkboard for me.

Without looking away from Eugene, I spoke. "*Landon*."

He shot her in the foot. In the knees.

Michelle's scream pitched higher.

I smirked at both of them screaming now.

"You two really shouldn't have put me in a bad mood. It tends to bring out the worst in me."

They threatened my family.

Threatened Nisha. My baby.

My *girls*.

And death?

Was *merciful*.

I didn't care how many operatives watched.

I had a unit of six right outside locking the damn place down.

And then they'd burn it all to the ground.

After I made sure they suffered in their final hours, the way they would've done to Nisha.

My *daughter*.

She's so small. She can't protect herself.

If the thought of Nisha being hurt ratcheted me up?

Anything happening to *my* little girl was like a match to a gasoline soaked warehouse.

My world erupted in flames at the idea of that little girl hurting.

And it was going to burn this entire place down.

I felt the dangerous grin spread across my face down at them, darkness coating my veins, ice flowing through them as I realized they were going to kill my world.

Nisha wasn't with a nice man or a good man.

But I was hers. The way she was mine.

Anything that threatened her? Would be eliminated.

"I'm not going to kill you, Eugene. Or your wife. Not for a long time."

Part of me screamed to go to Nisha, take her in my arms. But another part of me—the demons in me demanded blood. Demanded this.

I had plans. I went after these two first.

Because Nisha was with my brother now.

She was safe. Any lingering rage I felt for Kieran was gone.

I'd watched him run to her bloody self and I knew I'd get to her—he wouldn't leave her. But this?

I was going to get my cut in blood for what they did to her.

What they planned.

My smile stretched wider as I unsheathed my knife. "I'm not done with either one of you."

They tried to take my world from me.

I was going to tear into them for what they did.

61

NISHA

"SONYA'S AT THE HOSPITAL TOO WITH AIDAN." KIERAN MURMURED TO ME holding me to him.

I felt horrible because Eugene had gone after Sonya who was an easier target in her apartment.

He had known about her somehow.

"But she's asleep right now, taking it easy..."

"M-my f-f-fault—" I broke off as I cried. "She was hurt—"

"No, it's not your fault," Kieran held me tight, pressing his lips against my temples. "She's going to be fine. Aidan's got her. Alexei's her fucking guard, nothing's gonna happen to her...or you."

Half of my face was on fire and I was pretty sure I looked horrible.

"Once Aidan found her, he didn't leave her."

Kieran told me as he held me on his lap on the ride to the hospital.

I was shaking, out of it as he wrapped his jacket around me.

"I'm really sorry for breaking the news to you the way I did. I didn't think."

"It's okay."

He swore as he touched my bruised and bleeding face.

I was crying too hard and I thought one eye was swelling shut as I was changed into a hospital gown and checked over.

Afterwards, Kieran came back into the room his eyes pained.

"No wonder he lost his shit." Kieran's eyes were hard as he took my face in. His lips pressed into my temple as I shook. "How's the baby?"

I was trembling harder at the image of Killian's entire face. "Good." *She was. Thank God.*

Killian's face in my mind. He had looked like he'd been...enjoying it. Like he wanted to destroy them. And the strange feeling was. I didn't care. I wanted that too for what they'd done to me. To my daughter. I had been terrified of losing her.

I was crying too much to care about anything else.

"It's okay, I got you. I promise," Kieran hugged me a little brushing my hair back and holding the ice pack they'd given me to my face. "Jesus, you're having his fucking baby..."

At the hospital, Kieran stayed with me, his eyes darting between my stomach and me.

"I can call you Uncle now," it came out mumbled.

He shook his head. "Shit...Aidan told me it was serious. He never told me you were..." he motioned to my stomach processing.

We were both fine.

But that left...

"Killian...he..." I broke off at the look in Kieran's eyes. I couldn't feel one side of my face and I ached all over from what just happened.

Amber eyes met mine with something foreign in them. "He was worse growing up. Out for blood. All the time. Aidan talk to you about Gabriel?"

"Killian told me about him."

Kieran motioned around us. This facility looked different. Smaller.

"Smaller clinic for the shit Gabriel doesn't want to get out. He trained Killian to be a better weapon. That, in there, with your fucked up adopted parents, is the other side of who he is. The side he doesn't need you to see. That's how Aidan and I knew he was serious about you." He leaned in. "My brother? Who he is with you? That is one half of what that was in your parents old house..."

As he spoke he looked at me with wonder.

"He was wearing your fucking bandaids and shit. Acting like he was at peace. Because that's what he is. He finesses. That's who my brother is—without you."

I sat back feeling my heart pounding in my chest as he spoke.

"I feel like that man is so different from the man he is when he's with me."

"It's the same guy you put those heart-shaped bandaids on. He fucking loves you more than anything else. His life wasn't nice or kind to him and he wants to be good to you." Kieran ruffled his chocolate hair back staring at my belly. "Killian's not gonna let your parents live for that. It's disrespect at its finest and a fucking crime to touch you. Anybody who touches you? Good as dead. That's probably why you're not in danger from anyone in the city. Pretty sure now more than ever everyone will be terrified."

Kieran turned to face me fully and for once, I got a look at him. In all black. Weapons strapped to him.

Another person I didn't recognize anymore.

"If Killian ever steps into Aidan's shoes? If anybody does anything to you? That's what happens. And that's my brother being nice. I'm sorry you had to see that. But that's his world. I know he wants to be here. But he's gotta get his pound of flesh in."

I swallowed. "Because he looks weak if he doesn't?"

But what about being here with me?

"No," Kieran shook his head. "*Nobody*, trust me, nobody sees him as weak. But he's going to send a message. And that's not even when Aidan gets his hand on them for what they did to Sonya." He motioned to the door. "I feel like you two ladies are casting spells on my brothers."

"Sonya…" I mumbled.

"If Killian won't kill them. Aidan will. I don't envy that."

62

NISHA

It took Killian hours to come back.

And he looked different. Dressed differently.

When he walked in, Alexei out of all people had been next to me, the TV playing Sabrina the Teenage Witch out of all things.

Alexei had lazily watched it with me when Killian stepped into the room. His eyes finding me instantly. And just like that my heart ached.

Alexei looking between us quickly stood, giving us the room. I didn't even see anything else other than him as he looked at me.

His expression went dark at the sight of my face and I ducked my head.

"You're both good." His voice was gruff, as his eyes raked over my cheek.

I nodded, my throat tightening as he stepped closer, dressed in his usual all-black attire.

But beneath the familiar clothing, I saw him for who he truly was. He wasn't morally gray.

Killian is pitch black. But he was good for me.

Mine.

In every way, shape, and form.

My heart. My love. My everything.

And I was his.

I reached for him, holding my hand out. And that's when I saw it.

The unreadable mask of his dissolving as his eyes widened. He was surprised I accepted him. And that broke me a bit more and my eyes watered.

"Come here." I held out my arm as he approached me looking more tired than he ever had. The moment he got closer, I drew him into my arms in the bed. "Get in."

I moved aside, letting him settle until his head was buried in my neck, a sigh leaving him as he melted into me being careful of my stomach.

"I'm glad you're here."

My entire life I hadn't really been protected. Now I had it round the clock.

He nodded. Not saying a word. I felt my neck get wetter as he laid there half on top, his hand moving over my belly. He took a shuddering breath.

"You're okay."

In those quiet words, I heard the world. I couldn't stop crying. I knew in that moment if I asked him for the world he'd bring it to me. I knew.

I nodded, words failing me for once as I held him tighter, my fingers threading through his hair. "We're okay."

He nodded, not saying a word but I didn't know who was shaking anymore.

"Did you…" I didn't know how to ask. Did he kill them?

I didn't know initially how to reconcile the two parts of Killian. The mob and the Titan.

It was something I was adjusting to.

He shook his head. "Not yet."

My stomach turned imagining what he'd done. The implications of what he was saying.

"Are you okay?" It was a whisper out of my lips.

"No." His voice was low. "I saw you. I did. I just couldn't—"

"I know." I couldn't even wish he had because if not him? Kieran would've done the same.

"I have never wanted the way I want you…" the moment he said the words everything in my heart stopped. It did. I held him tight to me as he whispered it like it was a secret.

"I thought I never wanted to feel anything. I hated everything in the world. And then you came into my life and you took every single thing I believed in and turned it on its head."

His lips pressed into my pulse where I felt it fluttering wildly.

"Fuck, I thought you were dead," his voice was a croak.

"Nisha…you're my world. This is my world. Every part of you is made for me. From the first time I kissed you, I thought once would be enough. It wasn't. It will never be enough. I wish I had told you sooner. I'm sorry I didn't—I'm sorry I took so long to get back to you. But I promise you, I'm never letting you out of my sight ever again."

I didn't know my heart could crack open at those words.

It was all I had ever wanted in the world. Just him.

Just my little family.

And loving Killian felt easier than anything I had ever done.

"You're stuck with me."

At that a soft laugh left me. Is that what he thought? "Stuck, hm?"

He nodded into my neck. "Not going anywhere."

I wiped my eyes as I held him. "I was scared without you."

I didn't know what he was going to do, but my heart was racing at the thought of everything he could. His world.

This darkness. My entire life I thought I wanted one thing—he had turned it all on its head. Now?

I had this man.

And I wouldn't have asked for anything else.

"I'm sorry."

"But she's okay too. A lot better when she's around you."

His head lifted and I got a look at his red rimmed eyes.

"You'll take me home?" I whispered. "After?"

A beat passed and I felt him wiping his eyes. His fingers wiping mine. And for a moment—I realized I had always loved every version of this man.

Every version of him.

In every lifetime—I'd find my way back to him.

And I just wanted to go home to him.

"Yeah, I can do that."

63

KILLIAN

I hadn't left Eugene and Michelle broken and bleeding to let them die. No.

Aidan had wanted his fist in Eugene.

But he hadn't left Sonya's side.

I didn't know when he would—and if they bled out before then? Well, that would be a small mercy.

The moment I'd gotten blood out of them, I'd felt myself lose it. The image of Nisha's bruised and battered face in my mind.

"Aidan's been in there with her this entire time?" I asked Alexei who sat outside Sonya's room with Kieran outside hanging out together.

Closer in age, Alexei had become a younger brother to Kieran. To all of us.

"She's okay?" Nisha looked a little overwhelmed around all of us.

Aidan meanwhile was fluent in it. I looked at him like he had a third eye.

"Aidan?"

Nisha looked between us. "Did he just tell you what I think he did?"

I nodded, shaking my head. "He wants to remove Sonya from New York between this and her fucking ex."

Kieran snorted. "Like that's gonna go over well."

Alexei nodded. But I caught Nisha chewing her lip staring at the door. She wanted her friend. And what she wanted, she got.

I knocked on the door.

Alexei and Kieran both stood, shaking their heads.

I looked at Nisha meeting her wide eyes and did it again. Aidan swung the door open, his eyes dark and his jaw set as he looked at me. I saw Sonya quickly, ducking her head with her hair.

"Nisha needs to see her. You can spare a minute." He was taking her to fucking Chicago. He could have her then.

And Nisha didn't even wait, moving past me quickly, her smaller body padding to her friend and gingerly hugging her. The two of them crying. And any anger on Aidan's face was gone as he watched them.

I motioned him outside. "Come on. She needs it."

It was all right with both of them in there.

There was no other entrance and exit.

And the four of us were outside.

He stepped out looking more human than I'd ever seen him, his white dress-shirt unbuttoned enough to show all his tattoos. Kieran and Alexei moved down to make space for him in the seats outside the room.

All four of us hadn't really been like this in forever. And it took those two in there to bring us together.

I didn't know what the fuck to say to anyone.

Because I already knew what Aidan's plans were with Eugene. Graphically. And he wasn't going to relax until he got his revenge. Plus, there was Sonya's ex-husband delaying her divorce. He was in a pissy mood.

"Nisha wants all of you over for dinner."

That's what came out of my mouth.

All three of them looked at me and I felt heat on my face. I looked at Aidan. "You can take Sonya with you after. But she wants a family dinner." And she got what she wanted.

Alexei blinked. "Right now?"

Kieran snorted. "Nah, Alexei tomorrow."

"I cannot tell your sarcasm."

"Alexei," I stepped in. "At some point. She wants a family dinner."

"Nisha planning on cooking?" Kieran raised a brow as Aidan remained silent staring at me in confusion.

"I'll just get catering. I'm not about to let either one of them do anything." Sonya would try and help since they were good friends now it seemed. They all shut up as I said it.

The three of them looking confused as fuck. *No wonder Nisha wants us to have dinner. This is the first time we'd all talked in months. If not years.*

"Dinner." Aidan said finally.

I nodded. "Dinner." And then I paused looking around and feeling out of place for once. "I'm having a girl."

Kieran smirked at me and motioned to my stomach. "Pregnancy is flattering on you."

Alexei grinned at him and Aidan snorted.

"I will shoot you." I eyed Kieran. Even though he'd done me a solid and taken Nisha when he needed to. Gabriel had set him free for a bit from his usual duties with Watts at Titan Midtown to help us.

"Who's running Haven if you take Sonya to Chicago?" Kieran asked Aidan who was still confused about dinner.

Alexei's face scrunched up, like he was trying to remember a math problem. "She has personal assistants, Jess is great. Nurses and other people. They know what to do."

Kieran looked over at Aidan after exchanging a glance with me. "Does Sonya know she's taking a break?"

"She will when we get to Chicago."

All three of us eye'd him now. He didn't look the least bit phased. My brother was a man used to getting what he wanted.

Kieran smirked at me. "I have a kid too."

He pulled out his phone and Aidan groaned as Alexei smiled at a photo of a fucking cat.

And it was *huge.*

"What the fuck is that?" It was enormous. "Why is it *that* big?"

Alexei pitched in. "Everything is big in America."

Kieran looked offended. "He's delicate. And he's mine. His name is Cheddar."

All three of us snorted at *Cheddar.*

Aidan frowned at the photo. "You should rename him House because he's the size of a small one."

And Kieran grinned swiping to show photos of him holding his new obese cat. "Alisha gave him to me saying he needed a home. And now I finally have a cat."

Kieran's smile was mischievous.

"Not exactly what I envisioned but he *likes* me."

He has always wanted a cat...

I swallowed against my emotions and motioned for him to follow me. I needed to do this now. While Aidan was in his feelings about Sonya.

I pulled Kieran. "Thanks for taking care of her." Both Sonya and Nisha.

"I'm sorry—"

"I'm sorry—"

We both paused.

His smile was light. "Nisha got you to say that."

She had. I thought I might start there. But I had spent the last few hours curled into her and we'd both been emotional.

Things I never thought I'd be.

My throat worked as I looked at him. I didn't know what to say now. And his eyes wouldn't fully meet mine.

"I shouldn't have assumed she knew about our family—"

"No." I cut him off. " I didn't tell her. It was on me. I should've—"

"Heard Aidan got involved," Kieran's eyes went wide in a 'yikes' motion. I nodded. "He said he was coming to town to talk to Sonya."

We both eyed our brother sitting there looking grim and ready to bust the door down to Sonya's room.

His grin widened, a flash of his old self breaking through. "Big bro's invested. I think you got some sort of virus and now you're hitting us with it."

I wasn't upset about it.

"I shouldn't have said what I did—"

"Yeah, you should've..." Kieran trailed off, discomfort etched in every line of his face. "Glad you did. I needed it. I went to Gabriel talked to him. And he was good about it. Solid."

I blinked. "You..."

"I didn't tell him about Avani."

I let out a breath. Yeah. That's not gonna go over well. With *anybody.*

But that wasn't what I wanted to say. "I don't give a shit about the past and what our fucking old life was. It didn't matter then, and it doesn't matter now. You can choose to be better. So can I. We both can. That's why...Nisha...she—" I still struggled with my words.

I took a deep breath like Nisha had told me to.

"Stop punishing yourself for shit that wasn't your fault." My voice carried a strength I didn't know I possessed, born from months of learning to be with Nisha. Of *actually* being with her.

My anger at our old life had faded, replaced by the promise of something new. A future with Nisha and our daughter, waiting for me to bring home those damn basil plants she loved so much.

"None of what happened was our fault. We were fucking kids, Kieran. You ended up in the hospital because you didn't know how to be with Avani," I said, cutting to the heart of the matter. *"Why? Because you thought you weren't good enough."*

I pressed on, driven by a newfound clarity.

"I don't understand what you keep punishing yourself for. We didn't choose the life we were born into, but we can choose what we do now. Who we become. We don't have to be what we were. Or a product of our fucking family."

"You remember why Mom left?" His question caught me off guard.

I shook my head, my memories of that time fragmented and hazy.

"I barely remember her," I admitted.

He nodded, a shadow crossing his face. "Aidan does."

His amber eyes filled with an emotion I rarely saw in him—pain, raw and unguarded. Because everything left its scars.

"Sometimes I think I do. People who didn't want us—"

"It doesn't matter!" I cut him off, my raised voice surprising us both. "It doesn't fucking matter what those people did or thought."

The love I felt for her was overwhelming, unshakeable. It was a stark contrast to our own upbringing.

"Our parents, I gave up on them years ago. It stopped defining me. Even with Nisha, I learned to be better. You can too."

I leaned forward, willing him to understand.

"Fuck our parents. They don't define shit. You can choose to let it go or you can choose to sit there and fucking let Cormac win every single day. There is nothing wrong with you."

I let out a breath feeling the words trapped in my throat clawing their way out to Kieran. Something I'd learned over the course of my time with Nisha.

"I felt like a mess for my entire life. Like I kept waiting to be the better version of me. *All the time so* that *maybe*, life could happen for me. I thought I needed to change. But change isn't a big moment. Not *one* big moment. Nisha...she made me realize change is in all the little moments, all the choices I make with her. Every single interaction I had with her—I was *already* a better man. She loved me as I was. As I am. Just like Avani loved you."

I looked right at Kieran who looked at me like he didn't recognize me in that moment.

I didn't recognize me but something in me demanded to say the words.

"I don't know what the fuck you said or did to her. But you—*you* can fix it. *You* have that choice. Our father made his choices. You don't have to make his choices or push away someone you love. You don't have to feel like you deserve Avani, but it's about making every single moment with her *count*."

And that was the truth wasn't it?

I was going to be a better father than my father ever was. To my little girl. To Nisha.

Shit. I needed to get married…a breath left me in a huff as the emotions slammed into me. Nisha hadn't mentioned it and neither had I despite knowing she was pregnant. Why hadn't I mentioned it?

I swear to fucking God I'm an idiot.

I need to propose. How the fuck do I do that?

I need Lara.

His eyebrows lifted and a faint smirk tugged at one corner of his mouth, a shadow of his old mischief. "Nisha taught you that."

"Nisha taught me everything." That was the fucking truth.

He smirked at me. And I had to ask.

"Alisha got you the fucking cat?"

His eyes went dark as he shook his head. "Avani did. Both of them. I don't know how to talk to her," he interrupted, his voice flat. "Lish hits me up from time to time. Makes sure I'm good. I don't think she cares what we are. I think…I think Alisha wants me to date Avani."

His eyes met mine. "You know she told me if I decided to with Avani she wouldn't even be mad—because she says as long as Avani felt safe and was taken care of, Alisha never cared where I came from or what I did."

His eyes met mine and I saw how much Alisha's acceptance had meant to him. Reed and Gabriel didn't stand a chance if Alisha approved.

The darkness in his expression said more than words ever could.

"She didn't care what Reed thought because she said Avani's choice was hers. But the entire time I was with her, she didn't seem like she was into me..." He frowned. "She was too traumatized. I don't even think she saw me." But he saw her.

"What stopped you from just telling me."

He shook his head. "You know me."

I did.

And Avani hadn't seemed Kieran's type when I met her—too soft, too innocent. And I realized I didn't inherit Aidan and Kieran's avoidance. No.

I thought I hated everything until I met Nisha.

She made me realize how much love I had.

He frowned looking curiously at me then. "Why didn't you fight Nisha?"

"Why would I?" I shrugged.

He looked curiously at me like he couldn't believe I was right there. "You fight anything."

"Nisha is different."

Until Nisha, I hadn't been the type for a committed relationship or fatherhood. "She wasn't scheming or lying to me. She wasn't using me for her own gain. Nisha was there from day one. I never expected it. Never saw it coming. But once it did...it felt like she was everything I was waiting for." The words came easily as I said it to Kieran. "And I didn't know what to do, but I knew I didn't want anything. Or to fight her."

I looked at Kieran's surprised expression and felt my lips tip. "Why would I?"

"You just asked Nisha out?"

Well...after I'd made her come. But I wasn't about to tell my brother that. "Did you ask Avani? If she would..." Kieran like wild shit in bed. Nothing I would ever bring near Nisha.

His eyes widened. "Why?"

"Because maybe she's got more in common with you. You just don't know it yet." I added. "Nisha..." I motioned between us. "She trusts me. Like Avani trusts you. Just talk to her. She's back in school now? Yeah, go talk to her. Just tell her."

He looked like he was honestly considering it.

I couldn't fucking believe after years of seeing my brother in the most compromising fucked up positions possible we were actually talking about his love life. His sex life. Or lack of now.

Kieran was quiet.

"*You* didn't fight Nisha."

I shook my head at his quiet statement. He sounded almost impressed. Years ago Kieran and I wouldn't have dreamed of having this conversation.

"You really think if I...if I ask Avani...Cormac doesn't win?"

His question was simple. But it meant the world.

"I do."

He paused.

A beat passed between us.

"That was the most I ever heard you say."

I smirked not feeling it a bit. "Don't get used to it."

KILLIAN

Once Nisha settled?

I looked for the perfect ring at a jeweler Kieran said Teo liked since his family owned parts of it.

Davina&Co, high end luxury retailer I needed an appointment for. So Kieran texted Teo who just put in a request for me to go ASAP.

Once I stepped into the pale pink shop, the woman had eyed me up and down and directed me to bigger diamonds. But Nisha wouldn't want that. No, Nisha needed something else.

Something smaller.

I pointed at a pink diamond perfect for her.

Something simple for her hands.

Since she didn't like flashy shit.

"I'll take that one. But she needs a smaller band with it to wear. She won't wear anything heavy for long." Not with a baby.

Something easy for her to cook with without it getting lost while she frosted her strawberry cupcakes.

"How about this?" The lady suggested a tiny silvery band with it. I eyed the one next to it that looked like a tiny pink bow.

"That one."

"It comes with matching earrings." She motioned to a wall and I found the ones I knew Nisha would adore.

"I'll take two sets in case she loses the first one."

And I bought two of the bands in case she lost those too. Knowing Nisha who worked with her hands, she might.

And then I bought a tiny baby bracelet for my daughter.

She'd rang me up with dollar signs in her eyes as she packed it all up. At the sight of the black card I pulled out I would've thought she died a little, practically offering to carry the bags for me to my car.

I texted Nisha I was running a bit late ignoring her and taking the items out.

I picked up enough flowers to make the florist lose their damn mind and I drove to my penthouse.

Nisha had moved in there since it was bigger, safer, and Alisha had offered to redecorate it.

I didn't talk to Reed's girl much, but I knew she was a sweetheart and volunteered to make it feminine.

Now my entire penthouse looked like Nisha's old apartment. And I fucking loved it. Fucking pink *everywhere*.

Vibrant green plants. I lived in a fairy nest as Reed put it.

Get used to it. I love coming home to Lish and all this. It's great.

But I didn't know how to propose to my girl though.

Not a fucking clue. No internet search or anyone would know what to do.

Except Lara.

I wasted a few days beating around the bush unsure of how to even approach Nisha with the jewelry I got.

Instead I hid it somewhere too tall for her to reach and pretended like I wasn't dying. Nisha just rubbed my scalp thinking I was tense.

I didn't know how to propose. I wasn't good with words.

It was evening and I knew Lara would be up so I called her. It took her a few rings but she eventually picked up.

"Killian!" She sounded rushed but she answered anyway. "What's up?"

"You got a second?"

"I do."

I broke it down for Lara.

"I need your help," I said, cutting to the chase. "I'm gonna propose to Nisha." And so Lara gave me her two cents and helped squealing like a wild woman. On the call she sounded off. More quiet than usual.

"You good?"

She made a small noise. "Hmm, Liam's been busier than usual at Titan. I don't know if the work is getting to him. He's been acting strange."

"Strange?" I frowned.

"Mhm, like..." she broke off. "I shouldn't talk about it. But he's been off lately. I thought it was stress, but..."

"Want me to talk to him?" I didn't give a shit if he used a cane or not, if he did anything to Lara—he was a dead man.

"No," she was quiet. "I just think maybe whatever he's working on is weighing on him. He found that girl Lucy and since then he's been a little obsessed with the case. Did he say anything to you? I know you two were working together? Am I a weird girlfriend to ask you that?"

No. She wasn't. Nisha would do the same if something was off with me. "No. He hasn't told me. I can talk to him. I've been busy with Nisha so I didn't get a chance to focus on the Devereaux's."

"Thanks," she whispered. "Just worried..." I heard her shifting. "When are you going to propose to Nisha?"

"I don't know." I didn't.

I went about my evening routine, eating dinner and watching some movie she loved and I privately liked it.

Nisha put under-eye masks on both of us and rubbed my scalp while I laid on her occasionally checking on my...*daughter*. Kissing her belly during the movie.

Nisha munched on sour worm candy between us.

I passed her snacks and all the while, my heart was racing, my palms sweaty as I tried to find the right moment. But I couldn't say the words.

Later, as Nisha slept peacefully beside me, I pulled out the ring, watching it catch the moonlight streaming through the window.

Carefully, so as not to wake her, I slid it onto her finger, marveling at how perfect it looked. Her hands were small, but the ring itself was dainty.

I barely slept a wink, waiting for morning to come. When Nisha finally stirred, her eyes fluttering open, I was already wide awake, watching her.

She stretched, her hand coming up to rub the sleep from her eyes. And then she froze, blinking down at the ring.

"Killian…what…?"

"I wanted to do this right…"

Nisha sat up, her eyes never leaving mine. "Is this…are you…?" I nuzzled closer to her, aware my heart was pounding.

I had all fucking night to practice this like some psycho talking to myself.

"I love you. I should've done this a long time ago. I kept waiting for the right time, but I don't know why I didn't do it sooner."

I was finding the more I spoke the less I struggled.

"From the moment I met you, you made me feel like nothing else in the world mattered. You held me during my lowest and stayed by me. And when I let go of what I thought I was—I found what I could be. With you." I broke off feeling a little bit of that emotion catch my throat. And the worry resurfaced for once more than any job ever had made me feel. "*I practiced all night—*"

"You're doing great, baby," Nisha's smile was watery and full of pride as she held me tight to her.

I felt my lips tip at her encouragement. "You've been putting me back together every single fucking minute I spend with you. I wanted to be better for you. That was part of why I never told you. I didn't realize how fucking much I needed you until you came into my life. I never once thought I'd find someone like you. *Ever.*" I broke off as the realization hit me.

She saved me.

Every part of her saved my soul. Nisha always said she dreamed of someone to save her.

She never imagined it would be with my darkness.

But she'd saved me with her light.

"I was on the way to ruin, you stopped me right before I hit that. You gave me hope. A family. I felt like the moment you put your arms around me, telling me, everything was going to be fine—I believed you. I don't believe in many things, in many people, I hate more than I love —but I *fucking love you.*"

Her smile was watery but wide as she cried for me.

"And I love *her.*" I rubbed her stomach with a shaky hand. "Love you both. You're my girls. You're my love. My legacy. My future. Nothing will ever happen to either one of you as long as I stand. You have my word. I'm asking you. No, I am begging you. Be my wife."

She nodded, coming closer to me to kiss me over and over. I didn't know who was more emotional anymore.

She whispered it against my lips. "Did you practice all that?"

I nodded, my throat tight with emotion. "I did. All night."

"Yes." My heart exploded a little.

Nisha's eyes softened, her smile wide, her hands coming up to cradle my face. She peppered kisses across my cheeks, my nose, my forehead.

"You did so well, baby," she murmured between kisses. "I'm so proud of you."

I leaned into her touch, savoring the warmth of her skin against mine.

Her reassurances had always been calming. But now they were igniting flames under my skin. Her touch soft and warm and her lips moving over my neck.

Nisha's hands began to wander, tracing the lines of my shoulders, my chest. Her tongue darting out licking down a path from my chest to my navel.

"You've been so good to me," she whispered, her lips brushing against mine. "Let me take care of you now."

"Nisha, what about—"

She silenced me with a kiss, her tongue sweeping into my mouth. I groaned, my hips bucking involuntarily. It had been so long since we'd been together like this. Too long.

"Nisha—"

"Shhh, you met me halfway. I want to meet you too."

Nisha made quick work of my boxers, I hissed as the cool air hit my heated skin, but then her hand was on me, stroking, teasing.

"Fuck, Nisha…" I panted, my head falling back against the pillows.

She hummed in satisfaction, her grip tightening. She looked so beautiful, dark waves, dark eyes, moving over me.

Then, without warning, she dipped her head, taking me into the wet heat of her mouth.

I nearly came off the bed, a strangled moan tearing from my throat. Nisha worked me over with her tongue, hollowing her cheeks as she took me deeper. I swore holding her hair as she worked over me.

"Luv…" I warned, my fingers threading through her hair. "Fuck, your mouth feels…just like that, luv. Just like that."

She bobbed her head, taking me right to the edge before pulling off.

Only to straddle me, sinking down onto my length with a breathy moan.

"Oh God," she gasped, her hands splayed across my chest. "I forgot…"

And her thighs tightened around me. Tighter.

Nisha was barely taking the tip of my cock as she cried out, her head thrown back as I watched. I blinked rapidly unsure of what—

"Did you just…" I trailed off marveling at the way she trembled as her orgasm made her slick enough to slide down onto my length.

Oh. Fucking. *Shiiiit.*

Nisha whimpered, red faced as she blinked at me a little disoriented and shaking.

Struggling as she squirmed on my dick then the wet heat of her flooding around me.

"I think…" she licked her lips. "I found another side effect of pregnancy. I thought that first time we were together it was because it had been a while…but I think this is…normal now."

"Come here, luv. I got you." I gripped her hips, guiding her movements as she tried to take me. "Lean forward."

When she did, I held her close, thrusting up to meet her, hitting that spot deep inside her. Stretching her wider.

"All of it for me, luv. Take it."

"Ohhh, God." She whispered into my mouth. "Sensitive."

Hmm, I know.

"There you go, you can take it…good girl…" I held her tight to me, working my hips deeper in her. "Tell me when."

"*When.*" Over and over and over. I held her tight to me as she sobbed with every thrust. Nisha was losing it.

"Oh…fuck, you're soaking wet." I groaned feeling her wet heat around me. "That's so good, luv. You're close—"

"*Yes.*" Nisha cried out her agreement, her movements becoming erratic. Her pussy wildly clenching. I felt it.

Jeez, this is gonna be fun.

I growled. "Come for me, luv. I've got you."

With a cry, Nisha shattered above me, her walls clenching around me. Again and again.

I lost count of how many times she came as I fucked her through them.

392

Her hands laced with mine, the diamond glinting with sunlight and her naked body rocking, taking me further each time.

I followed right after her fourth or fifth, spilling inside her with a low groan. *"I love you. So fucking much."*

"I love you."

KILLIAN

ONE YEAR LATER

IT HAD TAKEN ME FOREVER AND A DAY TO GET HOME, BUT I MADE IT through the traffic coming in from Greenwich.

Every single time I hit the city limits my patience hit a nerve.

Lately I'd been considering getting a place in Greenwich which I didn't think Nisha would mind living it.

I spent half of my morning looking for nice houses for Kiara to grow up in. Maybe a summer home to take her to run around.

The neon streets of New York blurred past me as I weaved through the evening crowd, my mind fixed on one goal—getting back to my girls.

Nisha had been with Kiara, our daughter, all day, and I knew she'd be exhausted.

Despite running her blog full time, Nisha had decided to quit everything that she had done for survival, and do what she had always loved.

Now? I was running late.

My girls were expecting me. And I was not about to be a shit dad. To my wife or to my daughter.

I'd promised I'd help. Breaking promises wasn't something I did.

And my word was iron-clad.

When I finally reached my penthouse, I took the stairs two at a time, heading straight for the nursery where I figured Nisha would be.

Soft white noise drifted out before I even entered.

My heart swelled at the sight in the daybed we'd gotten for Nisha to feed her.

Both of my girls were there covered in the pink blanket, Nisha lying on her side, and I knew she was half asleep nursing Kiara.

Or she had been.

Nisha joked about a personal alarm clock in her. But I couldn't count how many times since she'd come into the world, I woke up to make sure she was good throughout the night.

Babies definitely did not sleep on schedule.

Her chubby fists were curled against Nisha as she held on like she never wanted to let go. I tore my shirt off since Kiara liked skin to skin contact whenever I was around.

She was fascinated by my tattoos and liked to gnaw on my fingers when she did find the ones there.

I was attuned to every single thing my girls did.

I'd be there for her. Unlike what happened to me. Make sure nothing happened to my girl.

The room was bathed in the soft glow of the cat-shaped nightlight Kieran had bought, casting shadows across both of their faces as I approached them.

Big and bright amber eyes bat up at me like she just realized she wasn't alone with her Mom anymore.

Slowly a wide gummy smile lit her lips and she pursed her lips up at me. A noise left her and a grin lit my lips at her excitement, the way her chubby arms and legs moved to get to me.

"I'm home, little luv. Did you miss me?"

And my *daughter*—I still never got over saying that—gave me another gummy smile.

And just like the first moment I met her, my heart, while full, expanded some more as I looked down at Kiara watching me.

She was just six months old and still *tiny*.

One of those fists reached for me and she let Nisha go to coo a little up at me.

Come here, little luv.

I gently reached over and picked her up, scooping her head up in one hand.

She'd been so small when she'd come into the world, I felt nothing but the need to make sure she and Nisha were safe from anything.

That had been one night I didn't want to relive if I could help it.

Without Sonya, Aidan, and my family I would've killed someone.

"Come on," I whispered inhaling her scent of milk and baby powder combined with Nisha's amber. "Let's give Mama a break."

I had her in my arms cooing and gurgling another moment later.

"Yeah? Sound good?"

Kiara made an adorable noise as she snuggled into me easily finding her little nook in my chest from day one she curled into it, and my heart fucking melted. *Just like that.*

Since she'd come into my life it did that all the time.

That gummy smile did me in every single time.

Because she was happy to see *me*.

I came home for her and somehow every single time she saw me she gave me *that* look.

I just eased off the bed, covering Nisha with a blanket. My wife was exhausted as I brushed her hair back.

And slowly I stepped out with Kiara in my arms.

"There we go, I'll take you to the kitchen, I'm hungry too. Usually your Mom's awake so I can have dinner with her, but I think she's tired tonight...did you get enough milk? No? Daddy can get you more."

It was oddly easier to talk to my daughter than anyone else. And I didn't know why.

I started doing it when Nisha was pregnant when she told me, Kiara could hear and understand my voice.

"You're getting so big, little luv. You might end up taller than Mama. Maybe you do take after my side of the family."

It didn't matter then what my past was. My future, my fucking everything was in my arms.

Dressed in a tomato print onesie, Kiara's inky black hair, so like mine, curled in tendrils around her face, defying any attempt at tidiness.

"I need something solid. I'm starving. Daddy had a long day with a bunch of idiots. Let me tell you about this nonsense..."

Talking to my daughter, I heated up some leftovers one-handed holding Kiara who had gone from sleepy to completely interested.

I knew I was completely hers and on my knees when I'd held her a few hours after she'd come into the world and she pursed her lips at me.

Like Nisha. The doctor wasn't wrong—babies did genuinely understand. She knew I loved her.

"You want boo's?" I couldn't fucking resist kissing her nose. "That's your boos."

I don't know why Kiara said kisses were boo's but we weren't arguing with her.

She was *adorable.*

She was all mine.

And I was fucking destroy anything that would try and hurt her.

My daughter looked up at me with those amber eyes of hers and I was *gone.*

"One day you'll sneak around the house with me and have dinner and snacks, hm? But for right now you're relegated to milk."

Nisha suspected she was teething with how much she kept us up at night sometimes.

I brushed her hair back as she made noises to communicate with me or try. Right now, I knew, she still couldn't be too far away from Nisha.

She was attached to my wife needing her more than she needed me.

But every so often she let me take her and it was the best feeling in the world to watch her beam up at me.

She knew *me.*

She grabbed my fingers trying to put them into her mouth, the little bows I got tattooed over my ring finger for her and Nisha.

I couldn't always wear my ring so I got their names on my wrist.

"You had a good day with Mama, little luv? I bet she kept you all snuggled and warm, huh? Plenty of boo's? You did? Tired Mama out now you're going to stay up with Daddy? Yeah? Is that why you put Mama to sleep?" I peppered her face with several as she squealed and giggled. *Fuck.* "Well, you got me little luv, I came home and found you."

She giggled again.

My heart was going to *explode.*

Lucas had said the same when he'd had his daughter who was the spitting image of Evie. He'd gone and lost his ever loving mind with how overprotective he was of both of them.

Lucas had hired someone to make Evie's transition to motherhood easier. And had given me the same advice.

Since we'd both became dad's within a month of each other our families were closer. As a joke for all the times I helped him, he stepped in to babysit Kiara.

Both of us discovered our girls dissolved into giggles at anything we did with them. And since then we'd become designated babysitters while our wives went off to whatever event had invited Nisha.

I moved to the couches in the living room cuddling her close to me as she eased up, her lips pursing again while I ate.

I held her while I took a bite of the gnocchi and chicken I had.

She looked at it and then at me opening her mouth. I didn't even hold back my laugh.

"I can't give you that, sweetheart. I don't wanna wake your Mom up. So all I got is kisses."

As *soon* as I said it, she pursed her lips again and I was beginning to see whose side of the family she took after.

She did it all the time. And if she didn't get kisses, she gave me that pout. She'd perfected it.

Nisha was beginning to think she took more after me. I didn't think so. Maybe she had my family's eyes but her features were all Nisha.

With my daughter, I had learned to grow as a father as much as a husband.

"This is what you do, huh? I say no and you give me those eyes and that smile and I'm gonna give you kisses?"

She cooed up at me until I got her a bottle and fed her first.

Halfway through, Nisha peered in sleepy eyed.

"I was wondering what happened to you." My wife's voice was soft as she padded into the living room and my head snapped up the same way Kiara's did. "Bartering daddy for gnocchi and kisses, hm?"

She beamed down at us rubbing her eyes a little.

"You two snuck off without me."

"Guilty, luv."

She bent down to kiss me only for Kiara to reach out and intercept. Or try to.

"You didn't have to get up, I would've come to you."

"I know, I was worried when I didn't feel someone..." Nisha kissed Kiara giggling in my arms, trying to lift up her head to get a kiss.

Both Nisha and I swooped in at the same time to kiss both of her cheeks as she squealed in delight.

I grinned up at Nisha. "She's all you."

And now, instead of an empty home, the walls of my penthouse knew this.

Nisha kissed me after. Twice. I sighed. "I would've put her down to bed, luv."

"I know, but you just got home too."

Nisha pulled back and Kiara did that little thing where she knew that was Mama and she was instantly reaching for Nisha. Who took her without question.

"Eat, I have her." She sat down next to me with Kiara cuddled in her arms.

Nisha's weary eyes met mine and she was still so fucking pretty.

"Did you have a good day today?"

"No," I smiled at her expression. "But it's fine. You look beautiful, baby. I spent another day with the recruits instead of you two. How was your play date with Evie?"

"Kiara and her daughter are inseparable..." Nisha talked about Evie's daughter while I listened. "I told Evie about that tallow balm Aidan got us for Kiara's rash on her cheeks...she said she'd try it."

"Lucas loves having this many girls to look out for—"

I took another bite food eating dinner with her cuddling Kiara close who was now dozing.

"I swear that man has baby proofed his entire home. He makes you look reasonable."

I laughed lightly. "He takes the cake."

"Yes, he does. Although, I've never felt anyone else more safe to leave Kiara around."

Lucas had lost a lot in his life. So had I. We both understood the lengths we'd go to keep our girls safe. My body reacted viscerally at the thought of anything happening to her or our daughter.

I didn't feel an ounce of concern when Kiara was with him since I knew he'd protect her with his life.

"He says he wants to his baby to work—"

"I tried that—"

"I have vetoed everything until she starts walking." Nisha looked at Kiara in her arms. "She's getting so big now. It won't be long before you're chasing after her. And I cannot imagine her at the manor. She would get lost."

"She might. But we'd find her." I grinned at the idea of her running

399

around Greenwich. "I was going to take you guys to Chicago when she's walking. Go visit."

"That sounds nice, I think she'd love it too. Something new for her to experience."

And not just her. I'd talked to Lucas to plan something for Nisha who had been through enough between having a baby and everything else. I just didn't know how to approach it.

"Want me to put on something for you, baby? Did you need something?"

"No, I got it, luv. Did you eat yet?"

She shook her head. "I'm not too hungry, more tired—" she yawned and I felt for her as I held up a bite of gnocchi. She took it without question and I alternated feeding her while I listened to her tell me about her day.

I went to get more food for both of us as we talked.

"...exhausted..." she murmured. "Evie asked me if I wanted her to keep Kiara overnight or for a few days..."

Yeah. That might've been because of me.

"I think she's teething more though. I can see little spots in her mouth and Evie recommended these icy toys to help."

"I was thinking," I started slowly, feeding her a bite of gnocchi. "We should take a break. Lucas and Evie said they'd look out for her for a week if you're comfortable with it. I planned it two months out so it gives us both some time to get ourselves together..."

"What?"

I smiled at her expression as Kiara dozed a little on her. "Lucas has a spot in Miami. I figured it's good beach weather and I could take you—"

"To Miami?"

"Yeah. It's sunny and warm—" her eyes moved to Kiara. "And it's for a week. We can take her, but Lucas said it would be solid for both of us to get a small break in."

Nisha laid her head into that spot Kiara had been on. Right over my heart.

"That sounds...wonderful. I'm just nervous to leave her."

"Like I said, we don't have to, we can take her. But I also want you to get a breather in and Evie doesn't mind."

"No, she does not. I think she wants another kid...Evie says it's nice to imagine her daughter having a sister."

"Lucas is having a heart attack—"

Nisha laughed lightly and her eyes met mine. "It would be nice for Kiara to have a sister."

I stopped laughing when I realized what she was saying.

"Or a brother," Nisha whispered.

"Luv," my throat worked. "I can't watch you go through that again. I'm not saying never—I just can't let you go through that."

I hadn't slept with Nisha in months. I felt like I didn't even know how to after spending ten hours with her in labor.

"Are you..." Nisha chewed her lip. "Do you not..." she looked down at Kiara. And I caught the unease in her shoulders, in her eyes.

"No," I set my food down reaching for her. "No, luv. I want you. I always want you. I don't wanna see you hurting. That's the only reason why I haven't—"

Ah hell, now I was embarrassed. I held her face. "Luv, you have no idea how badly I want you. But only when you're comfortable. Not because I wanted it. Only when she's good. Not because of me."

I didn't frankly fucking matter.

Her throat worked as I said it.

"Why do you think I want us to take a break?" I whispered seeing my daughter slowly falling asleep. "I just want us to take it easy for a week. It'll be good. Lucas says he did the same."

Nisha looked ready to cry as I said it.

"Luv," I held her tighter. "Nononono, don't cry."

"I'm just tired," she wiped her eyes. "I promise I'm okay."

I held onto her. Nisha had been emotional towards the last leg of her pregnancy and even now I could see the toll it took. Even if she wanted Kiara to have siblings—now was not the time.

"Come here." I snuggled them both like I had the entire night Nisha had her. "I know...I know, I'm trying, luv. I am. I promise. Just say yes, Evie will love to babysit."

Nisha nodded as I wiped her eyes.

"I'm gonna make you some dinner, and then I'm taking you both to bed, yeah?"

My wife could only agree. "Thank you."

"Luv, let's get you both to bed," I murmured brushing Nisha's hair back.

I carried both of my girls in my arms to the bedroom.

Setting Nisha down, before taking Kiara to her crib. Nisha didn't like sleeping without her and both of us looked out for her easier here.

She laid there curling into a ball as I put her tiny little pink blanket over here. Evie had gotten her one with little cherries on it.

This was my legacy. Nisha's. Something better. Something more. I turned to see Nisha turning to her side and curling in with the blanket because she knew I had Kiara safe and sound.

I did. I had both of them.

And I'd do anything for my girls.

AUTHORS NOTE

Thank you guys so much for reading Legacy.

Legacy was a lot of work and a lot of fun, but I hope you guys enjoyed and fell in love with Killian as much as I did.

Love,

Lilah

ALSO BY LILAH LANCE

∼

ABOUT THE AUTHOR

Lilah Lance writes romance for all the girls who dream of being seen, being *accepted*, and being loved for *who they are.*

Get exclusive content and giveaways by signing up for Lilah's newsletter on http://lilahlance.com where you can get sneak peeks and news before anyone else.